# Soul Sisters

## LESLEY LOKKO

PAN BOOKS

First published 2021 by Macmillan

This paperback edition first published 2022 by Pan Books
an imprint of Pan Macmillan
The Smithson, 6 Briset Street, London EC1M 5NR
*EU representative:* Macmillan Publishers Ireland Ltd, 1st Floor,
The Liffey Trust Centre, 117–126 Sheriff Street Upper,
Dublin 1, D01 YC43
Associated companies throughout the world
www.panmacmillan.com

ISBN 978-1-5290-6728-6

1 3 5 7 9 8 6 4 2

A CIP catalogue record for this book is available from the British Library.

Typeset in Sabon by Palimpsest Book Production Limited,
Falkirk, Stirlingshire
Printed and bound by CPI Group (UK) Ltd, Croydon, CR0 4YY

Visit **www.panmacmillan.com** to read more about all our books
and to buy them. You will also find features, author interviews and
news of any author events, and you can sign up for e-newsletters
so that you're always first to hear about our new releases.

# Soul Sisters

Lesley Lokko is a Ghanaian-Scottish architect, academic and bestselling novelist, formerly Dean of Architecture at The City College of New York, and now the founder and director of the African Futures Institute, Accra, Ghana. She has lived and worked on four continents. Lesley's novels include *Soul Sisters*, *Sundowners*, *Rich Girl, Poor Girl* and *A Private Affair*. Her novels have been translated into sixteen languages and are captivating stories about powerful people, exploring themes of racial and cultural identity, as well as love, loyalty and family histories.

By Lesley Lokko

*Sundowners*

*Saffron Skies*

*Bitter Chocolate*

*Rich Girl, Poor Girl*

*One Secret Summer*

*A Private Affair*

*An Absolute Deception*

*Little White Lies*

*In Love and War*

*The Last Debutante*

*Soul Sisters*

For Debs and Nic, who are always in my thoughts.
And for Megs and Lois, who keep them – and
me – so close.

Some mistakes can never be undone.

'The chameleon gets behind the fly, remains motionless for some time, then he advances very slowly and gently, first putting forward one leg and then another. At last, when well within reach, he darts his tongue and the fly disappears. England is the chameleon and I am that fly'

LOBENGULA

'[The British] happen to be the best people in the world, with the highest ideals of decency and justice and liberty and peace, and the more of the world we inhabit, the better it is for humanity'

CECIL RHODES

# TIMELINE

*Prologue*        Matabeleland, Southern Rhodesia        1921
                  George McFadden [23] b.1898
                  Nozipho [17]
                  Margaret [19] b.1902


**PART 1**                                               1949
*Chapters 1–4*    Edinburgh
                  Robert [13] b.1936
                  Aneni [16] b.1933
                  Margaret [47]
                  George [51]


**PART 2**                                               1978
*Chapters 5–7*    Edinburgh & Harare
                  Jen [9] b.1969
                  Robert [42]
                  Kemi [9] b.1969
                  Margaret [76]

**PART 3**                                                1987

*Chapter 8*          Edinburgh
                     Jen [18]
                     Kemi [18]
                     Robert [51]


**PART 4**                                                1997

*Chapters 9–27*      London & Johannesburg
                     Jen [28]
                     Kemi [28]
                     Solam [31] b.1966
                     Robert [61]
                     Oliver [58] b.1939
                     Iketleng [55] b.1942


**PART 5**                                                1998

*Chapters 28–47*     Edinburgh/London/Johannesburg
                     Jen [29]
                     Kemi [29]
                     Solam [32]
                     Robert [62]
                     Julian [52]
                     Alice [late 50s]


**PART 6**                                                1998

*Chapters 48–53*     Johannesburg
                     [same]

**PART 7**                                                1998

*Chapters 54–60*   Johannesburg
                   [same]


**PART 8**                                                2001

*Chapters 61–66*   Johannesburg
                   Jen [32]
                   Kemi [32]
                   Solam [36]
                   Robert [65]
                   Julian [55]


**PART 9**                                                2004

*Chapters 67–73*   Johannesburg
                   Jen [35]
                   Kemi [35]
                   Solam [39]
                   Robert [68]


**PART 10**                                               2004

*Chapter 74*       Almondsbury
                   [same]


**PART 11**                                               2005

*Chapters 75–81*   Johannesburg
                   Jen [36]
                   Kemi [36]

Solam [40]

Robert [69]


**PART 12**                                              2008

*Chapters 82–89*  Johannesburg

Jen [39]

Kemi [39]

Solam [43]

Robert [72]


**PART 13**                                              2010

*Chapter 90*     Johannesburg

Jen [41]

Kemi [41]

Solam [45]


*Epilogue*       Cape Town                               2010

Jen [41]

Kemi [41]

Solam [45]

# Soul Sisters

# PROLOGUE

*Matabeleland, Southern Rhodesia, 1921*

George McFadden listened intently as Reverend Grove outlined his plans for the new mission station at Marula, some sixty miles south-west of Bulawayo along the wavering, thinly tarred road that led to Bechuanaland. George gripped the back of the chair, his ruddy face screwed up as he struggled to suppress his rising panic at the pools of sweat forming under his armpits, sliding down his ribcage. His protruding knuckles showed white against his freckled skin, burned to an angry reddened stripe at the nape where the fierce African sun bore endlessly down upon him. He'd been instructed to wear a hat at all times, but no one had mentioned the wind. On his very first day, striding out confidently across one of the closely grazed fields, a breeze sprang up out of nowhere and whipped it off his head. He'd immediately given chase, but stopped after a few seconds, aware of himself as a figure of ridicule to the clutch of children squatting in a hollow in the sandy road running next to the fields. One of them stood up and pointed at him, covering his mouth with his hand in a universal gesture of amusement or amazement, hard to tell which. He was a strange sight in these parts. A tall, red-haired white man with a sparse, gingery beard and dark, close-together eyebrows . . . little wonder they stared. Apart from himself, Reverend Grove, Tim Bellingham and the occasional travelling salesman, there

3

were no other white men within a hundred-mile radius of the little mission village.

He was suddenly aware of a deepening silence. He looked up. Reverend Grove had finished talking and was looking expectantly at George, waiting for an answer. The sweat now pooled against his waist. He pressed his arms against his sides. It was the heat; the damned heat. He moved about it in a dazed torpor all day long, unable to think clearly. 'I . . . I beg pardon, sir,' he stammered, reaching for a handkerchief to mop his perspiring face. 'I . . . I'm afraid I didnae catch . . .'

Reverend Grove winced. George's heart sank. He knew how much his thick Scots burr offended him. Reverend Grove's carefully modulated accent spoke of a very different background to the Glasgow tenement where George had sprung from. George was one of thirteen children left penniless when his father, a dockyard worker, was hit by a swinging boom and thrown, already lifeless, into the murky waters of the Clyde. His mother wasted no time in presenting George, one of the brighter of her sons, to a distant cousin of hers, Alistair Corcoran, who somewhat reluctantly offered to pay for George's education. George rarely saw his uncle after that first visit. In due course, however, aged twenty-three with his degree firmly in hand, he was able to call upon his uncle in his elegant home on Law Crescent, in the shadow of the Dundee Law. He was shown into the dining room and his benefactor got up and embraced him. The lad had done well for himself, yes, indeed, it was clear. The investment had paid off. Emboldened by the warm reception and the glass of sherry pressed into his large hands, George hurriedly launched into further plans. He'd been thinking of something in the legal profession . . . perhaps even a barrister? His benefactor took off his glasses and stared at him. There was a moment's uncomfortable silence, during which George began to panic. Had he said something wrong?

His uncle cleared his throat. Had George perhaps considered Africa? Well, no, he had not. *Africa?* He remembered growing breathless. He'd tried to keep the panic out of his voice, much as he was doing now. *Africa?*

'George, I asked if you've any carpentry skills?' Reverend Grove's voice broke into George's painful recollections. The Reverend's weary expression gave him away. He already knew George's feeble answer.

'No, er, no . . . I have not,' George admitted. 'It wasn't . . . it wasn't on the, er, curriculum.'

Reverend Grove sighed. 'What *do* they teach you fellows these days?' he muttered. 'Well, we'll just have to make the best of it.'

'I'm sure I'll—'

'Well, I'm sure you'll—'

Both men spoke quickly, not wishing to linger. George paused; the right of way was the Reverend's.

'It was a gift from Rhodes,' the Reverend said, fumbling in his waistcoat for his pipe. He lit it carefully, a thin plume of smoke rising vertically towards the thatched roof of the hut that had served for the past five years as the mission school. It was the hut's replacement with a brick-and-stone building they were now discussing.

'That . . . that was very kind of him,' George murmured, not knowing quite what to say. Carpentry? He'd never held a hammer in his life.

'Indeed.'

The two men stood for a moment in the deepening silence. There didn't seem to be anything further to say.

'Well, you'd best be getting along,' Reverend Grove said finally. 'Darkness falls quickly in these parts.'

'Aye, that it does,' George agreed. He got up hurriedly and moved towards the doorway. Outside, the shadows were already long on the ground, dancing where the wind stirred the trees, sending their leaves into a whispering flurry. He crossed the patch of bare ground behind the mission, his feet biting into the warm sandy red soil, sending up little clouds of ochre-coloured dust. The sweet, thick after-taste of sorghum beer was in his mouth and throat – his mind, too – as he walked unsteadily towards the cluster of thatched huts that marked the beginning of the village. Hamlet? Settlement? Township? Even after eighteen months he found it hard to name it. Less than a village, more than a clearing . . . what *was* it?

A bird called out and a dog barked somewhere beyond the clearing where clumps of mealies were bunched together, desperate for rain. He glanced up at the sky. Not a cloud in sight. Clear and high, the *blue* of it – azure, cerulean, Prussian, cobalt, turquoise – stretched to infinity, beyond infinity. It made his eyes ache, dizzy to the point of collapse. It wasn't a blue he could recall ever seeing before. He was a Scotsman. His whole being was finely and permanently attuned to the quicksilver changes in weather that were a feature of his homeland. Clear skies in Scotland were a rare occasion. Usually the weather was thick and hanging, always threatening rain. Not here. Not a spit of rain in days, weeks, months. Oh, how he longed for it, and for the taste of something other than the sour, ferment-smelling pap they made from corn, a tasteless porridge with none of the gritty snap and bite of Scottish oats. Pap and wild spinach – that seemed to be the extent of their diet. No wonder the men, women and children were listless to the point of apathy. Out here, sixty miles from the nearest town and life beyond the near-futile scratching out of an existence for their daily food, there was nothing to sustain them nutritionally, materially or spiritually. He brought himself up abruptly. His thoughts were veering dangerously again. It was on account of the latter – spirituality – that they were here. Grove, Bellingham and himself. At the thought of Tim Bellingham, his gut tightened. Twenty years old, golden-haired, tanned and boyishly enthusiastic, he'd come out recently from Cambridge with his head full of new ideas, most – nay, *all* – of which filled George McFadden with dread. Dread because *he* hadn't thought of them. Dread because everything that came out of Timothy Bellingham's mouth seemed so . . . *clever*, so reasonable, so thoughtful . . . so *right*. The frightfully clever-sounding words tripped off his tongue. Latin, Greek, a touch of ancient Hebrew, when he was so inclined. And unlike George, afflicted with both a stammer *and* a burr, the natives appeared to have no trouble understanding him. In addition to his perfectly modulated Etonian English, in six weeks he'd mastered more Shona – an unforgiving, illogical tongue if George had ever heard one – than George had in eighteen *months*. 'Sawubona, *nkosi*.' That was what the elders called him. 'Nkosi'. 'The learned one', a term reserved for the most respected amongst them. Even Reverend Grove wasn't an '*nkosi*'. No, only Timothy Bellingham with his easy, loping walk and charming manner was *that*.

Suddenly a movement in the bushes to his left caught his eye. He stopped abruptly. Although the low scrub that surrounded the village could hardly be called jungle – not enough rain for that – he was still fearful. Here in the heart of Africa, a harmless-looking spider could inject enough venom into a man's hand to kill him in seconds. And it wasn't just the spiders. Although rarely glimpsed, snakes the size of yam tubers slumbered in the warm cracks of rocks, just waiting to be trodden upon. He'd seen what happened to a goat or a donkey bitten by one of those. Half an hour; that was all it took.

'Who's there?' he called out. His skin tingled unnervingly. There was a scuffling noise and then the unmistakable sound of giggling. He stared into the deepening gloom. Darkness fell so swiftly here, close to the tropics. The mealie stalks rustled. His fingers closed around the Bible in his left hand. 'Who goes there?' he all but shouted.

The stalks parted to reveal two faces. He almost let go of the Bible in relief. Two young girls, identical in their unspecified features. He still hadn't learned to distinguish between them, unable to recall who was who, in spite of Reverend Grove's masterful attempts to Anglicize their dreadfully long and complex names. He could scarcely tell the difference between boys and girls. If it wasn't for the fact that the men sported ragged beards and the women went bare-breasted, he wasn't sure he'd know which was which amongst his own age group, truth be told. But the two in front of him were girls. It was clear. Their pubescent breasts with thick, dark, puffy nipples were right in front of him. He cast his eyes downwards, his whole body being flooded with hot, awkward embarrassment. Would they not learn? It was so *unseemly*. So un-Christian.

'*Sawubona, bwana*,' they both sang in unison. His eyes fluttered upwards momentarily. He thought he recognized one of them, though he'd be damned if he could remember her name. The darker of the two. She was the Chief's daughter, or so he'd surmised. Hard to tell, what with their multiple women and everything. Who belonged to whom? They lived in compounds, not homes, and their language, such as he'd come to understand it, was no help. Everyone was a 'sister' or a 'brother', and the word for 'woman' could mean anything – wife, concubine, mother, sister, grandmother, aunt. It was all so loose and unfettered, so *unstructured*. Yes, the natives were unstructured in their ways.

He looked back down at the ground. What were they doing in the mealie stalks at dusk? He struggled to recall the Shona word. 'Home,' he said finally, pointing to the watch he carried on a chain. Would they understand what he meant?

'We went to fetch water, *bwana*,' the darker one piped up suddenly in clear, if accented English.

His head flew up, astonished. Where had she learned English? Chief Lobengula had flatly refused to allow the girls in the village to attend the mission school alongside the few boys he'd managed to spare. 'School is no place for women,' Reverend Grove had informed him haughtily when he first arrived. 'That's Lobengula's view, anyway. No use trying to persuade him otherwise, trust me.'

'You speak English?' he stammered incredulously.

She nodded. She was a bright-looking scrap of a thing, dark as you please, with skin the colour of a burned nut, or peat . . . he struggled to find the right words. Not for the first time, he wondered why the Chief was so against sending the girls to the one-room mission school. If this one was anything to go by, they were as bright – if not brighter and a darn sight more pleasant to look at – than any of the boys.

'Yes, *bwana*. I speak English.' Her voice was calm, unlike his, which had come out in a high-pitched squeal.

'How?'

'My brothers taught me.' She lifted her chin, a touch defiantly, he thought to himself. She was not like the other girls, shy, timid little things whose gaze fell away the moment his landed.

He cleared his throat. 'Well, that's . . . that's a good thing,' he said finally. *Guid*. He hated the way it came out, the long '*uuu*', like those insufferable Dutchmen to the south. He caught the look of stifled laughter that passed between them and felt the heat rise in his neck. The truth was, he'd had very little to do with women, African or otherwise. It embarrassed him now to recall the conversation with Bellingham of a few evenings ago.

'So, anyone special left behind?' Bellingham had asked, his lean frame sprawled out on the wicker chair in front of him. Unlike both George and Reverend Grove, who wore shirts and uncomfortably heavy trousers at all times, no matter how hot it was, Bellingham wore shorts. The first time George had seen him striding towards him in the mirage of heat and dust, he'd been scandalized. Those thick, muscular knees and finely turned calves ... disappearing into leather sandals? He'd blushed to his scalp, as if a naked woman had suddenly appeared in front of him. Even Reverend Grove, usually the first and quickest to defend Bellingham, had felt compelled to give a small sermon. 'Bellingham, it is not only that the requirement of modesty necessitates the provision of *some* sort of clothing, however simple, but Christian morality—'

'Sir, I'm afraid it's too *hot*,' Bellingham cut him short, smiling broadly. 'And whatever I'm wearing, it's a darn sight more than they've got on.' It was hard to argue with *that*.

Looking now at the scantily clad teenagers in front of him, George was forced to agree. He looked away, aware of his reddening face and neck. *Dammit*, he thought to himself, *no Scotsman is made for these parts*.

'What's your name?' he demanded suddenly.

'I am Nozipho.'

'Nozipho.' He pronounced it slowly. It was a pretty name.

'It means "gift",' she added. The other girl said something sharply to her, most likely admonishing her for volunteering information. All three stared at each other for a few seconds, then, without saying a word, the two girls suddenly turned and ran, their buttocks jiggling provocatively beneath the scrap of leather and beads they wore in place – and mockery – of a skirt. He forced himself to look away. The view it gave him of himself was disturbing. He was a sober man of impeccable moral truth. He didn't like the way the girl – Nozipho – looked at him. As if there were something in him that justified – or even encouraged – her scrutiny. As if he were other than what he appeared.

'Where've you been?' Bellingham looked up as he entered the room. It annoyed him, that lingering emphasis on the 'you'. As if he were incapable of going anywhere on his own.

'Nowhere,' he replied shortly. 'A walk.'

'A walk?' Bellingham's voice carried with it his amused disbelief. 'Where to?'

'Nowhere,' George repeated. He sat down on the edge of his narrow bed and began to unlace his boots. He didn't like to reveal his bare calves and feet in front of Bellingham but there was little choice. Until the new mission was completed, he was stuck there in the small, airless room with him and there was no escape. Bellingham's flesh had none of the dead marble whiteness of his own; it was burnished to a deep gold by the sun, as if polished to reveal the vitality within. He thrust his thin white toes away from view, sitting awkwardly on his hands, wishing he were anywhere but there.

'Ever been tempted?' Bellingham spoke up suddenly, not bothering to lower his book. *An Outcast of the Islands*. George noted the title immediately. He had no idea how Bellingham did it . . . managing to keep up with the latest titles and trends from Britain, which might as well have been the moon for all their contact with the outside world.

'Tempted?' George was momentarily confused. *Tempted by what?*

'By *them*.' Bellingham answered his unasked question,

lowering the book. He winked conspiratorially at George. 'I don't mind telling you,' he said chummily, 'I've been more than tempted. Held myself back, of course. Well, you have to, don't you? No knowing what the consequences might be. And they'd be pretty damn difficult to hide,' he chuckled.

George stared at him, aghast. 'Wh-what are you talking about?' he stammered.

'Oh, come on. I've seen your face when you think no one's looking. She's got a fine pair on her; I'll tell you that for free.'

'Who?' George felt hot and clammy, suddenly dizzy.

'Old Lobengula's daughter. The young one. I think they call her Nophizo, something like that.'

'Nozipho,' George corrected him automatically. 'It means "gift".'

'There you go.' Bellingham let out a lewd guffaw. 'You *have* noticed, you sly old dog.'

George shook his head firmly, although his face was on fire. 'She's the Chief's daughter,' he said sourly.

'All the more likely to comply,' Bellingham commented mildly. 'They'd sell their mothers if they thought it would gain them an advantage.'

George said nothing, too shocked to protest. Bellingham's tone was decidedly un-Christian. He stood up suddenly. The room was too airless to contemplate staying indoors and despite the mosquitoes, he wanted to be outside, away from Bellingham's prying eyes. He opened the door and breathed a sigh of relief. It was nearly dark and all around him, the land ran away to the horizon. There was nothing to be seen, only the appearance of the darkening sky. The bits of space between the smooth round mud huts came together in the darkness, ballooning out until he was lost in it. A few minutes later the village was gone, swallowed up entirely. Somewhere off in the distance he heard the cattle bellowing softly. The crickets had begun their night song. The land never slept. He ached for the silence of winter, the crying of birds as they migrated from place to place, season to season, the gentleness of it all. He sat down heavily on the edge of the step, forgetting for a moment that his feet were bare and that all it would take was one little sting, one little nip from an insect he could barely see, let alone name . . . and God only knew what might happen. That was the worst thing about being here. *God only knew what might happen.*

# PART ONE
# 1949

### Twenty-eight years later

• • •

Confession is good for the soul even
after the soul has been claimed.

MONA RODRIGUEZ

# 1

Robert McFadden, aged thirteen, pressed his ear flat against the wooden panelling and strained to hear the conversation taking place on the other side of the wall. 'You *cannot* be serious,' his mother said, her voice tight with outrage. 'Where is she?'

There was a moment's silence, then his father's voice came through the wall. Weak and placating. 'Well, that's just the thing . . . she's, er, here.'

'Here? Where's here? *Here?* Here in *Edinburgh*?'

'Aye.'

Robert frowned. It had been a strange week. His father, who had been away in Africa for most of Robert's life, was finally back. For good. But Mother seemed about as pleased to see him as she was to see the gardener. Or the coalman. Or the old hunchback who delivered vegetables once a week. *Not* pleased, in other words. Knowing Margaret McFadden, it wasn't altogether surprising. Robert's quiet, stern character, somewhat disconcerting in a child of thirteen, came almost exclusively from his mother, or so everyone said. She'd married 'down' – that was the word everyone used. For a time, Robert thought it meant 'Africa'; 'down there', as the servants kept referring to it. After a while, however, he grasped the true meaning of the word. It had to do with money, of which his mother had plenty and his father absolutely none. No one seemed to understand how or why they'd married in the first place and, since he was an only child, there was no one to ask, no one with whom he could speculate. All he knew was what Mrs Guthrie, the housekeeper, had told him in those odd moments when she'd relaxed sufficiently to pour herself a wee dram and ease off her shoes. His mother was the daughter of a Rhodesian landowner, originally from Scotland, who'd been travelling with his wife and two young daughters from Salisbury to Johannesburg when their train derailed and they were stuck for a week in Marula, a tiny mission station just south of Bulawayo where his father was stationed. He loved hearing the words. *Bulawayo. Marula. Gweru*. In Mrs Guthrie's mouth they took on an even more exotic ring. 'Bool-ay-waay-oh.' He'd looked it up on the map. He found it impossible to imagine his mother in anything other than the high-necked, stern dresses with full skirts, stockings, boots and sometimes even a tie that she wore year-round, even on the odd day when the sun shone brightly in Edinburgh and the air turned misty with heat and haze. Whatever had transpired in that week in the middle of darkest Africa, Margaret Strachan returned to Scotland betrothed. He was aware too that the word 'return' had a certain ironic ring to it. Before she'd set foot in the house in Abercromby Place, purchased for her and her new husband by an overly grateful father, she'd only once been to Scotland. She'd grown up on a sprawling estate in Rhodesia, had been home-schooled by her mother, an Englishwoman of her time and class, and as a result, sounded about as Scottish as the Queen, whom she adored. Unlike her husband, whose Glaswegian accent was as irrevocably wedded to his vocal cords as his tweed suits were to his frame, there appeared to be little of Scotland in the woman, and vice versa. Every chance she could, she boarded the steam train for London, taking Robert with her. When Robert was nine, she'd outraged everyone by declining to send him to Fettes College or George Heriot's, which was where his cousins had been sent. Instead, she sent him to Eton. When he first heard the news, he was secretly relieved. Neither school inspired anything more than outright dread. Fettes with its gloomy Gothic spires and George Heriot's with its turrets and cold, stone facade seemed more like prisons than schools. He *much* preferred Eton. The endless playing fields, the smiling house matron, and the fact that he was four-hundred-odd miles away from the frosty atmosphere of 3 Abercromby Place was enough to assuage any homesickness he might otherwise have felt. By the age of thirteen, he sounded for all the world exactly like all the other English boys in his year . . . there was nothing Scottish about him, which pleased Margaret no end but seemed to upset and astonish his father. In truth, it mattered little. He so seldom saw or heard from his father that by the time George McFadden returned to Edinburgh, Robert, who was on holiday from school, hardly recognized him.

'And what'm I to do with her?' he heard his mother ask frostily. He pressed his ear even harder against the wall.

'I . . . well, perhaps we could find some . . . employment . . .?'

'*Employment?*' His father might as well have blasphemed. 'What sort of *employment?*'

There was a moment's hesitation. 'Well, she could join the other servants . . . in the house?'

'The house?' His mother's voice rose. 'In our *house*? Whatever will people say? A Negro serving girl *in this house*?'

'She's not . . . well, I mean, clearly . . . yes, *of course*, she's a . . . a . . . well, I mean, the thing is . . . I can hardly send her back, can I?' His father appeared to be pleading.

'Robert McFadden! What in heaven's name are ye doing?'

He jumped guiltily. It was Mrs Guthrie, on her way to light the drawing room fire.

'I . . . I was just . . .'

'Eavesdropping, that's wha' ye're doin'! Runaway wi' ye, afore I tell yer mither.' Mrs Guthrie glowered down at him. Robert needed no second warning. He fled. His mother would take an extremely dim view of his eavesdropping. As he galloped up the stairs to his room on the third floor, two at a time, he wondered who they'd been talking about. A *Negro*. A servant girl, too, by the sound of it. Who was she and how had she come to be in Edinburgh, in his home?

# 2

His first thought, upon seeing her for the first time, was that she resembled nothing so much as a deer; a doe-eyed, frightened-looking deer, caught in the cross-hairs of a gun. His second thought, coming close on its heels, was that there was something strangely familiar about her, as though he'd seen her before. The two thoughts jostled uneasily at the forefront of his consciousness as he stared at her. It was a cold grey morning and the air was like smoke. Through the large sash window that looked onto the gardens at the rear of the crescent, the soft, muffled sky moved slowly and ponderously. Beyond the sloping rooftops and chimneys that fell to the Firth of Forth, the waters of the estuary glinted like steel.

She stood next to the large oak table, floury with the morning's baking, her thin, dark fingers resting trembling on its edge, as though she might otherwise fall. She was slight – so slight! – dressed in a long, dark brown pinafore frock that was several sizes too big for her and only a shade or two darker than her skin. He had never seen a Negro before. Once, in London, sitting in the back of a taxi with his mother, he'd seen an Indian man in a resplendent turban and a long, flowing robe that looked more like a dress than anything a man might wear. He'd craned his neck for ages, trying to catch the last glimpse of his dark skin and flashing white eyes, but his

21

mother had caught him out and reprimanded him for staring. Now, however, he couldn't help himself. She was unlike anyone he'd ever encountered. Her hair, escaped from the funny cloth hat she wore, was thick and springy, a soft dark cloud that shaped her head like a halo.

'Dinnae stand there gawpin' at each other,' Cook said briskly. 'Here, start wi' this, will ye?' she said to the Negro girl, handing her a rolling pin. Her own thick, meaty arms were covered in flour, sleeves pushed up to her elbows. The girl stood there, dumbstruck, though whether with terror or incomprehension, Robert couldn't tell. How old was she?

'Does she speak English?' Robert asked curiously.

'Aye, or so yer father says,' Cook said sniffily, as though the girl was invisible. 'I've nivver heard her say a word, mind.'

Suddenly the girl picked up the rolling pin and followed Cook's lead, batting down the soft mass and separating it into thick balls, ready to be rolled. So, she did speak English after all. He smiled, pleased with the discovery. To his surprise, she smiled back, offering the full charm of her face to him, like a shy gift. It was a pleasant shock. There was something about her, he discovered, that made him fear a rebuff. He had no idea how to talk to her. In his confusion, he turned away and quickly left the kitchen.

He climbed the stairs to his room on the third floor, just below the servants' quarters. It was lonely at home in the holidays. He missed the rowdy, rough-and-tumble atmosphere of school. Home was boring in a way school never was, could never be. Sometimes his mother came upon him in the library or the drawing room, 'idling without purpose', she called it. In Mother's eyes there could be no greater sin.

He sat down on the edge of the bed and tried to recall the girl's face beyond the shock of the new. Her features were smudged, any attempt at a precise recollection blotted out by her darkness. Eyes? Black, he thought, like the springy soft mass of her hair. Nose and mouth? He saw her in his mind's eye and frowned. There it was again, that strange sense of familiarity hovering on the edge of his consciousness. Was it possible he'd seen her likeness somewhere? A photograph, perhaps? It had been years since his father had opened any of the leather boxes that lay along the bottom shelf of the bookcase in his study. They contained a treasure of sepia-tinted photographs of Father's 'other' life in Africa, that place Robert had never seen and could scarcely imagine.

The clock on the landing suddenly struck eleven, the last chimes fading softly into the mid-morning gloom. On impulse, he stood up suddenly. Father had gone out earlier that morning and his mother was entertaining a circle of women from the church in the drawing room on the ground floor. He had a sudden longing to open those boxes and see for himself where the mysterious Negro girl had come from. He might even find a photograph that he'd once seen, long ago, that was now reasserting itself in his mind's eye, explaining why it was that he felt he *knew* her, as impossible as it seemed.

The dust motes spiralled slowly upwards as he pulled the first box towards him. It hadn't been moved for months, perhaps even years. No one ever came into the study other than Father and the maids, who hurriedly dusted and restocked the copper bucket of coals every other week. Somewhere inside him, a momentary twinge of unease surfaced but he suppressed it quickly, a little quiver of excitement running through him as he lifted the lid. The musty smell of old paper and tobacco rushed upwards to meet him.

There were perhaps a hundred or more photographs of

differing sizes and paper thicknesses, from tiny portraits with crinkled edges to more official-looking prints of groups of people: huddled under a tree, inside a mud-walled house, outside a church in what looked like the veritable middle of nowhere. He pulled them out carefully, picking each one up and studying it, trying to fathom the stern faces behind the moustachioed gentlemen in pith helmets and hats who were his father's colleagues, he supposed. There were no women. There was an old train ticket, yellowed and fading. He picked it out and turned it over. *Léopoldville–Brazzaville*. He didn't even know where that was. A dried-out nib of a fountain pen, a button . . . some sort of insignia. There was a letter in there, folded over thrice. He hesitated. He recognized his mother's looping, fanciful script whilst simultaneously hearing her voice. *Eavesdroppers never hear good of themselves*. Reading her letters was tantamount to eavesdropping, he knew. He carefully put the letter aside. A single portrait photograph lay underneath; he pulled it out and held it up. It was of a young woman with coal-black skin and shining eyes, who held her hand up to her mouth in a gesture of suppressed laughter. He frowned. There it was again. That whisper of something he'd long ago forgotten or buried, or both. He stared at the photograph. He turned it over. There, in his father's script, a single word. *Nozi*.

Suddenly he heard footsteps coming towards the study door. He hurriedly shoved the photographs back into the box and clumsily put it back in place. He scrambled to his feet and only just managed to slip behind the heavy damask silk curtain behind his father's desk before the door opened. It was one of the maids. He watched as she quickly scraped the remnants of the previous night's fire from the grate and restacked the coals, carefully sweeping away the ashes from the hearth before tiptoeing out as quietly as she'd come. There was something foreboding about the study with its endless books and air of dim, deathly calm. He waited until the last of her footsteps died away and then made his own escape.

# 3

Her name was Aneni, which he soon learned meant 'God is with me'. Mrs Guthrie snorted derisively. 'God or no, she'll be known as Annie in *this* hoos.' She seemed to have no idea why she'd been brought to Scotland. Her mother had died a long time ago, she told him. She'd learned English back where she'd come from, down there in Africa. She called Father '*bwana*', which Robert learned meant 'sir' or 'master'. *Bwana* had insisted she attend school, apparently angering her grandfather, the chief of the village where she'd been born. He could hear traces of his father's accent in amidst the schoolgirl vocabulary and the words she'd picked up from the other maids, quick as a flash. Was she pretty? He couldn't really say. Father said she was sixteen, three years older than he was. He noticed the way her breasts moved underneath the pinafore she wore in the same distracted way he noticed all the maids' – those near enough his own age, that was. She was certainly prettier than Dorcas, the chambermaid, and Lettie, who worked in the kitchen. She had smooth, shiny skin and the big, doe-like eyes were fringed with black lashes; a square, well-turned jaw and full lips that covered pearly-white teeth, the front one sticking out just a fraction so that the lips twitched every once in a while, a reminder of the slight imperfection in an otherwise perfectly pleasing face. He was instinctively attracted to what he didn't even know was beauty. He found it difficult to meet her eyes. The darkness there disturbed him.

She slept with the other girls in a room in the attic under Cook's watchful eye. Although they were wealthy enough to own both a townhouse and a house in the countryside, near Peebles, the family lived mainly in Edinburgh. His mother disliked the cold – and it was always cold in Peebles, even in summer. There were four staff in the New Town home, and perhaps a dozen in the countryside. He was aware, as children often are without being told, that it was his mother's private income that paid for it all. He found the words puzzling. What was 'private income'? How did it differ from 'salary'? And what was wrong with his father that he seemed incapable of generating wealth? It was all very confusing and different from most of his fellow Etonians, whose fathers were either 'in government' or 'the City'. As far as he could work out, Father didn't really seem to have a job. He'd been a school-teacher at a mission school, but many of the photographs showed him carrying a saw and a hammer, and the mud-and-brick building didn't look anything like a school to Robert.

# 4

The house was in a flurry of excitement. All day long the smells of Christmas wafted up the stairs. Cinnamon, nutmeg, cloves . . . scents that had been forgotten in the war years had suddenly reasserted their presence, despite rationing. Cook's voice could be heard shouting orders to everyone, including Mrs Guthrie, which made the servant girls smile and forced his mother upstairs with a migraine. There was to be a dinner that evening for several of their neighbours, including someone from Africa with whom his father had once worked, a man named Mr Bellingham. Robert eagerly anticipated the visit. Aside from Annie, he'd never met anyone from his father's past. He was due to arrive in the early afternoon, on the train from London. Angus, the footman, was dispatched in a taxi to pick him up from the station. Although Robert longed for one, his mother was adamant that they had no use for a car. 'A waste of money,' she declared firmly. 'Where would we go?'

A tap at the door interrupted his thoughts. It opened a crack. It was Annie. She wasn't allowed upstairs and certainly not to his room, but over the past few days the household rules had been relaxed on account of Christmas. 'Cook says you're to come downstairs,' she said timidly, hovering in the doorway.

'What for?'

'She wants you to taste something.'

'Can't *you* do it?'

She shook her head. 'I don't know what it's supposed to taste like.'

'Oh, very well. I'll be down in a minute.' He picked up his comic book again. Billy Bunter was in the midst of a dramatic rescue operation and he desperately wanted to find out what would happen. But Annie was still hovering at the door.

'She says you must come now. She's afraid it's going to burn.'

'Oh, bother! All right, all right . . . I'm coming.' Billy Bunter would have to wait.

By the time he got to the door, Annie had disappeared down the stairs, her tread as light and soundless as a feather.

Dinner that evening was a great success, bolstered enormously by the presence of Mr Bellingham, Father's friend. He was everything Father was not. Handsome, fair-haired and broad-shouldered with an easy smile and a deep, rumbling laugh. He'd even managed to make Mother laugh out loud. For once Robert was allowed into the dining room with the adults, although he was seated at the far end of the long table covered in white damask that was so bright his eyes hurt. It had been years since the house had seen such a gathering. Their neighbours were all there . . . it was glorious. The dining room had never looked so rich and warm. The curtains were drawn, and the glasses and silverware gleamed in the soft light. It was hard to believe it was only four years since the war had ended. The gamekeeper at their Peebles home had sent up two pheasants . . . it had been years since they'd had game on the table. There was wine and port for the gentlemen, sherry for the ladies. Afterwards, the maids came in to clear away the plates. The men were standing, waiting for the ladies to rise. The door was open, and in the hallway, hidden from the guests, was Annie, waiting to help Cook and the two footmen carry dishes to the scullery. She'd obviously been given instructions to stay out of sight. Unlike the two other maids, who were in uniform, their hair pinned tidily under their caps, Annie was in her habitual brown pinafore minus a cap. Whoever had told her to wait had forgotten about the large mirror just inside the dining room. From where he was standing, Robert could not only see Annie, he could see Mr Bellingham as well. Mr Bellingham caught sight of Annie as he turned to help Mrs Macpherson rise a little unsteadily from her seat, and in that moment, his eyes swivelled round to meet Father's. A look passed between the two men that Robert couldn't fathom . . . surprise? Anger? Shame? He couldn't tell. The moment passed as swiftly as it had come. When he turned back to the mirror, Annie was gone.

He wasn't sure what had woken him, the bark of a dog outside somewhere, the creak of a stair . . . whatever it was, Robert came through the layers of sleep to lie in bed, his heart thudding. The house was quiet and although he was warm enough under his eiderdown, the room was cold enough to force a reluctance to get out of bed. There it was again. A sudden noise. Somewhere between a muffled shout and a scream, cut off abruptly. He lay there for a second more, his heart beating faster now. He'd recognized his mother's voice. He slid out of bed, wincing as his bare feet touched the cold wooden floor. He bent down in the dark, fumbling for his thick woollen dressing gown and slippers. He padded carefully to the door and opened it, listening intently. On the floor below, a heated argument was going on, but not between his parents, he realized as he crept towards the source, but between his mother and *Mr Bellingham*! He stood in shock outside his mother's bedroom door. Downstairs in the hallway, the grandfather clock chimed twice. It was two o'clock in the morning! What was Mr Bellingham doing in his mother's bedroom? And where was Father?

'I don't care *what* you say!' It was his mother's voice, a low, hissing sound. The hackles on his neck rose. 'You're lying to me. You're both lying!'

'Mrs McFadden, please . . . please listen to me. It was not his fault!'

'Don't talk to me about "fault",' his mother sobbed. 'Don't you dare! How *could* he? And to think . . . she's here, in this house, under *my* roof!'

'Don't blame the girl,' Mr Bellingham urged, his own voice low and fast. 'She's only an innocent victim in all of this.'

'Victim? You call her a *victim*?'

'Mrs McFadden—'

'I want her gone, d'you hear me? I want you both gone!'

'Mrs McFadden, please! I beg you.' Mr Bellingham was pleading. 'Don't punish her. Blame me, if you have to blame anyone. I saw what was happening and I made no move to stop it. He couldn't help himself . . . you don't know what these native women are like.'

'You . . . you *knew*! All along, you *knew*!'

Robert's heart was thudding fit to burst. He brought his hands up to his ears in an unconscious gesture of protection. He knew what he was about to hear. Somehow, deep down, he'd known it from the moment he'd seen her. Aneni wasn't some 'puir wee lass' his father had rescued from obscurity. No, that wasn't it *at all*. She was blood. *She was his father's child*. Aneni was his half-sister.

# PART TWO
# 1978

Twenty-nine years later

. . .

Be slow to fall into friendship, but when thou art in,
continue firm and constant.

SOCRATES

# 5

'Sit up straight, Catriona. No one likes to see a slouching child, least of all *me*.' Her grandmother broke off her conversation to peer at her down the length of the mahogany dining table. The table's surface was like glass, light bouncing off in every direction. Jen McFadden sighed inwardly but did as she was told. Her given name was Catriona Jennifer McFadden. No one in the entire world called her Catriona, other than her grandmother and occasionally Mrs Logan, the cook, when she wished to tell her off. No one called her Jennifer, either. For as long as she could remember, she'd been called Jen. 'And hold your knife and fork properly. *Most* unbecoming.'

Jen adjusted her grip, but the reason she was grasping her cutlery tightly in the first place was on account of the conversation taking place at the far end between her mother and grandmother, a conversation she wasn't officially party to, of course, but which she could hear nonetheless. She waited with bated breath for her grandmother to answer her mother's question.

'So, when are they arriving?' her mother asked again. Patiently, as ever. No use hurrying Margaret McFadden.

Her grandmother took her time. 'Thursday,' she said, finally. 'They're bringing them directly here. They'll stay until Sunday and then they'll leave the child here.'

Jen's heart sank. So, it *was* true after all. Mrs Logan was right. There was someone coming to live with them. Someone she'd never met, didn't know, didn't want. She felt tears welling up in her throat and eyes. She looked down at her plate. She could feel her nose reddening and her cheeks growing warm. It was only a matter of seconds before her grandmother's eagle eyes would spot her distress. Children who slouched, chewed with an open mouth, failed to hold their cutlery properly or – worse – sobbed at table, were *not to be tolerated*. She tried to concentrate on her food. Scrambled eggs, two round slices of black pudding, a single piece of toast and a grilled tomato . . . she struggled to breathe. It was hopeless. Everything on her plate swam before her eyes; colours, textures, taste merging as a tear began to trickle down her face.

'What on earth is the matter with the child?' her grand-mother asked sharply.

'Jen,' her mother said quietly. 'You can leave the table. You're excused.'

'She is *not*!' Her grandmother's voice rose indignantly. 'I haven't given Catriona permission to leave.'

'Jen, leave the table.' Her mother was unusually insistent.

Jen looked nervously from one to the other. She slipped from her chair and quickly left the room. As she closed the door behind her, she heard her grandmother say, 'You'd do well to remember you married *into* the McFaddens, Alice Heatherwick, not the other way around.'

Jen hurried off. She had no desire to hear her mother's response. Her grandmother was a *bitch*. That was what Mrs Logan had said the other morning to Mrs McClenaghan, the housekeeper, when she thought Jen wasn't around. 'Tha' woman,' she'd said, drawing herself up to her full height of four feet, her large overripe bosom quivering, 'is a *bitch*. I dinnae mind saying it. I dinnae ken how Mrs A puts up wi' it.'

'Mrs A' was Jen's mother, Alice Heatherwick, the young Highlands girl who'd married Robert McFadden, sole heir to Mrs McFadden's fortune. 'Mrs M' was Margaret, Jen's grandmother. The wealth had come from *her* father, not her husband George McFadden, who'd died years earlier and for whom she seemed to have nothing but contempt. It was a miracle she even kept the man's name.

'Wheesht!' Mrs McClenaghan said sharply. 'She pays your wages, does she not?'

'Aye. But she's still a bitch.'

Jen was hiding in the pantry, crouched down with one hand stuck inside the glass jar of oatmeal biscuits. She stuffed a biscuit in her mouth to stop herself laughing out loud in glee. *Bitch. Bitch. Bitch.* She repeated the word softly to herself until she heard the two women move from the kitchen to the conservatory where they always had their elevenses. She'd slipped from the pantry with two biscuits in her pinafore pocket and a heart made lighter by their talk.

She ran upstairs to her bedroom on the third floor and closed the door behind her. She flung herself on the bed and rolled onto her front, pressing her face into her pillow, her hands balled into fists by her sides. She let out a muffled scream, beating her fists against the counterpane and kicking her heels, the way she'd done as a very young child in the days before Margaret McFadden had moved from her home in Peebles to live with them in Edinburgh. The family home was too large for her, she declared imperiously. 'Rattling around in there like the Snawdoun Herald.' Jen had wanted to know what the Snawdoun Herald was, but her mother was too distraught at the prospect of her mother-in-law coming to live with them to answer. Margaret was now seventy-six and in rude health. It was entirely possible she'd be with them for decades yet. Jen screamed into her pillow again. Her grandmother had been with them for four long years, a time without end. Jen, who had once been an only child and the darling of all the servants, had been peremptorily relegated to the sidelines, bound by a code of childhood conduct that seemed to belong to a different century. *Seen and not heard. Spare the rod.* And her favourite: *Protect yourself from other people's bad manners by a conspicuous display of your own good ones.* Nowadays Jen rarely saw her father and when she did see her mother, Margaret's shadow was somehow always hanging over them.

And now someone else was coming to join them and usurp her, sending her even further down the queue. Life couldn't possibly get any worse.

# 6

All day long, adults came and went, the murmur of their conversations punctuated by the sharp bang of the screen door as it swung to and fro. Some brought things – useless things, like goats (in one case) and a pile of traditional Ndebele blankets (in another). All were coming to say goodbye. Kemi sat with her grandmother on a low stool, sucking a boiled sweet that one of the aunties had given her, listening with half an ear to the adults talking. Most of her attention was elsewhere, taken up with the excitement of being the star attraction, rare in that household of real, and much more important, stars. She was leaving Rhodesia. The following night, she would board an airplane bound for London in the company of an *international aunt*. She would have preferred to go with one of her *real* aunts – Auntie Violet, for example, her mother's younger sister – but the terms of her mother's recent house arrest seemed to encompass all adult members of her family, even the ones Kemi didn't know. She'd memorized the three-letter codes of all the airports on the journey to London – from Salisbury (SAY) to Rome (FCO), and from Rome to London (LHR). The last part of the journey to Edinburgh would be made by train. Her Uncle Robert would meet her at Heathrow (LHR) and chaperone her to London's King's Cross where they would catch a sleeper train to Edinburgh's Waverley Station. The journey would take almost two whole days.

'Who is Uncle Robert?' she'd asked her grandmother. All she knew about him was that he had a daughter the same age as Kemi. Her name was Catriona Jennifer McFadden. Apparently, she couldn't wait to meet Kemi. Kemi wasn't so sure. If it were her, she reasoned, she wouldn't be thrilled at the prospect of sharing her room with a complete stranger, especially not a stranger from halfway across the world.

Her grandmother was oddly silent. She shrugged. 'He's . . . he's your grandfather's friend,' was all she would say. Kemi understood it to mean her grandfather Godspeed, her mother's father; not her father's father, Dumisani Mashabane. Her mother's father was only known by his first name.

Someone was weeping as she came out of the house, banging the screen door loudly behind her. Kemi watched with detached curiosity as she patted her cheeks dry and blew her nose – loudly – before coming over to where Kemi sat and placing the palm of her hand on Kemi's head. 'Poor little thing,' she said in Shona. 'So young. All that way. And when will she come back?'

Her grandmother made a strange, half-strangled sound that sat somewhere between a sob and a groan. She brought her own hands up to her eyes, pressing against her lids, but when her fingers fell away, Kemi was relieved to see her eyes were dry. She wasn't sure she could have borne seeing her grandmother cry. 'Come,' her grandmother said, getting to her feet. She wrapped her colourful *kanga* around her, tucking it firmly around her waist. It was a present from Kemi's mother, brought back from a trip to Tanzania in the days when Florence Mashabane was still able to leave the country. A bright turquoise background, a red flowered border, and the words *Sisi sote abiria dereva ni Mungu* printed several times in circular, flowing script across it. 'It means, "We are all passengers, God is the driver",' Florence told her delighted mother. Now, as a banned person, arrested for inciting resistance to white minority rule under Ian Smith's government, Florence Mashabane was not allowed to leave her front door, except to drive to the police station every day between midday and two o'clock, to report and record her presence.

'Come,' her grandmother repeated. 'Let's go inside and see your mother.' It was a subtle reminder that her mother wasn't allowed past the swinging screen door. Across the road, just hidden from view by the hedge, was the unmarked police car that drove slowly up and down the street at any and every hour, now parked under the shade of an acacia tree. Kemi caught the glint of binoculars as one of the policemen trained his gaze on the house. She opened the door and followed her grandmother in. Just before it slammed shut, she turned and stuck out her tongue at him, a childish act of defiance that would have earned her a slap from her grandmother, had she seen it. It made her feel better, just the same.

Inside the living room, her mother sat like a queen on her throne whilst various friends and family members fussed around her. To everyone else, the occasion would be tragic. Her only child, being sent away. A husband in jail down south, her daughter sent overseas to be raised by others, she herself under house arrest. How could she bear it? Florence's answer was produced under a smile so serene and beatific it seemed to come from a religious rather than political source. *We must all make sacrifices. I cannot exempt myself.* Her grandmother's hand on her shoulder guided Kemi forwards to the upright chair in which Florence sat, her elaborate hairdo, magenta-painted nails and elegant clothing a proud assertion of her identity as a beautiful, powerful woman and her refusal to be bowed. Kemi kneeled down dutifully at her mother's feet. The smiles that followed were an acknowledgement that she, too, could be counted on in this family, utterly united in their dedication to the struggle to overthrow white rule.

The house and its occupants (save one) were in a fever of anticipation and excitement. Their African guest would be coming directly from Waverley to 17 Jordan Lane, Morningside, any minute now. Breakfast had been prepared and was being laid out on the dining room table. Claw-footed tureens of creamy porridge stood alongside silver jugs of not one, but three – *three?* – types of maple syrup; there were bowls of thick clotted cream; silver racks waited impatiently for slices of hot toast. From the kitchen came the scent of frying bacon and the cook's own homemade sausages. Mrs Logan stood at the Aga, a huge bowl of beaten eggs in her floury arms, just waiting for the signal. All this for a 'puir wee African lass'? Jen was in a fever of mutinous jealousy. No one had ever – *ever* – made such a fuss over *her*.

She wandered upstairs and into her mother's bedroom. Her parents slept in separate rooms, an arrangement she thought everyone shared. It was only when she was invited to stay the night with Lizzie Macintosh that she noticed her parents didn't sleep separately. 'Where's your mum's room?' she'd asked Lizzie, as they crept into the bedroom to look for her mother's jewellery box.

'This *is* my mum's room,' Lizzie answered, puzzled. 'What d'you mean?'

'Well, where does your dad sleep?'

Lizzie pointed to the double bed. 'Right there. Where else is he supposed to sleep?'

Jen fell suddenly quiet. It was the first inkling she had that things in her own home might be the exception and not the rule.

'Why do *we* have to have her?' she asked her mother for the hundredth time.

Alice was in front of her dressing table, carefully combing and arranging her hair. She put down the silver-backed hair-brush and turned to face Jen. 'Listen, I know it's hard for you to understand, but poor Kemisa hasn't got anyone. Her dad's in jail and her mother's been arrested. Just think what it'd be like if Daddy and I weren't here. Who would take you to school? Who would cook your tea?'

'Mrs Logan would,' Jen muttered sullenly, picking at an invisible thread on her skirt. 'And Jock would drive me to school.'

Her mother was silent for a few minutes. 'Well, it'll be nice for you to have a sister,' she said finally. 'You're always saying you want a little brother or a sister.'

'Yes, but she's *not* my sister!' Jen burst out. 'She's *African*! How can she *possibly* be my sister? She's *black*! Everyone'll know it's a lie!' Jen's voice rose to a shout.

'Catriona McFadden! Just you stop that nonsense right now! How in God's name did we bring up such a selfish little girl? What does Christ teach us to be? Kind, compassionate, caring, that's what. Not selfish and mean-spirited. Now, go and brush your own hair and make sure you've a clean skirt on. And put a smile on your face. The wind'll change any minute and you'll be stuck with that scowl.' Her mother turned back to her own image. 'Go on,' she mouthed at her in the mirror. '*Go!*'

Jen fled. She burst into her room and slammed the door shut behind her. She dropped to her knees beside the bed and folded her hands in prayer. 'Dear God,' she began hesitantly. She paused for a moment, summoning up the courage to voice her innermost fears. 'Dear God, please make everyone hate her. Please make her mean and ugly and horrid. And please, God, *please* make sure Mummy and Daddy don't like her better than me.'

*A single colour.* All of England appeared as a single dull greyness that overwhelmed everything, especially the senses. Kemi sat in the back of the fancy car that bore them away from the airport and gazed out upon a landscape without any recognizable landmarks, no sense of scale or the passing of time. Fields, stone walls; more fields, more walls; steel electricity pylons running off to the horizon; the grey tongue of the motorway stretching in front of them; then, as they drew nearer to the city, small, neat bungalow houses, all painted the same colour. Presently they came upon taller houses, with square, boxy windows that looked out onto grey streets. Grey. It was a colour she couldn't ever recall seeing. Now she was to be smothered in it. She pressed her hands and legs tightly together and tried not to look at the man sitting next to her who had introduced himself as 'Uncle Robert'. She had no problem addressing him as 'Uncle' but adding 'Robert' seemed sacrilegious. At home, all adults were either 'Auntie' or 'Uncle', *never* 'Auntie Jane' or 'Uncle John'.

She turned away from the back of chauffeur's peaked cap and Uncle Robert's stern, bearded profile and looked out of the window instead. The streets of London that they passed through were filled with a strange electricity, a kind of suppressed liveliness that was very different from the bustle and chaos of home. In Mbare, every square inch was taken up with human activity – hawking, trading, gossiping, making and mending. There was an orange seller under every shady tree, a shoeshine boy at every kerb. When you pulled up at a traffic light, someone immediately appeared selling Lotto tickets and chewing gum. The air was full – shouts of welcome and good-bye, the cries of the iced-water sellers, the women selling peanuts and boiled maize ears – 'two shillings a piece!' But in London there was no such noise, no such signs of life. Instead, all of life's activity seemed to be tightly contained behind steamed-up glass windows – cafes, hairdressers, clothes shops, shoe shops, chemists . . . all hidden behind the same screen through which people peered, as though trying to work out what might be beyond. At a traffic light, when the car slowed to a halt she saw two children, separated by the foggy glass of a restaurant window. One was inside the restaurant and the other outside, waiting with his mother. She watched as they both slowly traced out a circle on the glass through which they could see each other. She stared at them. It seemed ineffably sad, almost as sad as the feeling pressing down on her when-ever she thought of her mother's face as she said goodbye, not even able to come to the airport in Salisbury. Her aunts and uncles were the ones appointed to take her. 'Be a good girl, Kemisa. Study hard. Listen to Uncle Robert. Remember who you are, always. No matter what happens, hmm? I will come for you soon.'

She'd nodded, afraid to speak. Her fear was so tightly wound inside her tummy that any show of emotion would burst it. Her mother's last words, shouted to her from behind the screen door, made everyone in the car laugh. 'Don't make friends with every African you meet!' There was little chance of that, she thought to herself glumly. She hadn't seen a single African. She was the only one. In time, would she too take on the cold grey pallor of those around her?

*

'They're here,' Alice said, and slipped off the window seat that overlooked the driveway. Jen looked up. Her mother smoothed down her skirt. It was an automatic gesture, applicable in all circumstances, all weathers, all moods. Jen had long since made up her mind never to smooth down her skirt or smooth back her hair, another of her mother's nervous tics. 'Come on, Jen. Let's go down and meet them.'

'*You* go,' Jen muttered sulkily.

'Come on. Don't be like that,' her mother said, holding out a hand. It was the hand that did it. Jen couldn't remember the last time she'd held her mother's hand. She slipped her own in it now, savouring the way her mother's soft, smooth palm fitted over her own, nice and tight. Her mother gave her a reassuring squeeze and for a moment, Jen's heart lifted. Things might be all right after all. 'Ready?' her mother asked, looking down at her. Jen couldn't help it; she too tucked her hair behind her ears, just like her mother, and together they walked down the stairs.

She could see the two shapes behind the frosted glass of the front door. Her father, tall and upright, and a smaller figure beside him. She swallowed nervously as the handle turned downwards and the door opened.

'Come in, Kemisa, come in. Mrs McClenaghan, will you take the young lady's coat?' he said to the housekeeper hovering behind Jen and her mother.

Kemisa Mashabane stood in the doorway. The midday light spilled around her. All Jen could see was masses of curly, dark brown hair; a small, heart-shaped face the colour of a Dairy Milk chocolate bar; enormous, jet-black eyes that slanted upwards and a full, soft mouth. She was wearing a tartan skirt, white shirt and blazer, as though dressed for school. A pair of knee-high dark blue socks and sensible black shoes . . . everything about her was neat and tidy, perfect in the way Jen would never, ever be. Kemisa Mashabane was *beautiful*.

Jen: *She's the most perfect girl I've ever seen.*

Kemi: *She hates me already.*

Jen: *She thinks I'm ugly.*

Kemi: *She's afraid I'll stay forever.*

'Jen, come and meet Kemisa. Don't be shy.' Her father's voice was full of an emotion Jen couldn't place. It was almost tender. 'This is an important day for our families. An important day.'

# 7

'Which side would *you* like?' Jen hung about in the doorway, suddenly shy. Her bedroom, which had held a single bed and a dressing table all her life, now held two beds, side by side, and a larger dresser, which the chauffeur had brought in the night before. Jen had carefully placed her own hairbrush and trinkets to one side, leaving exactly half its surface clear for Kemisa's possessions.

'I don't mind,' Kemisa said politely. Her voice, like everything about her, was soft and calm.

'Well, *I* don't mind either,' Jen said, unsure how to resolve the question of who slept where. 'I mean, they're both by the window and—'

'I think *you* should choose. It's your room,' Kemisa said politely.

Jen hesitated. 'OK, well, I'll sleep here,' she said, pointing to the bed next to her. Her mother had bought two new counterpanes and on the bedside table, in between the two beds, was a single rose in a small glass vase and a dish of wrapped boiled sweets. Her bedroom now resembled the spare room. It had been her mother's idea to make them share a room.

Kemisa picked up her overnight bag and put it on the bed that was now hers. 'I hope you don't mind having to share with me,' she said, releasing the double locks, accurately reading Jen's mind.

'Oh, no,' Jen said hurriedly, guiltily. 'Would you like one of these?' she held out a sweet, suddenly unsure of herself.

Kemisa shook her head. 'No, thank you. My mother doesn't allow it.'

Jen's eyes flickered upwards. 'But she's not here. How will she even know?'

'I can't do that. I would never disobey my mother.'

Jen carefully unwrapped a purple sweet and popped it in her mouth. 'Well, I never obey *my* mum,' she said cheerfully, her right cheek bulging pleasurably with the sticky sweetness. 'There's no point. She can never remember whether she's told me to do something or *not* to do it. She lives in her own head, that's what Cook says.'

Kemi looked startled for a moment, as if Jen had let a swear word slip. 'But she's your *mother*,' she said.

'So? Anyhow, I actually think she's *not* my mother.'

Kemi's eyes widened. She looked at Jen curiously. 'What do you mean?'

Jen shrugged. 'I don't think I belong here. On earth, I mean. I think I came from somewhere else, maybe another galaxy or something.' She sucked on her sweet. 'I mean, we don't even *look* alike. I don't look like either of them.'

Kemi said nothing. She busied herself carefully unpacking the few possessions she'd brought with her. Two pairs of everything – sweaters, socks, underwear . . . black and grey, nothing colourful, nothing fancy, nothing memorable. It was ironic. Kemi Mashabane was memorable regardless, and not just on account of her skin colour. 'So, you're an only child too?' Kemi asked finally, after the last piece of clothing had been tidily put away.

Jen nodded. 'That's what everyone says. But I don't believe

49

anything anyone tells me,' she added quickly. 'I'm sure I've got brothers and sisters somewhere. Is that really all you've brought with you?' she said, changing the subject.

'What else should I have brought?'

'Well, what if you have to go to a party?'

'A party?' Kemi sounded doubtful. 'What sort of party?'

'*Any* party.'

'I don't know,' Kemi said carefully. 'I've never been to a party.'

Jen stared at her. '*Never?* Never, ever?'

'Never.'

'Why? Don't you have parties in . . . where you come from?' She struggled to remember the name.

Kemi shrugged. 'Some girls do. But we're under house arrest.'

'What does that mean?'

'It means I can't leave the house except to go to school. The police watch us all the time. They sit opposite our house all day. I even know their names. Sometimes my grandmother makes me take them water. My mum can't. She can't even go into the front yard.'

Jen was stunned. 'Why?'

Kemi looked at her. Her gaze was steady. 'Because we're going to overthrow the government,' she said simply.

Jen was lost for words. The sweet in her mouth had turned into a hard, sharp sliver. She bit it slowly, letting the sweetness dissolve on her tongue. Kemi was unlike anyone she'd ever met. She had only the vaguest sense of what was happening 'down there' where she came from. A world of politics and police meant absolutely nothing to her. She tried to imagine life without the occasional excitement of a party, or being confined to her own house, but couldn't. There was a gulf between them that had nothing to do with the fact that she was white and Kemi was black, or the fact that Jen's hair was straight and Kemi's was curly. Those were just the most obvious signs. Beneath that, a whole world separated them which she was drawn to, yet instinctively feared. What did it mean to overthrow a government? Why did it mean something to the stranger, who was now about to share her room, and not to her? Something was being offered, she understood, that was tantalizingly, frustratingly out of her reach.

She was innocent, Kemi saw, in the way that only children often were, too preoccupied with their own lives to notice what happened to others. She had a strong sense of fantasy, too, inadvertently revealed in the silly idea of unknown brothers and sisters, and in her observation – which Kemi already knew was Jen's, not Cook's – that her mother 'lived inside her own head'. So did Jen. That much was clear. But there was also an affectionate eagerness about her that Kemi found touching. Jen wished to be *seen*. Despite their differences, Kemi understood the desire to be properly seen and heard only too well. Kemi couldn't remember her father. The man whose face stared back at her from the photographs she was shown was a stranger. Sometimes, when her mother's attention was elsewhere, she would pick up the framed photograph that lived on the side table in the living room and tilt it this way and that, searching for a hint of familiarity in the solemn, composed gaze. She knew she was *like* him; everyone commented on it – 'just like her father, ay?' – but it seemed a matter of composure, of manner, not looks. Jen looked nothing like her parents, either . . . another unexpected bond. She slid a quick, careful look at the girl sitting on the bed, twisting one end of a long auburn plait between her fingers. She had never been this close to a white girl of her own age before. Jen looked up suddenly. A tremor of recognition passed between them. Her eyes were neither blue nor green, Kemi noticed, an in-between colour, made more difficult to place by the fringe of light brown eyelashes and the red-blonde arch of her brow. They eyed each other warily. Then Kemi reached out her hand, palm turned upwards. 'You know,' she said shyly, 'I think I'll have a sweet after all.'

There it was. In the shared bedroom, a kind of comfort neither had known before was about to be built. Both girls recognized it without it having to be said.

# PART THREE
# 1987

## Nine years later

. . .

What I cannot love, I overlook.
Is that real friendship?

ANAÏS NIN

# 8

'You go.' Jen eyed the closed door of the study nervously.

'No, you go.' Kemi shook her head. 'You go first.'

'No, *you* go first.'

'Why?'

'Because I'm too scared to tell him.'

Kemi rolled her eyes. '*You*? Excuse me, you're the one who threatened to break Claire MacGregor's nose, d'you remember?'

Jen grinned. 'That was different.'

Kemi shook her head. She'd never forgotten her first day at Fettes, nearly nine years earlier. She'd walked into the classroom with Jen, her heart thumping with fear. There was no mistaking the look everyone gave her. 'Who – or what – the hell is *that*?' She slid into the seat next to Jen and waited for the murmuring to stop. Suddenly she heard the scrape of a chair next to her. She stole a look sideways. Jen was standing over a blonde girl sitting in the next row. 'You say that *ever* again, Claire MacGregor, and I'll break your fucking nose.' There was a sudden gasp and the class fell silent. Jen wouldn't tell her what Claire MacGregor had said. In the nine years since then, she'd asked her many, many times. Jen simply shook her head, stubbornly mute. But Claire MacGregor never said it – whatever it was – again. She felt a sudden rush of affection for her soul sister. It was Jen who'd come up with the term. 'We're more than *real* sisters. We're soul sisters.' It was true. She was closer to Jen than anyone in the world.

'All right, I'll go. But don't let him talk you out of it, d'you hear me?'

Jen nodded. 'I won't.' But her voice wasn't quite as convincing as it should have been. 'I *won't*,' she repeated. 'I promise.'

Kemi gave her a rueful smile. She secured her ponytail, making sure there were no loose, unruly curls, and knocked on the door.

'Come in.' Uncle Robert's deep voice came from within. She pushed open the door, letting it shut quietly behind her. She stood in the doorway, waiting for him to look up.

'Have a seat, Kemisa. I'll be with you in just a moment.'

Uncle Robert was Scottish – as Scottish as the Jacobites, as he often said – but his accent remained stubbornly Etonian.

'So, what can I do for you, Kemisa?' Uncle Robert looked up from the sheaf of papers he'd been studying. She would always be Kemisa to him, never Kemi. Theirs was an oddly formal relationship, given that she'd lived with the McFaddens for half her life. She'd seen more of Alice and Robert McFadden than she had her own parents. She spoke to her mother whenever the circumstances permitted – once or twice a year, if they were lucky. Their conversations were short and to the point. *Are you being a good girl? Are you studying hard? Do you have everything you need?* Kemi knew the calls were monitored. What could she tell her? Yes, she had everything she needed. When she and Jen turned twelve, it was Cook who explained to the girls what menstruation was, not Alice. As for her father, it had been so long since anyone had heard Tole Mashabane's voice that even his daughter wouldn't be able to place it.

'Uncle, do you have a moment?' *That* was the correct way to address him. Jen's approach was always combative, as though she expected to fight. It wasn't the way to approach one's elders.

'Indeed, I do.' He was sitting at his desk, its surface a field of dark green leather and almost-erased gold, a stack of legal papers spread out in front of him. He turned in his seat and indicated the chair opposite. She sat down, folding her hands in her lap. He looked at her, a finger resting in the soft folds of his bearded cheek, waiting for her to divulge whatever it was she'd come to see him about.

'It's about university, Uncle. I've made up my mind,' Kemi began hesitantly. He nodded encouragingly.

'Go on, Kemisa.'

'I'm going to go for medicine. I spoke to the careers advisor yesterday. He thinks I've got a good chance of getting into UCL.'

Uncle Robert was quiet for a moment. He nodded slowly. Then he got up from his chair. He walked over to the armoire beside the window and unlocked one of the drawers. He took something out, weighing it in his hand for a moment, then turned and walked back. He sat down and cleared his throat. Kemi looked at him expectantly, her heart beginning to beat faster.

'I've thought about giving this to you many times over the past nine years since you came to us,' he began carefully. 'Tole asked me to give it to you when I felt the time was right. It was the last conversation we had.' There was silence between them. He held out the little black box to her.

Kemi took it from him, blinking quickly and very hard. For a moment the room swelled and lurched alarmingly. 'Th-thank you, Uncle.'

'Go on, open it.'

Kemi prised the lid open carefully. Inside, nestled on a bed of simple white tissue, was a solid silver pocket watch. She took it out with shaking fingers, holding it up by the little chain hoop. *Parkin & Son. Doncaster.* She turned it over. There were the three embossed silver hallmarks and a date, 1887. She stared at it. It was solid and heavy in her palm. Her fingers curled protectively around it. 'Thank you, Uncle,' she said again. For a moment they stood looking at the antique pocket watch together. Neither was the type to let much show. In those first few weeks and months he'd had the habit of shifting his feet about uncomfortably whenever he came upon her in the hallway or in the kitchen, unused to her, uncertain about where it might lead. 'Thank you, Uncle,' Kemi said again softly, slipping the watch back into the box. Where had it come from? Why had her father asked Uncle Robert to give it to her? She sensed it was not the right time to ask. 'Shall I send Jen in?'

He nodded slowly. An expression crossed his face, so fast she wondered if she'd imagined it, a kind of inward-looking weariness, almost of defeat. 'Yes. Send her in.'

The word in her father's mouth might have been a swear word, a dirty word, a *blasphemous* word. He said it just the once – 'artist?' – with the question mark still trapped within, and turned away, patting his pockets for his pipe. Minutes ticked by, filled only with the worrying of a match into flame as he lit his pipe, the sound of rain hitting the windowpanes and the slow, curling hiss of smoke. Jen stood where she was in front of his desk, arms folded tightly across her chest whilst he smoked with his back to her, looking out across the garden to the misty view of Arthurs Seat just visible through the apple trees.

Finally, he cleared his throat and turned around again. Taking a seat, he laid the pipe carefully on its stand and brought his hands together, elbows resting against the desk's worn leather surface.

'So,' he said carefully, all the weight of the world – his expectations, her grandfather's dying wishes, the wealth of the McFadden family and her grandmother's steely contempt – contained in the careful manner in which he spoke. 'You've decided on it, have you?'

Jen swallowed. She nodded, not trusting herself to speak. Not just yet.

'And you're asking me to support you in this decision?'

'I . . . I'm going to do it anyway.' She was proud that her voice shook only a little. Bravado aside, it was about the most frightening thing she'd ever done.

'I see.'

'It's what I want to do, Father. It's all I've ever wanted to do.'

'Well, Jennifer, life isn't just about what one *wants* to do. It's also about what one *must* do. The right thing. The right choice. Even if it's a sacrifice.'

'What's *wrong* with art, Father? I'm *good* at it.'

'The wealth of this family wasn't built on anything quite so frivolous, Jennifer. You'd do well to remember that.'

'But I don't *care* about money!'

'You'll care about it soon enough. It's impossible to make a living out of art, Jennifer. Impossible.' It was a death sentence. 'Just like your mother. All talk. Nothing *but* talk. Well, I'll not stop you, Jennifer. And I'll not stoop so low as to fail to support you. But nothing will come of it, you mark my words. Yes, indeed. Just like your mother.'

Jen felt the blood rush to her cheeks. Her father seldom spoke of her mother, let alone to her, but it was an open secret in the house that he had little regard for her. It wasn't just the matter of separate rooms and separate lives – Alice McFadden didn't actually *have* much of a life. Her world revolved around the domestic spheres of the McFaddens' two homes – the house in Morningside and the large, empty country house just outside Peebles. There was no question of selling it, so Alice made the weekly trip down from Edinburgh to oversee the few staff who remained, making sure everything inside was in pristine working condition, held in trust for the generations who might one day follow. She opened her mouth to say something, *any*thing, but found that words failed her. They stared at each other for a wordless moment.

'You'll thank me right enough one day, Jennifer,' her father said finally. He picked up his pipe. The conversation, such as it was, was over. She swallowed hard and left the room.


'So, what did he say?' Kemi's face appeared between the bannisters. She was sitting on the third step from the top, hugging her legs to her chest. She'd pulled her curls free of her ponytail. The stained-glass window on the first landing streamed with multicoloured light. Kemi's halo of curls appeared to be on fire. *An angel. A beautiful black angel.*

'He hates the idea, of course, but he won't stop me.' Jen tried to shrug it off.

Kemi looked at her searchingly. She wasn't fooled. 'Are you OK?'

'Yeah, course I am.'

'Sure?'

Jen's eyes filled with sudden tears. It was impossible to cry in front of *him*, but she'd never been able to keep her feelings hidden from Kemi. 'He won't stop me. Th-that's the main thing,' she sniffed.

'Not stopping you isn't the same as actually supporting you,' Kemi said, ever practical. 'He's not going to cut you off, is he?'

Jen shook her head. 'No. He didn't threaten *that*.'

'What's the worst that can happen? The very, very worst?'

Jen looked up at her, blinking back tears. 'Wh-what d'you mean?'

'Exactly what I said. Look, if you're not going to be penniless, what's the worst that can happen?'

Jen's shoulders went up and down. 'I . . . I don't know. I might fail. I might not be any good.'

'Yes, but equally, you might succeed. Now, dry your eyes, stand up straight and start thinking about where you're going to go next.'

Jen looked up at her. The hallway began to swim again. 'I . . . I don't know if I can,' she began, worried that she would burst into tears. 'I'm not like you, Kemi . . . I . . . I think I'd better do something else.'

Kemi was quiet. Jen looked at her nervously. She didn't like it when Kemi was quiet. They looked at each other without saying anything. 'It's your life, Jen. Don't let anyone else tell you what to do with your life.'

'It's not that simple,' Jen said shakily.

'That's where you're wrong,' Kemi said slowly. 'It *is* that simple. It's *your* life. Not his, not mine. Yours.' She slid her long legs down the stairs and got up. 'Yours,' she repeated. And then she was gone.

Jen remained where she was, crouching on the bottom stair, afraid to move. Not for the first time she had the distinct sense of the two of them having come to a line together, only to watch Kemi cross it, leaving her behind.

# PART FOUR
# 1997

## Ten years later

. . .

Ambition is not a vice of little people.

MICHEL DE MONTAIGNE

# 9

'And for you, *Mamá*?' The waiter turned to his mother. Solam Rhoyi read the man's mind as if he'd spoken aloud. He noted the way the waiter's eyes quickly assessed his mother's expensive suit, colourful scarf and a watch that probably cost a year's wages, likely more. He threw Solam a quick glance, wondering if he was a TV star, a footballer? No, no . . . ah, yes, he had it! His eyes widened slightly as recognition dawned. *Solam Rhoyi. Is he a politician? I've seen his face on TV.* His manner softened. In someone like Solam Rhoyi there was the promise of better to come.

Solam darted a quick look at his mother. He noticed the frown. She hated being called *Mamá*, especially with that long, drawn-out 'a' at the end. *Mamá.* A sign of respect she could have done without, *thank you very much*.

Iketleng held the menu away from her as if offended by it. 'Fish? Do you have fish?'

The waiter nodded patiently. 'Yes, *Mamá*. There is a fish dish. No, I don't know the name. But it is tasty, yes, yes . . . very tasty.' Solam could read her impatience like an open book. She'd only been back from New York a few months and was determined to find fault with just about everything in South Africa – and everyone.

'I'm sure it'll be fine,' Solam said briskly, closing his own menu with a snap. 'Two of the fish, whatever it is. Grilled, not fried. Shall we have a glass of wine?'

His mother nodded. He chose a Sauvignon Blanc, a Tokara, not too heavy. When it arrived, he quickly took charge, relieving the poor waiter of any more of Iketleng's wrath. He poured them both a glass. 'Cheers.'

'Cheers,' she murmured, only partially mollified.

Solam took a sip, eyeing her warily. He never knew how to read his mother's moods. Not that it was surprising. They'd spent most of their lives apart. Even his parents had barely spent time with one another. His father was a recently qualified lawyer and trade union organizer with a young wife and a six-year-old son when he was arrested and held for six months at the notorious John Vorster Square prison in Johannesburg. When he came out, he was sent to the north of the country to start a union for mineworkers. Within a year, he was rearrested, this time for life. Solam remembered the day of his father's sentencing. It was at the High Court in Pretoria. He was passed from shoulder to shoulder, at the back of the courtroom where the blacks were squashed. The mood was jubilant, defiant. He remembered too the gasp that tore through the court when they were sentenced and the loud outburst from the hundreds who'd come to hear it pronounced. *Amandla! Awethu! Amandla!* The crowd's blessings fell like laurels upon his father and the six other young men who were being led back down to the cells. His father turned and raised a shackled fist, not at his wife and child but at the crowd. And then it was over. He was led through a door at the back of the courtroom and they were gone. Solam rode home sandwiched between adults who never stopped talking, staring at his mother's braided, elegant head. Within a year, his mother too was picked up and sentenced to ten years for 'conspiring to overthrow the state'. His aunt, his mother's youngest sister, stepped in to take care of him. He moved out of the modest house in Protea Glen, where he had his own room, and into his aunt's much more modest and crowded house in Jabulani, opposite the police station and next to the hospital. All night long the ambulances drove up and down Bolani Road, wailing into the darkness. At first, he lay stiffly in the bed he shared with his cousin, Moketsi, afraid to close his eyes in case he found himself dreaming of his mother and woke up crying. At the new school just up the road on Nkonyane Street, he kept himself to himself, trailing miserably behind his cousins in the dusty playground, longing for his old school, his old teachers, his friends . . . his *life*.

Then, one afternoon a little over a month later, he was summoned into the living room by his aunt. The smell of cooking wafted over the assembled gathering from the kitchen behind the beaded screen. There were perhaps a dozen men, none of whom he'd seen before, sitting smoking, drinking a little . . . there was an air of camaraderie and warmth, of the kind he understood now that he'd missed. His aunt was nothing like his mother. She was a nurse at the district hospital. She worked long hours and did not complain. There was no man in the house. No one spoke of an uncle or a father – his cousins didn't seem to feel or see the lack. She went to church three times a week but didn't press him to accompany her, for which he was grateful. She presented him to the men, both hands on his thin shoulders, pressing him forward. The conversation ebbed and flowed around him, snatches of the kind of language spoken in his old home, when his parents were around.

*I never trusted him. They infiltrated everyone, everything . . . I tell you.*

*Any news from Sweden? I thought they said there'd be money.*

*I just asked Johnny. You remember him? The one from the Star.*

*We should have been better organized back then. You know, too much in-fighting. That's our problem, man. We so busy fighting each other we forget who's the real enemy!*

His aunt's fingers dug into his shoulders. In that house, children were seen but not heard. He could feel her tension as she waited nervously for a gap in the conversation. Not like his mother. She would have been at the centre of the discussions or arguments, her flamboyantly painted fingernails waving as she underscored someone else's opinion, or, more likely, refuted it. There was a pause in the talk. His aunt pounced. She hurriedly nudged him forward.

'Mfundi, this is Oliver's son. The one they were talking about.' An older man looked up, his eyes blinking slowly. He looked Solam up and down.

'Oliver's kid, eh? You're Iketleng's son?'

Solam nodded. A shy obstinacy came over him. He watched closely as the group's attention slowly shifted, coming to rest on him.

'He's a big boy already!'

'Looks just like Iketleng. Man, that woman. Fearless. Fearless, I tell you! Did you see her when they came for her?'

'How old are you, son?'

'S-seven.' His stammer, long since suppressed, suddenly reasserted itself.

'Big for his age. Tall, eh? Just like Oliver.'

'So, how would you like to go overseas, young man?'

He blinked. Overseas? He didn't understand the word. He turned to look up at his aunt. There was an expression he hadn't seen in her face before. Anger? Her nails were piercing his skin. He shifted uncomfortably.

'Here, come . . . come here, son.' One of the other men beckoned him forward. The air was marbled with cigarette smoke. He slid out of his aunt's grasp and stood before him. The man, whose name he did not know, smiled at him encouragingly. 'Yes, overseas. To England. It's been decided.'

A few weeks later, aged seven, he made the long trip to England with a friend of his father's, a quiet taciturn man who mostly read and dozed on the flight from Johannesburg via Cabo Verde, somewhere out in the middle of the Atlantic. The man broke his concentration to explain that other African countries would not allow South African Airways to fly over their airspace. They had to stop and refuel on one of the islands still owned by the Portuguese. 'Not for long,' the man remarked cryptically. Dimly, Solam understood that the fate of the island nation was somehow tied to South Africa's own fate, the cause for which both his parents were in jail and, it seemed, prepared to die. He wasn't sure how to feel about that. He understood that his own importance as Oliver and Iketleng's son was intimately tied to their sacrifice, but he longed for his mother's touch, her easy smile or the warmth he remembered when her attention was on him.

They drove from London to the boarding school selected for him. Stowe School, about an hour's drive from the airport. He stared at the imposing facade from the car window, his breath coming short. He had never seen anything like it. It was as big and grand as the Union Buildings in Pretoria. This was a *school*? He was handed over to a Mr Jenkins, the housemaster, into whose care the seven-year-old was entrusted. Mr Jenkins briskly looked him up and down and smiled. He was a big, chalky man, with large, warm hands. He shook Solam's hand gravely but firmly – a double pump, up-down, twice, before letting go. There was something solid and comforting about that handshake. The man, whose name he still didn't know, and who had accompanied him for almost two days, seemed eager to leave. There was a muted, hurried conversation between him and Mr Jenkins at the door . . . and then he was gone. The last link to home.

He found that he fitted in surprisingly well in his new home. He was clever, good at sports, fair-minded, funny . . . the sort of qualities the English admired. Soon the nagging sense of being out of place left him. He was popular, both with his teachers and his classmates, which he sensed was unusual. But the real meaning of boarding school escaped him. What was it all in preparation for? What was he supposed to do with himself?

In sixth form, he shared a room with Charlie de Cadanet, the son of one of Britain's most famous sculptors. Charlie was new to Stowe, having left his previous school 'before he was asked to'. Good-looking, with a dry sense of humour, he and Solam hit it off immediately. He too was afflicted by the disease of being 'a son of', as he cheerfully put it. 'We're both our fathers' sons.' Both were defined by their fathers, although for entirely different reasons.

'There *is* no escape,' Charlie said to him good-humouredly on their first night in their new room. Their beds were at opposite ends of the small attic, all the way at the top of the boarding house. 'But let's face it, worse things happen at sea.'

'Why don't you change your name?' Solam asked after a moment. He actually had no idea who the sculptor was. People at school talked of Edward de Cadanet in hushed tones. Politicians, revolutionaries, statesmen . . . those were more in Solam's field. Artists meant little to him.

'Why should I? Would *you* change yours?'

Solam pondered his response. 'No,' he conceded after a moment. 'Mind you, it's not the same thing.'

'In what way? Your parents are famous too.'

'Yeah, but it's different with mine. They're in jail. Everyone feels sorry for me. And I'm African.'

'What does *that* mean?'

'It means most people are just relieved I can speak English. Or I haven't got a bone through my nose.'

Charlie let out a guffaw. 'Priceless!'

'It's true,' Solam said, beginning to laugh as well.

'Well, *I* won't let on if you don't,' Charlie said, and there was the sound of a smile in his voice. Solam began to relax. He liked Charlie, even if they barely knew one another. 'What're you doing at half-term?' Charlie asked suddenly.

Solam burrowed further down in his bed. At 6'3, with a duvet made for the average man, his toes were always cold. He pondered the question. Half-term was still a way off. 'Dunno. I usually go to Basingstoke. To friends of the family. Sort of.'

'Basingstoke? Where the hell's that? Why don't you come home with me? Mum and Dad'll love you. And not because you speak so well.'

Solam pondered the invitation. Home. He had no sense of home other than Stowe. 'Sure,' he said, as casually as he dared. 'Sounds good.' He had no idea what he would say to the very distant aunt whose two-up, two-down house on Hawthorn Way he'd gone to every half-term and holiday since he'd arrived in England. He liked his aunt well enough, but after a night in the cramped house where the number of residents seemed to change daily, depending on the situation 'down there', he itched to get back to Stowe.

Charlie was right. Edward and Libby de Cadanet *adored* him. For almost the first time, he sensed they were genuinely interested in him *as a person*, not as a token or a badge of honour.

There was no pity or surprise. They accepted him just as he was. It was his first taste of freedom.

For the two remaining years of school, it was to the de Cadanets' beautiful Pimlico home that he went every holiday, not to Basingstoke. If his aunt was hurt by the switch, she was gracious enough not to let it show.

'Any time,' she said to him over the phone. 'You come to us *any* time.'

He never went back. Pimlico, with its sophisticated wine bars, elegant high-ceilinged villas and beautifully manicured squares, was much more to his taste.


He was twenty-four when his parents were released from jail, alongside Mandela. With the unbanning of the ANC and the release of all political prisoners, the regime's days were numbered, everyone knew it. With his degrees in hand, he flew to Cape Town to meet his mother and father, whom he hadn't seen since he was seven, and to visit the country of his birth. He was a stranger. He'd *forgotten his own language*. England was his home now. He spent less than a fortnight in a hotel in Cape Town, bewildered by everything, unable to connect. He flew back to London with the taste of disappointment fresh in his mouth. South Africa was no place for him.

But a year later, with apartheid finally in its death throes and his parents moving rapidly up the political ladder, he began to change his mind. Part of it was to do with the new group of friends he'd met in London. Like him, they were Africans who'd attended the best universities in London, Paris . . . New York. They were bankers and doctors and engineers. They were well educated, well-travelled, full of confidence. Some of them were from the south, like him – South Africans, Zimbabweans, Zambians – but there were Ghanaians and Nigerians amongst them, as well as Kenyans, Ugandans, Senegalese. New Africans. People who were like him, who *liked* him . . . he'd found his tribe. And home was his for the taking, when the time was right.

Now he had a plan. He took another path. For the first time ever, he leaned on his parents for a contact. He wanted to live in London, and he wanted a place at the London School of Economics. Iketleng was galvanized into action. For her, it meant only one thing: their only son would soon be coming home.

A tiny basement flat in Kensington was found. It belonged to one of the many Jewish supporters of the ANC command-in-exile. Dr Feldman was only too pleased to let it out to the handsome young man whose parents had sacrificed everything for the cause, including their only child. There was no rent to be paid. No, absolutely not, he wouldn't hear of it. The place was empty most of the year anyway. A housekeeper would come in once a week. It would be a pleasure, no, an honour. Solam moved in. If anyone on the interview panel at the LSE was astute enough to connect Solam Mxolisi Rhoyi with Oliver and Iketleng Rhoyi, he had the good grace and manners not to bring it up. The young man sitting in front of them was impressive enough without parental connections. 6'3 of solid, sport-honed muscle, a keen intelligence and an easy, charming affability, he'd be an asset to the university. After the interview, the panel discussed the applicant.

'He's their only son, am I right?' Professor Galfard said, stirring his coffee reflectively.

'That's right.' John Wootten, head of the admissions committee, nodded. 'We've had a few like him. Worth their weight in gold. They'll all go on to key positions, mark my words.'

'Well, rather chaps like *him* than the sort we've been getting lately,' Professor Galfard said darkly. He didn't need to elaborate.

The recent scandal involving a despot's son who'd somehow obtained a PhD at the same time as the university had received several million pounds in funding pledges – none of which had materialized – had cost the vice chancellor his job and no one wanted to be reminded of *that*. Fortunately, Solam Rhoyi presented no such risk. He was the real deal.

A year at the LSE was followed by two years at Merrill Lynch, a year at Standard Bank's City of London HQ, and then, finally, the position he'd been waiting for – a transfer to South Africa, to the Simmonds Street HQ in Johannesburg. Professor Galfard was right. In the new dispensation after the fall of apartheid, men like Solam Rhoyi were like gold dust.

He said his goodbyes, moved out of the basement flat in Kensington, bought Dr Feldman a small painting by Gary Hume on Charlie's recommendation as a token of his appreciation, and flew straight to Johannesburg.

He spent the first few months at his parents' comfortable new home in Sandton. Straight after independence in '94, his father had been appointed ambassador to the United Nations and he and Iketleng had moved to New York. For three years, the new home on Wilton Road was empty. It made a comfortable landing pad for Solam, but he hated the suburbs. He missed the city.

He could never be sure who'd engineered it, his mother or his father. Neither would say. The approach was made cautiously, through his line manager at the bank. National Treasury was looking for young, qualified South Africans, something in tax analysis. He understood it had been Solam's specialization at university. His name had been put forward . . . was he interested perhaps? The salary was good – not as much as the bank, of course, but a position in the Treasury would lead to other things . . . in time, perhaps, an elected position. For now, there was a vacancy and he'd thought of Solam. It would be a wrench losing him at the bank . . . but, all things considered, a civil service appointment might be just the right move. Would he consider it? *I would. Oh, yes, I would.* Within a year, he was promoted to Deputy Director of Prudential Regulation, the government's youngest ever appointment. The journalists loved him. The newscasters loved him. The morning financial shows loved him. *Everybody* loved Solam Rhoyi.

By the time Iketleng and Oliver returned from New York, the tables were turned. It was Solam who was now in charge. He was the one with all the connections; he knew whom to call, when. In their absence, the city had transformed itself. He knew where all the best restaurants were, where Iketleng could find the coffee she liked and the shoes she could now afford. He knew which clubs Oliver ought to belong to and whom to avoid. And it was Solam who'd chosen the restaurant in Rose-bank where they now sat, mother and son, close in ways they'd never been before.

'So . . . where's this place you've been looking at?' Iketleng said, placing her wine glass down on the snowy white table-cloth. She looked around her. Yes, her son had taste. 'Is it close by?'

'Er, no. It's in Braamfontein, actually.'

She looked up at him in surprise. 'Braamfontein? Why on earth would you want to buy a house in Braamfontein?'

He shrugged. 'It's not a house, Ma, it's an apartment. A loft, actually. It's in a great building. Overlooks the Mandela Bridge, right in the heart of things. It reminds me of London. New York.'

She rolled her eyes. 'Don't give me that. Jo'burg's nothing like New York. Certainly not Braamfontein. Why don't you buy somewhere nice, like Sandton, or Rosebank? Who on earth lives in Braamfontein?'

'That's precisely the point. I don't *want* to live where everyone else lives. Look, much as I've enjoyed staying at yours, I hate the suburbs.'

'Don't be silly. What's to hate about security and rubbish collection and roads without potholes? You'll be broken into, or your car will be stolen . . . or worse.'

Solam shook his head. 'Listen to you. Now *you're* being silly. It's 1997, not 1987. Things are different now.'

It was Iketleng's turn to shake her head. 'I don't know what your father will say,' she said, lifting up her glass. 'Braamfontein? *Nobody* lives in Braamfontein.'

'Well, I'm about to,' Solam said, following suit. 'I'll have you both over for dinner as soon as I've moved in.'

Iketleng snorted. 'That'll be the day. Well, it looks like we'll be living in Pretoria soon.'

'So, what's going on? I'm hearing rumours.'

'What sort of rumours?' Iketleng asked, a small smile playing around the corner of her lips.

He looked at his mother. 'The inner circle. Or so I hear.'

Iketleng said nothing for a moment. 'Well, it's up to the old man,' she said finally. 'But, yes, there've been a few conversations.'

'And Dad? What does he say about it? I thought he wanted to stay out of the inner circle?'

Iketleng shrugged. 'You know what he's like. He doesn't say much. At least not until it's all been confirmed.'

Solam smiled. She wasn't about to give an inch. 'And you?' he asked slowly. 'You've done your time, surely?'

Iketleng met his eye. She drew in her lip, the way she did

76

when she wasn't sure how to answer something or needed more time. 'We'll see. We're still talking. There are some who feel two Rhoyis in government is too much.'

He nodded. He'd known that before asking. There was silence between them for a few moments. The waiter came back with a plate of warm bread, olive oil and balsamic vinegar. Iketleng made a great show of refusing the bread, then, unable to stop herself, picked at the crust. She was uncharacteristically nervous, Solam saw. He wondered why.

'So . . . when are you off?' she asked quickly. Too quickly, he thought. She was up to something.

'On Tuesday.'

'And where are you going again?' Her voice had the air of someone who knew the answer. He frowned. It wasn't like her to be coy. What the hell was she up to?

'London.'

'How long?'

'Few days, a week at the most. I'm going with the Director General. I can't stay away too long . . . you know what this place is like.'

Iketleng smiled faintly and he saw the irony wasn't lost on her. It was now her son's turn to tell her things were at home.

'You should look up Kemisa if you have the time.' Iketleng tried to sound nonchalant.

'Who?' He was puzzled.

'Kemisa Mashabane. Tole and Florence's daughter. Didn't you meet when you were children? I saw Florence in New York, just before we left. She's so proud of her. A doctor, just like her father. Imagine.'

'Imagine,' Solam said dryly. 'Anyway, I won't have time. I'm there for meetings, Ma.'

'Well, it won't hurt. We exiles ought to stick together. I was just telling Florence—'

77

'Ma, we're not exiles any more. It's over.'

Iketleng looked at him sharply. 'It's never over. Don't forget that. You think independence solved everything? My child, independence is only the beginning.'

'Sure, Ma, sure.' Solam knew better than to argue with her. She had a way of pursing her lips together that was the fore-runner to an argument or a sermon, he couldn't tell which . . . not that he wanted either. He glanced at his watch. It was nearly two thirty.

'You have someplace else you'd rather be?' Iketleng asked sharply.

He sighed. 'No, Ma. I said I'd meet the realtor at the flat at five, that's all.'

'So, you've made up your mind?'

'Yes, Ma. Yes, I have. Now, tell me what you want from London.'

Iketleng immediately softened. 'Ooh, won't you bring me back some digestive biscuits? You know, the dark chocolate ones. I miss them.'

Solam nodded. He understood her message. *You can't even get a decent packet of biscuits here.* He smiled. For all her con-victions, his mother was sometimes remarkably easy to read. 'Noted,' he said. 'Two packets.'

'No more than two. I'm watching my weight, remember?'

He suppressed a smile. She looked the same to him as she'd always done. A tall, striking woman, always with an elaborate, beautifully coiffed hairdo. The years in jail seemed to have had remarkably little impact on her. It was his father who had changed, so much so that his first sighting of him was a shock. He'd always remembered him as tall and thin but the years on Robben Island had worn him down, quite literally. He was thin to the point of emaciation. It was the first time the conse-quences of his parents' sacrifice had been hammered home to him. In the years since their release, however, his father had changed again. Now, like many men who'd existed on a Spartan prison diet, the rich food and wine post-release had produced a small but noticeable paunch, a little potbelly, which was the source of much teasing between his parents. The rest of him had remained lean, but the stomach gave it away. He was as fond of a good steak washed down with red wine as anyone else. 'You wait,' he said now, looking enviously at Solam's washboard stomach, 'it'll happen to you too.'

'Never,' Solam laughed. He wasn't given to vanity, not by a long shot, but he loved sport too much to even contemplate being out of shape. Running, cycling, rugby . . . *those* were his passions, not Cuban cigars or barrel-aged whisky.

He kissed his mother goodbye, leaving her on the phone. Her driver and bodyguard were waiting discreetly in the corner of the restaurant. He crossed the plaza, conscious of eyes on him as he went. There were precious few black faces in the Rosebank Mall who weren't waiters or security guards. He cut an odd figure, he knew, with his smart suit and polished brogues. He caught the eye of a waiter who turned to look at him as he passed, pride in his face. Solam knew that he represented a new kind of black man – educated, erudite, confident. He walked through the Mall as though he owned it, a whole generation and class away from those who'd carried the hated *dompas*, the piece of paper allowing blacks to be in urban areas for no more than seventy-two hours without permission. It had been over a decade since the pass laws were repealed, but their memory was hard to erase.

He crossed the road and jogged up the steps to the car park, ignoring the cluster of beggars who were permanently stationed at the entrance. He could get used to many things, but not the beggars. The high, hard summer light bounced off the sleek cars and the puddles left in the ground by the earlier sudden rainstorm. He was still getting used to the reversal in seasons. Winter in the northern hemisphere was summer in the south. Christmas in summer. It still didn't feel right.

He got into his car, enjoying the smell of new leather. Yes, a convertible BMW was something of a cliché, but it was also one of the finest cars he'd ever driven. He manoeuvred his way out of the parking lot and turned into Sturdee Avenue, enjoying the weight and thrust of the car's powerful engine. He drove fast, flying through the intersection of Jan Smuts, heading towards the inner city. In a few weeks' time, he thought to himself with a faint smile, he'd be coming home to his own place, his first home.

He felt his phone vibrate gently in his pocket. He tugged it out and looked at the message as he waited at the lights. *Don't forget to look up Kemisa Mashabane. I promised her mother.* He tossed the phone onto the passenger seat with a sigh. When would his mother realize that he didn't need her to organize his love life? He had plenty of expertise and experience in *that* department without anyone's help, least of all hers.

# 10

For a few moments, none of the surgeons clustered around the gurney spoke. Everyone's concentration was on the patient lying in front of them. Mr Fairbanks, the neurologist in charge, cleared his throat. 'Dr Mashabane, will you take over?'

Kemi swallowed nervously. There was absolutely no time to waste. It was only her second craniotomy, but she knew why she'd been singled out. She was in her first year of the neurosurgery programme and she was the only female on the team: she *had* to get it right. She adjusted the focus on the high-powered microscope and leaned over. From the screen to her left she knew the tumour was located just under the right temporal area. Fairbanks had guided the removal of the dura and the delicate pink mass of the brain was already exposed.

'Eleven, please,' she murmured to the theatre nurse hovering discreetly at her left elbow. A scalpel was passed along. She gripped it, remembering to relax her hold exactly at the moment of the first incision. The blade went in cleanly; not a flicker of resistance. A thin, angry stream of red traced the line of incision, whisked away before it could spread by the aspirator. Geoff Manning, second-in-command, peeled back the quivering mass of pulpy flesh with his pincers, giving her as much room as possible to view the brain. She saw it immediately. In contrast to the healthy-looking surrounding matter, the tumour was purplish and malevolent, exactly as one might imagine it. She cut away carefully at the sac covering it, Geoff holding back the flaps as she went. The melanotic tumour was nestled in the right upper corner of the exposure, glistening accusingly at her, pulsating in time with the patient's heartbeat. The veins were clearly visible, one slightly thicker than the rest, delivering the blood on which the tumour had been greedily feeding.

'Gently does it. Mind you don't puncture too early.'

'Yes, Mr Fairbanks.' Kemi's hand was steady.

'Relax into it. You're doing fine.'

'Thank you, sir.'

She leaned forward, all her concentration focused on the jelly-like tissue sac covering the tumour. A millimetre to the left or right would result in damage to the healthy brain tissue – and who knew what that would lead to? It fascinated her – the reduction of a life's worth of feelings, emotions and memories to the pulpy grey-pink matter that lay before her, its form giving no clues as to what lay beneath, buried within. An inadvertent slip of the blade might take out any number of experiences or skills . . . loss of language, the ability to recall, a person's motor skills? It was what had drawn her to neurosurgery in the first place, both the terror and the exhilaration.

'Well done,' Geoff murmured two hours later, as the team pushed through the operating theatre doors into the anteroom. 'Steady as she went. Couldn't have done a better job myself.'

She smiled at him. 'No, you couldn't,' she said, half teasingly. 'But I could feel Fairbanks's eyes boring through *my* skull, never mind the patient's.'

'He's hard to impress,' Geoff agreed, peeling off his surgical gown. 'But you're doing a fine job of it. Just watch out for those hands.' He lowered his voice. 'Wandering, apparently. He's got a bit of a reputation.'

Kemi laughed. 'Come on. He's old enough to be my uncle. No way.'

'Why d'you say that?'

'What?'

'Uncle. Most people say, "old enough to be my father", not "uncle".'

'I . . . I was brought up by my uncle,' Kemi said quickly. She knew exactly where the conversation would turn.

'I've always wanted to ask you . . . you're not related to Tole Mashabane, are you?'

'No,' she said smoothly, without turning around. Barely a week went by now without his name in the news. 'It's a common name,' she lied. 'A bit like "Smith", or "Jones".'

'Ah. I always wondered. Wouldn't that be something, though? If you *were* related.'

'Would it?' Kemi said politely. She picked up her handbag. 'I'm off,' she said firmly.

'Aren't you coming out for a drink with us? Come on, it's nearly Christmas.'

Kemi shook her head. 'I can't. I'm meeting someone.'

Geoff raised his eyebrows. 'Some*one*?'

'No, nothing like that. My sister.'

'Oh. I didn't know you had a sister. You've never mentioned her before.'

'Geoff, I've only known you for a couple of months,' Kemi said, only half in exasperation.

'Yes, but you know everything about me. Practically everything.'

'That's because you talk a lot. I don't.'

'Where are you meeting? Can I come along?'

'No.' And then more gently, to soften the blow: 'Maybe next time.'

'Promise?'

'No.' She smiled. 'Besides, haven't you got a date? With the lovely Pernilla, if I remember correctly.'

Geoff smirked. 'You know perfectly well I'd ditch her in a heartbeat if you just gave the nod.'

'Don't hold your breath.' Kemi pushed the locker door firmly shut. 'Have fun,' she said, twirling her fingers at him. 'I can't wait to hear all about it.'

'You're just saying that,' Geoff said, slinging his bag over his shoulder and following her out of the changing room.

'Yes, I am,' she grinned. 'See you Monday.' She blew him a mock kiss and disappeared through the swing doors.


It was raining outside. She pulled up the collar of her coat and tucked her unruly curls under its hood. She walked down Gower Street, past the peeling facade of the old Victorian teaching hospital, now under demolition. A sleek glass-and-steel phoenix of a building was supposed to rise from its dust, or so the billboards promised. She rather liked the old, red-brick Gothic pile – it reminded her a little of Fettes. At the thought of Fettes, her face brightened. It had been almost six months since she'd seen Jen. She was back from a three-month stint in New York, apparently the maximum time she could get away with, without anything as official as a work permit in hand. Kemi had forgotten what exactly she'd been doing in New York . . . an assistant to an assistant to an assistant curator? Something along those lines and something in the 'art world', whatever and wherever *that* was. It was hard to keep up with Jen. She spoke of the art world the way some people spoke of the Third World; a separate world 'out there',

disconnected from normal, everyday life. Wherever it was –
London, New York or Miami – it seemed to Kemi to be a
world fuelled largely by artists' egos, clients' money and a
bewildering, ever-increasing circle of 'contacts', not people,
friends or colleagues, whose every whim Jen sought desperately to please. It was amusing but exasperating, too. Better
than most, Kemi knew Jen was capable of so much more.
After graduating with a degree in art history, Jen had drifted
from one seemingly dead-end job to another, never quite settling, either geographically or professionally. The disastrous
conversation with Uncle Robert meant she'd never pursue her
dreams of being an artist. Kemi listened to her long list of
reasons why she'd abandoned the idea with as much sympathy as she could muster, but with little understanding. It
didn't make sense to her: why didn't Jen just do what she
*really* wanted? Who cared what others thought? But she'd
learned the hard way not to ask.

She pushed open the door to the Thai restaurant that Jen
had chosen and was shown to a window seat. It was still
early; just past five on a rainy Friday afternoon, two weeks
before Christmas. She looked outside; there was an *Evening
Standard* placard almost directly in front of her. *Winnie Mandela to Testify.* She looked away. It was the second reminder
of home in less than a couple of hours, though she wasn't sure
why she thought of it as home. How could a place she hadn't
been to once in nineteen years still be thought of as 'home'?
She picked up the menu, looking for something else to occupy
her. Jen would be late; she was *always* late.

Ten minutes later she looked up, sensing someone coming
towards her. It was Jen. She rushed to her in her usual flurry of
scarves, coat, jumper, handbag, her hands tugging impatiently

at her coat buttons as she dropped her gloves and shopping bags at her feet.

She got up. They collided. 'Sorry,' she murmured, hugging Jen tightly. 'Gosh, you're cold!' Her long red hair was damp at the ends.

'I'm late, aren't I?' Jen asked anxiously, throwing her coat over the back of a chair. Kemi stole a quick look at her before she collapsed into it. She'd put on weight, Kemi noticed. Jen's weight went dramatically up and down, depending on dozens of factors Kemi couldn't keep up with, anything from being in love to falling out of it; from finding a job to losing one. She lived at an emotional intensity that made Kemi slightly dizzy.

Kemi shook her head firmly. 'No, I'm early. Got out of surgery at four.'

Jen clapped a hand to her mouth. 'Oh no, I forgot! I'm such an idiot!'

'What?'

'I haven't seen you since you won!'

'Won what?' Kemi was puzzled.

'That place . . . the surgery thing. On the team. You know, the place you were hoping for . . .'

'Oh, Jen. That was *months* ago.' Kemi smiled. 'And it's no big deal.'

'I *always* forget,' she moaned. 'You must think I'm a complete flake.'

Kemi shook her head, smiling at her a little sadly. 'You know I don't think that. You've been busy . . . we've both been busy. Let's get something to drink. What'll you have?'

Jen brightened visibly. 'I'll have a glass of white,' she said decisively. 'No, make it a bottle. I've been waiting for this *all* day. I've just been run off my feet!'

'What's going on?' Kemi asked, picking up the wine list. 'I thought you said you were coming back home for a rest.'

'No, that's all changed. Parker found me the most *amazing* job at this new gallery in Mayfair and—'

'Who's Parker?' Kemi interrupted, looking at Jen closely. *A new man?*

'Oh, no, nothing like that,' Jen said quickly, reading Kemi's glance. 'He's gay.'

'So?'

'Plus, he's American,' Jen said breezily, as if *that* completely ruled him out. 'We met through Mindy . . . remember her? She was at Durham with me. I'm sure you met her. Anyhow, Parker's great. He used to work for Sotheby's, and he knows everyone, and I mean *everyone*. So, he spoke to Federico at Cube, and the next thing I know, I'm on the phone to Federico's wife, Isabella, and—'

'Jen, I don't know any of these people,' Kemi interrupted her again gently. 'But just tell me what it is that you're actually going to be doing?'

'Oh, I'm being silly! I keep forgetting you don't know any of them. They're art dealers. They've just bought Cube, you know, the new gallery that's just opened on Bruton Street . . . you must have heard of it? No? Next to Tiphâne de Boissy's gallery?'

Kemi shook her head again. She listened with half an ear as Jen rattled off a dozen names she'd never heard of. Tiphâne? Brooklyn? Federico? It was such a far cry from her own world, where people had simple, *normal* names, like Geoff and David and Anne. As Jen began excitedly describing the new gallery and her new job – which sounded suspiciously like all her other jobs where she was given a grand-sounding title but made to do all the donkey work – Kemi's mind drifted back to the *Evening Standard* headline she'd spotted in the window, and to Geoff's remark. She was uncomfortably aware of the fact that her parents were beginning to reassert themselves in her life in a way they hadn't for almost twenty years. Although her mother had been released from house arrest three years after Kemi's arrival in Edinburgh, it had been decided to leave Kemi with the McFaddens. There was little point disrupting her schooling, especially since she appeared to have settled in so well. Florence Mashabane continued the fight to free her South African husband, languishing on Robben Island with all the other ANC prisoners. Freedom in Mugabe's Zimbabwe, her home country, was matched across the border in South Africa by the defiant intensification of the slowly dying apartheid regime.

It would be another decade before political prisoners in South Africa were released. When Tole walked out alongside Mandela in 1990, Florence accompanied him to London a month later. Kemi was summoned by the headmaster at Fettes and told to prepare herself for a historic journey to London. There were likely to be reporters around, she was told, and no doubt journalists would be keen to talk to her. 'Why?' Kemi asked, alarmed.

'Well, they're your parents, too,' Dr Osborne said, smiling benevolently. 'As well as being heroes, of course.'

Kemi didn't know what to say. As soon as she walked into the hotel room in South Kensington, she understood that the part of her life that had existed before Edinburgh was firmly over. It had nothing to do with her. The regal, aloof woman in an elaborate headdress sitting in the upright chair at the window overlooking the gardens didn't belong to her. She didn't even get up! She sat calmly with her hands folded in her lap and waited for Kemi to cross the room, ignoring the assembled reporters and their noisy, clacking cameras. Kemi reached her mother. She accepted her mother's cool hand on her wrist in the same way she'd felt her hand on her head, aged nine, when she was sent away. Not even a kiss! Her mother's head moved once, twice, the same benediction. 'Welcome home.' Kemi had no idea what to say. The plush suite was no more a home than the bungalow in Harare with the swinging screen door had been. Edinburgh was home. Not Harare. Not the Bentley Hotel in Harrington Gardens. She stood back and allowed herself to be inspected slowly, head to toe and back again. Her mother's expression was unreadable, unreachable. Her father was 'out' and no one seemed to know when he'd be back. When he finally arrived, flanked by bodyguards, she suddenly felt the urge to hide behind her mother's skirts. She had no recollection whatsoever of the tall, thin man who stood before her, smiling widely. At the last minute, just before leaving Fettes, she'd slipped the pocket watch into her skirt. Now she fingered it nervously.

'Kem, you're not listening!' Jen's voice broke in on her thoughts.

'I am, I am, I promise! Sorry, it's just been a long day.' She took a sip of wine. 'Couple of tough cases.'

Jen was immediately contrite. 'Listen to me. I've just been sitting here prattling on about myself . . . sorry, Kem, honestly. I haven't seen you for six months and all I can do is go on about *me*.'

'No, don't be silly. Anyhow, your life's so much more interesting than mine, I promise you. All I do is go to work, go to bed, wake up and do it all over again. Now, tell me about next Saturday. What's the event again? Do I need to put on a dress?'

# 11

Something was definitely wrong, Jen thought to herself ten minutes later as she watched Kemi walk to the toilets. You couldn't see it in her face but Jen had long since learned to read the other signs – the flickering pulse underneath her right eyelid; the faint tremble in her hands when she reached for her glass – that spoke of the kind of exhaustion Jen could only guess at. Kemi's skin hid everything – every blemish, every flaw, every wrinkle – smooth dark satiny skin, stretching tightly over her cheekbones and jaw. When Kemi first came to live with them, Jen couldn't stop marvelling at how different they were. *One black, one white. One clever, one stupid. One slender, one plump. One calm, one excitable.* Yet it immediately became clear that the surface differences hid a closeness that neither girl had ever experienced, or hoped to experience. How was it possible for two creatures who were so alike that they practically finished each other's sentences to be so different? Jen's emotions were right there on the surface of her pale, almost translucent skin. Kemi's were hidden, buried underneath the smooth darkness that fooled everyone except Jen. Her normally short nails were longer than usual and her wild, curly hair was dry and frizzy, which meant she probably hadn't been to see a hairdresser in months. Her parents had been in the news over the past couple of days, too. Jen dimly recalled seeing Kemi's father being sworn in as Mandela's right-hand man on TV, and her mother had been in trouble for openly criticizing Mugabe. All the years under house arrest had done little to silence Florence Mashabane's sharp tongue.

'Have you seen the news?' Jen asked carefully as their food arrived.

Kemi gave a little shrug. 'Yeah. Here, try these. They're delicious.' She passed over a plate of grilled shrimps. It was her way of deflecting the question.

'D'you think you'll go?' Jen persisted.

Kemi paused, her chopsticks halfway to her mouth. 'To what? The swearing-in ceremony? No. Why? Should I?'

Jen hesitated. 'Well, it's . . . it's an important occasion, isn't it? I mean, Father's going.'

Kemi shrugged again. 'It's important for him, not me.'

'Why not?'

'I'm in the middle of my new rotation. I can't afford to take time off.'

Jen was silent. She could still remember the day it had first dawned on her that Kemi's dedication to the causes which both their families seemed to have been fighting for almost a century wasn't quite as strong as everyone assumed. It was in their final year at Fettes. Everyone knew Kemi would be made head girl. It was a foregone conclusion. She was Tole and Florence Mashabane's daughter, for goodness' sake. Even if she hadn't been brilliant in her own right, there was no denying the cachet she bestowed upon the school. Between them and the Mandelas, there were few political families with such pedigree.

But Kemi surprised everyone by turning it down. She'd marched into Dr Osborne's office after the announcement had been made in assembly, and emerged an hour later with reddened eyes but with that determined tilt to her chin that Jen had long since learned to recognize. She didn't want it. She didn't want the limelight. It was the second time that Jen felt the line separating them had been crossed, and that she'd been left standing in Kemi's wake. Dr Osborne made the announcement to a stunned school the following morning. In its entire history, no pupil had ever turned down the role. Kathleen Harris was ushered in as head girl. Jennifer McFadden, Kemi's 'sister', was her deputy. Kemi wished to study medicine, like her father. She needed all the spare study time she could get. It was only right that she'd given up the honour to Jen, her sister. Everyone applauded vigorously. Jen was well liked and the reasons given seemed fair enough.

But for the remainder of her time at Fettes, Jen couldn't quite shake off the feeling of being second best, the understudy to her infinitely more talented, more deserving and certainly more diligent sister, though few would have said it out loud. Then there was the other bond she and Kemi shared, which they rarely spoke about. Both had grown up with mothers who were shadows. The big difference was that Kemi's mother was made a shadow through her own strength. Alice was a shadow through an insipid weakness that secretly terrified Jen, partly because she knew it to be part of her own character, in the same way Kemi had inherited Florence's grit and determination. In her most private moments, when she was absolutely sure no one could see her, she stood in front of the bathroom mirror, anxiously checking her image. Had her mother's feebleness somehow rubbed off on her? At face value, it seemed unlikely: Alice was dangerously thin, pale and slender to the point of ethereality. Jen was plump and rosy, with sturdy calves and generous hips . . . anything *but* a waif. Kemi found the thought ridiculous. 'It doesn't work that way,' she said sternly. 'You inherit things like eye colour, or the colour of your hair. You don't inherit *character*. At least not in the way you're worried about it.' Jen wished she had Kemi's confidence. She herself wasn't sure.

'But won't they be expecting you?' she asked Kemi hesitantly.

Kemi shrugged. 'They'll get over it. And no, to be honest. I don't think anyone's expecting me.' She put down her chopsticks. 'I wish everyone would just stop.'

'Stop what?' Jen asked, although she knew what Kemi was about to say.

'Stop assuming that I want anything to do with it. I'm never going back. It's not my home. My home is *here*, Jen, not there. I don't know anything about the place any more. I don't know and I don't care.'

Jen was quiet. It was the first time in years she'd seen Kemi agitated. Her normally smooth brow was furrowed. 'Well, promise me you'll come and see the new gallery?' she asked brightly, changing the subject. 'The opening's next week. At least come for a drink. Bring someone from work. I never get to meet any of your friends.'

'That's because I've hardly got any,' Kemi said with a quick, rueful smile.

'Well, you've got me. And it's my first big opening in London. So, *please* come.'

'All right, all right, I will. Tell me what you're doing again?'

'Oh, I'm just the organizer. Wine and canapés, invitation list . . . stuff like that. But it'll lead to other things, I know it will. You always have to start at the bottom.'

'Why do you always sell yourself so short?'

Jen flushed. 'I don't. You've got it wrong. You don't know what it's like, Kem. The art world . . . it's just so competitive. You've got to start somewhere.'

'Ordering drinks?'

Jen looked down at her empty plate. She helped herself to

more rice, partly to give herself something to do. 'It's not like that,' she said, uncomfortably aware she was beginning to sound defensive. 'It's different for you.'

'No, it's not. You're brilliant, Jen. You got a *first*, for God's sake.'

'Yeah, well, fat lot of good it's done me,' Jen said, a touch of bitterness creeping into her voice. She tried unsuccessfully to squash it. 'He didn't even come to my graduation.'

Kemi sighed. 'He was away on business, Jen. It wasn't on purpose.'

'He came to yours, though, didn't he?'

'Because he happened to be here, that's all.'

'That's what *he* says. *I* know why he came to yours and not mine. He's *proud* of you. Look at you! You're a surgeon! It doesn't get better than that. But he's ashamed of me and everyone knows it.'

'Jen . . . stop it. This is supposed to be a catch-up dinner, not an argument about Uncle Robert. You're *brilliant*. *I* know it; *he* knows it; *everyone* knows it. The only person who doesn't seem to believe it is you.'

Jen swallowed the little angry knot of resentment that seemed to appear in her throat every time she thought about her father. She looked down at her plate again, blinking furiously. She nodded. 'You're right,' she said after a moment. 'I'm sorry. It's just—'

'I know,' Kemi interrupted her gently. 'I know how angry he makes you. But I keep telling you . . . it's *your* life, not his. Live it for *you*, not for him. Stop worrying about what he thinks of you. Worry about what you think of yourself.'

Jen nodded again. She blew out her cheeks. 'You're right. You're always bloody right.'

Kemi smiled. 'There you go again. I'm not always right. Half the time I don't know what I'm doing either. But I don't spend the other half worrying about it, that's the difference. Just follow your instincts.'

'That's just it,' Jen said unhappily. 'I feel as though I don't have any. Most of the time I've got no idea what I'm meant to be doing with my life.'

'Just take it a step at a time. Find something you love and stick with it.'

'Well, I love *this*,' Jen said hesitantly. 'I love bringing people together . . . I know it sounds silly and boring but—'

'There's nothing silly and boring about it, Jen. It's what you love and it's what you're good at. Now, for God's sake, drink up. I can't finish this bottle on my own and *you* ordered it. And tell me what to wear next week. I don't want to wind up looking like the hired help.'

Jen giggled. 'You never look like the hired help. But I've got just the thing,' she said, casting her mind back to her own wardrobe. 'It's been a few years since I could squeeze my way into it. It'll look brilliant on you.'

Kemi knew better than to comment on Jen's recent weight gain. She'd never met anyone who went up and down a size or more in the same year. 'Just promise me you won't make me look ridiculous.'

'I promise I won't. *Everything* suits you.'

'Not true. You clearly haven't seen me in my scrubs. I look like a cucumber. With a hairy head.'

Jen giggled. 'Speaking of hair . . . when was the last time you went to a hairdresser?'

Kemi put up her hands in mock defeat. 'You've got me. I honestly can't remember.'

'So why don't you come around to mine on Saturday? Before the opening, I mean. We can go to the hairdresser's and then get ready for the show together. Go on, it'll be like old times. You can take an afternoon off, surely?'

Kemi nodded. 'All right. You win. I'll come over around lunchtime. Now, tell me more about this new friend of yours, what's his name? Barker?'

'Parker.'

'Parker. Who is he? What does he do? How did you meet him? I want to hear *everything*.'

# 12

It was nearly 10 p.m. by the time she opened her front door. Despite her protestations, they'd polished off two bottles of white wine between them – well, Jen had polished off most of it – and Kemi's head was pounding faintly. She shut the door behind her and leaned against it for a moment. She looked down at her left hand and smiled faintly. She was still holding on to the half-finished cigarette she'd started as soon as she came out of Warren Street. It had been months since she'd had more than half a glass of cider or wine and even longer since she'd smoked. She put down her bag, shrugged off her coat and hung it up on the back of the door. She walked down the hallway to the kitchen, threw away the cigarette and poured herself a glass of tap water before going into the living room. The small one-bedroom flat had been a graduation present from Uncle Robert, though it was technically his, not hers. He used it once or twice a year when in London on business. 'I can just as easily stay in a hotel,' he said breezily. 'It's yours as long as you want or need it.'

'But what about Jen?' was Kemi's first thought. 'Won't she want it?'

'I'll get Jen something else,' Uncle Robert said resignedly. 'To be honest, I can't see Jen wanting to live in Fitzrovia.' He was right. Even Kemi couldn't quite imagine Jen in the midst of Fitzrovia with the elderly, blue-rinse ladies who were her neighbours or the silent, uniformed maids who cleaned the corporate offices around the square each day. True to his word, Uncle Robert bought Jen a small studio flat just off Fulham Road, which was much more in keeping with Jen's tastes. Fitzrovia's inhabitants were light years away from the lovely, fair-haired girls who frequented the cafes on the King's Road. Jen's flat, all floating curtains, dark dramatic colours and sheepskin rugs, was the opposite of Kemi's. Kemi had barely done a thing to it since she'd moved in. She didn't have the time, for one thing, and she really didn't care about her surroundings for another. As long as it was reasonably warm, dry and comfortable, it was fine. The fact that there were mismatched cushions on the sofa or that the kitchen hadn't been done up since the seventies was neither here nor there. 'It works,' was all she would say whenever Jen pulled a face. 'I haven't got time to think about sheepskin rugs.'

She walked over to the window and stood looking down onto Conway Street below. A couple were crossing over, the girl clinging possessively to her boyfriend's arm. There was a Christmas tree in the square, blinking green, blue and gold, sending streams of coloured lights across the wet pavement and into the night sky. She watched as they stopped to look at it, the girl's face turned up towards his in a moment of shared pleasure. It had been so long since she'd shared a view or a sight with anyone, let alone a boyfriend. What must it feel like? she wondered. She had almost forgotten what life outside work was like. She looked enviously at the couple again, but at that exact moment, something went wrong. They'd stopped almost directly underneath her window; an argument was breaking out. Even from where she was standing, she could feel the boy's impatience. His girlfriend tugged on his arm; he shook it off, annoyed, and walked away. She half smiled to herself. So much for romance. She turned away from the window and switched on the TV. Time for the news, and then straight to bed. For once, she wasn't on call. She sank into the sofa. The newscaster's voice washed over her rhythmically . . . 'Kyoto Protocol signed . . . Myra Hindley has lost her appeal . . . a massacre in Algeria . . . the ANC's fiftieth national congress is to be held in Mafikeng . . . In Zimbabwe, Dr Florence Mashabane, the wife of Mandela's right-hand man, Dr Tole Mashabane, is being considered for a top-level IMF position in Paris.' Her mother's face suddenly filled the screen. She was wearing a boldly patterned head-scarf. The darkness of her skin was another colour complemented by the starkly beautiful indigo and black markings, symbols of fish, birds, abstract geometries. Kemi stared at it, willing herself to feel something – *any*thing. It was like looking into the face of a stranger. Then the image disappeared as quickly as it had come. The newscaster was back. 'In other news today . . .'

She drew her knees up to her chest, the way she'd done as a little girl. Her mother was leaving Africa, something she'd always sworn she would never do. 'Leave? Me? Never! I was born here, I grew up here, I will die here.' A typically dramatic Florence Mashabane statement. The sort of statement that invited – and required – no response. Her mother. *My mother.* She rolled the unfamiliar word around on her tongue. It was the second time today she'd thought about her mother. Most unusual. Months, sometimes years, went by without any reminder of her mother and now, today, twice . . . she was left feeling slightly unnerved by it.

She switched off the television and reached for her stack of medical notes, which were always kept on the side table next to the sofa. She needed something to distract her. She pulled a sheaf of papers out of the pale green folder and removed the paper clip. Her upcoming cases: two complex and one relatively straightforward. She began to read the admission notes.

The first case was a thirteen-year-old girl with trigeminal neuralgia, most likely caused by nerve compression. She ran over the procedure in her mind's eye: a small opening in the skull behind the ear, opening the lining of the brain and inspecting the origin of the affected nerve. If they found it, they would remove it very carefully from the site, using a small piece of Teflon fabric to cushion the nerve. The whole procedure could – if things went well – take under an hour. If it didn't . . . she stopped herself in time. It was something Fairbanks always said to the junior doctors. *Don't think about what might go wrong. Focus on your training, procedures and protocols.* She wondered who the surgeon directing the team would be. Fairbanks and his ilk rarely made an appearance on the weekends. She knew from overheard gossip that the most senior consultants played squash on Sundays. It seemed a fitting game for surgeons. All that aggression.

# 13

Halfway across London, safely in her own flat and unable to sleep, Jen poured herself a shot of whisky and wandered into her own living room. She looked around with a sense of satisfaction that came rarely to her during her working hours. She loved her flat. It was on the second floor of a handsome, red-brick Victorian building on Bishop's Road. Father had bought it – somewhat reluctantly, it had to be said – as soon as she'd graduated. 'No sense wasting your money on rent,' he'd said down the phone. 'The trust will make the purchase.' And that was that. Still, whilst the trust might *own* it, she'd furnished it out of her own savings. She'd done a bloody good job of it, too. Kemi had absolutely no interest in aesthetics but even she had remarked on its tasteful, exuberant air. Father had seen it once, taken off his glasses and pinched his nose between his brows, and that was that. When he replaced his glasses, the issue was closed. Her mother had never seen it and most likely never would. It had been years since Alice had left the house on Jordan Lane. She'd retreated into a suite of rooms on the second floor and rarely ventured outside. After the long-awaited death of Jen's grandmother, there'd been a small window of hope that finally, after so many years of silent oppression, Alice might resurface . . . but it wasn't to be. If anything, she'd faded even more into the background.

She wandered across to the oversized blue velvet sofa, glass in hand, and sank into its soft folds with a sigh of equal parts pleasure and exhaustion. She'd spent the last three months living on someone's couch in a tiny apartment in Long Island City, across the East River from Manhattan. Whilst it had done her the world of good – at least in terms of making those all-important contacts in the art world – she'd been so home-sick for her flat and her London friends and the cosy familiarity of the Kensington-and-Chelsea way of life that she'd contemplated leaving pretty much every weekend. New York terrified her. She'd struggled to hide it, turning up duti-fully every morning to the stark white gallery on Spring Street where Parker had pulled in a favour to get her a job as assist-ant to the glamorous Lu Wai-Shen. Every morning, she'd braved the dirty, noisy and chaotic New York subway, packed to the rafters with the most motley assortment of people she'd ever seen, hustling like millions of others to secure a bit of standing room and avoid catching anyone's eye. She'd seen rats the size of small dogs scurrying along the platform, dis-appearing into the dark tunnels that ran up and down the island like capillaries, feeding the city with its workers who came in from the Bronx, Brooklyn, Long Island, New Jersey . . . The whole world converged on Manhattan between 7 a.m. and 9 a.m., only to be disgorged in the opposite direction eight hours later. The New York subway made the London Underground seem luxurious beyond compare. It was a crazy, schizophrenic place, in spite of the wealth and glamour that existed above ground on avenues like Fifth and Lexington, whose shops made her dizzy just to look at. Living in New York, irrespective of whether she was on someone's couch or not, was the sort of experience most of her friends would have killed for. The fact that she'd bagged an *actual* job, at an *actual* art gallery, was almost too good to be true. She was paid cash in hand – not very much of it, but she'd happily have done it for free.

Lu was from Hong Kong – beautiful, rich, Bedales-educated and sent to finishing school in Switzerland. She'd done a degree in art history at Parsons and considered herself to be a global citizen. Her father was 'richer than God', according to Parker. Aged thirty-five, she owned a gallery with the German collector Jürgen Scheuler, appropriately named Scheuler Lu, in the fashionable heart of Soho, with a roster of up-and-coming artists. She was sufficiently intrigued by Parker's description of a 'dreamy Scottish redhead' to agree to a meeting.

Parker took her to meet Lu at Balthazar, just up the road. Jen was so nervous she swallowed half a Valium beforehand, which made her appear even dreamier than usual. To her surprise, Lu hired her on the spot. Although 'hired' wasn't quite the right term. There would be a weekly envelope containing five $20 bills, which was barely enough to keep her in subway tokens.

'You haven't got a work permit, darling, and besides . . . it's not as though you need the money,' Parker drawled. 'Think of it as an investment. After this you'll be able to work anywhere.'

It wasn't quite true on either count, but Parker had organized it and Jen would have done anything for Parker. Whilst one or two of Jen's friends *might* have had the wherewithal to survive for three months in New York on little more than air (and a monthly stipend from a trust fund that wasn't really worth mentioning in polite company), most couldn't. Jen could. It continued to be a source of barely suppressed tension between herself and Father. *When are you going to get a proper job?* It was a constant refrain. It didn't help that Kemi was now on her way to becoming one of the youngest and most talented surgeons in the world, or so Father boasted.

Just another little reminder of the ways in which they were so different. She'd swallowed her pride and asked Father for a small advance against her trust fund to cover the cost of three months' work experience in New York.

'Work experience, did you say?'

'Yes, Father.'

'And, if I may be so bold . . . why aren't you earning? Or do you intend never to earn?'

'No, Father. It's . . . it's not quite like that. In the art world—'

'Oh, the *art* world. Yes, I'd forgotten. In the *art* world nothing operates the way it does in the *real* world. Well, it's your inheritance. You do with it as you see fit. Once it's gone, it's gone. You do understand that, don't you?'

'Yes, Father.' Jen waited for the closing rebuke that she knew was coming.

'Strange how Kemisa's not touched hers,' he went on. 'Not a penny. She's saving it for something useful, no doubt. She's got a head on her, that one.' Jen said nothing. Five minutes later the conversation – if it could be termed such – was over. She had her money. She was on her way to New York.

Paid or not, she did *everything* at Scheuler Lu's, from answering the phone to picking up Lu's dry cleaning. Lu walked – or stalked – the gallery in her high-heeled Blahniks, phone clamped to her ear, screaming instructions. She'd overheard one of the girls who also 'worked' for Lu saying that back in Hong Kong, she had three personal maids whose job it was to ensure Lu had everything she wanted, whenever and however she wanted it. Small wonder she bossed everyone around as if to the manor born. She was.

Jen learned very quickly to stay out of her way. In some

respects, it was a little like the house in Morningside. She kept her head down, did what she was supposed to and spoke only when spoken to. And Parker was right. She met all *kinds* of people in New York; artists, gallery owners, collectors, clients . . . the sort of people who not only made up the art world, but who made it go round. At parties she rubbed shoulders with Upper East Side divorcées, swathed in furs and dripping with diamonds; women who, despite their air of bored indifference, knew their Rothkos from their Rauschenbergs. She met young, newly minted bankers, freshly arrived in the city from places like Idaho and Iowa, who clearly didn't. She met old-school dealers and curators who could size up a potential client from a hundred yards and whose expressions went from snarling to serene in the blink of an eye. Parker seemed to know everyone. 'This here's Jen . . . all the way from Edinburgh.' He pronounced it *Ee-din-borow*. No one seemed to know the difference. No one cared how it was pronounced. They all adored Parker, with his neat white shirts and colourful bow ties and braces. He wore a different pair of spectacles every single day and had more tan brogues than her father. 'English shoes,' he said proudly, lifting up the sole. 'I buy 'em by the truckload. If there's one thing you guys know how to make, it's a damn fine pair of shoes.'

'I'm not English,' Jen said primly.

He smirked. 'Same difference. You sound English to me.'

'Well, I'm not.'

'What*ever*. Now, see that girl over there? The one with the blue fur coat? That's the mayor's niece. Go talk to her. Make nice. Bring her to the gallery. Lu'll be pleased.'

Still, no matter how many contacts she made or how many potential clients she reeled in, two months of working ten hours a day at the gallery, followed by cocktail parties, had taken its toll. Despite the fact that there was no real time to eat, she'd begun putting on weight. Breakfast was a salmon and cream cheese bagel, wolfed down after coming off the 7 from Vernon Boulevard-Jackson at Grand Central–42nd Street before disappearing into the A, which took her to Fulton and then up to Spring. Sometimes she had another one from the van at Spring and Sixth if she'd had a particularly hellish ride. Lunch was a takeaway bowl of noodles or sushi from any one of the dozens of shops on Spring or Varick Street, usually gulped down as she ran back to the gallery. There were parties every night at which she drank far too much on an empty stomach, which she refilled walking up Vernon Boulevard before collapsing on Cindy's sofa in the apartment on the thirty-fifth floor that she shared with her girlfriend and three cats. The view from their living room was spectacular, but she was usually so exhausted by the time she got back to the apartment that she had no time or appetite to take it in. Aside from Cindy, who was the sister of someone at university, she had no friends. Everyone was effusive and charming, but it never seemed to go any further than that. Most of the people she met were in love with themselves, not with each other. They showed up at galleries and openings, drank champagne and ate the odd canapé – when no one was looking – but nothing about them seemed *real* to Jen.

Now, without Kemi's reassuring presence, she was lonely again, the sort of hard, desperate loneliness she'd experienced as a child. It terrified her. She tried to confide in Parker, but realized soon that Parker simply wasn't interested in her fears. Parker was a conundrum. He was overwhelmingly open and charming, but also oddly aloof. He was generous to a fault, a damn good listener and everyone's closest friend, but he also had the knack of keeping everyone both enthralled and at the same time, at arm's length. It began to dawn on her that all New Yorkers were exactly the same. No one actually *wanted* intimacy. They wanted only the appearance of it – the air kisses and the loud, overly exaggerated cries of welcome and departure – but when it came down to it, it was each man (or stilettoed woman) for himself. *That* was how you got ahead, at least in the rarefied circles of the New York art scene. People simply clambered over each other, spiking each other through the heart or head on their way to the top – although it was hard to see what the 'top' actually *was*.

Finally, it was over. After three months she went home, crushed inside perhaps, but with a Filofax full of names. Wasn't that the point?

She took another sip of her whisky, feeling it burn all the way down her throat. She began to think about the following Saturday. Was everything organized right down to the last detail? Had she forgotten anything? She ran over the invitation list in her mind's eye; over three hundred people, culled from everyone's mailing lists. If they were lucky, half that number would show up. She'd organized the catering, double-checked on the cleaners, made sure all the assistants would be on hand. The works were hung, the floor was polished, the lighting was all in order. She'd taken care of all the last-minute details, like flowers, champagne and wine, canapés ... everything was in hand. What would she wear? She drained her glass and stood up. She'd find something in that vast closet of hers.

Twenty minutes later, she had both outfits ready. For herself she'd picked out a pleated burgundy velvet skirt (elasticated waistband) with a white silk blouse and a pair of black high-heeled pumps. Conservative enough to placate Isabella, the gallery co-owner, who hated her assistants to outshine her. With a pair of ornate earrings and a chunky bracelet, she'd look fashionable enough to fit in. For Kemi she chose a long, fitted knit dress in Missoni-style stripes. With Kemi's colouring and a visit to the hairdresser's beforehand, she'd look stunning. She shut the wardrobe door with a snap and began to get ready for bed. She was actually looking forward to the opening. It would be a chance to show Kemi that she, too, was good at *something*.

# 14

'No, *no*, not that one. It's far too long on you. Turn around, but slowly . . . I want to see how it fits.'

Kemi patiently did as Jen asked, risking a glance at her watch. It was almost four thirty. They'd been at it for an hour and the bed was a rapidly rising mound of discarded clothing. There was less than an hour to go before Jen was due at the gallery and so far, nothing seemed to please her. The dress she'd originally picked out was so long and trailing that Kemi was afraid she'd trip and break her neck if she wore it. Despite the choices Jen put in front of her, even Jen wasn't satisfied. Skirts were either too short, too frilly or too fussy . . . dresses were either too plain or too tight . . . something wasn't quite right. Kemi couldn't remember the last time she'd tried on so many clothes, *ever*.

'OK, try this.' Jen fished out something from the back of her closet. A black chiffon skirt with gold tassels. Kemi looked at it in alarm.

'I'll look like a Christmas cake,' she said quickly. 'I hate those tasselly bits.'

Jen shook her head firmly. 'It's Christmas. You're *supposed* to look like a cake. Or at least you're supposed to look good enough to eat.'

'Rubbish. Why can't I wear that one?' she asked, pointing

to a just-discarded, inoffensively blue jersey dress. 'It was quite . . . nice.'

'Precisely. I don't want you looking *quite nice*, darling. I want you looking spectacular.'

'Oh, Jen. Give up, won't you? I hardly wear anything other than black trousers. You already know that.'

'This *is* black. And I've got the perfect shirt for it. Here.' She rummaged around and produced a glittery top with a pussy-bow neck and long, billowy sleeves. Kemi stared at it as though it might bite. 'Try it on,' Jen said firmly. 'Trust me.'

Kemi took the shirt and slipped it carefully over her newly straightened hair. She turned to look at herself in the mirror. 'It looks ridiculous,' she said quickly. 'I hate it.'

'Well, *I* like it. And you promised you'd go with whatever I chose. So, that's it settled. Put on those shoes . . . yes, the high-heeled ones. You can't wear flat shoes with an outfit like that.'

'But I won't be able to walk.'

'Yes, you will. Don't be so feeble. It's not easy, being gorgeous. And you *are* gorgeous. So, wear it with pride.'

Kemi looked at her reflection unhappily. Yes, it was certainly different. She slipped her feet cautiously into the ludicrously high-heeled black shoes Jen had picked out for her and took a few unbalanced steps. 'I'll never get used to them.'

'Yes, you will. Now, let's get a cab. It'll take ages to get there and I've still got a ton of things to do before the show opens. Oh, blast . . . is that your phone?' There was a muffled ringing from somewhere deep beneath the pile of clothes. Both women struggled to reach it. 'It's yours,' Jen said, handing it over. 'But hurry up, I'm going to get us a cab.' She scrambled off the bed.

Kemi quickly looked at the screen. It was an unlisted number. 'Hello?' she said breathlessly, tugging impatiently at the hem of the offending skirt. It was about six inches shorter than she normally considered wearing. It made her feel naked.

'Hello, could I speak to Kemisa Mashabane?' It was a man's voice. Deep, unfamiliar.

She frowned. No one other than Uncle Robert called her 'Kemisa' and it certainly wasn't him. 'This is Kemi. Who's calling?'

'My name's Solam Rhoyi. My mother's a friend of *your* mother's, from way back. She asked me to give you a ring—'

'Kem? Come on, taxi's here,' Jen shouted up the stairs. 'Let's go. We're going to be late!'

'I'm sorry,' Kemi interrupted him quickly. 'I'm busy at the moment. Could you ring back later?' She put the phone down without waiting for an answer, mildly irritated. Who the hell was Solam Rhoyi? She had no idea. Florence was always telling people to ring her – why? 'I'm coming,' she yelled, and grabbed her handbag. She took a final look at her image and winced. The whole thing was so not *her*. She opened the door and ran down the stairs. Jen was waiting impatiently with the front door open. There was a black cab idling on the street.

'Who was it?' Jen asked, hurrying her along.

'Some bloke from home. My mother gave him my number. I wish she'd stop doing that. I've no idea why she bothers.'

'She's playing matchmaker, you idiot. What did he sound like?'

Kemi shrugged. 'I wasn't paying attention.'

Jen rolled her eyes. 'Your mum and I have more in common than you think,' she said, closing the door behind them. 'Can you get us there by five?' Jen asked anxiously through the partition. The driver pulled away from the kerb and took off down the road at speed.

'I'll do me best.'

# 15

In his room at Claridge's, Solam put his phone away, slightly irritated. Well, at least he'd tried. He could report back to Iketleng that he'd done exactly as she'd asked. Wasn't *his* fault she'd hung up on him as soon as he mentioned his name. Oh, well. He'd done as told and phoned her, enough to get his mother off his back.

He got up, stretched and yawned. It was nearly five. He had a dinner meeting at seven. It would be over by ten thirty at the latest. He hesitated for a moment, then picked up his phone again. He had less than forty-eight hours in London, which wasn't really enough time to look up old friends. There was one person he'd have time to see, however, no matter how fleeting the visit. He scrolled through the list of names until he came to it. Edward. He hurriedly tapped out his message. *In town for a couple of days.* He tossed the phone on the bed and rummaged around in his luggage for a pair of sweatpants and his running shoes. Edward would get back to him within the hour. Time enough for a run to clear his head before his business meeting.

# 16

After just half an hour, Kemi wished she'd never come. She didn't know a single person apart from Jen, who was so busy overseeing everything that she'd barely seen her since they arrived. She hovered for a few moments on the edge of a number of small groups, sipping her white wine as slowly as possible and trying to look inconspicuous. She was the only – the *only* – person of colour in the entire room. She was also the only one who looked like a Christmas cake, she thought to herself miserably, catching sight of herself in one of the oversized mirrors. She found it difficult to join in conversations about which she knew nothing, much less subjects that she cared little about. The gallery was tiny and packed to the rafters. Everything was white, from the polished white concrete floor to the dazzling, crisp white walls. Diamond-hard pinpoints of white light radiated from the ceiling, and in one corner stood an enormous white Christmas tree festooned with all-white decorations. The paintings, however, were the opposite – giant, brooding images in black or dark brown with a single thick line or stripe bisecting them. It was hard to know what to make of them. They *looked* simple enough . . . but that probably wasn't the point. Or was it?

A waiter brushed past her elbow with a plate of delicious-looking canapés. She reached out and picked up a giant shrimp with a dollop of wasabi strung along its tail, and popped it in her mouth. She was immediately rewarded with a searing rush of horseradish. She almost choked. She swallowed it whole, her nostrils and eyes flooding with tears. She fumbled in her bag for a tissue. She had to get some fresh air. Her whole face was on fire. She pushed past the thick knots of people standing around the paintings until she reached the door. It was open. She stepped onto the pavement, blinded by the tears streaming down her cheeks, and ran slap bang into someone jogging down the street with his headphones on, his attention anywhere but on the people gathered at the entrance to the art gallery from which she'd just escaped. She gave a little yelp, twisted on her blasted high-heeled shoes, and went crashing to the ground.

# 17

About a minute earlier, Solam had exited Claridge's at a comfortable pace and turned the corner, lost in the music thumping through his headphones. He was oblivious to the chilly evening air, nimbly dodging the late-night shoppers who crowded the pavements along New Bond Street. After a twelve-hour flight from Johannesburg, it felt good to be out in the open air, running. He turned left onto Bruton Street, which was quieter, except for a crowd gathered about halfway down. He slowed a little, weaving lightly in between the well-dressed women in high heels and no coats – were they *mad?* – and was just about to speed up again when a figure came barrelling out of the doorway. He tried to avoid it but he was aware of cars on his right-hand side, and the last thing he wanted was to end up under a set of wheels. They collided. It was a woman. She gave a short cry and pitched headlong onto the pavement. He grabbed hold of her arm, trying to steady her, but the impact sent them both sprawling. He was aware of a shout and a car swerving to avoid hitting them and the commotion on the pavement behind him.

*Ohmigod! Watch out!*

*Jesus! Is she hurt?*

*Someone, help her up!*

People rushed forward to help them both. Solam shook his

head to clear it. It had happened so quickly . . . He looked down. The girl was wearing a short black skirt with gold tassels which had ripped. One of her heels was broken. She looked absolutely dazed. He immediately crouched down to help her. A black girl, exceptionally pretty, with long straight hair parted in the middle and huge, expressive eyes. He stared at her. She was stunning.

'Are you all right? I'm so sorry. I didn't see you . . . my fault completely. I should've been paying more attention.'

She shook her head, still dazed. 'No, no . . . it was me. I'm fine, I'm fine.' She struggled to stand.

'Give her a bit of air.' Solam turned to the crowd who were hovering anxiously around them. 'She's fine, I think. Not hurt, just dazed.' He turned back to look at her, frowning suddenly. That voice . . . where had he heard it? 'Can I get you anything . . . a taxi, maybe? I'm afraid I've ruined your dress. And your shoes.'

She shook her head. 'No, please don't worry. I'll be fine. I'll grab a cab and go home. I wasn't enjoying it much anyway.'

A ripple went up the back of his neck. 'What's your name?' Solam asked, still frowning. It couldn't be . . . no, surely not?

She looked up at him sharply. 'I said I'm fine,' she said testily. 'Absolutely fine.'

Suddenly the penny dropped. 'You're not Kemisa Mashabane, are you?' he said incredulously, beginning to laugh.

She shot him a suspicious look. 'Do I know you?' she asked coldly.

He couldn't stop laughing. The throng of people on the pavement began to drift away, turning back to their cigarettes and their conversations. The girl was obviously unhurt and the two seemed to know each other. 'We spoke about an hour ago on the phone. I'm Solam. Solam Rhoyi.'

Kemi stared up at him. Her mouth dropped open.

# 18

The man standing in front of her, looking at her anxiously to make sure she was in one piece, was beautiful. No other word would do. Even in a sweatshirt, jogging pants and running shoes, he was beautiful. Almond-shaped, dark black eyes, high cheekbones, a killer smile . . . perfect teeth. He shoved his earphones and Walkman into his pocket and held out his hand. 'This isn't quite how I pictured meeting you,' he said, still smiling, 'but it's nice to meet you all the same.'

She shook his hand, still stunned. 'How . . . how did you know it was me?' she asked.

'Your voice . . . it's pretty distinctive. Not quite English, not quite . . . you know, from back home. Our parents know each other.'

'You're South African?' She was surprised. He sounded English.

He nodded. 'Raised here, though. Like you. It was my mum who gave me your number. Look, let me get you a cab so you can at least go home and change. Is it a party?' He gestured to the gallery behind him.

Kemi shook her head. She was trying unsuccessfully to balance on one leg. She *knew* she shouldn't have worn these blasted heels. 'No, it's a gallery. Tonight's the opening. Yes, I suppose I'd better go home.' She looked down at her torn skirt. 'I should tell my sister.'

'I'll go,' Solam offered immediately. 'You just stay here for a second. I'll find her. Have you got a coat? You must be freezing.' He looked across at the crowded room through the enormous glass window. He grinned suddenly. 'She won't be hard to spot. There aren't too many like us in there.'

Kemi shook her head. 'Oh, no . . . she's not . . . she's not my real sister. I mean, my biological sister. Oh, it's too complicated to explain. She's in there, somewhere. She's got red hair, quite tall. Her name's Jen.'

'I'll find her.' He looked at his sweat-stained jumper. 'I'd give you this, but . . .' He gave her a quick, rueful smile.

'Oh, don't worry. I'll get a cab and wait inside. I don't live far away.'

'Give me two seconds. And I insist on paying for it.'

Kemi smiled weakly, too tired to argue. Her knee was throbbing from where she'd hit it on the pavement. She longed to get home.

# 19

Everything was going so well! Jen could scarcely believe it. The tiny gallery was packed! More and more people seemed to arrive every minute. No sooner had one group left than another arrived. She ran back and forth from the tiny galley kitchen to the front room, making sure glasses were topped up, coats were safely fetched or stored, and that the key buyers were being looked after. Her feet ached. There were only two waitresses on duty. She looked around for either of the gallery assistants but they were nowhere to be found. *Just like bloody New York*, she thought to herself in exasperation. No matter how refined things appeared, she was *still* the dogsbody, the lowest person on the rung; the person whose job it was to make sure everyone did theirs, and her own as well. Federico and Isabella were at the front, doing what they did best – charming the pants off everyone – whilst she was at the rear, emptying champagne glasses and ashtrays, despite the stringent NO SMOKING signs.

'Excuse me . . . are you Jen?' someone said behind her.

She turned around. A tall, *extremely* handsome young black man, dressed somewhat incongruously in running gear, stood in the doorway to the tiny kitchen. 'Yes, I'm Jen.' She wondered who on earth he was.

He sensed her confusion and smiled, revealing a row of

stunningly white teeth. He shook his head. 'No, we haven't met. I was out jogging and collided with your . . . with Kemi. She's broken a heel, unfortunately. I'm just going to put her in a cab and make sure she gets home safely. She's fine . . . just a bit shaken, that's all.'

'Oh my God!' Jen put up a hand to her mouth. 'Is she all right?'

'Jen! Will you get a move on! There's a whole group of people without drinks!' It was Carolyn, one of the assistants who'd been strangely absent all evening. Jen whirled round in embarrassment. The gorgeous young man, whoever he was, was quick to react.

'Don't worry about Kemi. You've got your hands full. I'll make sure she gets home safely.' He flashed a smile and was gone. Jen's mouth was still open.

'*Jen!*' Carolyn hissed at her, more urgently this time.

'I'm *coming*,' Jen said through gritted teeth. Christ. Would it kill *her* to pick up a tray?

# 20

He was as good as his word, waving her protests aside with such good grace that she just had to give in. Within minutes, he'd found Jen, her coat, her handbag *and* a cab. He was clearly someone used to giving orders.

'You were pretty rude over the phone earlier,' he chuckled, as the cab sped towards Fitzrovia.

She felt her face grow hot. 'Sorry,' she said ruefully. 'It's my mother . . . she's always giving out my number.'

'Mine too.'

There was a quick smile of understanding between them. 'Sorry about that,' she said after a moment. 'I'm not usually that . . . well, rude.'

'I bet you are.'

She turned to look at him, frowning in protest. 'No, I'm not, I promise. I'm very well behaved.'

He grinned. 'All the time?'

She felt her face grow even hotter. Was he . . . *flirting* with her? 'Yes,' she said primly. 'All the time.'

He grinned. 'I doubt that very much.'

He *was* flirting. She felt her face grow even hotter. She wasn't used to his easy manner. Most men found her too intimidating to flirt with. 'I . . . I'm just . . . busy most of the time.'

'You're a doctor, aren't you? Like your father?'

She nodded. 'Surgeon, actually.'

'Ah. Aren't you all sociopaths?'

She looked at him in surprise. 'Whoever told you that?'

He laughed, flashing those impossibly white teeth again. His physicality was disarming. She was uncomfortably aware of his thigh next to hers. 'Relax. I'm only joking. It's what they all say.'

'You shouldn't believe everything you hear.'

'I don't.'

They stared at one another for a second. Kemi was the first to look away. 'So, what do *you* do?' she asked politely, wishing her voice didn't sound quite so prissy.

'Me? I'm in banking.'

'Ah. I should've guessed.'

'Do I look like a banker?'

She pulled a face. 'No. But I don't suppose *I* look like a surgeon, either.'

He smiled faintly. 'Yeah, well, there's that. What d'you think *he* thinks of us?' He gestured discreetly towards the cabbie.

She was surprised. 'What does it matter?'

'Ah, I was right.'

Kemi stared at him again. His manner was both off-putting and intriguing. She'd never met anyone quite like him. 'Right about what?'

'You. You're . . . prickly. Feisty. You're no pushover.'

She felt the heat in her face again. She turned to look outside the window, unsure how to respond. 'I'm not very good at this,' she said finally, reluctantly.

'Good at what?' There was a knowing amusement in his voice.

'Small talk. You know, chit chat. *This.*'

He chuckled. 'Relax,' he said again. 'You're doing fine. Considering you tried to kill me earlier.'

'I did *not*!'

'Could've got me run over, racing out of the place like that. I never asked you . . . what made you bolt in the first place?'

She began to laugh. 'Horseradish,' she giggled. 'I ate a prawn that was thick with horseradish.'

He smiled. 'Well, it's a pleasant surprise,' he said. 'And a relief.'

'How d'you mean?'

'Well, you know how it is. Parents say, "oh, you must meet so-and-so . . . he's great, she's great" . . . and then you meet each other and you can't stand each other. Happens all the time, especially to people like us.'

She was intrigued. 'People like us?'

'"Exile kids". We don't know whether we're coming or going. People think we're so cosmopolitan and easy-going, but we're not. We're just confused. We've no idea who we are, half the time . . . the other half, we're trying to be someone else.'

She was silent. He'd hit the nail so hard on the head it was painful to hear. The cab turned off Tottenham Court Road. She was nearly home. She turned to him. 'It was really nice of you to bring me home. I'm fine now, honestly.'

He looked at his watch. 'I've got a meeting in about half an hour,' he said, pulling a quick face. 'Otherwise I'd ask you to dinner. Are you free tomorrow? I'm only here for a couple of days before I head back. Let me take you out. Just so I can say sorry properly and tell my mum we've met.'

Kemi hesitated. The cab slowed to a stop. The Christmas tree in Fitzroy Square was in front of them. She suddenly thought back to the couple whom she'd spotted the week before. Yes, it had been so long since she'd shared anything with anyone. She opened her mouth. 'You've got my number,' she said simply. He made her nervous.

He chuckled, reaching across her to open the door. 'Then I'll see you tomorrow. Eight o'clock. Now that I know where you live.' He signalled to the driver to continue. 'Eight o'clock,' he repeated. 'And wear a pair of sturdier shoes.'

She watched the cab speed off, too stunned to respond.

# 21

It took Jen a moment or two to work out that it wasn't her alarm clock shrieking its head off – it was her phone. She fought through the thick layers of sleep, her head pounding. She'd taken one of the bottles of leftover champagne home with her, polishing it off in the cab before stumbling up her front steps. She rummaged around in the duvet for the damn thing, willing it to stop ringing. Morning light showed through the crack in the curtains. She looked across the room at her clock. It was 8:03. Who on earth was ringing at 8.03 a.m. on a Sunday? She peered under the bed. Ah, there it was!

'Hello?' she croaked. It was probably Kemi. She remembered dimly the calamity of the accident on the pavement and the gorgeous young man who'd taken her home. Perhaps she was phoning to tell her something? It wasn't Kemi, however. It was Federico, her new boss.

'Did you lock up last night and put on the alarm?' he was shouting. She struggled awake. What was he saying?

'Yes, yes . . . of course I did. What's the matter? What is it?'

'Are you sure? Did you lock up after you?'

A cold bolt of fear ripped through her. 'I . . . I think so . . .'

'You *think* so?' His voice suddenly went cold. 'We're here with the police. You'd better get here *now*.' The phone went dead.

LESLEY LOKKO

She sat bolt upright, fear pushing the pain in her temples to one side. Her heart was pounding. For a second she thought she might be sick. She struggled to recall her last moves as she frantically looked around for a pair of jeans and a sweater. Was it possible she'd actually *forgotten to lock the door*? She grabbed her handbag and her coat and ran out into the road.

# 22

Whoever was downstairs at the front door was pounding on it as though trying to break it down. Kemi could hear the dull thuds through the walls. She closed her laptop with a snap and walked to the intercom. 'Who is it?' she called out, grabbing the key from the rack. It was Jen. She was sobbing uncontrollably. Kemi flung open the door as Jen came up the stairs.

'Whatever's the matter?' she asked in alarm. Jen was sobbing hysterically. She wasn't even wearing a coat. 'What's wrong? What happened?'

Jen couldn't get her words out. Her teeth were chattering but with something other than the cold. 'Gone,' she kept repeating as Kemi led her inside. 'All gone.'

'What's gone? What happened? Where's your coat, Jen?'

'P-p-paintings . . . everything. Computers, phones . . . everything! They cleaned us out and *it's all my fault*!'

'What are you talking about?'

'The g-gallery . . . I forgot to lock the door last night. Thieves got in and everything's gone. Everything!'

Kemi looked at her, aghast. 'You *forgot* to lock the *door*?' she repeated incredulously. 'The *front* door?'

Jen's head went up and down. Her face was blotchy, made ugly through her tears. 'I don't know how . . . I just forgot.

Federico rang at eight o'clock and made me come down to the police station. I've never seen anyone so angry. I thought he was g-g-going to h-h-hit me,' she stammered, tears coursing down her cheeks.

Kemi hurriedly led her into the kitchen. 'Here, sit down. I'll get you something. Just have a seat.' She pulled out one of the chairs. 'Go on, just sit for a moment. I'll be right back.' She ran into the living room and opened the sideboard. She hurriedly poured a small shot of whisky and carried it back through. 'Here. Your teeth are chattering. Have a sip – just a sip – and calm down. Tell me *exactly* what happened.'

Jen lifted the glass. It clattered loudly against her teeth. In between gasps and sips, she managed to get the story out.

# 23

Kemi listened to her with a sinking heart. How much had she had to drink before locking up? Kemi wondered. Even in the thirty or so minutes before she'd stumbled outside and bumped into Solam Rhoyi, Kemi had seen Jen lift one glass of champagne after another as she rushed around the room, trying to keep everything together.

She let Jen sob herself into exhausted submission and then very carefully led her into the living room and onto the sofa. 'Here,' she said, pulling up a blanket and covering her. 'Just rest for a bit. Don't worry, darling. It'll all be insured, I'm positive.'

'He fired me,' Jen sobbed, hiccupping softly, like a child.

'Well, you did say you were worried it would turn out to be a bit of a dead-end job.'

'I know, but it was still a *job*! What's Father going to say?'

'Don't tell him,' Kemi said reasonably. 'You'll find another one. Just chalk it up to experience.'

'That's all I ever seem to do,' Jen moaned. 'One bloody bad experience after another.'

'That's absolutely not true. Now, I bet you haven't eaten anything yet. Did you have breakfast?'

Jen shook her head. 'I'm not hungry.'

'Maybe not, but you'd better eat something. I'll make you some scrambled eggs.'

'Can I stay here for a bit?' Jen asked tremulously. 'Just for a couple of days?'

'Of course you can,' Kemi said automatically. 'Stay here as long as you want.' She hesitated. 'I'm . . . I'm out this evening,' she added quickly. A little frisson of excitement ran through her.

'Out?' Jen looked up, surprised. She'd finally stopped crying. 'Are you on call?'

'No, not work, no. I'm actually . . . I'm going to dinner with someone.'

'*Who?*'

'Oh, no one. I mean, not like that. It's just the guy from last night . . . the one I bumped into.' She tried to shrug nonchalantly. 'We sort of know each other. Well, our parents do.'

Jen's mouth dropped open. She'd forgotten all about the robbery. 'The black guy? The one who took you home?'

Kemi nodded. 'Yeah, him. His name's Solam. Solam Rhoyi.'

'He's *gorgeous*!' Jen said breathlessly. 'He came over to tell me he was taking you home. You never said a word!'

'It's not like that,' Kemi said quickly. 'We're only going to dinner.'

Jen let out a dramatic sigh. 'At *last*!'

'Oh, for goodness' sake! I'm only going to dinner. Besides, he lives in South Africa.'

'It's perfect. You're perfect for each other.'

Kemi shook her head. 'Such nonsense you talk,' she said affectionately. 'Such nonsense. Now, lie down. I'm going to make you something to eat.'

'What are you going to wear?' Jen asked, as Kemi opened the fridge door in search of eggs.

'Oh, I'll find something. Now, stop worrying about me and start focusing on feeling better. Tea or coffee?'

*

By seven thirty, however, the tables were turned. She was now a bundle of nerves, and for once she was glad of Jen's advice.

'No, no, *no*!' Jen looked up as she came out of the bathroom. 'You cannot possibly go out wearing that!'

Kemi looked down at her perfectly serviceable black jeans and Doc Martens. 'They're brand new,' she offered by way of explanation.

Jen rolled her eyes. 'Jeans? Doc Martens? Are you *kidding* me?'

'What's wrong with them?'

'Jesus, don't get me started. Quick! We've only got about twenty minutes. I knew I should have checked what you were going to wear earlier.'

'Jen . . . it's only a dinner!' Kemi wailed. But there was no stopping her.

With minutes to spare, Jen finally looked her up and down and nodded. 'Not what *I'd* have chosen for a first date,' she said sniffily. 'But it'll do. You didn't give me enough warning.'

Kemi looked down at her slim-fitting black trousers, high-heeled black boots and white shirt, and shrugged. Heels aside, there wasn't much difference between what she was wearing now and what she'd had on thirty minutes earlier. 'It's not a date,' she corrected her. 'And I still don't see what the difference is.'

'Jeans send out the wrong message on a first date. Too casual. Unless they're designer jeans, of course. And I don't see too many of those in your wardrobe.'

'I keep telling you, it's not a date!'

Jen shrugged. 'Call it what you like. I'm just looking out for you, sister.'

Kemi had to laugh. 'And I appreciate it, sister.' And at that moment, right on cue, the doorbell went. She picked up her coat and bag. 'I won't be late,' she called out, walking down the hallway.

'Stay out as late as you want,' Jen called back. 'I'll be asleep by the time you get back. And I'll sleep in the living room. Just in case.'

Kemi ran down the stairs. She was still chuckling as she opened the front door. She looked up. Her heart missed a beat. As gorgeous as she'd found him the night before in his sweat-stained jersey and running shoes, he now looked as though he'd stepped off a catwalk. He was wearing a dark blue suit with a charcoal polo-neck sweater, a thick overcoat thrown over one arm. He wore thick, black-framed glasses that on any other man might have seemed frivolous, even vain, but not on him. She closed the door behind her. 'You're on time,' she said, not knowing what else to say.

He leaned forward, brushing her cheek very lightly with his. She sank for a moment into the cushion of his cheek, smelling his aftershave, and felt her knees go weak. It had been a long time since she'd been close enough to any man to smell his aftershave. 'I'm always on time,' he said, offering her his arm. 'Come on. Cab's waiting; the restaurant's booked and I'm *starving*.'

'Where are you taking me?' she asked, tucking her arm into his. It felt good. No, more than good. She swallowed nervously.

'Wait and see.'

# 24

She was a revelation, he had to admit it. Her obvious beauty aside, behind the rather frosty facade there was a person of depth, humour, wit. He'd been attracted to her the minute he saw her lying dazed on the pavement below him, but by the time their meal was halfway through, he saw that there was something more there to be found. She aroused his curiosity. He couldn't recall ever feeling anything like it and that was perhaps the biggest surprise of all. He, Solam Rhoyi, who'd had more relationships than he could remember or count – not that the vast majority could be described as 'relationships', he reminded himself quickly – he was intrigued. He'd had more than his fair share of clever, independent women, but none had managed to capture his interest, once the initial attraction wore off. He chuckled to himself as he poured them both another glass of wine. She wasn't much of a drinker either, he noticed. He liked that. She wasn't one of those women who set out to get drunk as quickly as possible, thereby absolving themselves of any subsequent lapses in judgement. There was a measured slowness to her movements and speech that was oddly calming. She took her time with things – with her answers, her judgements, her jokes. Her second glass of wine sat untouched. Something in her manner restrained him, prevented him from doing what he would normally have done . . . turned on the charm and taken her home to bed, whether his or hers.

Dessert was offered. She wasn't one to refuse, prattling on about her weight whilst simultaneously helping herself to his, either. She ate her crème caramel with relish, savouring every mouthful. There was nothing in her manner that could be described as even faintly flirtatious. It was a cliché, perhaps, but Kemi Mashabane was *not that type of girl*. Woman, he corrected himself. It seemed almost insulting to think of her as a girl. 'How old are you, again?' he asked.

'Twenty-eight. Why?'

'I was just thinking . . . you're pretty young to be a fully qualified surgeon,' he said, suddenly hoping she wouldn't take offence.

She did not. 'Well, not *fully* qualified, not yet. It's a long haul.'

'How long?'

She shrugged. 'It depends slightly on what you want to do. Eight years, sometimes longer. Neurosurgery is one of the longer ones.'

'And did you always know you'd wind up doing it?' he asked, curious. Eight, ten years? It seemed like a lifetime.

She shrugged again. 'Not really, but I doubt anyone knows exactly what they want to do. I sort of fell into it . . . fell in love with it, you might say.'

He experienced a sharp contraction in his stomach. He shook his head sharply to clear it. 'Lucky you,' he murmured, not knowing what else to say.

'How about you? You said you were a banker. Which bank?' she asked, twirling her half-full glass of Shiraz between her fingers. Her nails were short, clean and blunt, he noticed. Capable-looking hands. They had to be, he supposed. She held people's lives in those hands, probably in the same firm but gentle way she held her wine glass. He felt again the unexpected pull somewhere in his gut.

'Me?' he parried, deadpan. 'Well, not really "in" banking. I'm a civil servant now. Just joined National Treasury.'

'So, you're back.'

He hesitated, then drew in his lip. 'I never *wanted* to go back. I always thought I'd stay here. When my dad was released, I went back for the first time and hated it. I couldn't wait to get back to London.'

Kemi smiled. 'Me too,' she said quietly. 'But I suppose it's different for me. I grew up in Zimbabwe, not South Africa. I speak Shona, not any of the South African languages. My dad was never around to teach me his language.'

'I've forgotten how to speak Zulu. But in a way, that's also an advantage.'

'How so?'

He took a mouthful of wine, savouring it slowly before answering. It wasn't something he would readily admit to, much less to someone he hardly knew. 'It feels strange, even disloyal, to say this out loud,' he said after a moment. 'But things are still so new back home. It hasn't even been five years . . . everyone's still finding their way.'

'So, what does that have to do with speaking Zulu?'

He looked her straight in the eye. 'Most whites don't see me as South African. Or even African, for that matter. They see me as one of them, whatever that means. I'm someone they can . . . trust?' He said it almost hesitantly. 'The fact that I'm as clueless as they are when it comes to that . . . speaking Zulu or Xhosa, or whatever . . . they see it as a sign that I'm just like them. And that's a good thing, for now.'

'I don't understand.'

'The economy is still in their hands, no matter who's in charge. Blacks still own less than one per cent of the country's wealth. It's taken the English and the Dutch two hundred years to amass their fortunes . . . they're not about to hand it over. Yes, we might have won political power, but the *real* power – the economy – that's going to take another hundred years. And that's why people like you and me are valuable. More valuable than you think. We're the inbetweeners, the ones both sides can trust.'

Kemi was quiet. She smiled faintly and shook her head. 'It seems a whole world away, nothing to do with my life. For me, we're all the same, thank God. Blood is blood, organs are organs . . . one sick person's the same as any other. When they're lying there on the operating table, you don't think about any of that. A human being is a human being.'

'Not where we're from,' Solam said, also smiling faintly. 'Come home. Come see for yourself. We need people like you.' He stopped himself, stunned by where the conversation had gone in such a short space of time. 'Listen to me,' he said, trying to laugh it off. 'I sound just like my mother.'

'And mine,' Kemi said dryly. 'And that's probably why she sent you.'

# 25

She stopped on the last step and turned round to face him. 'Thanks,' she said softly, looking down at him for once. 'I really enjoyed dinner,' she added with a smile. 'And apologies for knocking you over.'

'It was worth it,' Solam smiled. They looked at each other in the sodium glow of the street light.

'Well, I'd best be going,' Kemi said, fishing her key out of her bag. 'Safe journey back.'

He hesitated for a second, then leaned forward and kissed her. For a long moment, they stood locked together, although he didn't touch her with his hands. It was the sweetest kiss Kemi had ever received. She could feel his body move towards her, laying its caress alongside hers, even though they were standing up. He broke away first. She looked up, trying to read his expression. She couldn't. His beautiful face was closed to her.

'Goodnight,' he said quietly. 'I'll call you.' There was no push for anything more. She didn't know whether to be relieved or disappointed.

'Goodnight,' she said softly, putting her key in the lock and opening her door. She heard him clear his throat and begin to walk away, his footsteps growing fainter by the second. She closed the door reluctantly and leaned against it.

'Kem? Is that you?' Jen's sleepy voice drifted through from the sitting room.

'Yes, it's me. Go back to sleep.'

'You alone?'

Kemi suppressed a laugh. 'Yeah, of course I am. I'll tell you about it in the morning.'

'Night, Kem-Kem,' she said, sweetly reverting to an old childhood name.

'Night, Jen-Jen. Sleep tight. I'm up early but I promise I won't wake you if you're still asleep.'

'I won't be. I want to hear all about it.'

Kemi smiled to herself as she walked up the stairs to her bedroom. All? There was nothing to tell . . . and yet there was everything.

# 26

The door burst open, sending a trolley of notes and surgical equipment crashing to the floor. Kemi was furiously typing up her case notes. She looked up, irritated by the intrusion, and recognized the young houseman from the general surgery team.

'Is Fairbanks here?' he asked breathlessly.

She shook her head. 'No, he's in theatre. ER sent a head trauma up. What's the matter?'

'There's a patient on the general ward . . . he had a heart transplant a few days ago . . . he's been doing fine but he started coughing up blood, his chest tubes are full of it . . . Carrick's not in yet so the duty nurse sent me up to get Fairbanks.'

Kemi jumped up. 'Well, he's not here either. Which ward?' she said, already halfway through the door. He ran after her.

'C. We need a cardiac surgeon but she thought Fairbanks could do it in a pinch.'

'So can I.' Kemi ran down the stairs two at a time, the houseman hard on her heels, along the corridor towards the ward. They burst through the swing doors together. As soon as she saw the patient, she knew there wasn't a second to waste. The whole bed was covered in blood. 'Get me a chest kit,' she shouted to the nurse who was standing helplessly by. 'And call theatre. What's the flow?'

'Three-twenty millilitres,' the nurse said, sounding tearful.

'There's no clot?' she asked the nurse, as she felt the man's abdomen as gently as she could. The nurse shook her head dumbly. She was young, Kemi noticed, and probably frightened out of her wits. The orderlies arrived moments later with the gurney. 'Right . . . you . . . take that side . . . lift him up . . . gently, *gently*. OK? Which theatre?'

'First floor. They're ready for you. Who's assisting?'

'Him.' Kemi pointed to the houseman. 'Is the anaesthetist prepped?'

'Everything's ready.'

'Let's go.' She ran with the team helter-skelter back down the corridor towards the lift. Every second counted. She knew that the key to keeping the man alive was to ensure he bled out into the tubes, away from the heart and lungs, not internally. It was too early to tell what had caused the bleeding, but they had to stop it. They wheeled him in, the anaesthetist came forward, and she gowned and masked up in an instant.

Forty minutes later, it was all over. Two layers of absorbable mesh, a sterile intravenous bag, and a series of staples across the damaged vessel had succeeded in stopping the blood flow.

'Pressure's back down,' the houseman said, watching the monitor. 'One thirty over ninety. We'll keep an eye on it.'

Kemi was conscious of her heart thumping hard inside her chest as they wheeled the patient out. Someone was standing in the corner of the room. She pulled off her mask and saw that it was Julian Carrick, the resident cardiologist. He walked over, nodding to the junior houseman who was hovering at her elbow, seemingly unsure of what to do, or what had just happened.

'Good work,' Carrick said briskly. 'I got here five minutes after you'd started. It went well.'

'Were you watching?' Kemi asked. She hadn't been aware of him at all during the operation.

'Observing, not watching,' he demurred. 'Close shave.'

Kemi nodded. 'First time I've done it on my own,' she said, wondering as soon as she'd said it if it was the right thing to say.

'Well, I couldn't tell. *He* certainly couldn't,' Carrick said with a chuckle. 'Lucky chap. Could've easily gone the other way.'

Kemi looked down at her hands. 'I suppose I'd better get changed,' she said, not knowing quite what to say. She felt a little awkward, having taken over his case in such dramatic fashion.

'Would you . . . d'you feel like a drink?' he said suddenly. 'You look a bit shaken. It's past six, I just realized. Traffic's terrible at this time of day. I'm going to head to the Stag and Hound for a quick one, if you fancy it? You look as though you could do with one.'

Kemi looked up at him, surprised. Consultants of his rank rarely even spoke to registrars or housemen who weren't on their team. Mr Fairbanks, with whom she'd worked for over a year, was certainly not in the habit of joining them for post-work drinks. 'Are you sure?' she asked hesitantly.

'Positive. I'll see if Harry wants to join us. That's my house-man,' he added. 'The one who came to get you. He's only just started, sod's law. This'll have been a bit of a shock for him, too.'

'Well, if you're sure? It's really kind of you,' Kemi said. 'I'll . . . I'll just get changed.'

'Good. See you there.' Kemi stared after him for a second, then gathered her wits. He was right. It was nearly quarter to seven. After the sudden rush of adrenaline that had carried her through the surgery, a drink with colleagues was exactly what she needed. There was another reason, too. It had been three days since Solam had kissed her on her doorstep and since then, she hadn't heard a word from him. Not a peep. Was it normal to wait a week before getting in touch? She had absolutely no idea. Whatever the case, she couldn't bear the thought of sitting at home waiting for the phone to ring. She'd never had any sympathy for those girls in books and films who waited with dwindling hope for the man to call back . . . now she was one of them. Perhaps *she* was supposed to make the first move, not him? No, it didn't feel right, somehow. *I'll call you.* Those were his exact words. *So, call me!*

Twenty minutes later, she looked up to see Carrick and his houseman, Harry Johnson, weave their way across the crowded room towards her, beer and crisps in hand. The Stag and Hound was packed with medics and nurses, all winding down after a hard day's work. She let her fingers graze her mobile phone, tucked away in her pocket. She tried not to think about it.

'Thanks, Mr Carrick,' she said, as he carefully placed a half-pint of lager in front of her.

'Julian, please. We don't stand on ceremony in cardio,' he said with a smile. 'Not like you lot. Very formal on the fifth floor, or so I hear. Not that there's anything wrong with being formal,' he added hastily. 'I've known Mark Fairbanks for years. He's always been that way.'

Kemi wasn't sure how to respond. Julian Carrick was in his late forties or early fifties, she guessed, perhaps a decade younger than her own boss. Suddenly she felt her mobile vibrate in her pocket. Her heart skipped a beat and she pulled it out, her fingers shaking. It was Jen. Disappointment crashed over her like a cold wave, but she struggled to keep her composure.

'Boyfriend?' Julian asked, as he manoeuvred himself into the seat opposite. 'Or husband?'

'Oh, no, no, just a friend,' she said quickly, embarrassed. 'I'll . . . I'll call her back later.'

'Well, cheers. Here's to one helluva day.' He lifted the glass. 'And what a day it was. Well done, by the way. You kept your head, and your nerve. Good job.'

'Yeah, good job,' Harry echoed. He still seemed dazed. He drained his half-pint almost immediately.

'Thanks,' she said, feeling slightly uncomfortable. Suddenly, someone shouted her name. She turned around. It was Geoff. He waved at her, surprised to see her in the Stag and Hound.

'What're *you* doing here?' he asked, coming over. He was alone. He grinned at the other two men. 'Unbelievable. I've been asking her to come out for a drink with me for nearly three months and she's never once agreed.'

'Well, you're obviously not persuasive enough,' Julian chuckled. 'Julian Carrick. Cardio.' He held out a hand. 'You two obviously know each other.'

Geoff slid onto the bench next to her. 'Same team. Nice to meet you.'

'What're you having?' Harry got up. 'I'll get the next round.'

'Not for me,' Kemi said quickly. 'One glass is about all I can take.'

'Oh, come on, a half-pint won't kill you,' Julian said, smiling at her. 'Drink it slowly. We're celebrating her first embolectomy. Cool as a cucumber, in and out. Patient didn't feel a thing.'

'Course he didn't,' Geoff said, raising his glass. 'He was asleep, I take it?'

She laughed. 'Yes – Harry just burst in, Fairbanks was out . . . there was no one else.'

'Your dad would've been proud of you. I remember watching him at the Royal Infirmary in Dundee when I was a lowly registrar. Same hands.'

Kemi felt the heat rise in her face. She could feel Geoff's eyes on her.

'Who's your dad?' Geoff asked her, frowning.

Kemi turned to face him. 'Sorry,' she said with an apologetic grimace. 'I . . . I just don't like people knowing.'

'I'd have thought it was obvious?' Julian said, surprised. 'Everyone knows.'

Kemi squirmed uncomfortably. 'Oh, no, hardly anyone knows.'

'I *thought* it might be,' Geoff said, still looking confused. 'But you were so adamant it wasn't. Why on earth did you hide it?'

Kemi made an impassioned face. 'I just don't like people knowing, that's all. Can we drop it? Please?' Her mobile buzzed again. She tried to ignore it but couldn't. She got up clumsily, almost spilling her beer. 'I . . . I'll be right back,' she said, retreating from the table. 'Just give me a minute.' She pulled her phone out. It was Jen again, not Solam. She felt suddenly close to tears. She pushed her way through the crowded bar, looking for the sign to the toilets. 'Hello?' she pressed the phone tight against her ear. It was so loud in the bar she could barely hear her. 'What? I can't hear you!' She struggled to get to the stairs. The toilets were on the first floor. 'What did you say?' she shouted again, taking the stairs two at a time. Thankfully one of the stalls was empty. She ran inside and bolted the door.

Jen shouted something but she couldn't catch it. Suddenly, the line went dead. Kemi looked at the phone in disbelief. She'd run out of battery. Now she'd have to wait until she got home to hear from him, *if* he called at all. She promptly burst into tears.

# 27

Solam looked at the man sitting opposite, sweating with a combination of heat and drink, and wondered dispassionately if the distaste he felt for him showed anywhere on his face.

'I don't mind telling you, it's a relief.' Dirk Coetzee waved his brandy glass affably.

Solam sighed. He knew what was coming next. 'Why? What were you expecting?' he asked. He glanced discreetly at his phone. Twice in the past couple of days he'd been on the verge of phoning Kemi Mashabane but something had come up. He wanted to be in the right frame of mind to call her, not irritated and distracted, like he was now. He let out a barely perceptible sigh. Dirk seemed oblivious.

'Oh, you know how it is. One's never sure. Word comes from on high that you've got to take at *least* one, but you never know who or what you're going to get. I don't mind telling you—'

'I don't think you should,' Solam said quickly, evenly, interrupting Dirk's whisky-induced confessional flow. It wouldn't do him any favours to pick a fight now, not when he'd barely been in post for a year. *Don't make waves*, his mother had warned him. *Especially not in the beginning. Go where you're told, do as you're asked. It'll pay off, just you wait and see.* He wasn't sure. He would never say it to her face – or even behind her back – but things were different now. He looked around the bar at the gracious Saxon Hotel, one of the finest in Johannesburg, and tried to focus on the task at hand. He'd been instructed by his boss to charm the pants off the private sector bankers. *Take them out, get to know them.* Those were his orders. His division was staffed almost exclusively by rugby-playing, beer-drinking Afrikaners. He was probably the first black senior banker they'd ever come across, never mind shared a drink with. No wonder poor Dirk was knocking back the Laphroaig. It was far more of a shock to him than it was to Solam. He was well accustomed to throwing back drinks with white men. Until recently, it was all he'd known.

'Another one?'

Dirk peered at his glass as though he'd never seen one before. 'Yeah . . . another one, why not? You're a good man, So-So . . .?'

'Solam,' Solam finished helpfully for him. He signalled to the waiter. 'Another one for my friend here.' He turned to Dirk. 'Just nipping to the gents. I'll be back.'

He left Dirk and walked towards the toilets. He pushed open the door to one of stalls and sighed. Socializing with well-fed white men was by far the most stressful part of his job. Two glasses in and they suddenly all felt comfortable enough to tell him what they *really* thought of the changes sweeping through the country. It didn't occur to them that he had no interest in knowing what they thought. Dirk was a nice enough bloke when sober, but like so many, he was too dim to fully grasp what the changes actually *meant*. Their days were numbered. It might not happen now, or even within the next five years, but it would happen. The old guard would have to make way for the new. Those idiots who couldn't pronounce let alone remember his name were going to have to adjust the way they viewed things, especially business.

What *had* worked in the protected and isolated apartheid era no longer worked.

He flushed the toilet, watching the water swirl around and around, then zipped up his trousers. He looked at his watch. It was just past eleven. Another half an hour and then he could go home. Maybe then he'd find the space and time to call Kemi. It had been almost a week since he'd kissed her. He was aware of an unfamiliar longing to hear her voice again. He washed his hands, still thinking about her, and pushed open the door to the corridor. A woman was standing just by the entrance to the bar, fingers curled around a wine glass. She was tall and blonde, stunningly beautiful.

'Hi, Solam,' she murmured as he passed. He stopped and looked at her in surprise. Was she talking to him? 'Hi there, Solam,' she said again.

'Hi . . . have we met?' he asked, confused. How did she know his name?

'I'm a friend of Dirk's,' she said, with a quick toss of her head in Dirk's direction. 'He thought we ought to meet.'

He looked past her to the bar where Dirk stood with a brunette draped across his chest. He winked at Solam, suddenly not quite as drunk as he'd seemed. Solam turned back to the blonde. 'What's your name?'

'What would you like it to be?' she asked, her eyes widening. Her accent was hard to place.

Solam suppressed the urge to laugh out loud. The blonde was still staring suggestively at him. He felt his cock stir. It had been a while. One way to keep his mind off Kemi. 'Anything,' he said finally, almost wearily. 'Call yourself whatever you want.'

She smiled and tucked an arm through his. Her perfume closed over him, thick and heady. 'Let's start with "A". Call me Anna. That's easy, isn't it?'

He shrugged. 'OK, Anna. Whatever you like. So where are we going?' She steered him towards the bar where Dirk had his tongue down the brunette's throat. The bar had suddenly emptied.

'Come and meet my friends,' she said, reaching up to speak close to his ear. 'We're all Dirk's friends.'

'Popular guy, Dirk,' Solam murmured.

'*Very.* You have no idea who he knows.'

'Where are we going?' Solam asked, as Anna expertly manoeuvred the car out of the tight parking space. It was a Jaguar. Red, with black leather seats. Was it hers? He glanced at her. Her long white skirt was parted to reveal a firm, tanned thigh. She must have sensed his gaze. As she swung onto Rivonia, she opened her legs a little wider. She was wearing nothing underneath. His eyes widened. She turned and gave him a faint but knowing smile. 'Where are we going?' he asked again, only just managing to resist sliding his hand in between the soft folds of her dress.

'There's a party at a friend's place. It's not far. Dirk thought you might enjoy it.'

He caught the trace of an Eastern European accent. 'Are you Russian?' he asked, as they sped down the road towards Sandton City.

'Does it matter?'

He shook his head. 'No. Just curious.'

'Don't be curious. And don't be worried. Dirk is very discreet. Nothing will happen to you unless you want it to.'

'I'm not worried,' he said, leaning back into the plush leather seat. It was true. For some odd reason, the thought that it might be dangerous hadn't even crossed his mind. He smiled to himself. He'd underestimated Dirk.

She turned left and pulled to a halt in front of a security hut. They waited for a second whilst the security guard jotted the car number plate down and then the gate swung open. He sat up as they sailed through. It was a long driveway, thick with plants and trees, curving round at last to a neoclassical portico.

'So . . . here we are,' she said, pulling up the handbrake.

He looked around. There were least a dozen cars in the enormous driveway . . . Mercedes, Jaguars, a couple of luxury 4x4s, a Bentley . . . even a Hummer. He let out a low whistle. 'Some party.'

She laughed and got out of the car. 'Come on. Let's go inside.'

The house was lavishly decorated in the way only a house which was usually empty could be. The living room was vast, stretching across several sunken pits towards a garden that was lit up like a Christmas tree. There was a long glistening pool, palm trees, loungers, and those ridiculously pruned round hedges that looked like a row of poodles on guard. He looked around him. There were perhaps a dozen men sprawled on the endless white couches, with drinks and plates of half-eaten food everywhere. And women. There were more beautiful women than he'd ever seen in his life in one room at the same time. Brunettes, blondes, a redhead or two . . . black girls, white girls, two Asian girls sitting with a large, florid man sandwiched in between them. There were champagne bottles everywhere. A door opened to his left and a girl walked into the living room, naked save for a tiny black thong and a pair of leather high heels.

'Drink?' Anna had appeared beside him, holding a tumbler of pale whisky. 'Or drugs?' She pointed to a side table with several neat lines of coke hospitably lined up.

He shook his head. 'Nah, a drink's fine for me.'

'Then there's more for *me*,' she said happily. She handed him the tumbler and sank gracefully to her knees, bending her head to the glass. A minute later, the coke was gone. She straightened up and held out her hand. 'Come on. Party time.' She led him through the room, seemingly knowing her way around. She pushed open a door at the far end to a small study, dominated by a huge television screen and yet another white leather sofa.

'Whose house is this?' he mumbled, as she pulled him down onto the sofa next to her.

'You ask so many questions,' she replied, her fingers busy at his zip. 'What does it matter? You're here. I'm here. Just relax and have a good time. Everybody else is.'

She slid down on the couch until she was kneeling right in front of him. Her blonde hair spilled over his thighs. He was about to say something when he felt her warm hand slide right inside his boxers, shaking him free. He felt the day's tension flood right out of him, making his head spin. He was glad he was sitting down. He closed his eyes. For a brief, startling moment he thought of Kemi. Then the blonde's mouth was upon him and for a few minutes he was unable to think of anything at all. She was expert at her job. Within minutes he exploded in her warm, willing mouth.

# PART FIVE
# 1998

## Three months later

. . .

The past, the present and the future are really one;
they are today.

HARRIET BEECHER STOWE

# 28

A half-eaten Kit Kat and two empty cappuccinos lay between them. Kemi had finished talking and for once, Jen couldn't think of a single thing to say. They were sitting in a small coffee shop around the corner from the hospital.

'So, he just never called back?' she asked incredulously. 'Not once?'

Kemi shook her head. 'Nope. I left three messages. I wondered if something had happened to him . . . you know . . . maybe he'd had an accident, or he was ill or something? But my mother was at some function or other and she saw him. Apparently, he's well. Very well. He's just been promoted.'

Jen was speechless with indignation. 'What an *arsehole*!' she said hotly.

Kemi shrugged. 'Well, one dinner and a kiss . . . doesn't mean a thing.'

'Kem, it's not *that* . . . it's just so bloody *rude*! I mean, who does he think he is?'

Kemi shrugged. 'Oh, forget him. He's not important. Anyhow, that's not what I wanted to talk to you about.'

Jen eyed her warily. 'So, what did you want to talk about?'

Kemi reached down into her satchel and pulled out a folder. She placed it on the table. 'This,' she said, opening it to the first page.

Jen looked at it. It was an application of some sort. *The J Taft Funding for Surgical Residencies in Southern Africa*. She frowned. 'What is it?'

Kemi looked at her. She drew in a breath. 'I'm going to ask you something,' she said slowly. 'Something big. It's a lot to ask, I know, and I won't blame you at all if you say you can't.'

Jen looked at her in surprise. Kemi never asked her for anything, let alone anything big. 'What?'

Kemi's eyes met hers. Slowly, as she watched, Kemi's face changed. There was a small fold of skin beneath each eye that sank away, drawn tightly over her cheekbones. It was a look Jen had seen many times before, a look of quiet, steely determination. Her mind was made up, whatever it was. When she spoke, Jen had the feeling she'd known all along what was coming. 'I want to go back,' she said, tracing a line on the patterned tablecloth with the tip of her teaspoon. 'And I want you to come with me.'

Jen blinked. 'Back? Where?'

'South Africa. Johannesburg. Will you?'

Jen's mouth dropped open. 'Go with you? Why? What on earth will I do there?'

'Do whatever you like. It's only for three months. I've already been accepted. I just . . . I just think if I don't go now, I never will. It was one of the things I . . . I liked about him. He'd gone back. He was – he *is* – doing something useful. He's needed.'

'Jesus, Kemi. You're needed here. If *anyone's* needed, it's you. Look at the job you do.'

'Yeah, but there are hundreds of surgeons here who could do the same thing. I want to be properly useful.'

Jen swallowed. It had been three months since Federico had fired her. She'd taken on a series of dead-end temping jobs just to fill the time – and to keep Father from asking yet again what she intended to do with her life. She was suddenly reminded of the day she and Kemi had sat outside her father's study, eleven years earlier, Jen trying desperately to summon the courage to tell him she wanted to be an artist. What had Kemi said to her? *It's your life, Jen. Don't let anyone else tell you what to do with your life.* Sound advice, which she'd failed to take. And now here it was again. Only this time, Kemi was setting a test for *herself*, not for Jen. There was no question Kemi would fail it the way she had.

'I'll come,' she said suddenly. 'I'll find something to do, don't worry about me. You're absolutely right. If it's something you feel you have to do, then you should do it. You told me that once, and I didn't do it then. I want to do it now.'

Kemi looked at her. Her eyes were shining. 'Really? You'll come with me?'

'Course I will. You don't think I'd let you go out there on your own, do you?' Jen said lightly. 'No . . . if you're going, *I'm* going. Even if it's only to stop you throwing yourself at that idiot, what's-his-name?'

Kemi laughed shakily. 'Solam? No. This has nothing to do with him.'

Jen saw then that the shine in her eyes wasn't just happiness, it was tears beginning to form. She swallowed down hard on the lump in her own throat. They were soul sisters. She felt it now, again.

# 29

For the first few moments after waking, Julian Carrick almost forgot where he was. He lay in bed, aware only of the tremendous ache in his groin and a head that felt like lead. He reached down to adjust the waistband on his pyjamas and found that they were damp, sticky. He lifted the covers and nearly laughed out loud. He'd had a wet dream. He was fifty-two years old. He hadn't had a wet dream since he was a teenager!

He slid out of bed, careful not to wake his wife Rosemary, who was snoring softly as she always did, and walked on tiptoe to the bathroom. Once inside, he peeled off the damp pyjamas and thrust them to the bottom of the laundry basket. He switched on the light and looked at himself in the mirror. His face stared back at him, utterly wrung out, and it wasn't just the mild hangover from the night before. He turned on the tap and splashed cold water over his face. Two aspirin would certainly get rid of the hangover but as for the other matter, the wet dream . . . well, there, for once, he had no answer, no clue. He was horrified, mortified. For the first time in twenty-six years of marriage, he found himself adrift. Oh, he'd had the odd moment . . . which man his age hadn't? Once or twice, nothing he'd ever acted upon. An overly grateful patient, and a waitress on holiday in Greece. Both times it had crossed his mind, but he'd either been too preoccupied or too afraid of the consequences to do anything other than shake his head regretfully, passing up the opportunity, as he should. But this . . . this was different. He couldn't even pinpoint the day or moment it had first hit him. She'd crept up on him slowly, almost imperceptibly, and then his awareness of her gathered steam until it was like being hit by a roller coaster and he could think of little else. *Idiot. Idiot. Idiot!* He stared at his face in the mirror. She was young enough to be his daughter, if he'd had one. Was that it? Some subliminal longing for the child he and Rosemary had failed to produce? *Don't be ridiculous.* There was absolutely nothing parental about his feelings for Kemisa Mashabane. He was just thankful she wasn't on his team. As the resident cardiac surgeon, he only came across her in theatre every once in a while. Thank God. She reduced him to the incompetence of a junior houseman in her presence and that wouldn't do at all—

'Julian? What on earth are you doing?'

He whirled round. It was Rosemary. Sleepy-eyed, she'd come into the bathroom without him even noticing. She stood in the doorway, staring at his naked bottom half. He flushed.

'I . . . I was just heading to the shower,' he stammered, pulling his top off. 'I couldn't sleep, for some reason. Thought I'd . . . I'd go for a run.'

'And you're taking a shower *before* you run?' Rosemary sounded amused. 'That doesn't make sense, darling.'

'I . . . I know. I . . . I had a bit too much to drink last night,' he said quickly. 'Just thought a cold shower would clear the old head.'

'Were you out with the team?' She yawned, going over to the toilet. He ducked into the shower and closed the door. When they were first married, it was one of the things he'd loved most about her – a complete lack of self-consciousness about her own body and its functions. Now it embarrassed him. He turned on the shower tap and stood for a moment in its warm steady stream. Christ, what was happening to him?

'Changed my mind,' he said fifteen minutes later, walking into the kitchen. Rosemary was already at the kitchen table, buttering a slice of toast.

'Oh? Feeling better?'

He nodded. 'Shower did the trick. What've you got on today?' he asked, going to the fridge.

She looked up. 'You've forgotten, haven't you?'

He turned around. 'What?'

'The Pritchards are coming to dinner. You said you'd cook.'

He stopped, fingers on the door handle. His heart sank. 'Damn,' he said, louder than he should. 'I mean . . . yes, I forgot. Do we have to?'

Rosemary looked at him in surprise. 'I thought you liked having them over?'

'I do. It's just . . . I don't know . . . it's been a really busy month.'

'I could cancel,' she said, looking doubtful. 'It's a bit late, but I'm sure Kate'll understand.'

'No, no, it's fine. I'll just pop to Waitrose and get what I need.'

'D'you want me to come?'

'No.' That too came out louder than he intended. 'But thanks. I know what I'm cooking . . . I won't be long.' He had to get out of the house. He shut the fridge door.

'Aren't you having any breakfast?'

'No, thanks. I'll grab a coffee somewhere. See you soon.' He left the kitchen before she could ask any more questions.

He started the car engine and sat for a few moments, waiting for the interior to warm up. He was skating on very thin ice. He put his hands on the steering wheel and for a moment let his head rest on it, closing his eyes. A loud tap at the window made him jump out of his skin. It was Rosemary.

'Whatever's the matter with you?' she asked as he rolled down the window. She was holding out his wallet. He'd left it on the kitchen table.

He struggled to raise a weak smile. 'Head's worse than I thought. Thanks,' he said, taking the wallet. 'Must've emptied my pockets last night when I came in.'

'Is everything OK?'

'Yeah, yeah, everything's fine. Just the old head.' He tapped his forehead lightly. 'It'll have cleared by the time I get back. Thanks,' he said again, and put the car in reverse.

She stood by uncertainly as he manoeuvred his way out. He ought to have been more reassuring . . . given her a kiss, a pat on the hand. But he couldn't. He couldn't bring himself to touch her. *Jesus Christ*, he swore at himself under his breath, what the hell was wrong with him? Kemisa Mashabane hadn't so much as *looked* at him but he couldn't get her out of his head.

# 30

'Ma'am? Ma'am?' Alice awoke with a start, her heart pounding. Someone was pressing on her arm. She opened her eyes and tried to focus. It was one of the maids, but she couldn't remember which one. What was her name? All these girls. She just couldn't keep up. Traipsing in and out of the house all these months and years. The damn girl wouldn't stop shaking her.

'What? What is it?' Her tongue was heavy and thick.

'Mrs Smith sent me up, ma'am. Your daughter's here.'

'My daughter?' Alice gripped the side of her chair, levering herself upright. As usual, she'd fallen asleep in front of the television. 'Which daughter?'

The girl seemed puzzled. 'It's Jennifer, ma'am.'

'Oh, of course. Jennifer, did you say?' The girl looked even more confused. 'Will you send her up?' Alice asked, glancing around. 'No. Don't send her up. Tell her I'll come down.'

'Are ye all right to come downstairs?' the maid asked, clearly alarmed.

Alice put up a hand to her hair. Why was the maid so worried? Did she look a mess? 'Of course I'm all right,' she snapped. 'I'm not an invalid. Who did you say it was again?'

'I . . . I'll just go and get Mrs Smith, ma'am.'

'Oh, for goodness' sake, don't bother Mrs Smith!'

But the girl was gone. Alice sighed and leaned back in her chair. Catriona was here. How long had it been since she'd seen her? she wondered. She tried to remember. A month? Six months? Maybe even longer? Nothing seemed to make sense these days, least of all the passing of time. She reached for the little plastic box of pills that was never far from her chair and picked up the half-empty cup of tea. It was cold, but no matter. She swallowed two Nembutals and then took a Valium, just for good measure. She hated being woken up like that in the middle of her afternoon nap. The news that Catriona had arrived had set her nerves on edge. 'I'll just close my eyes for a second,' she murmured, making herself comfortable in the chair. 'I'll go down in a minute.'

The maid looked rather flustered as she delivered the news that her mother would be downstairs directly.

'Downstairs?' Mrs Smith, the new housekeeper, gave a snort. She bustled around her, fetching teacups and saucers. 'Aye, that'll be the day. I cannae remember the last time she came downstairs.'

Jen's heart sank. Would she ever be able to return home like every other person she knew and expect to find anything approaching normal? She'd been dreading coming back for a whole host of reasons, chief of which was her mother's deteriorating grip on reality. 'Losin' her marbles' was how Mrs Smith put it. Kemi was kinder. 'It sounds like early onset dementia. It's not her fault. Don't be *too* hard on her.' It seemed to Jen as though her mother had always been in the process of 'losing her marbles', dementia or not. She couldn't even recall a time before the pills and the headaches and the slow retreat to the rooms on the second floor. She sighed. At least her father wasn't in yet. She wasn't looking forward to *that* conversation.

LESLEY LOKKO

'Ye should look in on Mrs Logan while ye're here. She was ever so fond of the two of ye, ye know,' Mrs Smith said, setting down a heavy brown teapot. Jen looked at it in surprise. She remembered it from childhood. The only thing that appeared to change in the Morningside home was the staff – there were fewer of them now, just Mrs Smith and the new girl. Mrs Logan had retired nearly five years ago and the gardener only came in once a week.

'I will. I'll go round tomorrow after church.'

'Och, that'll make yer da happy, so it will. Goin' tae church, I mean. I dinnae ken the last time he had someone tae go wi'. Yer ma's no bothered wi' church any more.'

Jen took a sip of tea. 'How is she?'

'Same as ever. She's nae bother as long as she has her pills and her telly. She takes a wee drop every now and then, granted, but she's nae bother at all.'

'I suppose I'd better go up,' Jen said, looking at the clock above the Aga. It was nearly three. Her father would be home around five, Mrs Smith had said.

'Aye. She'll no be comin' down now.'

'Shall I take her anything?' Jen asked, sliding off the kitchen stool. She finished her tea, and took the cup and saucer to the sink.

'Dinnae bother. I'll take her supper up in a wee while. Off ye go. Dinnae ye bother wi' them cups, either. Lisa'll do it.'

Jen took the chance to escape. Mrs Smith's accent was thick enough to cut with a knife. Half the time she had no idea what the woman was saying.

She walked up the stairs, letting her fingers trail loosely along the gleaming bannister. It was like stepping back in time, she thought to herself, as she made her way slowly to Alice's rooms on the second floor. The dark carpets and the sombre wallpaper were exactly the same. The same pictures of Scottish landscapes and the framed portrait of her grandmother as a young bride hung on the turn at the first landing. The door to her father's study at the far end of the corridor was closed. As she passed it, a strange, morbid sense of déjà vu stole over her, something half remembered, half forgotten, deeply buried. She stopped. There was a curious, uncomfortable prickling at the nape of her neck, like a shiver of wind across the surface of a lake. The house was calm and quiet, yet a strange crystallization was taking place, heard in every tiny creak of the floorboards, in the sound of the rain outside, even in the muffled noise of Mrs Smith moving around downstairs. She drew in a deep breath. Something was hovering at the far reaches of her concentration. Her heart was racing and her palms felt sweaty and clammy. She drew in a breath, then another, breathing fast. And then, all of a sudden it vanished, as quickly as it had come. She put a hand on the bannister to steady herself. A dull pressure was beginning to build up at the base of her skull. She put a hand to her nose in disbelief. It was bleeding. She hadn't had a nosebleed in years. In fact, the only place she ever had them was in this house. She pushed open the door to the toilet at the top of the landing and grabbed a handful of toilet paper to staunch the flow. There was no telling what the sight of blood might do to Alice.

She found Alice sitting upright in a chair by the window, fast asleep. Her hair, always fair, was now snowy white. She looked like a woman in her seventies, not her late fifties.

'Mum?' Jen put out a hand, touching her lightly on the forearm.

Alice woke with a start. For a second she stared at Jen, her eyes completely blank, as if she couldn't recognize her. Jen felt her stomach contract. The vacant look in her eyes was more than she could bear. Recognition dawned slowly. Alice blinked. 'Catriona? Is that you?'

'Hi, Mum. Yes, it's me. Jen.'

'Oh yes, yes . . . Jen. Of course. Of course it's you. When did you get back? Are you home now?'

Jen swallowed. 'I just came up for a couple of days, Mum. To say goodbye, really. I . . . I'm actually going away for a bit. To South Africa. Kemi's taking up a place at a hospital out there and—'

'Africa?' Alice interrupted her suddenly. She began picking agitatedly at the sleeves of her cardigan. 'Why on earth would you want to go *there*? I'd have thought it'd be the *last* place you'd want to go.'

Jen looked down at her, puzzled. 'Why? It's perfectly safe, Mum. I'll be with Kemi.'

Alice gave a little derisive snort. 'Oh, *her*. Well, she'll only get what she deserves, I'm sure of it.'

Jen was stunned, not just by the words, but by the sudden look of venomous spite on Alice's face. It was a look she'd never seen before. And then, just as quickly as it had appeared, it vanished. Alice turned her face up to Jen's. 'Won't you ask Mrs Smith to bring me up a cup of tea, darling?' she said, her voice and face as sweet and innocent as a child's. 'And a biscuit. I've just realized . . . I'm starving. Isn't that odd?'

Jen said nothing. Yes, her mother was losing her grip, and her mind. Where on earth had *that* outburst come from? She was mixing Kemi up with someone else, surely?

The conversation with her father was surprisingly easy. 'Well, you'll be with Kemi. I dare say she'll make sure you get something out of it. How long will you be away?'

Jen bit down on the urge to snap at him. 'Three months,' she said, as calmly as she could.

'And I dare say you'll be looking for another advance?' The slight emphasis on the word 'another' wasn't lost on Jen.

'If that would be all right, Father,' she said, just as calmly. No point in getting into an argument.

He sighed. 'I've little choice, have I? I don't know why you always leave these silly requests to the very last minute. It was exactly the same as that last little caper you went on . . . where was it? America?'

Jen looked beyond her father to the twilight horizon. It was eight o'clock in the evening. With a bit of luck, she'd be out of the house by nine, on her way to meet a couple of old schoolfriends on George Street. The following morning she'd be on the train back to London, having survived both parents and with the knowledge that, for the next few months at least, she'd be free. 'Yes, New York,' she said quietly. 'But it *did* lead to a job,' she added. She couldn't help herself.

'And how long did that last?' Robert asked, going to his desk. He didn't seem to expect an answer. He sat down and opened the drawer to his left. He made a great show of opening his blue-and-gold chequebook, picking up a fountain pen with a sigh.

Two minutes later it was all over. She walked back downstairs, a sizeable cheque in her hand and the bittersweet taste of freedom in her mouth.

She boarded the London train at Waverley Station, slung her overnight bag onto the rack above her seat and sat down. The carriage was surprisingly empty. She put her coffee and sandwich on the foldout table and picked up her magazine. As the train pulled slowly out of the station, the tall, dark granite buildings on either side that formed the canyon of the city's heart began to fall away. The hills were golden-orange in the unexpected sunshine, tufts of egg-yellow gorse flashing through as Arthurs Seat appeared, and passed. After years in London, the stillness of the Scottish landscape never failed to move her. She let it work lightly on her, over her, struck again by the space it gave you to breathe. The tightness in her chest that always came over her at home began to ease. It was as if the open, empty landscape was preparing her for her return. She looked out on the stretch of fields and flowering scrub, broken here and there by a clump of dark trees and small, jutting platforms of craggy rocks, and was grateful.

# 31

Kemi's enormous, battered suitcase lay open-jawed in the middle of the living room. All around it was the debris of her packing choices: T-shirts, cardigans, jeans, underwear . . . make-up, hair products, books, a pair of trainers with the laces missing, odd socks rolled into mismatched balls. She rested on her haunches, sifting through the piles, deciding what to take, what to store, what to throw away. It was years since she'd done a thorough clear-out . . . in a way, it was oddly cathartic. She glanced at her watch. It was nearly six o'clock. She'd been at it pretty much all day. There was less than a fortnight to go until their departure. Jen had gone up to Edinburgh the night before to break the news to Uncle Robert that not only was Kemi leaving for three months, she was too. Why she'd left it to practically the last minute was beyond Kemi. 'Just pick up the phone and tell him,' she'd said, only half a dozen times. But Jen stubbornly refused.

'It'll be better if I talk to him in person.'

'Well, just *do* it. What's he going to say?' It was sounding eerily like their conversation of more than a decade ago.

Jen shrugged. 'I don't know. I still have to ask for an advance, you know. I won't be working.'

'You'll be staying with me and you'll be painting every day . . . you won't need much. It's only three months.'

'I know, I know. But I'd still prefer to talk to him face-to-face than over the phone. He'll probably just put the phone down on me. If I'm standing in front of him, he won't have much choice.'

Kemi said nothing. She'd just hoped Jen would actually do as she promised and go up to Edinburgh. If not, she'd be spending the long plane journey down the length of Africa alone.

She stood up, yawning. She had another week of work and then four glorious days off. She couldn't remember the last time she'd had more than a day off . . . whole weekends off and bank holidays and the like seemed to belong to another lifetime. Her rotation had come to an end, but UCH was one of the capital's busiest hospitals and there seemed to be no let-up to the stream of emergencies that came flooding through the doors. For a moment her mind drifted to the previous night's conversation with Carrick. *Most* odd! She'd bumped into him coming out of theatre. He'd rushed up to her, already breathless, as though he'd been running.

'I just heard the news!' he said, startling her.

She pulled her mask aside. She hadn't even stepped out of her surgery boots. 'Sorry?'

'Mark just told me! You're leaving!' The look of distress on his face was almost comical.

'Er, yes . . . it's only temporary. I . . . I applied for a fellowship in South Africa,' she answered, bewildered. Why should it even matter to him? She wasn't on his team.

He stood there, looking utterly dejected. 'You . . . you never said,' he said finally, his voice trailing off.

Kemi was even more puzzled. Aside from the one time they'd had a drink together and the occasional encounter in the hallways or the medics' staffroom, where she couldn't recall ever saying more than 'hello', she'd barely spoken to him. 'I didn't . . . well, I just didn't think it mattered—'

'When are you going?' he interrupted her.

'In about a fortnight. I'm finishing up with Fairbanks on Saturday, then I'm on call for a week . . . and then we're off.'

'We?'

She felt her face grow warm. It seemed ludicrous to even *think* it. No . . . surely not? 'My sister. She's coming with me for the three months.'

'Oh.' He seemed to be struggling to speak. 'I . . . I was rather hoping you might consider cardiology,' he said finally. 'Once you'd finished with Mark, of course.'

Relief flooded through her, followed immediately by embarrassment. Of course, it was professional interest. How on earth could she have even *dreamed* it was anything else? 'Oh, I'd love to,' she said quickly, aware as soon as she said it of how silly she sounded. You didn't just jump from neuro to cardio on a whim. 'To . . . to chat about it. Once I get back, I mean,' she added lamely.

'Yes, of course. Well, I . . . I hope you'll, er, stay in touch. Here . . . I'll give you my email address. I've only just got one, although I must confess the whole thing seems like a rather bad idea to me,' he said with a short laugh, fishing a card out of his pocket.

'Yes, all our case notes are being digitized. I spend more time at my computer than I do with patients,' she agreed.

'Exactly. Well, I suppose you've got lots to do,' Carrick said briskly. 'I hope you enjoy it. Look forward to hearing about it when you're back.' He gave her a quick farewell salute and turned around. Before she had a chance to respond, he'd disappeared through the swing doors.

She felt embarrassed thinking about it now. He was old enough to be her father . . . in fact, hadn't he said he'd actually worked with her father? She walked into the kitchen, wondering if there was anything edible in the fridge. What would Jen be doing at that very moment? she wondered. She suddenly felt a pang of longing for those long Edinburgh summer nights when the light stayed in the sky until almost eleven, and the pubs and street cafes were full. It had been years since she'd been back.

Her mobile gave a faint ping. She smiled. It was probably Jen, either tearful or triumphant. She walked back into the living room and bent down to retrieve it. Her heart missed a beat. It wasn't Jen. She stared at the little square screen in shock. *Solam Rhoyi.* There it was, flashing out at her from the backlit screen. She hadn't heard from him in three months! She pressed the 'read message' button with shaking fingers. *Hi, how're things? Past couple of months have been busy. Hope all's well. Solam.* She stared at it. *How're things?* She almost threw the phone across the room. Jen was right. He was a prick. A world-class prick. She shoved the phone angrily into her back pocket and walked back to the kitchen. There was a bottle of wine on the top shelf. She pulled it out, unscrewed the cap and poured herself a glass. It was totally out of character but she didn't know what else to do. She carried it back to the living room and continued her methodical packing. One folded T-shirt after another, a pair of folded jeans, another sweater . . . a hat. Anything to take her mind off the phone and the fact that she longed to text him back.

# 32

As soon as he pressed send, he regretted it. What had possessed him? Either to send it or to have ignored her for the past twelve weeks in the first place? He didn't have a good answer. He didn't even have a bad or weak answer. He'd been an asshole, plain and simple. After that night with the hookers when he'd lost control, he'd felt so angry with himself for giving in that he'd deliberately stopped himself from reaching out, at least until the memory of his loss of control had faded. She'd tried to call him during the week and he'd been too ashamed to answer, thinking he'd ring back at the weekend, when things had calmed down. But the weekend came and he found himself out with Dirk once more, with a different group of women this time, equally beautiful, equally willing . . . and then a week had stretched to two, and then three. And by then he felt too stupid to call her, so he'd done nothing. It niggled him like a toothache. What would he say? *Sorry, I've been busy? I miss you? I've had sex with a whore, not once but twice, and I've been an asshole?* None of the above. At least three times in the past few weeks he'd pulled out his phone, hoping for a message or another voicemail from her, wondering how to break the ice until finally, after nearly three months, he'd had enough to drink and pressed send before he could change his mind.

Cursing, he got up and walked to the window. He dragged

the sliding pane open and looked down onto the street below. It was nearly midnight but the heat of midday was still trapped in the smooth black tarmac, wafting upwards, making him sweat. The sky fluttered eyelids of lightning, briefly competing with the neon sign across the road, *Best in Africa Life Insurance*, sending flashes of green light down onto the crowds below. Midnight was midday; day was night. Braamfontein throbbed like a giant, human pulse. In a city that had been emptied from the inside after the fall of apartheid, it was fast becoming *the* place to be. The mix was heady. Students from the nearby university poured out of lectures on Friday afternoons, taking up residence in the streets – or so it seemed – until Monday morning. Abandoned buildings had been taken over as squats by white hipsters, looking for more adventure than the gated suburbs could provide. They hung out on street corners, openly smoking, revelling in the mayhem. Aspiring models and actors from the township prowled the clubs and bars. In amongst them all, the security guards and parking attendants hustled everybody, all day, all night. It was a spot that never seemed to sleep. Someone shouted out to a passerby. He watched as two men tried to shake down a woman who'd parked her car in the wrong spot before being chased off by her friends.

He pulled the window shut, despite the heat, and turned to go back through the loft. His phone was still silent. He looked at it for a moment, then put it away. It was his own damn fault. He wouldn't blame her if she never replied. He looked around. The loft was vast, made even bigger by the almost total absence of furniture. Directly in front of the building, work had begun on the new Mandela Bridge, linking up the two business areas of Braamfontein and Newtown. The inner city was slowly coming back to life. Given time, Johannesburg would become the Manhattan of the south, the beating heart of the continent. He stopped himself. He was beginning to sound like the realtor who'd sold him the loft. He looked at his phone again. Nothing.

He walked over to the dining table where his briefcase and laptop stood waiting for him. He pulled out a sheaf of papers and sat down. *1997 Minerals Yearbook. Niobium (Columbium) and Tantalum (Advance Release)*. He read it through quickly at first, frowning as he concentrated. Dirk had tossed the file his way the night before with a breezy, 'Have a read through, tell me what you think.' What did he think of what? The report was part-technical, part-economics. Domestic data surveys, production figures, consumption . . . what did this have to do with anything? He read on, wondering what he was supposed to be looking for. About halfway through, a headline caught his eye. *World Minerals Review*. He frowned. It was a listing of all the world's niobium-containing carbonatite deposits: Australia, Brazil, Canada, Democratic Republic of Congo. He forced himself to concentrate. He dimly recognized some of the place names from geography lessons. Katanga, Kivu, Maniema and Orientale Province. The report mentioned coltan several times. Coltan? He frowned. Where had he heard of it before? What was it used for?

He pulled his phone out and dialled a London number. A man picked up on the other end. He asked a couple of questions, listened intently for a few minutes, then hung up, tapping the phone thoughtfully against his front teeth.

So, there it was. Dirk had singled him out for a *reason*. For the third time in as many months, he realized the man's cheery buffoonery was calculated, and calculating.

# 33

Julian pulled into the driveway and switched off the engine. He sat there for a few moments, his heart thumping. Upstairs Rosemary would be waiting for him, her face cleaned and scrubbed of make-up, her cheeks and neck smelling of one or other of those face creams she used. A terrible reluctance washed over him. He opened the car door and got out. His legs felt heavy and tired. He walked up the steps to the front door feeling more exhausted than he had done in months. He slid the key in the lock and opened the door. The house was quiet and fragrant with Rosemary's cooking. He closed it behind him as quietly as he could and stood for a few moments in the hallway. It was just after 9 p.m. These days, unless there was something specific to do – a dinner party or a work function – Rosemary went to bed early, thank God. He put down his bag on the rug, taking care not to make a noise, and walked into the living room. He looked around as though trying to see it for the first time, through someone else's eyes. It was a long, narrow room with high ceilings. Rosemary had chosen a deep, dark blue for the walls which contrasted beautifully with the snow-white ceiling and ornate covings. A single brass bowl lightshade hung over the heavy wooden coffee table, placed right in front of the fireplace. The floors were a light knotty pine, covered with plush sheepskin rugs in creamy white and chocolate brown. An L-shaped leather sofa ran the length of the back wall and at the far end, tall double sliding doors opened out onto a conservatory which they'd added the previous year. A giant plasma television disappeared into the blue of the wall; it had been a while since the two of them had sat together on the sofa, watching anything other than the news.

He eased off his shoes and walked over to the drinks cabinet in his socks. He poured himself a small brandy and took it to the sofa, sinking into it with a semi-audible sigh of gratitude. He took a sip, leaned back and closed his eyes. He couldn't stop seeing her face, all dark, smooth skin and those bright, almond-shaped eyes. He lifted a hand to his nose . . . he could smell her too, that faint, lemon-sweet fragrance that she wore. He knew Rosemary's perfumes – Dior, Chanel No. 5, and occasionally Opium – he'd been buying them as presents for years. He took another sip, and then another. How on earth was he meant to go upstairs, take off his clothes and slide into bed beside Rosemary, acting for all the world as if nothing had happened? The irony was, nothing *had* happened. *Nothing has happened. I've done nothing.* He'd come close to making a fool of himself, that was all, that was the extent of it.

He reached up a hand to his chin, feeling the rough bristle underneath his fingertips with a strange sense of relief. His face was exactly as it had been that morning, when shaving. He remembered looking at himself in the mirror, just out of the heat of the shower, the blood drawn freshly to the surface of his skin. Without his glasses, he'd looked at himself, seeing in his face a younger version of himself and, with some pleasure, took it to be his definitive self . . . but of course it wasn't. He was fifty-two years old, he reminded himself harshly, frowning at his image. What was he *doing*? One last, desperate kick of the prostate? He dropped his hand, shame breaking over him like a wave.

'Julian?' Rosemary's voice brought him back to himself. She was standing at the top of the stairs.

'Coming. Just got home.'

'What time is it?' she called out sleepily. 'I thought I heard the car but then you didn't come up.'

'I'll be right there. Go back to sleep. I'll be up in a minute.' He drained the last of his brandy – Dutch courage? – and walked slowly upstairs, somehow remembering to switch off the downstairs lights.

# 34

From the pressurized cabin, thirty thousand feet in the air, Kemi looked down upon the earth, hours and hours of empty landscape unfolding beneath them as they flew south. Every now and again, she pushed up the eyelid of the oval window, as if to remind herself where they were. Every so often a wave of turbulence jolted the aircraft and her view of the golden sands, soft ridge following soft ridge, was temporarily dislodged. Algeria, Niger, Chad, then the vast expanse of green-black that was Congo, great plumes of smoke from a thousand bushfires trailing listlessly below. Beside her, Jen slept, oblivious to the world. In her lap lay her books and magazines, mostly untouched since take-off. Her mind was in turmoil. She didn't know what to expect when they landed. Her parents were delighted with the news that she was coming 'home', as they put it. Never mind that it was only for three months. No doubt her mother had sensed an opportunity to mend a bridge, but in truth there was no bridge to mend. There had never been a rift. How could you fix something that wasn't broken? When she thought about her father, there was simply an absence, a void where there should have been the presence of something – love, loss, anger, even resentment . . . *anything*. There was nothing. Just a vague, faint memory of the solidity of a father's embrace, the scratchiness of a beard, the whispering sound of a voice. When it came back, all those years later, it had changed beyond recognition.

Nowadays, when she heard her father's voice on television or saw his words in print, it was the voice of a man addressing the masses, not her. That was how it had always been. That was how it would always be. She'd made her peace with it long ago. In the same way that she'd pushed all thoughts of her family well below the surface of her everyday consciousness until they'd all but disappeared, she had done the same with Solam. If she were being completely honest with herself, she would have to admit to the fact that all this was partly down to him. It had happened so unexpectedly. A single evening's conversation had turned her upside down. Never mind the obvious and undeniable attraction; much more importantly, she sensed, he'd stirred an all but forgotten longing in her to pick up the threads of a past she'd grown to think of as dead and buried. But it wasn't. Not by a long shot. And for that, she mused, she ought to thank him. Once the sting of rejection had passed, she would reach out again. It was the right thing to do. Some things went beyond love and sex and all the rest of it, including, perhaps most especially, heartache.

'Ladies and gentlemen, welcome to Johannesburg International Airport, where the local time is now nine thirty. Please remain seated until the seatbelt sign has been switched off. Please take care when opening the overhead lockers . . .'

The flight attendant's professionally neutral voice wafted over them. The furze of blond grass on the side of the runway bounded into view as the plane touched back down upon the earth once more. The view was distorted by the convex slope of the window, but it was real, exactly as it had stayed in her mind without ever thinking about it. Her heart began to beat faster as they edged towards the exit. The aircraft doors opened and voices from the outside were borne in on cold gusts of wind. It was March, the start of autumn in the southern hemisphere, and in spite of the blazing sun, the air was crisp.

She and Jen emerged alongside all the other passengers in that special daze that comes from sitting in the same position for twelve hours as the metal bird carries its load across time zones and whole continents. A cleaning woman, her bucket and mop appearing as an extension of her body, threaded her way absentmindedly between the passengers. Two young customs officials, their tight, high buttocks wiggling sexily as they walked purposefully towards the arrival hall, flicked a bored, professionally male glance over the two women, one tall and red-haired, the other short and dark. The immigration officer with long shiny red fingernails looked at her burgundy passport without comment. '*Sawubona, Sisi*,' she said, closing it with a snap.

'What did she say?' Jen whispered, as they both passed through.

Kemi smiled. '"Welcome". She must've thought I was South African.'

'Well, you are, aren't you?' Jen grinned back. Her eyes were sparkling. Their fellow passengers were all strangers again as they spilled out, no longer connected to each other but to the welcoming hands and faces. Kemi scanned the crowd, looking for the driver whom the guesthouse said they would send. Ah, there he was! *Dr Mashabane*. He was holding a handwritten sign. She gave a wave and the portly man came forward. His smile was wide and bright enough to power the whole terminal building.

'Good *morning*, ladies! My name's Derrick, yes, I'll be taking you to the Lucky Bean Guesthouse. Let me take your luggage, no . . . please don't worry, I've got it.' He grabbed both suitcases with ease. 'This way, ladies . . . this way, please. This way.'

They drove out of the airport parking lot and joined the late morning traffic heading towards the city. The sky was a dazzling, blinding shade of blue. Jen stared out of the window, open-mouthed. It was all so unfamiliar to her. To Kemi, it was the opposite. As strange as it seemed, it was as if she'd never left. Johannesburg wasn't Harare, but the quality of light and the smells and the sounds were the same. The past had come crashing into the present, turning things upside down. Perhaps that was why she enjoyed surgery so much – there was absolutely no room for confusion. She leaned her head back against the seats and closed her eyes.

# 35

It was nothing like she'd been expecting. Huge, bustling, modern . . . and so bright! After the damp smog of London, the fresh, sharp air of Johannesburg was invigorating and uplifting. They'd been booked into a charming guesthouse in Melville, a pretty, tree-lined suburb close to the university. Derrick unloaded their bags and pushed open a door set into a high, ivy-covered wall. She gasped as they walked in. The garden was lush and beautifully kept, with borders of the most vibrant flowers she'd ever seen, and a water feature that sent a tinkling sound reverberating all the way to the open front door. They'd been given two adjoining cottage suites tucked away at the back of the guesthouse, hidden from the main house by a willow tree that overlooked the pool. It couldn't have been prettier. Their rooms were large and spacious. A giant spray of Oriental white lilies stood on a wooden table in the centre of hers, filling it with their heavy perfume. There was an ensuite bathroom and a patio . . . it was gorgeous.

'Ohmigod, it's absolutely *perfect*!' Jen exclaimed, bouncing happily on the enormous bed. 'You never told me it was this . . . this beautiful!'

'It's not *all* like this,' Kemi said dryly, surveying her from the doorway. 'You'll see.' Brilliant sunshine streamed in through the French doors, bouncing off the glossy concrete floor.

'I don't care! It's just perfect.'

'Are you hungry? I'm *starving*. The owner said there's a restaurant just around the corner. The driver'll take us.'

'Why? Can't we walk? I feel as though I've been sitting down for a week!'

Kemi shrugged. 'He said it's too dangerous to walk.'

Jen frowned. 'Dangerous? It's the middle of the day!'

'Well, that's what he said. See the barbed wire?' She turned and pointed to the razor-wire fence surrounding the property. 'Apparently they get broken into all the time. There's a security guard outside,' she added hastily.

Jen looked around doubtfully. It was hard to think of anyone breaking into the little paradise in front of them. 'OK, well . . . I'll take a shower and meet you at the front,' she said, getting off the bed. 'I suppose we'd better do as he says. Father'll go mad if we get mugged on our first day.'

Kemi nodded. She put up a hand to free her curly hair from its clip, shaking it loose. 'Meet you in half an hour. I need to wash the plane air out of my hair.'

The Service Station Cafe at the bottom of the hill was equally delightful. They chose a table next to the window, overlooking a ragged line of hills and some of the most sumptuous homes Jen had ever seen. The sun was high in a splendid afternoon. They ordered a bottle of white wine and two enormous salads. She was aware of how active her brain had become since their arrival. Ideas and images interlocking and colliding . . . her love of colour, light, form and texture had suddenly come alive again, after having been buried for so long. She slipped her cardigan off her shoulders, enjoying the feel of warm sunlight streaming through the glass.

'You'll burn,' Kemi said, laughing at her. 'Even through the glass. It's not Edinburgh.'

Jen grinned, putting her hands up in mock despair. 'I know, I know. Red hair and freckles . . . not a good combination.'

'In the right climate, it is. You always looked so . . . so at *home* in Scotland. As if you shouldn't ever be anywhere else. It just suited you. I always used to think that.'

Jen looked at her in surprise. 'Really?'

Kemi nodded. 'I always felt so out of place. When we used to walk to school, I hated the way everyone looked at me. They all knew I didn't belong.'

'That's rubbish. They were staring at you because you're gorgeous. That's what I thought. I always felt so . . . so washed out next to you!' Jen protested. 'It's true! Next to you I just fade away.'

Kemi shook her head. She took a sip of wine and leaned back in her chair. 'I know what I know,' she said firmly. 'Anyhow, I suppose that's always the way. We always remember childhood differently. Everyone does.'

Jen nodded. 'D'you remember the Croswells? Sam and Stacy? Identical twins and yet you'd think they'd been born into different families. Sam's version of events was always the opposite of Stacy's.'

'And yet they're both true. That's what psychologists say.'

Jen looked at her. 'What d'you mean?'

'Well, just that if you asked two siblings to describe the same event, you'd get two completely different stories. But both are true. That's what family psychologists spend most of their time doing . . . making sure each side knows their story isn't necessarily the only one. You can both experience the same event completely differently. It's all about your interpretation of things, not really about what happened.'

Jen was quiet for a moment. She was aware of her breath

quickening and of a sudden look of concern on Kemi's face. She put up a hand to her own face. Her nose had started to bleed again. Something long buried was beginning to surface in her. She could feel it and was afraid.

# 36

Solam landed in Chingola, in southern Zambia, in a tiny four-man aircraft, just before seven. The airport – no more than a bungalow – was only just awakening. He was waved through customs without question and directed to a desk with a hand-painted sign – *Car Rentals* with the majuscule 'R' missing. He was served by a sulky-looking girl whose magenta-tipped hands stabbed out a vicious rhythm on the keyboard as she typed his name and details.

'*Sign. Here.*' She ripped the form from the printer and shoved it at him. He signed as requested. She was not to know the signature was not his own.

Ten minutes later, he was behind the wheel of a brand-new Land Cruiser, complete with mini bar and a satellite navigation gadget that sat awkwardly on the dashboard. It was a two-hour drive from the border to Lubumbashi, assuming the border was open. It was 7.30 a.m. on a low grey morning that he knew already would lift to a scorching hot day. The humidity was intense. He loosened his tie and threw it onto the back seat, freeing his collar. The car was air-conditioned but the heat still seemed to seep through the floor.

He drove out through the main street of the town, heading

for the T3 road that would take him north to the border with neighbouring Congo. All along the roadside, vendors of wooden animals were polishing them under flamboyant red flame trees, preparing their wares. He'd never been to Zambia before; the town quickly began to unravel as he drove north, one flowery roundabout after another, until the houses gave way to a dense collection of shacks, a shanty town of the kind that could be found all over Africa. Soon there was nothing in front of him except the smooth black tarmac, the trees, and occasionally a long-tailed bird that rose up from the long-haired grasses on either side of the road. He drove without stopping, passing one village after another, meeting every now and again one of those heavily laden lorries that made the journey between capitals, bursting at the seams with bags of produce or building supplies. Every now and then he passed a sack of wood or charcoal leaning against a makeshift table by the side of the road, waiting for a buyer. People lived deep inside the landscape as they might live in a house, he thought to himself. Individual shelters and mud huts were flimsy, make-shift objects – it was the landscape that protected them, not their structures.

As he drew closer to Kasumbalesa, the border crossing, he noticed that the villages grew larger. Smoke rose through the forest in small spirals and there were large patches of chopped-down trees, cleared to make way for subsistence farms everywhere he looked. The tarred road had been left behind and as he got out of the vehicle to stretch his legs, he saw that it was like all the cars he'd passed on the road – covered in red laterite dust, already looking battered and old. The undersides of the fenders were rimmed with red clay and the bonnet was a graveyard of dead insects. At the border post itself, he joined a short queue of cars and lorries, and was told by a customs official to wait while he called for his superior after handing over Solam's British passport. There was some confusion. A black man with a British passport? He produced his business card and a bank brochure with a twenty-dollar note deftly folded between the pages. *Ah . . . yes, yes . . . no problem.* Ten minutes later, he was waved through. It was probably equivalent to a week's wages, Solam thought to himself, as he pulled past the rusted sign saying, '*Bienvenue en République Démocratique du Congo*'. Aside from the mines to the south and east of the town and the border crossing, there was little else here by way of employment.

He put his foot down and made it to the merging of the Zambian T3 road with the Congolese N1 in just under half an hour. The village of Lumata passed by and soon, just before nine, he began to make out Lubumbashi, the country's second-largest city, emerging from the flat scrubland that surrounded the outer suburbs.

His hotel was on Boulevard Kamanyola in the centre of town, a bland, nondescript building that could have been anywhere in the world where businessmen meet to trade or make deals, legitimate or otherwise. He parked the car under one of the canopied shades and got out, stepping into the heat the way he might have stepped into a shower. It smothered him from head to toe. He picked up his bag, slung it across his shoulder and made his way to reception, sweat pooling in the waistband of his trousers and on his neck.

The manager was seated behind a desk at reception. He got up as Solam approached, snapping his fingers for a bellhop. A young kid appeared silently; within minutes, he'd been registered and was shown the way to his room. The air conditioner wheezed ineffectually in one corner of the room. He tipped the kid a dollar and was rewarded by a megawatt smile of gratitude which embarrassed him. A disproportionate return for a commonplace gesture. The door clicked shut behind the kid and he was alone. He peeled off his shirt and trousers, heading for the shower. His meeting wasn't until six that evening and the overnight flight, coupled with the heat, had worn him out.

The shower was tepid but exactly the right temperature for the tropics. Any cooler and he'd have begun sweating again. It was just past noon, the hottest time of the day. He opened the door to the small veranda. Heat and silence fell upon him. There were borders of orange flowers in the garden in front of him, and the air was thick with their scent. A pair of guinea fowl wandered across his line of vision, pecking at the ground with short stabbing movements, looking for grub. A vast, strange sense of unreality swept over him. He was so far from home, in every sense of the word. *This is how it starts*, he thought to himself grimly. *A favour here, a debt to be repaid there, and the opportunity to make more money in a single week than most people would make in a lifetime.* If he were honest, it was also the excitement that had attracted him. He'd watched his mother and father – and countless others like them – sacrifice everything they had, including him, their only child, only to be pushed around like flimsy pieces of paper, subject to another's will. Where had it come from, this sudden desire to do things differently? He couldn't tell, couldn't say. All he knew was that he wasn't about to be pushed around by anyone, least of all by a government in whom he couldn't quite bring himself to trust and a future he couldn't quite see. *Yes, this is how it starts.*

Solam shook hands with each of the men in turn. '*Merci, m'sieur, merci,*' he murmured, one by one. The tall, thin one, who went by the name of Gloire, was the only one to return his greeting.

'*Au revoir, M'sieur Rhoyi.*' He pronounced it the French way, swallowing the 'r'. 'I 'ope to see you in Johannesburg one of this day.'

He left the hotel lobby. He was sweating, in spite of the air conditioners blasting out icy air from every corner of the lounge. His shoes made a brisk clipping noise as he strode across the tiled floor. At the far end of the room, a pianist was hammering out a medley of Dionne Warwick songs and – absurdly – Christmas tunes. It was March! No one seemed to notice. Waiters in red fez caps scurried in and out of the groups of tables, balancing trays aloft, looking every bit as harried as waiters anywhere in the world, faced with a crowded room. And it was certainly crowded. The Grand Hôtel Lubumbashi was clearly the centre of all the city's activities. Behind him, like a piece of taut turquoise satin, the hotel's swimming pool shimmered through the gauzy curtains. Families sat by the poolside, parents talking to each other across the heads of their children or across tables, as nannies watched over their offspring. Fat businessmen sat almost immobile with very young girls who ate methodically and silently whilst their bene-factors spoke quietly into their mobile phones. A few white faces, just the usual smattering of local diplomats and busi-nessmen, the latter identifiable by the hungry, almost feral look on their faces. They were all hustlers. Lubumbashi was a city in which deals were made, in their hundreds, in their thou-sands. Every second of every day. From diamonds to guns to copper to coltan.

He ran lightly up the steps and crossed the upstairs lobby. From behind the long reception counter, he was being watched, he knew. He'd been in town less than twenty-four hours and he could practically smell the tension in the air. It was the scent of money. Money and greed. Two men passed him on his way out. Solam felt their mood of confidence, the tense composure of men who are always alert and ready for a deal gone south, a double-cross . . . even for death. He walked out into the thick-headed humidity and flagged down a cab. He had the sensation of stepping into a boxing ring or the gladiators' pit, only he didn't know who he was fighting, or why.

*Yes, this is how it starts.*

# 37

The last stretch of the new freeway linking Johannesburg to Pretoria had been completed since he'd last driven there. The shanty town that had once crept up close to its edges had been bulldozed to make way for a new park, freshly planted trees blowing unsteadily in the autumn breeze. He drove fast, concentrating on the road and not the afternoon ahead. Sunday lunch? His mother had been insistent. A few old friends of his father's had been invited . . . they never saw him any more . . . what else was he doing on a Sunday afternoon? He'd put the phone down and gone to take a shower, his mood already dark. There were countless other things he'd rather be doing on a Sunday. He'd turned away from his own reflection in the bathroom mirror. There was another reason he was reluctant to meet his parents. He'd never been able to hide anything from Iketleng, and the knowledge of what he'd been up to over the past couple of weeks was etched into his soul. She'd take one look at him and read it, practically every sordid detail.

He tried not to think about the afternoon ahead. The drive set him between hills of brilliant, verdant green. To his left, the brooding shape of the Afrikaner *Voortrekker* Monument, and, to his right, a signpost leading to a hotel. The city was come upon almost instantly, no transition from the dry hills to the steel-and-glass canyons that marked its downtown. He drove on past the graceful Parliament that was now his party's official home, past the line of huge palm trees and the prison, and out through the other side of the central business district, towards the elegant suburbs where his parents now lived. The house was an official residence, paid for by the state; no expense spared, he noted. It was his first time at their new Pretoria home. Now that Oliver was the Gauteng Premier and a member of the Executive Council, he could be reasonably assured that he and Iketleng would be taken care of for life. Still, no matter how luxurious it was, it was still small compensation for the long, lonely years spent languishing in jail, Solam thought to himself. The house was at the top of one of the long, winding roads that branched off into cul-de-sacs, each with a more spectacular view than the other. It was in the Cape Dutch style, two handsome bays on either side of an enormous, studded wooden door with beautiful, sweeping gardens falling away down the hill.

He parked the car on the side of the street and nodded to the two uniformed officers standing stiffly to attention as he approached. He had been recognized, he saw from their faces, but protocol was protocol . . . he handed over his driving licence and government ID badge and walked through the small metal detector before being allowed through the gate. There were four other cars in the driveway. A couple of sleek Mercedes, his mother's Audi and a small Kia, looking lost and incongruous amidst the bigger, flashier engines. He jogged lightly up the steps to the garden, wondering who else had been invited to lunch.

A uniformed maid took his jacket, showing him through the hallway to the patio at the rear of the house. The previous incumbent's artwork was still on the walls, he noticed, as he followed her. Someone – an interior designer, no doubt – had tried to give the place a more contemporary, African feel by adding splashes of bright colour and pattern, but the cushions and fabrics sat awkwardly alongside the oil paintings and watercolours that must have belonged to the previous owners. The inside of the house had been knocked out to make an enormous, comfortable living room, overlooking both the rear and front gardens on either side. The plush chairs were grouped together in easy intimacy and there were fresh flowers everywhere. A low glass table held the morning's papers and a cup of coffee, half drunk. He ducked under the eaves that led to the patio. He could hear voices from the garden. He wondered if he should have worn a tie, perhaps? He glanced down at his dark blue jeans and thick cable-knit sweater . . . too casual? He shrugged. Too late now.

He stepped off the patio and onto the thick, soft grass. There was a small knot of people standing by the pool. He walked towards them, preparing himself to greet and be greeted . . . and froze. He felt the smile drain from his face.

It took him a few minutes to recover from the shock he'd felt as soon as he realized it was Kemi standing beside the pool, her expression hidden behind a pair of oversized sunglasses. His mother came towards him with a playful smile on her face, unable to conceal her pleasure at finally having brought the two of them together. 'Look who's here!' she called out gaily, waving him over. He recognized Dr Mashabane, tall and regal, and the mother, her head wound up in one of those elaborate headscarves that the wives of Nigerian diplomats liked to wear, practically a self-standing sculpture in its own right. Kemi was standing next to a tall redhead whom he recognized as the girl he'd met in London . . . what was her name? Jane? Jen? 'Come and meet the daughter of our closest friends,' she urged.

He walked up to the group, aware of everyone's eyes on his face. Kemi's face was partly hidden by her mother's headdress but it was obvious she hadn't said anything about having met him already. He felt his heartbeat quicken. She was wearing one of those off-the-shoulder floaty dresses that brought film stars like Brigitte Bardot to mind . . . her hair cascaded around her head and shoulders like a dense, dark cloud.

'At last,' Florence Mashabane said, stepping forward. She embraced him warmly, kissing him on both cheeks. 'You were about this high when I last saw you,' she said delightedly, looking up at him. He was passed from mother to mother, father to father, embracing and being embraced in turn. The mood was ebullient and joyful, in stark contrast to the sense of foreboding that came over him as he looked down at Kemi, her eyes still hidden. She didn't offer her cheek but her hand instead.

'And this is Kemi's "sister", as we call her. Darling Jen. Daughter of *another* very close friend.' Florence smiled beatifically, nudging Jen forward. They shook hands. Her grasp was firm and cool. There was no sign in her face either that they'd met. He swallowed uncomfortably.

'So, let's go through,' his father said, shepherding the group towards the patio.

'We brought our housekeeper,' Iketleng was saying, as the women picked their way in heels across the lawn. 'Did I tell you about the one who was here when we arrived? Oh, she was terrible! I kept having to put salt in everything. No taste!' Their chatter washed over him. He followed them, still dazed. There was an enormous tangled grapevine hanging low over the patio roof, its leaves as pale and translucent as tracing paper. A couple of birds skimmed by, looking for fruit, but it was autumn and the grapes were small.

'Now, we'll put the young people at this end of the table,'

his mother said, taking charge as usual. 'If I let Oliver and Solam sit next to each other, no one will get a word in edge-wise!'

He darted a quick look at Kemi. She'd taken off her sun-glasses. Her expression was neutral. She took a seat next to Jen, put her elbows on the table and laced her hands together, making a bridge for her chin. She seemed utterly composed. He sat down opposite, wondering how on earth to break the ice.

# 38

She couldn't believe her eyes. She looked up and there he was, walking towards them, all 6'3 of him, dressed casually in jeans and a thick sweater, a pair of sunglasses tucked in the roll-neck, looking for all the world as if he'd stepped out of the pages of some glossy men's magazine. She had no idea what to say or where to look. It was clear he'd been intended as some sort of surprise. When she and Jen had been introduced to his parents, they'd embraced her warmly but said nothing about Solam having met her before, or about him coming to lunch. Clearly, their London encounter hadn't been important enough to report on.

She stole a look at Jen. Her eyes widened slightly, enough to convey her own surprise, and her anger too, Kemi noticed. There was a faint tightening of the skin around her eyes when she looked at him. It was a feature of hers since childhood. That, and a shiny nose when she was about to cry.

They were seated together at the end of the table, set slightly apart from the parents. Solam looked completely at ease. He made no attempt to speak to her alone. In fact, he seemed to pay Jen more attention. Food was brought to the table by a succession of uniformed maids, but she'd lost her appetite. She didn't want to appear rude or churlish – too much her father's daughter for that! – but neither did she have any intention of letting him in again, in a manner of speaking. Cool, calm, professional. That was the way to handle men like Solam. He was someone to be kept at arm's length; the longer the arm the better. She wouldn't give him the satisfaction of seeing how hurt she'd been, but neither would she play the coquettish game she'd seen so many of her girlfriends play. She despised it, just as she despised all forms of deceit.

'What brings you to South Africa?' he asked finally – a touch insolently, she thought.

She lifted her gaze. 'I've got a fellowship,' she said evenly. 'Just for a few months.' She made no reference to the fact that it had been the major topic of conversation between them, before.

'You should have told me you were coming,' he said, lifting his wine glass. 'I'd have organized a few things . . . I don't know . . . a tour, or dinner with friends . . . show you around a little.'

She shrugged. 'Jen's here,' she said simply, brushing off his lame offer. 'And besides, I'll be at work most of the time.' It was a snub, but a subtle one. Let him work it out.

He took it in his stride. She had to give him that. He wasn't one to sulk. 'Where are you working?' he asked curiously.

'Baragwanath.'

He raised an eyebrow. 'Well, you'll certainly be thrown in at the deep end. Good for you.'

So, she *had* rattled him a little, she saw with the tiniest thrill of satisfaction. She looked at Jen, who appeared to be studying her chicken hard enough to dissect it telepathically. What was the matter with her? She'd barely said anything. She turned her attention to her parents and the conversation unfolding on the other side of the table. Politics and prison. She listened with half an ear to her father and Oliver Rhoyi discussing prison rations and felt immediately ashamed. It was the same feeling she'd had as a child, afraid to complain about anything for fear of seeming selfish, or worse. Whatever her silly childish troubles were, they paled in comparison to what her parents were facing; she'd learned very early on to bottle her frustrations and hide her pain. She coped with whatever was thrown at her. End of story. It meant that when the very worst thing that *could* happen did, she knew better than anyone what to do: nothing. She did and said nothing. She had always done nothing.

She stopped, shocked by the path her thoughts had taken. She got up from the table, mumbling her excuses, and walked a little unsteadily down the hallway. The guest toilets were at the far end of the corridor. She yanked open the door, locked it, and walked over to the sink. The first wave of nausea rolled over her and she stumbled to the toilet, barely making it in time before her stomach heaved and her lunch came hurtling out.

# 39

Jen just couldn't help herself. She couldn't stop staring at him. He was the most beautiful man she'd ever seen. The two-minute encounter they'd had at the gallery in London that night did him no justice at all. She'd clearly been too harried to take him in properly. He was chatting half-heartedly to Kemi, who was doing her level best to ignore him, but Jen wasn't fooled. Kemi had long been the mistress of her own silences, leaving others to look for the gaps and opportunities in conversation that she declined to own.

She studied him covertly as they ate. His lips were clearly drawn, defined by a darkened, bevelled scroll at the edges, and his nose was beautifully curved, almost haughty-looking, the nostrils finely etched as though by some careful sculptor. His cheekbones were wide and high, and his jet-black eyes were hidden by the fold of his eyelids at the corners. It was an unusual face. It spoke of a mixture of races that she couldn't identify, like many others in this part of the world, she supposed, whose ancestry could only be guessed at in the complex vortex of history and circumstance. She understood now why Kemi had been so bowled over.

Afterwards, she couldn't have said what the conversation was about. The usual pleasantries, spoken within earshot and for the benefit of the parents, engrossed in their own conversations, but curious enough to throw a glance towards them every now and then, as if in confirmation of what they'd long desired. The younger generation . . . Kemi and Solam . . . *this* was what they'd fought for. She could feel their desire as if they'd spoken it aloud. It wasn't often that the differences between her and Kemi were drawn so starkly, but she felt it now. Kemi and Solam belonged to one side of an invisible but unshakeable barrier of history and she was on the other. She saw now what she'd been unable – or perhaps unwilling – to ever fully grasp. When Kemi first came to live with them, people often referred to 'her life out there', as if it were different in some fundamental way to the life she now had. In some ways, perhaps it was? But to Jen, in the ways that *counted* – friends, family, school, homework; all the unvarying routine of childhood – it couldn't have been all that different. How else to explain the ease with which Kemi slotted in? After the first term, it seemed as though she'd always been there. If there were adjustments or accommodations to be made, Kemi made them, without fuss or complaint. But now, for the first time ever, she was beginning to grasp just how wide the distance between them might be. Kemi's parents sat on the other side of the table but they were strangers to Kemi. There was none of the easy intimacy that characterized all parent-child relationships – even her own. No wonder she'd been so drawn to Solam. He came from the same world, the same place and time.

She looked down at her plate, feeling suddenly dejected. What was she doing here? A sudden irrational jealousy took hold of her. Was she jealous of Kemi or Solam? But before she could question herself, Kemi suddenly stood up, her hand to her mouth as though she were feeling unwell. She got up and hurried to the bathroom, leaving everyone looking awkwardly at one another. What had just happened?

'Oh, dear . . . is it something she ate?' Mrs Rhoyi said, looking concerned. 'I hope it wasn't my chicken?'

Jen hastened to reassure her. 'It's probably too spicy for her,' she said quickly. 'We're not used to it.' She realized her mistake as soon as the words were out. 'In Scotland, I mean,' she added quickly. 'The food's pretty, er, bland in our house.' She looked unhappily at her own plate. Her words had come out wrong. She'd implied Kemi was now Scottish, not South African. She'd implied a bond between herself and Kemi that didn't really exist. She'd implied she knew more about Kemi's tastes than her parents did. Things in South Africa were more complicated than she'd anticipated. She felt completely out of her depth. As usual.

# 40

Kemi rinsed her mouth several times over, wetted her hands and ran them through her hair to tame it. She'd been gone for nearly fifteen minutes . . . any longer and someone would come looking for her. She looked at her reflection in the mirror, anxiously seeking signs of the storm that had blown up inside her without warning. She traced the fine line of her eyebrows, moulding them back into shape. If you didn't look too closely, she seemed fine. A little tightness around the eyes, perhaps, but that was it. She blew out her cheeks, squared her shoulders and opened the door. It was time to re-join the others, assure everyone she was OK.

The corridor was quiet. She could hear the maids chattering in their language as they washed up in the kitchen, down the hall. She walked slowly back to the patio, her arms wrapped around her waist, hugging herself tightly. Something was hovering at the edge of her consciousness, a premonition or foreshadowing of some kind . . . it fluttered back and forth, like a capricious bird looking for somewhere to land. She tried to catch hold of the feeling – excitement or dread? But before she could examine it properly, it lifted again. She was left feeling rather breathless, as though sensing the lull before a thunderstorm. She looked up at the sky as she crossed the garden to join the others. Clear, azure, high-*veld* skies. Not a cloud in sight. It was not the season for storms.

# 41

By the end of her second week at Baragwanath, Kemi could scarcely remember what her working life at UCH had been like. It was exhilarating, terrifying, all-consuming. Here there was no early morning coffee with colleagues before beginning a day's shift. You walked straight into whatever emergency had found its way to the front door. Baragwanath – or Bara, as everyone called it – was the third-largest hospital in the world and she had never in her life seen anything as big or chaotic. Nothing worked as it should. There were chronic shortages of almost everything you could think of, from beds to essential equipment. On her second day, she'd found a patient eating his hospital meal with a tongue depressor. 'No cutlery,' one of the bad-tempered nurses informed her shortly. 'They steal everything.' Half the time, machines were either out of order or they hadn't been serviced, or someone had stolen the spare parts. If she hadn't seen the chaos with her own eyes, she wouldn't have believed it possible. And yet, for all that, there was a closeness and camaraderie between the staff that she'd never before experienced. Everyone – from the most junior medical student to the most senior consultant – pulled together, extracting miracles on a daily basis. The nurses, for all their gruff bad humour, were saints. No one was turned away, no matter how long the wait. She'd spent the first six hours of her first day wondering how *she* would survive, never mind the patients who arrived at death's door.

Now, two weeks in, she felt as though she'd been there all her life. It was nearly nine o'clock in the evening. She'd been on call for almost forty-eight hours and it was finally time to go home. She walked dazedly to the staffroom and was just changing her rubber-soled shoes when the door burst open.

'Stabbing's just come in! Third door down . . . can you assist? I've got another emergency.' A harried-looking junior doctor looked wildly around for someone – anyone.

'Sure,' Kemi gasped, the usual surge of adrenaline kicking in at the mention of an emergency. She ran down the corridor after him, looking for the third door. It was open. She walked in and clapped a hand to her mouth. A man was sitting on the wooden bench with a knife sticking out of his head, the blade buried deep in his skull. His hair and face were matted with congealing blood and the stench of alcohol was overpowering. He was completely still. There was no one else in the room. She gulped, and approached him. 'Sir?' She touched him as gently as she could on the arm. 'Sir?'

'Don't waste your time. He's gone,' someone said.

She turned round. It was a woman. She was wearing a smart black suit. Kemi couldn't tell if she was a doctor or a visitor, perhaps neither. 'Gone?' she repeated blankly.

'Dead.'

'Oh.'

'Who're you?'

'Kemi Mashabane. Mr Dissanayake's my supervisor.'

'Ah. I'd heard you'd arrived. Welcome.' The woman looked closely at her. 'Come with me,' she said abruptly. 'You look as though you could do with a coffee. Maybe something stronger.'

Kemi hurried after her as she marched down the corridor. She pushed through the exit doors at the end and walked down a flight of stairs, passing nurses and medical students running off in all directions. The canteen on the ground floor was almost empty. There were two other junior doctors slumped over their coffees. Judging from their blood-stained coats, they were coming off a long shift. The woman motioned for her to sit down. She fetched two cups of coffee from the vending machine and brought them over. 'I'm Dr Mkize, by the way. Ayanda Mkize. I'm one of the directors. How long have you been up?'

Kemi shook her head. She'd lost track. 'What time is it?'

'Dr Mashabane, I'm going to send you home. It takes time to get used to the pace here. Go home, get a good night's sleep. I'll see you back here on Monday morning.'

Kemi was too tired to argue. Dr Mkize was right. It wasn't just the hours she was putting in; it was the frenetic pace. Everything moved at twice the speed of anywhere else, including death. Since she'd arrived, three patients had died on the operating table, right there in front of her, often from such minor complications that it seemed absurd. An elderly woman waiting for hip surgery had developed a bed sore. It wasn't seen to and within a week, it had turned septic. She died of blood poisoning. Pointless. A young girl in the advanced stages of labour had come to ER. She'd been told to wait her turn in the long queue outside. She wound up giving birth in the toilets, haemorrhaged and bled to death. The other doctors shrugged. She would get used to it. There was a young Nigerian registrar named Ogundare. He smiled at her. 'Johnny-Just-Come. That's what we call people like you. You've been overseas for too long. Welcome home.' She'd smiled weakly.

'Thanks, Dr Mkize,' she heard herself saying. 'I'll be fine. It's just—'

'It takes some getting used to, as I said. Where did you train?'

'UCH.'

'Ah. I was at Bath. Yes, it takes a while. Do you have a car?'

She shook her head. 'No, the guesthouse where I'm staying has a driver. I'll just ring them.'

'I'll run you back, if you can wait for half an hour. Where are you staying?'

'Melville. But please don't go out of your way. It'll take him half an hour to get here and—'

'I'm not. It's on my way home. Just wait here. I'll be back shortly.'

She was too tired to argue. She could only nod in assent.

They drove out of Bara, turning right onto Chris Hani Highway. It was pitch dark; the street lights weren't working. The car was brand new and smelled of leather and perfume. Ayanda was in her forties, Kemi guessed, with a no-nonsense, brisk air that presumably kept her team in check, and in awe.

'So how long have you been back?' Ayanda asked, coming to a stop at the traffic lights. She looked left and right and quickly powered through. No one stopped at red lights, especially not at night, and especially not in the townships. Kemi didn't answer for a second. She turned her head briefly to look at the street. How was it that the neat, clean, grass-edged streets of places like Melville and Emmarentia could give way so seamlessly to the rutted and potholed roads of Orlando West, Diepkloof? She felt herself slipping back into something that was at once wholly familiar and yet strange. It had been years since she'd crossed the divide separating *this* world – the world of lean-to shacks, corrugated iron, enclosures made of sacking and loose bricks, and the open grassy *veld* in which whole cars had been left to rust and rot – from *that* world where she now lived, whether in London or here in the spacious guesthouse in Melville, a world of tended gardens, street signs, neighbourhood watch schemes and azure swimming pools. What did you call these broken streets with their rows and rows of institutional housing – two windows, a door in the middle, a parody of a child's drawing of 'house' – and the yards filled with the cast-off debris of white suburbia? Half the houses had no electricity, the other half no running water. What *was* this place? A town? A village? No man's land?

'Back?' she said slowly, turning to Ayanda. She smiled faintly. 'Everyone asks me that all the time. But the truth is, I never really spent much time here. I was born here, but I left when I was two, when my father was jailed, and I grew up in Salisbury. Well, Harare. I left when I was nine, so I've spent most of my life outside.'

'Does that matter?'

Kemi considered the question for a moment before answering. 'I suppose I've chosen *not* to remember. We actually lived somewhere near here. I don't remember where exactly.'

'Meadowlands. You were living on Nkosi Street when your father was arrested. I remember hearing about it from the grown-ups. I must have been about seventeen at the time. We heard the whole story. How your father tried to jump the fence at the back of the house but the police dogs got him. Apparently, he showed the officer how to stitch his own hand in the back of the police van. He was bleeding all over the place and they didn't know how to stop it. They wanted him alive, you see.'

Kemi looked at her in surprise. 'I didn't know that,' she said slowly.

'I suppose you were too young. For the longest time it was one of the photographs on the wall of my grandmother's house. You, going up the steps of the aircraft with your mother. Heroes of the struggle.'

Kemi shifted uncomfortably in the seat. 'I don't feel that way,' she said, wondering if she dared confide in Ayanda. 'I . . . I don't really feel anything. It feels as though it happened to someone else, not me.'

'Do you remember your father at all?'

Kemi looked down at her folded hands. 'No, not really. A few things . . . the sound of his voice, his accent. Mostly I remember everyone else's reaction, not his or mine. It's as if it didn't happen to me. It's as though it happened to someone I read about, not my own father. Isn't that strange?'

Ayanda shook her head. 'It's not uncommon,' she said, her voice suddenly gentle. 'It's to do with the way we process memory. You should know all this. Long-term memory is particularly sensitive to emotional trauma. That's why you sometimes find a blank in your own memory if there's been a particularly stressful or traumatic event.' She smiled. 'My first degree was in psychology. When I first came home, I was put on the Truth and Reconciliation Committee, listening to people's accounts of trauma under apartheid. We saw a lot of that sort of memory loss.'

Kemi's hands were shaking a little. She put one hand over the other to stop the trembling. 'I always thought memory loss was physical,' she said slowly. 'Like a blow to the head or something.'

Ayanda shook her head, smiling a little. 'That's the surgeon in you. You're trained to think primarily in terms of the physical. Find the problem, cut it out . . . that's how you measure a successful intervention. But the brain is so much more than its physical reality. That's what fascinates *me*.'

Kemi was silent. The urge to unburden herself came upon her crudely, like the urge to vomit. She turned her head away, concentrating fiercely on the low houses shut tight against the night, battened down hatches, a lone eye in a window pane that was a candle . . . the low, endless, rag-tag density of the township without a single tall building to puncture the horizon, until the strip of sodium lights announced the beginning of the highway, and the elegant finger of the Sentech Tower could be seen silhouetted against the sky.

The door to Jen's suite was shut by the time Kemi got back. She was probably fast asleep. She wondered what, if anything, Jen had done during the day. Florence had insisted on organizing a driver and a guide to take Jen around. 'It's the least I can do,' she said firmly. 'Her parents looked after you for half your life, this is nothing.' Kemi saw immediately that there was no point in arguing. The relationship between her and Florence would always remain distant, each careful to keep the other at arm's length for fear of what might be said out loud. For all her mother's self-assuredness and outward air of extreme confidence, Kemi somehow sensed that she too was at sea. Florence was not the type to admit to mistakes or to give voice to regrets. Under the circumstances, they'd done the best they could. And it had turned out well, thank God. Kemi was back now, with the coveted education and training her parents would have given her, had they been able. She had no idea what the financial arrangements had been, or if there had ever been a debt to be settled. Uncle Robert was wealthy enough and discreet enough to close down the possibility of even a discussion. It was simply never mentioned and Kemi learned not to ask. Now, however, the tables had been turned and it was Jen who was in need of support. Florence stepped in without a murmur, and it pleased Kemi to see her fussing over Jen the way she'd never fussed over Kemi. She'd never had the opportunity.

'What does she want to do?' Florence had asked, in one of

their rare telephone calls. 'Surely she can't just hang around whilst you're here?'

'I'm not sure,' Kemi said honestly. She hesitated. It wasn't her place to divulge Jen's ambitions, or lack thereof. 'Maybe she'll talk to you about it. Her own mother isn't much help.'

There was a moment's silence. 'I heard she's not well,' Florence said delicately. 'I didn't know.'

'She's been that way for a long time,' Kemi said carefully. 'But ask her. She admires you, I know.'

It was Florence's turn to remain silent. Yes, so much was left unsaid.

She unlocked the door to her room and shrugged off her coat, letting it fall to the ground. She felt her way to the bedside lamp and switched it on. She turned around to pick up her coat and stopped. An enormous bunch of red roses, still wrapped in paper and cellophane, sat on the small table next to the bathroom door. She walked over, her heart beginning to beat faster. She picked them up, inhaling their heady, rich scent deeply. A few drops of cold water still clung to the thick, velvety petals. There was a small card attached. She pulled the flap open and drew it out. *Please forgive me. Solam.* She stared at it. She put the flowers down carefully and walked over to her bag. She fished out her phone. It was not in her nature to be churlish or coy. She quickly tapped out a single word. *Forgiven.* She switched off the phone and headed for the shower. What now?

# 42

A stripe of sunlight filtered through the blinds and came to rest on Jen's face. She surfaced slowly, listening to the sounds of birds in the garden outside chattering excitedly, and to the faint bustle from the kitchens in the main house. She yawned, bringing tears to her eyes. Every morning was the same. She woke long after Kemi had left for work, ate a leisurely breakfast on the small patio outside their cottage, and spent the day mostly lounging by the pool, reading or daydreaming. To her surprise, Florence Mashabane seemed to think it was her responsibility to make sure Jen's days were filled. She had organized a driver, a string of local guides, contacts in the blossoming art scene – nothing was too much effort. At first, Jen was bemused and slightly embarrassed. 'I feel terrible,' she wailed to Kemi. 'Surely your mother's got better things to do than worry about *me*?'

'Oh, she loves it. She wouldn't be doing it otherwise, trust me. I actually had no idea she knew anything about art. She's thrilled she can talk to you about her favourite artists. You know me . . . I can't tell one end of a painting from the other.'

'If you're sure . . .?' Jen said dubiously.

'I'm sure. She's always complaining my father doesn't want to go to galleries with her. Go and enjoy yourself. Meet a few new people. *I'm* the one who feels terrible . . . I haven't had a spare moment since we got here.'

She glanced at the clock beside her bed. It was just after 9 a.m. Florence had organized lunch with the daughter of one of her friends – Kellyanne or something along those lines – who had just opened a new gallery in town. It was in Braamfontein, Florence said, a part of town that *no one* went to. Apparently. Jen couldn't work out why anyone would open a gallery in such an undesirable location, but there was no one to ask and Florence didn't seem the type to take kindly to questions. The driver was coming at ten thirty. Enough time for a quick swim and a shower.

Braamfontein didn't look *that* bad, Jen thought, as the driver slid into an empty parking bay. In fact, it reminded her of New York. The new development – 44 Stanley Avenue – was about the size of a city block, just off the main road. It looked as though it had been a sprawling factory at one point, with multiple entrances and little workshops, now boasting appropriately rusted signs in bold letters and yards of trailing wisteria and bougainvillea. It was charming. She got out of the car, intrigued. She walked through the main entrance, which opened onto a delightful little courtyard full of olive trees, small shops, and with a charming cafe at one end. Florence was wrong. The cafe was almost full. Far from being a place where no one went, it seemed to be the place where everyone went. She looked at Florence's message. *The gallery is to the left of Salvation Cafe as you come in the main entrance. You can't miss it. Ask for Kellyanne Simpson.* She walked past the cafe and the clusters of trendy, gorgeous people drinking coffee and nibbling distractedly at slices of cake . . . and there it was, just as Florence said. Room Gallery. The door was open. She walked in and caught her breath. It was like being back at Scheuler Lu. The familiar, heady scent of new paint and new wood . . . the stacks of paintings lined up neatly on the floor, waiting to be hung . . . the smell of coffee and cigarette smoke . . . the white walls and high ceilings. She felt immediately at home.

'Hi, can I help you?' A young woman came out from a door to one side. She was dressed in jeans with a beautiful paisley-print silk shirt, huge blue eyes, and one of those ultra-trendy micro fringes that Jen secretly longed to be brave enough to wear.

'Hi, are you Kellyanne? I'm Jen. I think Florence Mashabane called you earlier . . . she wanted us to meet?'

Kellyanne looked surprised. 'You're Jen?'

Jen nodded. 'Yes, that's me. Were you expecting someone else?' Kellyanne was frowning, as if something didn't add up.

'Oh, she said she was sending her daughter. I just assumed . . . *are* you her daughter?'

Jen smiled. 'No, not quite. I grew up with . . . well, it's a long story.' She looked around the gallery. 'This is *great*,' she said enthusiastically. 'Florence was a bit funny about the neighbourhood. She said *no one* ever comes here.'

Kellyanne laughed. 'That's what everyone *thinks*. It used to be completely derelict. It's an old factory, hasn't been active since the seventies, but it's coming back to life. It's an amazing place. We love it here. Welcome to the new South Africa!'

Jen walked over to the stack of paintings waiting to be hung. They were beautiful, vibrant paintings of Johannesburg's inner city, some obviously painted from a rooftop or a high vantage point. 'Who's the artist?' she asked, her eye caught by the strong, bold colours and confident, sweeping lines.

'Stanley Hermans. He lives just down the road. Some of these are of the train yard just across the road, and then there's his dinner party series. They're a sort of ironic take on *The Last Supper*, but with contemporary politicians as guests. It's a bit risqué, even for us. He's brilliant, though. We're super excited he's agreed to show here.'

'They're beautiful.'

Kellyanne nodded. 'The art scene has really taken off in the last couple of years. It's such an exciting time for us. We've been pariahs for so long . . . it's great to finally be back on the map. So, what brings you here? Florence said something about looking for work? Have you worked in a gallery before?'

Jen nodded. 'I worked for a small gallery in New York for a bit. And then in London, before we came out here.'

'You lucky thing. New York, London, Edinburgh . . . all these amazing places. I've never been out of South Africa.'

Jen looked surprised. 'Really? But you look . . . you sound . . . almost British?'

Kellyanne waved a hand. 'Oh, we all do. English-speaking whites, I mean. We all like to pretend we're from somewhere else . . . anywhere but here. You'll find out. Everyone's going to *love* you. You're the real deal, not like most of us. We're just pretending.'

'Pretending to be what?'

Kellyanne shrugged. 'We don't even know yet. That's the problem with this place. We don't know who we are . . . and we've no idea who we want to be.'

Jen was silent. She felt suddenly awkward. The undercurrents of tension that were always present in South Africa tugged at her constantly. An image suddenly swam into her mind's eye. It wasn't the slipstream of a jet, that powerful current of air produced by an object travelling through space and time . . . it was its opposite, the wake turbulence that an aeroplane generates at take-off: dangerous, unpredictable, disturbing.

# 43

'Do you have a reservation?' The head waiter looked Kemi up and down.

Before she could answer, a man's voice broke in. 'Yes, of course we've got a reservation.'

She spun round. It was Solam. She caught her breath. The waiter clearly recognized him, becoming his most unctuous self.

'Oh, good *evening*, sir. Sorry, if I'd known—'

'Known what?' Solam asked evenly. He leaned forward to kiss Kemi on both cheeks. A second waiter was hurriedly summoned to lead the way to their table. Solam stood back to let her go first. She was conscious of his gaze burning a trail down her spine. She'd ignored Jen's look of incredulity when she announced where she was going, instead asking her advice on what to wear. It had the temporary effect of stopping Jen's protests dead in their tracks, but she wished now she'd chosen something slightly less revealing. Jen had pulled out a long, clingy black jersey dress by a designer Kemi had never heard of. It had a mid-thigh split, which on Kemi's shorter frame actually mean upper thigh, but Jen was insistent. 'No, you're *not* wearing jeans! Let him see what an idiot he's been!'

'You can practically see my underwear!' Kemi protested, looking at herself anxiously in the mirror.

'Rubbish. Besides, if you *had* any decent underwear to begin with, you wouldn't be worried. Now, turn around. I want to put your hair up.'


'Is this fine, sir?' The waiter hovered anxiously, fussing over the placement of the table relative to the other diners, the patio, the light, the breeze.

'We're fine,' Solam assured him, looking at Kemi for confirmation. 'Now, bring me the wine list and leave me alone to enjoy my date.'

'Sir?'

'Just the wine list, please,' Solam laughed. He turned to Kemi. 'Not too cold? Not too hot? Not too tired?' He grinned, mimicking the departing waiter.

Kemi smiled and shook her head. 'I'm fine, and this isn't a date,' she said sternly.

He put up his hands. 'Mea culpa. I've a feeling I'll be saying that a lot from now on.'

'So, what happened?' Kemi looked at him straight in the face. There was little sense in pretending. 'Why did you just disappear?'

He sighed. 'I . . . I don't know,' he said slowly. 'I got back and then work just started piling up and—' He stopped suddenly. The waiter had appeared with the wine list. 'Red or white?' Solam asked her.

'You choose.'

'We'll have that one.' He pointed out a bottle, dispatching the waiter quickly, and then turned back to her. 'Look, I'm not going to pretend. I was pretty shaken by you. I mean it. You're not like anyone I've ever met. It was partly my parents putting pressure on me, yes, I'll admit it, but I . . . you scared me.'

'*Me?*' Kemi retorted incredulously. She couldn't believe

what she was hearing. 'How on earth did I scare you? We went to dinner, we talked, I went home. End of story!'

He shook his head. 'That's just it. It's *not* the end of the story. The opposite, in fact. It's the beginning. And that's what I suddenly got scared of.'

Kemi was silent. She had the sudden urge to kiss him. No man had ever been that open and honest with her, especially not after a single date. She drew in a deep breath, trying to steady her racing pulse. 'We talked, that's all. And a single kiss.'

He jerked forward suddenly, placing a hand on her forearm. He exerted a gentle pressure, pulling her towards him. She leaned in, her eyes never leaving his face. The kiss was slow and soft and strong, all at once. 'There,' he said, releasing her suddenly. 'That's my first mistake corrected.'

'Solam—' she began, aware of the blood rushing through her throbbing veins.

'Kemi,' he interrupted her, and it was as though she'd known his voice forever.

# 44

She wasn't one of those women whose sparkle becomes diminished with alcohol. He'd known many of those. In her, it had
the opposite effect. She only burned brighter, the blood rising
to her cheeks, giving her a dusky glow beneath the smooth,
dark skin. Her eyes were liquid pools of aubergine-tinted darkness. She had a way of listening with her head tilted slightly to
one side, her forefinger pushed gently into the soft pad of her
cheek with her chin resting lightly on her hand . . . it made him
want to reach out and stroke that cheek, an odd gesture of
endearment coming from *him*.

'What's it like?' he asked, more to cover his confusion than
anything else. 'The hospital, I mean.'

She laced her fingers together. 'Different. It's *much* more
chaotic. Everything's in short supply. Drugs, equipment, nurses
. . . you name it. Yet somehow we manage, don't ask me how.'

'When did you decide to do it?'

She looked at him quickly, catching him out. 'I'd been
meaning to for a long time,' she said, smiling slightly. 'Long
before I met you. But after we spoke . . . I don't know, it
seemed like the thing to do. I didn't want to be one of those
people who say "I'm going home" forever and never go.'

'And is it home?'

She pulled a face. 'It's too early to tell. Yes, there are some things you never forget. The sounds . . . language, the way people walk and stop and talk . . . that sort of thing. But could I live here forever? I don't know.' She fiddled with the stem of her wine glass. 'What about you? What made *you* decide to come back?'

She was testing him, he realized. She was no pushover. He'd never before considered whether he liked it in a woman. He'd simply never met one like her. He smiled. 'You asked me that last time.'

'I know.'

'Same answer. Nothing's changed.'

'But you've changed jobs. I overheard your mother telling mine. You're with International Relations . . . something like that.'

He laughed uneasily. He had the feeling she could see right into him. 'Yeah, something like that.'

'What does it entail?'

He shot her a quick glance. His heart missed a beat. What if she'd guessed what he'd been up to in the past few weeks? But she was looking at him with what seemed to be genuine interest. He felt again the conflicting tug of emotion. There was something about her that made him feel he could unburden himself of everything – yet he could not. There was no way to explain to her the confusion in his own head. She would see through that, too. 'Nothing much, to be honest. I go where I'm told.' He remembered his mother's phrase. 'It's six months here, a year or two there . . . they try you out in different posts.'

'And where d'you want to end up?' she asked, smiling at him. It was as if no one had ever asked him the question. He felt a quickening of his pulse, the thrilling, insistent pull of his own ambition.

'At the top,' he said slowly. 'Where else is there?'

# 45

Jen stirred her coffee and tried not to take another bite of red velvet cake. It was ironic that the gallery was located next to a cafe named Salvation. With its gorgeous cakes and desserts, it was her downfall, not salvation. Opposite her, in the way of all thin girls, Kellyanne polished off a brownie with ice cream *and* whipped cream.

'I love it here,' Jen said after a moment. 'Everyone's been so friendly and welcoming . . . I don't know why Kemi didn't come home sooner, to be honest. It's an amazing place.'

'You've only been here a few weeks!' Kellyanne laughed. 'And you've probably only seen the nice bits.'

Jen shook her head. 'No, I've been to Soweto and one other place . . . I can't remember the name. We drove through it. It looked a bit like Beirut. Not that I've ever been to Beirut,' she added quickly.

'Probably Hillbrow,' Kellyanne nodded. 'It's hard to imagine what it was like before.'

'Before?'

'Well, before everyone left. It used to be just like London or New York.'

'It looked pretty full to me,' she said, wondering what Kelly-anne meant. 'The streets were packed.'

'Oh, I meant whites. Yes, of course it's full of Africans. But that's different.'

Jen stared at her. 'How?'

Kellyanne shrugged. 'Well, *I* wouldn't live there, would you?'

'Don't you have any . . . er, *African* friends?' Jen asked, as delicately as she could.

Kellyanne looked genuinely surprised. 'No, of course not. We don't really mix, you see. And there's our . . . history.'

Jen was quiet for a moment. 'It's hard for someone like me to understand,' she said slowly. 'Kemi's my closest friend, closer than a sister.'

'Oh, but that's different,' Kellyanne said hurriedly, clearly worried that Jen had misunderstood her.

'How?'

'Well, she grew up overseas. She's just different. She doesn't come with baggage.'

Jen didn't know how to respond. Was that how Kellyanne saw it? Baggage? 'What about you?' she asked. 'Don't *you* come with baggage?'

'Oh, God yes . . . that's the problem, you see. We've *all* got so much baggage. I don't think we'll ever be free of the past. Not people like us. Most of my friends left after '94. They were terrified.'

'Of what?'

'Revenge. They all thought a war was coming. They've all gone to Australia or Britain.' She hesitated and looked at Jen almost shyly. 'Is it really better over there?'

Jen shook her head. 'It's funny. Everyone thinks somewhere else is better. But it's not. Things are pretty much the same everywhere. Everywhere has problems.'

'But not like ours, surely?'

Jen shrugged. 'I don't know . . . I've only been here a couple of weeks but there's a kind of energy here that's different. It feels as though you're all trying to *build* something. Back home . . . well, all we do is plaster over the cracks and pretend everything's fine. There's something honest about this place. You can't plaster over anything. It's all here . . . it's all in your face.'

Kellyanne nodded slowly. 'Yeah, I suppose you're right. I'd love to go overseas. That's the thing about us whites. We're not really from here, but we're not from anywhere else, either. Our parents and grandparents and great-grandparents came from Europe, but most of us have never been there. People say, "oh, you Europeans," but most of us have never set foot in Europe. But we're not African, either. We're stuck in the middle. We can't go back, but we don't know how to go forward. Especially now.'

'Well, not talking to each other can't help,' Jen said carefully. 'I mean, I can't help noticing . . . just look around. There aren't *any* black customers. The only black people here are the waiters.'

'That's why I love the gallery. I just love working with young artists. They're all trying to figure it out . . . just like we are. They're not afraid to say what they think, what they feel . . . I . . . I envy them, you know. They know how to be . . . free.'

Jen didn't know what to say. She'd learned more about the complex history of South Africa in a fortnight than she had in the past ten years. 'To be free takes guts,' she said slowly. 'Kemi taught me that. She's got guts in spades. Me, I'm too scared to take risks.'

'But you came here,' Kellyanne pointed out.

Jen shrugged. 'Only for three months.'

Kellyanne smiled. 'You know, that's what everyone says when they arrive. "I'm only here for a holiday," or "I'm only here for a couple of months." You wait, it'll get under your skin. You won't ever leave.'

Jen shook her head firmly. 'Not me. I'm just here keeping Kemi company. As soon as she's ready to go home, I'm gone.'

'Florence said you might be looking for a part-time job, though?'

Jen's eyes widened. 'How? I don't have a work permit or anything.'

'Oh, don't worry about that. I'd pay you cash under the table. I've been looking for someone to help me out, two or three days a week if you can spare the time?'

'Of course I can,' Jen said, smiling widely. 'When?'

'How about starting next Monday?'

'Deal.'

# 46

The plane banked sharply to the right, dipping just below the thin cloud cover. The whole majestic coastline suddenly came into view. Kemi put a hand to her mouth. It was stunningly beautiful. The jagged lavender-blue mountains rose almost directly out of the peacock sea, white-crested waves rolling lazily towards the shore. The pilot righted them, and the mountains gracefully sank away. The seatbelt signs came on and she fastened hers, fingers trembling with happy anticipation. It was a public holiday and she was on her way to meet Solam. It was her first proper holiday in years. The night before she'd been too excited to sleep. She and Jen had sat up half the night, talking. She'd never seen Jen so happy. Her part-time job seemed to suit her down to the ground. She was making friends – there was always some barbecue to go to, someone's house-warming to attend, or a gallery opening someone had heard about. They'd been in South Africa for a month and already it felt like home to both of them, to their immense surprise.

After landing, she collected her small overnight bag and made her way to the car rental desk. Solam had booked a room at one of the new boutique hotels that were beginning to spring up in the city centre. The Grand Daddy. She'd laughed out loud when he told her the name. It was on Long Street, he'd said, right in the heart of things. They would spend a night there, then drive down the coast to a small town called Betty's Bay. It sounded almost too perfect to be true. Three nights, four days ... and then it was back to work. She couldn't remember the last time she'd been so excited.

Twenty minutes later, she was on her way into the city. She took the N1 freeway towards the centre, struck by the sheer beauty of the mountains. No one had told her Cape Town was so beautiful. As she joined the morning traffic trickling slowly into town, her attention was momentarily distracted by a vast collection of scrap metal, corrugated tin and tattered plastic sheeting that lined the freeway – a shanty town, she realized, right up against some of the wealthiest real estate in the country. Then the freeway curved towards the left and the steel-and-glass silhouette of downtown and the harbour replaced it. She tried to concentrate on the road, careful not to miss the turn-off towards the city. The desperation of the shanty town was made all the more tragic by the stunning beauty of the landscape all around.

She found the hotel easily enough and handed over the keys to the valet. It was an old Victorian building with a beautiful, plush lobby, all dark wood panelling and thick Persian carpets. Solam knew a thing or two about luxury, she thought to herself as she waited to check in. It was just before noon. He would be at a meeting at Parliament until 3 p.m., he'd told her. Just enough time for her to settle in, take a shower, and spend a delightful hour or so in anticipation of his arrival.

He was late. She waited in the suite until just after half past three, but the anticipation was unbearable. She picked up her bag and headed down to the bar. A quick drink would take the edge off her nerves.

The stiff gin stole about her body, finding its way through her like a torchlight in the darkness. She looked around her. It was nearly four o'clock in the afternoon and the hotel bar was practically empty. From the street outside came the sounds of traffic, car horns hooting every once in a while, snatches of conversation, the odd shout from one side of the road to the other. It was peaceful inside. The barman methodically polished the glasses one after the other, hanging them carefully on the rack above his head. Her mobile rang suddenly. She glanced at it. It was Solam. Her heart missed a beat as she picked it up.

'I'm running late. I'll be there in half an hour. What're you doing?'

'I'm in the bar,' she said guiltily.

'Good for you. Make mine a whisky sour. I'll see you soon.' He hung up before she could say anything else.

# 47

The drive down to Betty's Bay took them through meandering cliff passes, down a sheer drop to the cobalt sea, then back up again through pine forests that brought Switzerland to mind. Every now and then Kemi stole a look at Solam's profile, the beautifully curved nose and square, determined chin, the gentle swell of his Adam's apple and the faint darkness that was his mid-morning stubble. He drove fast, concentrating on the road, his eyes flickering to the rear-view mirror, occasionally catching hers. They were both quiet, enjoying the sensation of being together without the distractions of work or family. It was a month since their first date in Johannesburg, almost four months since they'd first met. They hadn't yet slept together – out of an old-fashioned sense of courtesy, he hadn't pushed her for more than she was prepared to give. She was ready now, and the touch of his hand on her thigh as he changed gear or slowed down was enough to let her know that he was, too.

The guesthouse was everything a guesthouse in the country-side should be. Charming, beautifully furnished, tucked away into the hillside with sweeping views over the ocean. He parked in the empty car park at the front of the house and took their bags up to the front door. It was an old farmhouse with a beautifully landscaped garden and a modern wing overlooking the pool. The craggy mountain rose dramatically behind it, all dark greens and greys, with a thundery-looking sky.

'It's beautiful,' Kemi breathed, looking up. The wind rushed down the mountain pass, skimming over the surface of the sea, sending frothy waves hurtling towards the shore.

'Come on,' Solam nudged her. 'Water's usually cold here, no matter what time of year it is.'

The owner was on hand to meet them; a tall, elegant blonde, just divorced. 'I got the house; he got his secretary. I think I had the better deal,' she said, laughing, as she showed them to their room.

She was right, Solam remarked as soon as she'd closed the door behind her. It was a spectacular house. He put the bags down beside the enormous antique bed and for a second, they stood looking at one another. A wave of shyness flowed over her.

'Come here,' Solam said, sinking into the bed and patting the space beside him. She dutifully walked over to the bed. He took hold of her arm and pulled her towards him impatiently. He gave her no time for surprise or shyness. His warm, soft mouth covered hers, and any instinct in her to resist simply melted away. She became aware of an extraordinary sensation of longing, rising from her breasts through her neck into her mouth. When he drew back to draw breath, her mouth followed his, nuzzling at him like a child for milk. He laughed deep in his chest, and the sound reverberated through her body, her nerve endings alive with pleasure.

He was an experienced lover, bold but not aggressive, taking what he wanted from her in a frank, uncomplicated way but sensitive to her needs and mood. She felt herself released in some way, very different from the lovers she'd had before, with whom there was always the need to hold something back, some essential part of herself that she kept hidden, protected, preserved. There was none of that with Solam. When he came at last, his groan of release exploding close to her ear, she thought she might actually cry. It was what she'd been waiting for without knowing it. *He* was what she'd been waiting for, all along.

'Are you OK?' His voice broke the tender silence in which they were both held.

She nodded, not quite trusting herself to speak. They were both still half clothed, sweaters and jackets strewn across the bedcovers. He pulled the thick eiderdown over them both, folding her into his embrace. 'Yes,' she whispered, sinking into his warm, faintly scented body. 'Yes.'

'You're quite something, Dr Mashabane,' he said softly, tracing a line down the small of her back. 'Quite something.'

She didn't know how to respond, offering something else instead . . . the willingness and assurance of her kiss.

# PART SIX
# 1998

## Two months later

. . .

Love is the master key that opens the gates of
happiness, of hatred, of jealousy, and most
easily of all, the gate of fear.

OLIVER WENDELL HOLMES, SR

PART SIX

1998

Two months later

# 48

He came out of Parliament and ran down the steps, two at a time. He'd nearly reached the bottom when someone called out his name. He stopped and turned round impatiently. It was a young woman, dark-skinned, long braids . . . he frowned. Where had he seen her before? She hurried down to meet him.

'Sorry, sir,' she apologized, reaching him. 'I've been asked to give you something.' She held out a white envelope. He looked at it suspiciously. In the upper right-hand corner were the words 'Hélène van Roux' in a scrawl. He frowned. Hélène van Roux was the no-nonsense, straight-talking leader of the ANC's opposition, the Democratic Party. She was in her late fifties, the daughter of an Afrikaans minister who'd gone into politics very young as the wife of a city councillor, who'd later been killed. She struck Solam as a South African Margaret Thatcher, a combination of schoolteacher and autocrat.

'Thanks,' he muttered, taking the envelope from her. He turned and rushed to his car, tearing the envelope open. It was a handwritten note on her personal notepaper.

*Dear Solam (if I may)*
  *Forgive the presumption, but I've followed your*

*career since your return with keen interest. I would
like to discuss something which may be of mutual
benefit. If you are willing, I'd like to propose a meeting. I will be at my country home in Wemmershoek
until Sunday. Please let me know if I may expect you. I
would prefer to meet there.*

*Sincerely,*

*Hélène*

There was a telephone number listed and an address. He got into his car, still frowning. What on earth could she possibly want with him? The Democratic Party, whilst certainly the largest opposition party, had grown out of the now-defunct National Party, the government responsible for apartheid. Through a complex series of mergers and splits, it had finally broken away from the old National Party and reformed under a new name, hoping to erase the past. But in South Africa, Solam knew, history was hard to erase. No matter how hard they tried, the Democratic Party had about as much hope of winning a national election as the Green Party. Not a hope in hell, in other words. Still, he was intrigued. Wemmershoek? It was about an hour outside Cape Town. He was due to leave the following morning for Johannesburg, but he could slip away for a couple of hours. He hesitated before starting the engine; he needed time to think. There was a reason she'd asked to meet him away from Parliament, behind the scenes. He just didn't know what it was.

# 49

'Won't you have a cup of tea? And some cake? It's an old family recipe. I don't bake myself – no time, sadly – but Dora does it beautifully.' She beamed at him as if she were one of his aunts, offering a treat. He took both a slice and a cup from her, wondering what she was up to. Why had she invited him? They sat in the living room, tastefully furnished with antiques, comfortable chairs, rugs, and the kind of artwork that brought his teenage friendship with Charlie de Cadanet to mind. He looked at her closely, trying to work it out, but she revealed little. It was as if he was the one who had come to ask something of *her*, not the other way around. He felt the skin at the nape of his neck prickle, as though someone had run a hand down his back. She popped a piece of cake in her mouth with a monkey-ish, almost naughty gesture. She was a handsome woman, with a short, feathered cap of silver-grey hair and piercing blue eyes. Like many middle-aged women, that long, lovely stretch between breasts and stomach had shortened, but her legs were still slender, encased in black trousers and smart high-heeled shoes. A capable-looking woman able to withstand the rough-and-tumble sucking mud of politics, she'd weathered more political storms than most.

At last, she turned to him. She cleared her throat and began to speak. He listened intently, not interrupting, until she was finished.

'What sort of time frame are we looking at?' he asked carefully, standing up. He needed to stretch his legs.

She smiled. He saw that by saying 'we', he'd inadvertently communicated his assent. It was a small slip on his part, but she didn't react. 'A few years. Maybe five at the most, until we're confident enough of a win at the polls. That's the long play. So, there's time. Not *too* much, but enough.'

He walked over to the window. He was thirty-two years old. In five years' time, he would be right where he needed to be. 'And what guarantee do I have that you'll keep your word?'

'What guarantee do *I* have that you'll keep yours?'

'Touché.'

'So, we'll have to trust one another. And wait and see. But you know this makes sense. On your own, you'll wait decades, maybe more. Maybe never. The inner circle is growing each year. What makes you think you'll ever be let in?'

Solam said nothing. He tapped his forefinger against his mouth gently, reflectively. He knew what it was she'd seen in him that caused her to risk an approach. It was exactly what Dirk Coetzee had seen in him. Someone who was willing to risk it all to move ahead.

'There's one more thing,' she said, leaning forward slightly. 'And before you tell me to mind my own business, I think you should hear me out. It's about your girlfriend. I hear she might even one day become your wife. Before you make *any* kind of move in that direction, here's what I've been thinking about.'

Solam turned around, surprised. She motioned for him to sit down, and over the next few minutes, told him exactly what she thought he should do.

# 50

It was the middle of June. Jen woke with her teeth chattering every morning. The houses simply weren't designed to cope with cold. No heating, no insulation, no double windows. 'It's only another month or so,' everyone cried. 'There's no point!' It would have to be the three months that she and Kemi were visiting, she thought to herself crossly every morning when she got dressed. But, in a couple of weeks, they'd be gone. She was dreading their return. In the three short months they'd been in Johannesburg, she'd almost come to think of it as home. She couldn't imagine going back to work as a temporary secretary in an office somewhere in the City, waking up at six o'clock and standing cheek by jowl, hanging on to a strap as the Tube clanked and jerked its way towards Liverpool Street with millions of other miserable commuters. No more sunlight, no more weekends filled with pool parties and barbecues – *braais*, she corrected herself – no more gallery and the thrill of putting an exhibition together. And Kemi . . . she'd never seen her so happy, so fulfilled. She rarely saw her and Solam together. Both worked long, unsociable hours and any spare time they had, they seemed to prefer spending it away from Johannesburg. Kemi had been to places Jen hadn't even heard of – Franschhoek, Betty's Bay, Durban, Pietermaritzburg. Solam seemed determined to show her the whole country. Aside from the odd

LESLEY LOKKO

evening after work when she and Kemi bumped into one another on their way in or out of the guesthouse, she'd hardly seen her for weeks. She didn't begrudge them their happiness . . . far from it. Kemi's joy was infectious. She seemed almost a different person to the reserved character she'd known for half their lives. Solam had managed to bring out something in her – a lightness, a sunniness – that Jen saw now might actually have been her true character all along. He'd done the impossible: he'd brought her back to herself, brought her home.

She began tidying the gallery, picking up the few paper napkins and paper cups that had been discarded at the opening that evening of their latest show. It was another thing she loved about Johannesburg. The art 'scene', if you could call it that, was so different from the staid complacency of London. Their latest offering was more installation than art. Two young black women had set themselves up as though they were in a salon, inviting passers-by to assist with the de-braiding of their hair. Like Rapunzel, the two beauties sat immobile in the window as people queued up, either to take part or to watch the spectacle unfolding. Jen wasn't always sure she understood the concepts behind the avant-garde work, but Christ, it was a lot more interesting than trying to sell a stripe of blue paint on a black canvas.

She smiled faintly at the memory of her last London show. How embarrassed and terrified she'd been! One of those artworks would have sold for enough to cover the cost of her current gallery, all its holdings and their salaries for a year. But she wouldn't have traded in one for the other, not at any price. No, she didn't want to go back to London, that was the truth. And yet she *had* to. This was Kemi's country, not hers. As painful as it was to admit to, their time in Johannesburg had brought home a truth that they'd both avoided. They *were* different. Jen was enjoying her time in someone else's country, whilst Kemi had found a way to return home.

She put the cups in the bin, hauled out the trash bag and switched off the lights. There was a municipal dump just around the corner. She would deposit the bag and then call Derrick, the driver who'd somehow become her personal chauffeur, and head back to the guesthouse. She locked the door carefully behind her – it wasn't a mistake she'd ever make again – and turned to walk up the street.

At the corner she almost collided with someone in the dark. 'Oh, I'm sorry,' she apologized quickly. 'My fault.'

'Jen?'

She looked up in surprise. It was Solam. 'Hi,' she said, taken aback. 'What are you doing here?'

He looked down at her and smiled. 'Me? I live here. What are *you* doing here?'

'You live here?'

'Yeah, right up there.' He pointed to the building on the corner. 'Didn't Kemi tell you?'

She shook her head. 'No. But I thought you were in Zambia or Zimbabwe or something like that.'

He laughed. 'Ah, so you *do* talk about me.'

Jen blushed. 'No, I didn't mean it like that . . . I just meant . . . oh, never mind.'

'But what *are* you doing here?' he repeated.

'I work here.'

'Where?' It was his turn to look surprised.

'In that gallery.' She pointed to the brightly painted yellow door. 'That one. The art gallery. Didn't Kemi tell you?'

He shook his head and smiled, his perfect white teeth gleaming in the dark. It was six thirty but the street lights hadn't worked for months. 'Well, I suppose that makes two of us she doesn't tell anything to,' he added, still laughing. 'So, are you on your way home?'

She nodded. She indicated the bin bag. 'Just going to drop this off and call my ride.'

'You must be the only white person in Braamfontein who disposes of her own trash,' he said dryly. 'I bet the domestic workers around here have never seen the like.'

She blushed again. 'Well, I do it in London . . . why wouldn't I do it here?'

'Quite right.' He looked at his watch. 'So, are you in a hurry?' he asked.

Jen hesitated. 'Well, no, not really . . . but I don't know when—'

'She's in ER tonight,' he interrupted, reading her thoughts. 'She probably won't be back until much later. If you're free, would you like to go for a drink? I know you're probably leaving soon and we've never had the chance to meet properly.'

Jen hesitated again. He was only being polite, she was sure, but she hated to think he felt obliged to entertain her. 'Are you sure?' she asked. 'I'm quite happy to call the driver and just go back . . . you don't have to.'

'I know *that*. But if you'd like to have a drink, I'd be delighted if you'd join me,' he said with a mock bow.

Jen had to laugh. 'OK, well . . . in that case, since you asked so nicely.'

'There you go. Come on then. The Metro Bar it is.' He pointed to the bar across the road.

'I've always been too terrified to come in here,' Jen said as they walked in. 'I only ever see it on the weekends and it's absolutely packed with students.'

'That's the weekends. During the week it's perfectly respectable. You can even get a decent bottle of wine.' He led the way to the raised dais at the rear of the bar. 'It's quieter up here.

Students are mostly at the door or on the street. I don't know how they stay warm.'

Jen smiled as she sat down. 'It seems like decades ago when we were students,' she murmured.

'Only a decade,' he said with a grin. 'Not decades. So, what'll you have? Red or white? Or something stronger, maybe?'

Jen drew in her lower lip, catching it with her teeth, caught in the moment of indecision. Why not? It was only six thirty. A couple of drinks . . . she'd be home by nine. From the sound of it, he and Kemi would probably meet up when her shift was over, whenever that was. 'All right,' she heard herself say. 'I'll have a whisky sour.'

He raised an eyebrow. 'Good choice. I'll join you.' He sauntered off to the bar. She couldn't help but stare at him as he went. He was wearing a tan sweater. The stomach beneath the sweater was washboard-flat. She quickly averted her gaze. He was Kemi's boyfriend!

He came back with two tumblers. 'Cheers,' he said, lifting his glass.

'Cheers!' They clinked glasses lightly. The whisky burned its way down her throat, sending a pleasurable rush of warmth through her. She hadn't eaten since breakfast, she remembered suddenly. Better to take it slowly.

'Kemi says you've enjoyed being here,' he said, more of a statement than a question.

She nodded. 'I'm loving it. I can't bear to think about leaving.'

'When do you go?'

She sighed. 'I only managed to get a three-month visa, so I've only got a couple more weeks.'

'And what do you go back to? Job? Boyfriend?'

She laughed. 'Neither, sadly. I was just doing secretarial work. I screwed up the gallery job I had.' She pulled a face. 'But I'd rather not talk about that!'

'Fair enough. So, tell me about you.'

She glanced at him uncertainly. 'Me? Oh, there's nothing much to tell.'

He looked at her curiously. She felt herself go warm under his gaze. 'I doubt that,' he said evenly. 'I think there's probably rather a lot.'

The warmth spread slowly upwards through her neck and throat. She took a gulp of whisky to steady her nerves. He was the most disconcerting person to be around. The knowledge that he was Kemi's lay between them but it did nothing to stop the secret heat that rose from another part of her body, a different kind of wetness from the taste of whisky in her mouth.

'One more?' he asked. Jen's eyes went to her watch. It was nearly eleven. Her head was spinning. How many had she had?

'I . . . I think I'd probably better go. Kemi'll be wondering where I am.'

'Oh, she texted about an hour ago. Looks like they'll be there overnight. Some pile-up on one of the freeways. Sounded horrendous.'

'Oh.'

'So . . . one more for the road? Then I'll run you back.'

'No, no . . . I'll call Derrick. It's fine. You've also been drinking,' she said quickly. 'I'll be fine. He's completely reliable.'

'No, I insist. I've only had two. I've been drinking soda water. Not that you'd notice,' he chuckled. 'You sure you don't want another?'

She shook her head. 'No, I'm actually starving. I didn't have lunch.'

He made a small 'tsk' sound, pulling down the corners of his lovely mouth. 'Silly girl. Come on. There's nothing open at this time. I'll make you a sandwich at mine then I'll run you home. I'm only across the road.'

'All right,' she said, getting up unsteadily. 'But only if you're sure? I don't want to put you to any trouble.'

'You're not. Come on. Let's get you fed.'

She allowed him to take her arm and shepherd her out of the door, following dutifully, like a child.

The cold air and the short walk across the street did little to steady her. By the time she followed him into the large, empty apartment, the whole world was spinning. She felt sick. 'I . . . I think I'd better sit down,' she said shakily. 'I . . . I don't feel so good.'

'Here.' He quickly helped her to one of the chairs. 'Take a seat for a moment. I'll get you some water.'

She sat down abruptly. The room swam in front of her. She could feel her stomach heaving. She looked around her . . . there was a door at the far end of the room . . . probably the toilet. She was going to be sick. She stood up, swaying a little, and began to walk towards it. 'I need . . . I'd better . . . the toilet,' she mumbled. Out of the corner of her eye she could see him standing by the kitchen sink. He seemed to be pouring water into a glass but his movements were slow and unhurried. She put a foot out in front of her, then another, and then she felt herself beginning to fall. She opened her mouth to cry out but it was too late. She crumpled, her legs giving way underneath her. As she fell, she looked helplessly across the room at him . . . but Solam didn't move a muscle. She watched him watching her fall. That was the last thing she *thought* she remembered – Solam standing by the sink, watching her fall.

# 51

Kemi looked around, drinking in the view of the city spreading out to the north. She and Ayanda were sitting at the bar at the Tsogo Sun Hotel, at the top of the Sandton City tower, drinking expensive cocktails. Although they'd come to know one another well, at least in a professional context, she was only just beginning to see beneath the rather formal, offhand mask she wore, and sensed that there was an opportunity for a real friendship to develop, despite the fourteen-year age gap between them. She was both funny and wry, an odd but winning combination. She didn't suffer fools gladly. There wasn't a nurse or doctor in the entire hospital who hadn't felt the sharp end of her tongue at some point, but she was also capable of great generosity and empathy. The story of how she'd come to be so successful was more remarkable than Kemi could have guessed. Her mother had been a domestic worker and she'd never known her father.

'It's a familiar story,' she said matter-of-factly. 'Happens all the time. I was lucky, though.' Her mother's employers had taken a shine to Ayanda, sending her to a private school in Johannesburg along with their two daughters. She'd been one of only five black girls at the school. 'It taught me a thing or two about resilience,' she said, in the same dry tone of voice she used to admonish nursing students for failing to do things right. It was one of the qualities Kemi most liked about her. She had an utter disregard for hardship: 'Hardship's what made me.'

'Don't you ever want to get married?' Kemi asked curiously.

'Been there, done that. Twice.' Ayanda was brusque. 'No kids, thank God.' She refused to elaborate. 'And you? Do you have a boyfriend?'

Kemi traced the rim of her wine glass. 'Yes, actually. It's quite recent. In a strange way, he's the reason I came back.'

'Is he South African?'

'Yes, but he grew up in England, like me. His parents are friends of mine. His father and mine were in prison together.'

'Don't tell me . . . it's Solam Rhoyi!' Ayanda's eyes widened. 'I should have guessed!'

Kemi looked at her in surprise. 'Do you know him?'

'Put it this way: he's hard to miss if you're in our circles!' Ayanda chuckled. 'Solam Rhoyi. Well, well, well. Good-looking devil, mmnh?'

'I suppose so.' Kemi tried to sound disinterested.

'Oh, don't give me that look. Is it serious?'

Kemi hesitated. 'I think so. I mean, we've only been dating a couple of months. But . . . yes, we're pretty serious.'

'Tread carefully, my girl. Don't rush into anything. Guys like Solam are rare. I should know. I married two of them. They're called "black diamonds" here, and not just because they have expensive tastes. They're rare beasts. *Everyone* wants a black diamond in their pocket. Corporations, government, big business and women, too. Black *and* white. They've got it all. I don't know him personally, but I know the type. Just be careful. Don't lose your head too soon.'

Kemi nodded slowly. 'I'll try not to.'

'Good girl.' Ayanda raised her glass. 'Now, there's something

I want to ask *you*.' Her tone was suddenly business-like. 'What would you say if we made you an offer to stay?'

Kemi looked at her in surprise. 'Stay? What d'you mean?'

'Dr Khotsoane and I were talking the other day,' Ayanda said, mentioning one of the hospital's many directors. 'And we both came to the same conclusion. We'd love to have you for longer. You'd be an enormous asset to the hospital, not just in terms of your abilities – outstanding as they are, don't get me wrong – but as a person. A team player. A role model, if you must know.'

'Are you offering me a job?' Kemi asked, not quite following Ayanda's train of thought. 'A *permanent* job?'

'More than a job. A chance. A *real* chance to make a difference. I can't tell you what a boost it's been for some of our young doctors to see you at work. I'm not sentimental, you know that already, but I can tell you . . . you've really touched the team. We'd be honoured to have you. The money probably isn't as good as it is in—'

'Yes.' Kemi put out a hand to touch Ayanda's, cutting her off abruptly. 'Yes.'

The two women looked at each other. There was a sudden upsurge of feeling between them. Ayanda brought her other hand to lay it on top of Kemi's. She squeezed it hard.

'Welcome home,' she said, smiling widely. 'Welcome home, girl.'

# 52

She woke in the early hours of the morning, her head and heart pounding. She sat up slowly, gingerly. She looked down at her wrist but her watch wasn't there. She frowned and looked around. It was on the bedside table, lying face up. She put up a hand to her aching head. She couldn't remember taking off her watch. She usually slept with it on. She pulled back the bedsheet. She was naked except for her panties. She lay back, trying to piece together the previous evening. She remembered running into Solam and going off to have a drink . . . feeling as though she'd drunk too much . . . but she couldn't quite grab hold of the chain of events. Fragments of it came back to her. Feeling sick, the sharp winter air, holding on to his arm, getting up to go to the toilet, and then an odd sensation of falling, and of someone watching her . . . that was all. She picked up her watch and peered at it. It was nearly 5 a.m. She swung her legs out of bed and gingerly stood up. There was a packet of paracetamol in the bathroom cabinet. She walked over to the small fridge, took out a bottle of water and walked into the bathroom. She switched on the light. Her pale, smudged face stared back at her in the mirror. She hadn't taken off her make-up and there was an ugly crease down one cheek where she'd obviously slept on the pillow. She sat down on the toilet and pulled down her panties . . . and then she saw it. A thumb-sized, dull red bruise on the inside of her thigh. She stared at it. She must have fallen after all. She touched it lightly. It hurt. She reached for the toilet paper and then saw another bruise, this time on the inside of her forearm. She flushed the toilet and stood up, her head beginning to pound. She began examining her body carefully . . . there was a scratch mark just above her knee. What the hell had happened to her?

# 53

Kemi waited until the end of the week to break the news to Jen. She hadn't seen much of her – she was spending long days and evenings at the gallery, trying to wrap things up before their imminent departure. At lunchtime on the Friday, a full ten days before they were due to leave, she decided she had to tell her. She picked up her phone and quickly typed in a message. *Meet me at the Lucky Bean restaurant this evening. 7-ish? Got something important to tell you.* There. She pressed send and slipped the phone back inside the pocket of her green surgery gown. She heard her name being called out on the tannoy. She was needed in theatre. She pushed her way through the heavy swing doors, already running. She'd learned not to waste a single moment at Baragwanath. Every second counted, quite literally.

Jen was already waiting at the restaurant. She looked tired. She glanced up as Kemi walked in. There was an expression in her eyes that Kemi hadn't seen for ages and it startled her. A kind of inward-focused wariness that she remembered from so long ago she wondered if she'd imagined it.

'You look shattered,' Kemi said, bending down to hug her. 'Long day?'

Jen smiled faintly. 'Yeah . . . I can't believe we've only got a week left. It feels too soon . . . as if we've only just started to get things going.'

Kemi's heart sank. The waiter hurried over with the menu, giving her a few minutes to work up the courage to say why she'd asked Jen to meet. A few minutes later, with a large glass of red wine in hand, she turned to her. She drew in a deep breath. 'Jen, you're not going to like what I'm about to say.'

Jen looked at her and frowned. 'Why not?' she asked carefully.

Kemi let out her breath slowly. 'I've decided to stay,' she said quietly.

'Stay?'

'Yes. I've decided to stay. I'm not going back to London.'

Jen's face fell. 'You're not coming home?'

Kemi was quiet for a moment. How best to say it? 'This . . . this *is* my home now,' she said carefully. 'Or at least I want it to be.'

'It's because of him, isn't it?'

Kemi looked at her, surprised. 'Solam?' She shook her head. 'No, this has nothing to do with him. I've been offered a job . . . a permanent job—' She broke off. 'Don't cry, Jen . . . please don't cry. What is it? You'll come back to visit . . . I'll come to London on holiday. We'll probably see more of each other than we did when we were both living there.'

The reassurance only seemed to make things worse. Jen's face was blotchy with tears. 'But it won't be the same,' Jen sobbed. 'You're moving on . . . you know what you want to do with the rest of your life. I'm . . . I'm just . . . I just feel so *lost*, Kem.'

'Jen, you're not lost. It's just taking you a little while longer to figure things out,' Kemi said, grabbing hold of her hand. She squeezed it hard. 'It's not a race, Jen. You'll find your way.

I know you will. You had such a good time here . . . you'll find something in London. Call up that friend of yours when you get back . . . what was his name? Barker?'

'Parker.' Jen smiled shakily. She picked up a napkin and dabbed her eyes. 'Yes, he's back in London now. He'll have something, I'm sure. You're right. I'm being pathetic.'

Kemi shook her head. 'No, you're not. Stop putting yourself down all the time, Jen. You're going to miss it here. That's natural. And you don't know what's coming next . . . it's normal to be nervous. You're not pathetic at all. Not in the slightest.'

Jen nodded and blew her nose. 'I knew it wouldn't last forever,' she said after a moment. She straightened up and tucked her hair behind her ears. 'You're right. I just need to figure things out on my own.'

Kemi frowned. 'You're missing an earring, Jen. Did you forget to put it on?'

Jen touched her left lobe. She shook her head. 'I don't know . . . I must've taken them off somewhere but I could only find the one.'

'You never take them off.'

'I know. I don't remember taking them off but this one was lying beside the bed, beside my watch. It'll turn up.'

Kemi gave her hand another squeeze. 'So . . . you're not angry with me?' she asked anxiously. 'For not coming back with you?'

Jen shook her head vigorously. 'No, of course not. You're right . . . this is your home, not mine. I need to get back to London and sort out my own life, not try and live yours.'

Kemi smiled. Then she noticed something on Jen's face. 'Jen,' she said, alarmed. 'Your nose. It's bleeding. Here, put your head back. I'll get some ice.' She looked around for a waiter. The news must have upset her more than she was letting on, Kemi thought to herself. It had been years since Jen had had a nosebleed. When they were still young enough to have shared a room, Kemi had woken up a few times to find Jen's pillow soaked with blood. There seemed to be no explanation for the bleeds and in time, they simply disappeared. She held the napkin gently against Jen's nose, pressing firmly until the flow stopped. 'There,' she said, wiping away the last traces of blood. 'All gone. Poor you, Jen. I can't remember the last time you had a nosebleed, can you?'

Jen was quiet. There was something else, Kemi saw. She had an odd, faraway look in her eyes that meant something was puzzling her. She squeezed her hand, hard. Whatever it was, it wouldn't be long before she shared it. That was the thing about Jen – she was incapable of deception. She couldn't keep a secret for even a few hours, let alone weeks or months. When they first met, Kemi was astonished at the way Jen's emotions rose straight to the surface of her skin. She wondered if it was the case with all white people – the dark blush of embarrassment; the faint pink glow of pleasure . . . even the ugly, mottled blotches of shame or anger. It fascinated her. In time, of course, she recognized that the transparency was all Jen's. She kept hold of her hand. *I'm here*, she signalled with her touch. *I'll always be here. You can tell me anything. You know that.*

# PART SEVEN
# 1998

Two months later

. . .

For me, I always wonder what's worse: an
emotional betrayal or a physical betrayal?
That's a really tough call.

HILARIE BURTON

# 54

She stood in front of the racks of test kits, her heart thudding. She looked at the various products – Clearblue, First Response, Pregmate. She picked up a packet and walked to the counter. She paid, slipped the package in her handbag and walked out of the chemist's. She walked slowly down Fulham Road, oblivious to the sounds of the street around her. It was a dull grey summer day, not cold, not warm, with the occasional short drizzle of rain. She felt the presence of the test kit in her bag like a lead weight, equalled only by the weight in her heart.

At home, she carefully put the little white packet on the kitchen counter and made herself a cup of tea. She glanced at it from time to time, but she already knew what the result would be. She was pregnant. The only night she couldn't account for in the past six months was the night she'd left the bar with Solam. Fragments of the evening kept coming back to her, none of which made any sense. A fall; a sharp burning sensation between her legs; something hitting her teeth . . . nothing that she could hold on to. She remembered his beauty and her strong sense of attraction; she'd shoved it away it immediately – he was Kemi's boyfriend – but was it possible that drink had got the better of her and she'd lost control? A wave of shame swept over her. There was only one way out of this. An abortion. She would have to bury the evidence as deeply and thoroughly as she could. Kemi would never, *ever* know.

Her phone rang suddenly, shattering the silence. She picked it up and peered at the screen. *Unknown*. It was probably a sales call but she needed the distraction. Her own thoughts were too shameful to bear. 'Hello?'

'Jen.'

Her stomach gave a sudden, painful lurch. She gripped the phone and closed her eyes. It was Solam.

There was a moment's silence. 'How are you?' he asked finally.

She opened her mouth in astonishment but found she couldn't speak. It had been two months since she'd left Johannesburg. She hadn't said a word to Kemi about the evening they'd spent together. Out of a cowardice she didn't know she possessed, she'd waited for Kemi to bring it up . . . but she hadn't. After a few weeks, she realized Solam hadn't said anything either. She'd wondered why, but by then, too much time had passed. Kemi's text messages were as warm as they'd always been. Nothing was amiss. As far as she could work out, Kemi and Solam were as strong as they'd ever been. Only a week or so before, they'd flown to Durban together for a long weekend. She read the text messages with a growing sense of unease.

'Solam,' she said finally, exhaling slowly. 'I . . . I'm fine.'

'Where are you?'

She was taken aback. 'I'm at home.'

'Are you alone?'

'Er, yes. Why?'

'I'm in London.'

'Solam, it's not . . . a good time,' she said weakly, looking around her as if for support.

'Just give me the address.'

Time seemed to stand still. She gripped the phone tightly to her ear. '14 Bishop's Road,' she heard herself saying. 'Second-floor flat.'

'I'll be there in an hour.' He hung up the phone. She stood rooted to the spot. Her mind was in turmoil.


She opened the door. He was exactly as she remembered. Beauty beyond compare. His face was sombre, as though he too knew what was coming. She felt as though her legs might suddenly give way beneath her.

'Do you want to come in?' she asked, aware of how absurd the question sounded. Who flew from Johannesburg to London to stand on a doorstep?

'Yeah. Thanks.' He followed her in. He looked around and then his eyes came back to rest on her face.

She flushed. 'Wou-would you like something to drink?'

He shook his head. 'No, thanks. After last time, it's probably safer not to,' he said with a faint smile. 'But more importantly, how are you?' he asked.

She swallowed. 'Wh-what are you doing here? In London, I mean. Kemi didn't say you were coming.' She hesitated. 'How did you get my number?'

He smiled again. 'Don't worry about that. I was in Paris for a couple of days and I just thought I'd better check on you . . . see how you're doing. Last time I saw you, you weren't doing so well.'

'I wasn't?' Fear rose in her throat.

'Jen . . . don't you remember *anything* about that night?'

She shook her head. 'Not really. Did I . . . did something happen?'

Solam looked at her. He shook his head. 'I can't believe you don't remember a thing,' he said slowly. 'I . . . I've thought about pretty much nothing else.'

Jen swallowed. 'Was it my fault?' she whispered. 'Did I do something wrong?'

He drew in his lip. He lifted his hands, palms turned outwards. 'Look, however it started, I'm as much to blame as you,' he said slowly. 'I could've stopped myself. I could've stopped us both.'

Jen's legs felt as though they'd give way. She looked down at the ground. Embarrassment burned over her like a fever. She swallowed. 'I'm sorry,' she began, casting around for a chair.

'Hey, take it easy . . . don't fall over! You did that last time, remember?' Solam jumped forward and pulled a chair out from the table. 'Here, sit down. Can I get you something? A glass of water?'

She nodded, but as he turned to walk to the tap, she suddenly remembered what she'd left lying on the counter. 'No!' she blurted out, half rising from the chair. 'No . . . I'm OK . . . I don't—'

'Jen?' It was too late. He picked up the packet lying on the counter and turned to her. 'Jen?'

And there it was.

# 55

Kemi stood in front of the wardrobe, tapping a finger against her teeth, trying to decide what to wear. Solam was back from Paris and she had a rare night off. Unusually, he'd promised to cook. Since Jen's departure, they'd fallen into an easy routine, seeing each other when they both had space in their equally busy schedules, which wasn't all that often. But Kemi certainly didn't mind. She wasn't the possessive or demanding type. Solam joked that she was even less of a romantic than he was, which was difficult to imagine. They'd laughed about it. Kemi shrugged. Theirs was a match of equals. She had just as much of her own life and career as he did. But there was something else, too, something deeper. They both carried the same stubborn streak of selfishness. Like many exile children, they were self-sufficient to a fault, able to happily exist without others, free of the complex demands of parental and sibling relationships. She understood him well. Jen had softened Kemi's edges, allowing her to drop her guard a little, but Solam had had no one. He was entirely his own man, self-possessed in ways she both understood and respected. They were an unusual couple in more ways than many would ever see.

She pulled a black-and-white striped skirt off the hanger and rummaged around for a clean shirt. Without Jen's expert eye, Kemi would happily have lived in the utilitarian combination of jeans, trousers and shirts that had served her so well for most of her life. Jen had other ideas. Nestled amongst the shirts and blazers were a number of simple but elegant outfits that meant Kemi now had a choice. Although choosing was *work*, she thought to herself, smiling a little. She found a pretty white silk blouse with slightly flared sleeves and a pair of wedge espadrilles – done. She laid the clothes on the bed and headed to the shower.

The lift doors opened to the smell of steaks on the grill. She smiled. Solam's apartment, on the fourth floor of an old industrial building in the heart of Braamfontein, was spectacular for a number of reasons. It was enormous. She'd asked him several times just how big it was – three hundred square metres? Four hundred? She could never remember the exact figure. Whichever it was, it was huge. It was also spectacularly empty. There was a large leather sofa marooned in the middle of the space with an equally enormous television screen against one of the pillars . . . and very little else. A double bed in one of the three bedrooms off the central space, a makeshift desk in another, and a giant Weber grill on the patio at the rear . . . that was it. 'All a man needs,' Solam said with a grin. Kemi had to agree. She was in no position to comment. She was still living in the same guesthouse her mother had organized when she first arrived. She kept meaning to look for a more permanent solution but there never seemed to be any time . . . and besides, she'd grown to like the little guesthouse, and the fact that the staff all knew her name and how she liked her eggs in the morning. No, in so many ways, she and Solam were uncannily alike.

\*

The door to his place was open. She walked in and put her bag on the concrete kitchen counter. She could see him on the patio, barbecue tongs in one hand, phone clamped to his ear with the other. He gave her a quick wave – 'Two minutes,' he mouthed. She nodded. There was an open bottle of Shiraz on the counter and a single glass, clearly meant for her. She poured herself a measure and walked over to the couch. She sank back against the cushions, took a sip and closed her eyes for a second. It was the first time in a couple of days that she'd had the chance to relax.

She woke to the feel of his hands on her shoulders, gently kneading the knots of tension that seemed to be a permanent side effect of working at Bara. She reached up and caught hold of one of his hands, pushing it against the side of her neck. 'That's perfect,' she murmured. 'Just perfect.'

'Steak's ready,' he said, planting a kiss on the top of her head. 'Medium rare, no?'

She nodded. 'I'll get up in a minute. Don't stop . . . right there. Ouch . . . yes, right *there*.'

He chuckled. 'Sounds like an invitation to something else.'

'After my steak,' she said firmly. 'Food first.'

'Coming up.' He touched her neck lightly and walked back to the patio. She got up, stretching her arms, and walked to the bathroom at the far end of the space. She switched on the light but saw there was no toilet paper. She shook her head and closed the door. His own bathroom was just off the main bedroom. She walked in and switched on the light. It was marginally better stocked and at least there was a clean towel hanging on the shower door.

She flushed the toilet and walked over to the sink. There was a floor-to-ceiling mirror on one side of the bathroom and she quickly checked her appearance before turning on the tap to wash her hands. She reached for the small bottle of handwash . . . and then she saw it. The earring. She froze. There was absolutely no mistaking the small gold-and-diamond stud. It was Jen's. She stood still for a moment. Her mind jumped back to the restaurant. Jen tucking her hair behind her ears. Kemi noticing one earring was missing. Jen's response. *It'll turn up.* She swallowed. There *had* to be an explanation. Jen had never been to Solam's apartment. She'd have told her if she had. He must have found it somewhere . . . but where? She picked it up, turning it over carefully in her hand. There was a sudden loud knock at the door.

'Kem? You OK?'

She jumped. 'I'm . . . I'm fine. I'll be out in a minute,' she called, turning on the tap again. She splashed a little cold water over her face and patted it dry. Then she closed her fist around the earring and went to the door. He was standing outside, looking concerned.

'You OK?' he asked again.

She opened her mouth but couldn't find the right words. She opened her palm. She watched as he looked down at the stud and then at her face. She searched for the smallest change in his expression but there was none. They stood there together in silence, looking at the earring. It was the silence that told her what she needed to know. And then he spoke. What followed was worse.

# 56

'This *is* a surprise,' Iketleng murmured as the waiter showed them to their table. 'You *never* ring me.'

'Not true. Now, are you happy here or would you prefer a window seat?' Solam said, pulling out her chair.

'No, this is fine.' She looked around her. 'Nice place. I haven't been before.'

'Food's good,' Solam said, sitting opposite her. 'And they have fish,' he added quickly.

'Good. So, what's this in aid of?' Iketleng said, shaking out her napkin.

'Why does there have to be a particular reason?'

'Solam, I'm your mother.'

He sighed. 'All right. I wanted to tell you myself, before you heard it from anyone else.'

Iketleng looked at him sharply. 'What's happened? It's not Kemi, is it?'

Solam nodded slowly. 'It's complicated.'

'What happened? I can't believe it. You two are *made* for each other. What am I going to tell Florence? Or does she already know?'

Solam sighed. 'I don't know what she knows.' He looked at his mother. He chose his words carefully. 'I think that was part of the problem,' he said slowly.

'What?'

'Exactly what you just said. Everyone thinks the same way you do. That we're made for each other. The perfect couple.'

'Didn't *you* think so, too?'

Solam shook his head. 'It's hard to explain.'

'Solam, I'm your mother. If you can't explain it to me, who can you explain it to?' As soon as the words were out, Solam could see the conflict in her face. Theirs had never been the sort of relationship where such things could be discussed. She'd always respected the boundaries he drew so carefully around himself. It was partly out of guilt, he knew, which gave him the upper hand, but it was also not in her nature, or her culture, which was now so different from his.

'She's great, Ma. She's brilliant and ambitious . . . she's from the right family. We come from such similar backgrounds . . . yeah, it ought to work. But I need someone who needs *me*, Ma. Kemi doesn't need anyone.'

'I see.'

'And I did something. Something I'm not exactly proud of, but it happened.'

There was silence for a few moments. 'I won't ask you what you did,' she said finally. 'You're a grown man and it's not my business.'

'No, it's not. But I wanted you to hear it from me, not from anyone else. Least of all her mother.'

Iketleng nodded. 'It's not my place to judge. And you're right . . . no one really knows what goes on between a couple.' She twisted her own wedding ring in an unconsciously sentimental gesture.

Solam looked at her curiously. He had never really thought about his parents' marriage. They'd spent most of their lives apart. Was it possible . . .?

Iketleng seemed to read his mind. She shook her head

almost imperceptibly, though whether as an answer to his unasked question or a refusal to be drawn any further it wasn't clear. 'Whatever you did, I hope you will find a way to remain friends. Our families are too close.'

Solam pulled a face. 'In time, maybe. It's . . . complicated. Now, what'll you have to drink? There's a very good Chardonnay on the list.' He bent his head, hoping she would do the same. He was about to steer the conversation in another direction and he wanted her to relax.

'Chardonnay's fine,' she said, picking up the menu. Iketleng was nothing if not pragmatic. He could read her like a book. He chose his next words carefully.

'There's something else I want to ask you,' he said, still studying the wine list. He could feel her attention on him.

'What?'

'I've been approached by Mbete,' he began. 'He wants me to move to Economic Development. They're talking about a possible deputy minister role.'

'I see.'

'It's a big jump for me. I'll be the youngest deputy minister they've ever had. Can I trust him? I just need to be sure they're not setting me up for a fall.'

'Mbete's no fool,' Iketleng said thoughtfully. 'He won't go against you whilst your father is on the Executive. D'you want me to ask him?'

Solam shook his head. 'No, keep him out of this.' She said nothing, but he saw from her eyes that his decision met with her approval. 'It might be useful in the short term. In the long run, though, the less he knows about my path in government the better.'

Iketleng nodded. 'Mbete's not the one you need to watch out for. It's Mbatha. If he's pushing Mbatha out to make room for you, you'd better hope he's been given something good.

That younger crowd are ruthless, I'm telling you. All they think about is lining their own pockets as fast as they can, every single one of them. That's the danger.'

Solam said nothing. He felt a prickling at the nape of his neck. He pushed the uneasiness away. The first hurdle had been overcome. The first and possibly most difficult.

# 57

Ayanda carried over two glasses from the bar. She set them down, waving away the waiter, and slipped into the seat opposite Kemi.

'Cheers,' she said, lifting her glass. 'Now, tell me everything.'

Kemi picked up her glass. It had been a week since she'd found out about Jen and Solam. She'd walked out of his apartment in a daze. Derrick had come to pick her up. The following morning, she'd called in sick for the first time ever in her career. She lay in bed in the guesthouse, too stunned to speak or think.

'He cheated,' she said slowly, carefully. 'He's been with someone else.'

'I'm not going to say, "I told you so",' Ayanda said after a moment. 'But I did. And I told you that it's just the way things are between men and women, here. You'll never survive here if you think *your* relationship will be different. It's complex. Our history is so complicated. Apartheid damaged everyone, especially our men. Was it a fling? A one-night stand? Can you forgive him?'

Kemi shook her head. 'He's not the problem.'

Ayanda looked surprised. 'What d'you mean?'

'I'm not stupid. Solam's a good-looking man. Women practically throw themselves at him all the time. I see it every time we go out. Even *I* could see that it would just be a matter of time before something happened. He's out of the country half the time . . . we don't see that much of each other. Like you said, it's what happens. At the back of my mind, I think I always knew there was that risk. *That's* not the betrayal.'

'So, what is?'

'It's the woman he slept with.' Kemi took a gulp of wine. 'I don't think I can forgive her. Ever.'

'Who is it?' Ayanda looked puzzled. 'It can't be a friend of yours . . . you don't have any.' She put out a hand. 'Here in Johannesburg, I mean. You haven't been here long enough to make those kinds of friends.'

'It's not a friend,' Kemi said carefully. 'It's much worse than that.'

'Who?'

'It's my sister. Jen. My soul sister. That's what we used to call each other. Soul sisters.'

'*Jen?*' Ayanda couldn't possibly have looked more shocked. 'How?'

Kemi nodded. 'Yes, Jen. Apparently it was only the once, just before she left. But that's not the worst part.'

'What on earth could be worse?'

'She's pregnant.'

# 58

'Ah, Julian. Some good news at last,' Gareth McElhone, the senior neurologist at UCH, said as Julian walked into the staffroom stirring his cup of lukewarm coffee.

'What's that?' Julian asked mildly. McElhone was known to his colleagues as someone who was somewhat lacking in the humour department.

'Dr Mashabane's coming back. Got an email from HR this morning. Seems she's had enough of working out there.'

Julian's heart missed a beat. 'Interesting,' he murmured, taking a seat opposite. 'How come?'

Dr McElhone shrugged. 'No idea. Main thing is, she's back.'

'When does she start?'

'Week on Monday. It'll be good to have her on the team again. She's been missed. Now, about that patient who came in this morning. I'd like you to take a look at her, if you can. It's clearly an aneurism but there may be some underlying cardiovascular symptoms we're missing.'

Julian nodded, his mind already racing ahead. He was gripped with a longing of the sort he hadn't had since child-hood, a longing so acute he found his hands shaking. *Ridiculous*, he kept thinking to himself. Ridiculous, plain and simple. She'd been gone for nearly six months, but not a day had gone by when he hadn't thought of her. And now she was coming back.

The night before her arrival back at the hospital, he lay beside Rosemary, stiff with the tension of holding himself in, listening to her breathing softly, gently, peacefully, in and out, in and out, cursing himself for his inability to do the same. Rosemary had no inkling of the storm that had been brewing inside him for the past nine months. As before, when he finally entered sleep, he found himself in a place of such delightfully erotic longing that when he woke in the early hours of the morning, his pyjamas were once again damp to the touch. He buried them in the laundry basket again, thrust to the bottom of the pile. He showered and shaved and kissed his still-sleeping wife, leaving the house well before the usual time. He walked through Regent's Park, oblivious to the signs of autumn in the falling leaves around him.

There was no real reason to be in the staffroom on the fifth floor where the neurology team met every morning, but he found himself pressing '5' instead of '4' in the lift without realizing it. He had a full morning's surgery scheduled but it was one of the reasons he'd left home so early. If he were to catch a glimpse of her at all, it would be there, at that time, before the morning's caseload began. The doors opened with their usual hiss and he stepped out. He saw Fairbanks at once, walking towards the staffroom.

'You're just in time,' Fairbanks called out, waiting for him to walk down the corridor to join him.

'In time for what?'

'You'll never guess who's here!'

'Who?'

'Dr Mashabane. Come in and join us, we're just having a cup of tea to welcome her back.'

His heart was thudding. He hoped his voice and expression were steady. 'Really?' He fell into step alongside Fairbanks.

'We haven't seen you around in a while,' Fairbanks said, as they both entered the staffroom together. It was just the opening Julian needed. He was able to say, quite calmly, that he'd been away on holiday the previous week, so that when he caught sight of her, it was as if he was engaged in a conversation with a colleague, and was surprised to see her.

'Oh, *hello* . . . I just heard you were back. Lovely to see you.'

She looked up. Her face was the same, he noticed immediately, though there was a sudden tightness around the eyes. She'd lost weight. Her cheekbones were sharper, and that little hollow at the base of her throat between the clavicles was more pronounced. Around her mouth were tiny lines of tension, which relaxed as she smiled. 'Mr Carrick! How are you? It's really nice to be back.'

He held out a hand. Her touch sent a small thrilling shock through him. 'Mark was just telling me you're back with us. Well, it's good to see you. We must chat about your adventure some time. It'd be interesting to hear how things are out there.'

She nodded eagerly, it seemed to him, but before he could say anything further, someone else came over to talk to her and he turned away, elated. He chatted to Fairbanks for a few minutes. Luckily no one asked him what he was doing amongst them and he slipped out without anyone noticing, and began to whistle lightly as he walked back down the corridor to the lift.

# 59

They were sitting so close that their heads were almost touching. They had been there since six o'clock. It was nearly ten. Kemi had bumped into him on her way out of the hospital's main door and they'd fallen into step walking up Grafton Way. They'd started chatting about this and that ... by the time they reached Warren Street, it seemed the most natural thing to duck into the bar at the hotel on the corner and order a drink. He carried the glasses over to the corner table and sat down opposite her. The thread of conversation they'd started outside was picked up again. She found his questions so thoughtful. The shared professional language between them calmed her. It gave her something else to focus on.

'Will you have another?' he asked, pointing to her glass. 'A small one? It's still pretty early.'

She nodded. *Yes, well, why not?* There was only the empty flat to go back to and the telephone that never rang. The welcome she'd received from her former colleagues had touched her more than she was able to express. No one had asked her why she'd cut her appointment short. There was only pleasure at her return.

'A small one.' She smiled her thanks.

'Be back in a sec,' he said, getting up. She watched him

walk towards the bar. After Solam's almost overwhelming physical presence, Julian was a relief to be around. Solam consumed the very air around him. Julian was the opposite. He was quiet and self-contained. She couldn't imagine him getting angry or throwing his weight around . . . not that there was much weight to throw. He was of average height, slim build, grey-haired, with light blue eyes that shone from behind his wire-framed glasses. A serious face, deep grooves than ran from nose to chin, a faint salt-and-pepper shadow of stubble. She looked up as he approached, two small beers in hand.

'Thanks.' She curled her hand around the base. 'I'm not keeping you, am I?' she said, suddenly worried. She'd spent most of the evening talking about herself.

'Oh, goodness no. I'm . . . I'm just enjoying listening to you,' he said quickly. 'It sounds fascinating. I've never been to Africa. But . . . if you'll allow me to say something out of turn . . . there's something else, isn't there? There's another reason you came back. And please just tell me to mind my own business,' he added quickly. 'I don't mean to pry.'

Kemi was silent, struggling between the desire to tell someone and the knowledge that he was her superior. She had always been so careful to respect the boundary between her professional and personal life. Sometimes the distance she created was mistaken for aloofness but her cautiousness had served her well. Jen's betrayal had cut her to the bone and there was no one to tell. Her mother was only interested in Solam . . . why on earth had she thrown everything away? *He's just a typical man, for goodness' sake! What did you expect?* She didn't know how to tell her that it wasn't Solam's betrayal that hurt . . . it was Jen's. Florence simply couldn't understand. Even Ayanda's brisk sympathy did little to assuage the pain. And now here was Mr Carrick – *Julian*, she corrected herself – offering her a shoulder to cry on and a sympathetic ear . . . nothing more than that. She opened her mouth, and suddenly she couldn't hold back.

'I'm sorry,' Julian said quietly. Their beers were long ago finished but he made no move to fetch another. 'What rotten luck.'

Kemi gave a wan smile. 'Luck? I don't know that luck had anything to do with it, good or bad.'

'You mustn't think like that. That's all it was. Bad luck. Him, I mean. The other thing, with Jen, now that's different. You can get over a man, you know. But you can't get over the loss of a sibling. From what you've told me, it sounds as though that's what you really are . . . sisters. Deep down, I mean. Forget the biology.'

Kemi looked at him gratefully. He'd been able to put into words the pain she'd been feeling for weeks now. He was right. You could mourn the death of a relationship but there was no pain like that of a sister's betrayal. 'I just can't get it out of my head,' she said slowly. 'All that time after she left. . . we used to phone or text each other every other day. Sometimes nothing, just little things, you know. "I saw this film," or "Do you remember that" . . . silly things. And she never said a word. I can't bring myself to call her. She's three months pregnant. I should be there with her, but I can't be. It's been weeks since we've spoken. That's what I miss more than anything.'

'It'll take time, Kemi. Probably more time than you think you have. But if you love her, you'll forgive her. That's what love is, Kemi. It survives. *You* survive. But it's really up to her now.'

'You sound as though you speak from experience,' Kemi said hesitantly.

It took him a while to answer. 'Well, you don't get to *my* age—'

'You're not old!' Kemi protested, interrupting him.

'Old enough to be your father,' Julian said, smiling gently. 'Or near enough.' He looked at her sharply. 'What's the matter?'

Kemi suddenly couldn't speak. Her mouth filled with saliva, flooding her tongue and teeth. She was going to be sick. She got up clumsily and pushed her way past him, clutching a hand to her mouth. She looked around desperately for the toilets. One of the doormen caught sight of her, pointing to the stairs. He'd probably seen many young women like her. She made it to the stall just in time. His words had struck something inside her that had to be purged, released, revealed.

He was standing at the table when she returned, their coats in his arms. 'Are you all right?' he asked anxiously. 'Was it something you ate?'

She shook her head, swallowing to rid herself of the sour taste in her mouth. 'It was probably the beer,' she said shakily. 'I'm not used to drinking more than a glass.'

'Come on, I'll get you a cab. It's late. I'm sorry, I shouldn't have kept you out.' He was genuinely apologetic.

'No, of course not. I only live up the road, on Fitzroy Square. I'll walk. It's less than five minutes away.'

'I'll walk you home. I'm in Primrose Hill. The walk'll do me good. Come on. Are you sure you're all right?'

Kemi nodded. 'I'm fine. I don't know what came over me.'

He escorted her from the bar, his hand touching her elbow gently in a chivalrous gesture, making sure she was fine to walk. She was grateful. It had been quite an evening. The mood between them had changed. He was no longer Mr Carrick to her, she realized. The formality she'd insisted upon had gone, replaced by a warmth that was comforting, if unfamiliar. She'd never been one to make friends quickly. Ayanda had been an exception.

'Thank you,' she said, as they reached her front door. 'I mean it. I feel a little foolish now. I hardly know you but you were very kind. You *are* very kind.'

Julian looked down at her. His eyes were smiling. 'Goodnight, Kemi. This will pass, I promise.' He watched as she walked up the steps and put her key in the lock. She turned and waved. He carried on up the road.

# 60

Jen woke suddenly, jolted from sleep by a sharp, stabbing pain in her lower abdomen. It took her a second to understand that she was lying on wet sheets. She lay still, panic rising in her throat. There was a bedside lamp just beside her. She reached out and switched it on. She let out a muffled scream. The dark red stain pooled around her legs, spreading outwards. She touched the sheet. It was red and sticky with blood. Her blood. *No . . . please God, no.* She tried to sit up. She was three months pregnant. Her phone was on the dresser across the room. Why hadn't she thought to keep it by her bed? She began to cry. The stabbing pain in her stomach intensified. She had to call for help. She pulled the pillow from behind her and put it between her legs, then tried to stand up. She staggered across the room and grabbed her phone before sinking to the ground. She felt dizzy, though whether with pain or fear she couldn't tell. Her finger hovered over Kemi's number. It had been nearly two months since they'd last spoken and she had no way of knowing how much Kemi knew. Solam had been adamant. *Leave it to me to tell her. Yes, I know you feel guilty, even more than I do, but it's best if she hears it from me. When she's ready, she'll reach out to you. Don't force things, Jen. That's your problem . . . you're always in such a hurry.* He was right, she supposed. But there was only one person whose voice she wanted to hear right now. Her finger hovered. What on earth would she say? Solam was in Lusaka on a trade mission. She couldn't bring herself to disturb him. Another sharp pain coursed through her. With shaking fingers, she pulled up Parker's name. 'Parker? It's me. I'm sorry to call you so early but I'm . . . I'm bleeding. Can you come round?'

'Jen? What's the matter?' Parker was instantly awake.

Jen closed her eyes. She began to cry again. 'I'm bleeding. I'm . . . I think I'm losing the baby.'

'Hold on, Jen. I'll be right there. Just hold on. I'll call an ambulance and I'll meet you at the hospital. Jen . . . have you called Kemi?'

She couldn't answer. She let the phone slip out of her hands. Some mistakes couldn't be rectified. She'd brought it on herself. She'd seduced her sister's boyfriend . . . this was what she deserved.

# PART EIGHT
# 2001

## Three years later

. . .

If I get married, I want to be very married.

AUDREY HEPBURN

# 61

Kemi slowly turned the invitation over in her hands. It was on thick, luxuriously embossed card, a beautiful stippled cream colour, with spidery black writing.

*Mr & Mrs Oliver Sibusiso Rhoyi request the pleasure*
*of your company at the marriage of their son*
*Solam Samuel Rhoyi to Catriona Jennifer McFadden*
*Saturday 11th August 2001, at eleven o'clock*
*in the morning*
*Saint Michael's Church, Bryanston, Johannesburg.*
*Reception to follow.*

There was an RSVP; a second, smaller card, tucked discreetly into the fold of the beautifully inscribed envelope. She turned it over again. *S & J*. With a fancy scrolled flourish. His parents, not hers, were hosting the wedding.

'What was it?' Julian came into the bedroom, towelling his hair dry. 'I heard the doorbell.'

'Special delivery.' Kemi held up the card. 'A wedding.'

'Whose wedding?' he asked, going through to the dressing room.

'Jen's. They're finally getting married.'

He stuck his head back through the doorway. 'Really?'

He looked at her closely. 'Are you OK? How d'you feel about it?'

She smiled faintly. It was typical Julian. Her first assessment of him had been the right one. He *was* the kindest person she'd ever known. 'It's fine,' she said, giving him a reassuring smile. 'Really. It's absolutely fine.' It was true. Things would never be the same between her and Jen, but it was true what they said about time. It really did heal most wounds. She marvelled at the way the mind worked, weeding out pain, replacing it with other, less hurtful memories. It had taken her nearly two years to begin speaking to Jen again, but with distance and her own newfound happiness with Julian, the pain had turned to regret and then finally to acceptance.

Jen didn't come to their wedding. She had gone back to Johannesburg at that point and Kemi wasn't sure she was ready to face her. But that was a year ago, after Julian's divorce finally came through, and now . . .? Now they'd all moved on. She often saw Solam's face in the newspapers and on television. He was now an elected politician and the party's rising star. The role seemed to suit him. Jen was careful not to talk about Solam in anything other than the most pragmatic terms, which explained the invitation that had come by courier, not by phone call, Kemi thought to herself.

'Where's the wedding going to be?'

'Johannesburg.'

He gave her a searching look. 'D'you want to go?'

She nodded. 'Of course. I'll have to think up a present. What do you buy the couple who have everything?'

'You'll think of something. So, it'll be Johannesburg for our summer holidays. Well, I suppose it's a relief. I was beginning to think I'd never get to see the place. Now, which tie? Blue or red?'

'Blue. It matches your eyes.' Kemi was relieved to have

something else to focus on. She got up from the bed and walked over to the window. The garden below stretched all the way to Horniman Gardens at the back, giving them a swathe of greenery that few homes in the area could match. The builders were nearly finished with the kitchen extension – once it was done, there'd be a glass-fronted conservatory at the rear of the house with enormous sliding doors that opened directly onto the garden. She tugged back the curtains, letting sunlight flood into the room. It was May. The sky was clear and blue. She turned back to the room. Julian was humming to himself as he finished dressing, some mindless ditty he'd picked up from the radio. Their bed was a mess of sheets and blankets. She walked back towards it, automatically picking up discarded clothing and cushions and straightening the sheets.

'You don't have to do that,' he said, coming through. 'The maid'll get to it.'

She gave an embarrassed laugh. 'I can't get used to having a maid in here. I don't mind her doing everywhere else but not here. It's too private. I'd rather make my own bed.'

'Nonsense. It's what she's paid to do.' He fastened his tie and picked up his jacket from the back of the chair. 'Right, darling, I'd better run. I'll be late. Dinner this evening with the Cartwrights, don't forget.'

Kemi nodded absently. She kissed his cheek, which smelled of fresh soap and aftershave, and calmly continued making the bed. The house shuddered lightly as he ran down the stairs and slammed the front door shut. She heard the car start up, a loud, throaty purr, and then the tyres crunching on gravel as he reversed out. Then all was quiet again. She had a rare day off from work.

She reached for her phone on the bedside table and quickly tapped out a message. *Just got the invitation. Congratulations!*

*Looking forward to seeing you both.* She hesitated, then signed off, *K & J.* She smiled a little wryly. *S & J. K & J.* There was a rhythm to their combined initials.

Downstairs she heard the front door open again, carefully. It was Magda, the maid, who came four days a week, including Saturday. Kemi would have preferred the weekends alone, free of the need to speak to anyone other than Julian if she didn't feel like it, but he was adamant. Friday nights were generally spent either at a dinner, or hosting one. He certainly wasn't going to spend Saturday morning clearing up, and neither was she. Julian loved to entertain. After a hard week, he liked nothing better than cooking for friends with Kemi perched on one of the kitchen counter stools, keeping him company. Since his divorce, it was as though he'd rediscovered a whole new persona. 'I don't know how I existed before you,' he would say to her, over and over again. She finished making the bed, tied her dressing gown more tightly around her waist, and went downstairs.

'Morning, Magda,' she called out as she walked into the kitchen.

'Good morning, Mrs Carrick.' She was already busy hauling out the vacuum cleaner and brooms.

She plugged in the kettle. She would never get used to being called 'Mrs Carrick'. No one at work called her that. There she was Dr Mashabane, as she'd always been. It was only Magda and a handful of other people – the newsagent on the corner; one or two of Julian's senior colleagues, who presumably had never known the original Mrs Carrick, or who didn't care. For two people who'd been married as long as Julian and Rosemary, it was strange how quickly it had all unravelled and with seemingly so little fuss. It had been a remarkably civilized divorce. They parted after twenty-four years together with some regrets, but no real anger. 'But how can that *be*?' Kemi was astounded. 'She just agreed? Just like that?'

'It's just the way she is. Our kind, I suppose.'

'What does *that* mean?'

'We're brought up not to make a fuss. Stiff upper lip and all that.'

'It doesn't make sense.'

'Not to you, my darling. You're not English.'

She took her steaming mug of tea upstairs and walked through to her side of the dressing room. She opened the wardrobe door and stood in front of it, biting her lip. Julian spoiled her. Buying her expensive clothes seemed to be his second-favourite activity. From Valentino to Dior, the closet was bulging with barely worn gowns, dresses, trouser suits. Fortunately for her, his taste was impeccable. Although she could easily have afforded the clothes herself, it seemed to give Julian so much pleasure to buy her quality garments. She accepted the gifts as gracefully as she could.

She pulled out two Valentino dresses, both in wool crêpe. One was long and sleeveless in a deep, daring crimson; the other was shorter, falling to an asymmetric mid-hem, in a delicate blush stretch-silk georgette. She held both against her. The midi dress was less dramatic. It seemed to suit a dinner party better. She would keep the red dress for another occasion. She looked down for a pair of shoes. Her eye fell on the simple black high-heeled sandals. They would do. She slid the wardrobe door shut, relieved, and headed to the shower. She had a whole briefcase of case notes to go through before the upcoming week's surgeries. No time like the present.

# 62

Jen picked up the neatly typed list and began to count. Solam's assistant had ringed a total figure at the bottom in bold red pen – 351 – but she wanted to make sure. 267, 268, 269, 270 . . . She mouthed the numbers silently to herself, checking the names as she went. She hardly recognized anyone, aside from her parents and Kemi and Julian, of course. The few people she'd met when she and Kemi first came to Johannesburg were no longer in her circle. Her circle was Solam. She put the paper down. She'd been back for nearly three years, although it was hard to tell what she'd actually accomplished by moving to South Africa, other than being with him. They couldn't have carried on like that, meeting every other month, for a day or a weekend at a time. She'd been so relieved when he suggested she move.

'But what'll I do?' she asked, as though it wasn't the question that occupied her every waking moment.

'Whatever you like. What are you doing here?'

'Nothing much,' she said, trying to appear nonchalant. 'I mean, it's not like it's a *career* or anything.'

'Well, there you go.'

'I could start painting again,' she said slowly. 'I've got my inheritance. I could do anything.'

'You don't need to worry about money,' Solam said, sliding

out of bed. 'Have you seen my phone?' he asked, his mind already moving ahead. Jen pointed to the floor.

She knew when to let a subject drop. Pushing him for an answer to a question he wasn't interested in simply didn't work. He just wouldn't allow it. He disliked what he called 'scenes'. 'It's no use shouting,' he said to her after one of their first proper arguments. She could no longer remember what it was about. 'We can talk about it later.' By then, she knew him well enough to know it meant they wouldn't talk *at all*. 'But I *need* to talk,' she would say to his disappearing back. No matter. He was gone.

Later, when he came back, he'd look at her sideways, as if to say, "Have you calmed down?" She hadn't, but there was little she could do. She learned quickly that there were boundaries in him that she simply couldn't cross.

She looked back at the list again. There were hundreds of acquaintances; people Solam knew mostly through political channels. There were precious few whom Jen would happily have chosen to spend an afternoon with, let alone her wedding day. She couldn't get over their surprise at the fact that she was white: 'Oh, you're *white*. I didn't realize.'

'What did she *mean*?' she'd asked Solam incessantly when she first moved in with him.

He shrugged. 'Exactly that. You're white.'

'No, it was the way she said it. Like it was . . . I don't know . . . some big disappointment or something.'

'Well, it probably is.'

'But why?' Yet he wouldn't answer. It was up to her to figure things out.

She tossed the list aside impatiently. It was a Saturday. Solam was at golf. The house was completely silent. The day stretched out in front of her, endlessly, without purpose. She looked around, half wishing Solam hadn't moved almost as soon as she arrived. She'd liked his loft in the centre of town, a floor above the noise and grit and drama of the street. Now they lived in leafy Parkhurst, behind six-foot razor wire and a wall thicker than any she'd ever seen. There was a patio off the master bedroom which was the only place you could see beyond the property walls. She often stood up there in the evenings before Solam got home, looking out over the hundreds of other identical properties with their countless security devices supposedly keeping them safe. The northern suburbs stretched as far as the eye could see, endless trees and manicured gardens. In the spring, the jacaranda trees burst into their annual spectacular lilac-and-purple haze. Someone had mentioned once that the city was home to the world's largest urban forest. From where she stood on the balcony in the spring and summer evenings, she could believe it.

She got up from the couch and walked to the kitchen. It had become something of a luxury to have the house to herself. During the week it was full of staff. There was a cook, a maid, a laundry lady and the gardener, as well as the two drivers who worked in shift rotation. Solam's job as an elected politician meant he was entitled to a bodyguard, but he'd shrugged it off. She was relieved. It was quite enough to have six people on call practically 24/7, let alone a team of bodyguards. Most of the people they employed were distant – *very* distant – relatives, he told her. It was part of the way things worked out here. Loyalty aside, there was 75 per cent unemployment in some areas . . . it was what well-off family members did, no questions asked. And there was certainly no question they were well-off. She actually had no idea how much money Solam earned. It was another area that was off-limits to her, not that she particularly cared. She had her own income and inheritance. But money was never an issue between them, never discussed. There was simply enough for whatever was required. In the first year, she went back to the UK four times. She simply told Solam when she wanted to go and his PA dropped off a business-class ticket for her without being asked. For Christmas the second year, they flew to Melbourne to see one of Solam's old university friends. They flew first class on Qantas Airlines and stayed in a suite at the Park Hyatt. 'Why would we stay anywhere else?' Solam asked, seemingly baffled by her question. 'What's the point?' For Jen, more accustomed to her father's Presbyterian approach to wealth management, it seemed almost decadent. It was surprising how quickly she'd acclimatized, she thought to herself with a wry smile. Aged thirty-two, she had more house help than her entire family combined.

She took out a bottle of San Pellegrino and slowly wandered upstairs. Perhaps she should go to yoga? Or the hairdresser's? She stopped to look at her hair in the mirror, flicking her ends up for closer inspection. No . . . any more hairdressing and it'd start to fall out. A massage? She nodded to herself. Yes, that sounded more fun. She'd book an afternoon's pampering at the Saxon, her favourite spa. Now, where had she left her phone? She went into the bedroom. It was lying on the bedside table. She picked it up and scrolled through until she found the number. 'No, there is nothing available at the moment, unfortunately, but there is a slot at one thirty. Could Madam come in at one?'

'Yes, sure . . . who's the therapist?' She knew them all by name.

'It'll be Marie, ma'am. What would you like to have done? We can do a full body, hot stone massage . . .' She ran through the options. Jen cast around for a piece of paper. There was a yellow Post-it pad lying next to the novel she'd been reading.

Solam must have left it by mistake. She tore off the first page and quickly scribbled the details. *Marie. Hot stone & apricot body scrub.* She hung up and picked up the note she'd torn off, turning it over. It was Solam's handwriting. *Hélène van Roux.* There was a mobile phone number, a time and an address. She looked at it for a moment, frowning. Hélène van Roux was the chairperson of the Democratic Party, the ANC's opposition. The two parties loathed each other. Why would Solam meet her? Nothing in politics was ever as it seemed but she preferred that to any other explanation. The thought did cross her mind from time to time. What was it Jimmy Goldsmith had said once? *When a man marries his mistress, he creates a job vacancy.* She pushed the thought away irritably. She replaced the note carefully on top of the pad.

# 63

Solam stood up and excused himself from the group of men who'd finished their round of golf. He walked away from them, reaching into his pocket for the note on which he'd scribbled Hélène's number that morning. It wasn't there. *Shit.* He swore under his breath. He could have sworn he'd stuffed the note in his pocket just before leaving. Hélène would be waiting for his call. He looked at his watch. It was nearly one. Home was a ten-minute drive away. He'd better go. The call was important. He jogged back through the clubhouse to the veranda.

'Gotta run,' he said to the assembled group. 'Wedding drama.'

There was a round of good-natured ribbing. Someone said something about marrying a white girl. 'That's what happens.' There was a guffaw of laughter. He nodded, smiling. 'Yeah, yeah, yeah.' He left them, still chuckling and shaking their heads, and hurried down to his car.

Fifteen minutes later, he pulled up outside the house. He left the car parked by the kerb and walked through the sliding gate. Jen's car was gone. She was probably at the gym or the mall. He unlocked the front door and ran upstairs to the bedroom. The note was lying where he'd left it, although it had clearly been torn off. He frowned. Jen must have used the pad after him. It was a silly slip. He dialled the number and ran downstairs again. In the kitchen, as the phone rang on the other end, he switched on the gas. He quickly burned the note, flushing the ashes down the drain.

'Hélène? Sorry I'm late. I got held up. Can we talk?'

The road to the secluded farmhouse was rutted and pitted with potholes and deep grooves, fissures in the earth that forced the vehicles to bump and sway drunkenly from side to side. Sitting in the back of the second Land Rover, Solam's arm kept banging painfully against the door as they advanced slowly over the terrain. They were deep in the Hottentots-Holland mountains, somewhere between Paarl and Stellenbosch. It was dusk and the rosy winter sun was sinking in a graceful arc behind the jagged profile of the highest peak.

They stopped at a pair of wrought-iron gates set into one of the thick white walls that the early Dutch settlers had built all across the valley to demarcate their farms. Two men got out of the car in front, speaking into their walkie-talkies. The sound carried across the silence, crackling in the frosty air. The gates swung open and the cars passed through, one by one.

'Nearly there.' The driver at the wheel of Solam's vehicle turned his head briefly. 'House is just up ahead. It's a fantastic view.'

Solam nodded. He peered out of the window. It was true. *God's country.* The forgotten schoolbook phrase came back to him. The winter-green vineyards spread outwards in rows around them, hugging the slope of the mountain, pushing towards the peak for the last possible reaches of arable land. The ploughed earth stretched away in fan-shaped waves, closing in on its own horizon. It was an intensely cultivated landscape, shaped, pruned and organized according to human whim. Only the rocky silhouette of the surrounding mountain peaks retained anything of the former wilderness. Whatever else, he thought to himself with half a smile, they were a plucky bunch, those first settlers. The vehicles pulled into a gravelled driveway, parking under huge oak trees planted a century before, providing a natural canopy to the farmhouse. The doors were opened and he stepped down onto the ground, his boots biting into the earth, making the sound of a biscuit breaking. Pieter Hofmayer, the party whip, walked ahead, going through the hallway first. He saw Hélène in the shadows. Tall, very upright, her silvery bob catching the light from inside.

'Solam,' she said as he walked in. She held out her hand. 'Welcome to Vrede en Himmel. Glad you could make it.'

The rest of the group left them alone in the small study off the main living room. It was warm inside. A fire had already been started in the fireplace in the centre of the room. He looked around as he sank into one of the two leather chairs that had been carefully positioned in front of it. There was a small coffee table between them. Someone had put out two crystal tumblers and a plate of oatmeal rusks.

'Would you like a drink?' Hélène asked, indicating the decanter.

He shook his head. 'After. If there's to be an after, of course.'

She smiled. 'Of course.' She sat down opposite him and leaned forward, clasping her hands between her knees. They began to speak, each giving way to the other at first, then growing more animated and heated as the minutes went by. An hour passed, then another. Every now and then, to ask a question or make a point, she tucked a loose curl of hair behind her ear, showing a flash of her discreet diamond ear-rings. Everything about the woman was discreet, but the discretion hid a steeliness that was matched only by his own. Yes, they were more alike than anyone would ever have guessed.

'So, let's talk timing. I've got another term ahead of me, but in about a year's time, we'll start looking for my successor. If you were to jump ship around that time, it'd give you enough time to start building your alliances. How will you do it?' she asked. 'Press announcement?'

He shook his head. 'No, it has to be more public than that.'

'What, then?'

He leaned forward. 'I'll cross the floor.'

She sat back. Neither said anything for a moment or two. She looked at him thoughtfully, reflectively. 'It'll certainly be public,' she said. She got up suddenly and walked towards the fireplace. She held out her hands to warm them, rubbing them briskly together.

'When's the wedding?' she asked, changing the subject.

'August.'

She came back to her chair. 'Good move. Glad you took my advice. She'll be an asset.'

'I hope so,' he said, smiling faintly.

She looked at him. 'Can I ask you something? You don't have to answer it, of course, but if we're going to work together, it'd be useful for me to know.'

'By all means.' He returned her frank stare.

'How long have you been planning this?' The question hung in the air between them for a few seconds.

'All my life.'

# 64

'Ma'am, do you have a moment?' Iketleng turned round. It was that pesky journalist from the *Mail & Guardian*. What the hell was his name? 'Ivor Kowalski,' he supplied helpfully, sensing her irritation. 'If I could just have a minute of your time,' he continued quickly.

She turned back to the assembled diplomats. 'Gentlemen, please excuse me for just one second.' She flashed an angry look across the room at her press officer. He ought to have made sure there were no journalists in the room. He returned her glare impassively. *Idiot*, she thought to herself. *What is the matter with him? Doesn't he know it's his job to stop incidents like this?* 'How can I help you,' she asked, as evenly as she could manage.

'What was your son doing—'

'Come now,' Iketleng interrupted him immediately, putting a hand on his arm and steering him out of earshot. 'This isn't the right place for this sort of conversation. Why don't you ring my office tomorrow morning? How did you get in here anyway? Come.' She gripped his arm more forcefully. They were almost at the door.

'Look, we both know you're not going to let me in tomorrow,' the journalist hissed. 'I'm just trying to corroborate— Hey! Get *off* me!' Two burly men had suddenly appeared as if out of nowhere.

'Deal with him, will you?' She quickly brushed the sleeve of her jacket down.

'Your son was seen with Hélène van Roux on Thursday,' the journalist hissed as he was roughly manhandled out of the door.

Iketleng stopped. She half turned in surprise, but the French Ambassador was walking towards her. She turned to face him with her professional smile firmly in place. 'Apologies, Mr Claudel. An unwelcome guest. Please, let's go in. No, after *you*.'


Oliver looked up from his side of the bed, peering at her over the rim of his glasses. 'What the hell is he thinking?' She burst into anger, freeing the waistband of her trousers and yanking her confining silk shirt over her head. He put his report down.

'It's probably nothing,' he said patiently, trying to calm her.

Her straightened hair broke loose from its combs as she flung her clothing onto the floor, every inch the raging child. 'How can you say that? What the hell was he doing with her, anyway?'

'Did you ask him?'

'No! How could I? Stuck with those diplomats all day!' She broke into their language, which was only ever the tongue of intimacy between them. 'If he's up to something, I'll kill him!'

'What could he possibly be up to?'

'How would I know? He says nothing these days! It's that woman, I tell you. She's put him up to something. How could he put us at risk this way?'

'Oh, Iketleng, please. Let's not go into that all over again.'

Anger made her ugly. 'Why not? You refused to speak to him about it when I asked you. No, when I *begged* you. Why not the Mashabane girl? What was wrong with her? Does he realize what sort of an asset she would have been? Instead, he takes this . . . this—'

'Iketleng!' Oliver raised his voice. 'Stop it! It's his choice. Not yours, not mine . . . *his*. We gave up the right to make those sorts of demands years ago. Leave it alone, I'm telling you.'

It only seemed to make her angrier. 'You're telling *me*? Since when do you tell me what to do, what to think?'

He switched back to their language again. 'That's not what I meant and you know it. I'm just saying leave it alone. There must be a good reason why he went to see Van Roux and he'll tell us about it in due course. Now, it's late. We both have to be up early tomorrow. For God's sake, let's sleep.'

She threw her nightdress over her head and tugged it down. She got into bed beside him, stiff with rage. 'I can't sleep,' she said angrily. 'I can't just forget about it, like you.'

'Listen, woman. Keep your mind focused on your own affairs. Leave our son to sort out his.' He reached across her and switched off the light. She lay in the dark beside him, her breath catching on angry sobs. She always cried when she was angry. What the hell was Solam up to? She hated being left in the dark about things. Especially things of this sort.

# 65

Jen and Kemi turned together to look at Jen's reflection in the long mirror. The gown was by Stella McCartney, from her very first collection. It had been flown out by courier and Iketleng had personally overseen the fitting with two of her trusted seamstresses. It was simple, yet beautifully elegant. Made of stretch-crêpe satin, it had long fluted sleeves and a flowing train, and it opened from the neckline to the waist at the back, skimming gracefully over Jen's milky white skin. With her hair teased into looping ringlets and simple gold jewellery, she looked beautiful. Solam was in black. It was hard to think of a more glamorous or photogenic couple. The newspapers and magazines would go wild.

Jen looked at Kemi. There was still an echo of shyness between them that would probably always be there, she thought wistfully. Kemi was wearing a short-sleeved red lace dress with a delicately scalloped hem. Her hair was long and straight, pulled back into a high ponytail, making her cheek-bones stand out even more. Her nails were scarlet to match and she wore a pair of strappy black high-heeled sandals. She too looked radiant. It was mid-August, and although the air was cool, the day was flooded with brilliant, clear sunshine. It was exactly the right sort of day for a wedding.

'Ready?' Jen asked, biting her lip.

Kemi nodded. 'Let's go down. They'll all be waiting.'

Jen stood up. In her silver high heels, she towered over Kemi. She put out a hand to steady herself. Kemi laid her own hand over hers. For a moment they stood in front of the mirror together: one short, one tall; one black, one white. There was a powerful uprush of feeling between them. Kemi squeezed her hand, hard. A strong sense of her own being flooded through her, leaving her trembling. Jen felt her eyes flood with tears, which she hurriedly blinked away. Then the moment passed and they walked out of the bedroom together.

The church was packed. There was standing room only at the rear. To address the imbalance between the bride and groom's respective guest lists, the wedding planners had done away with tradition and guests were seated according to importance, political to the last. Jen was passed from cheek to cheek, hand to hand, arm to arm, embrace to embrace. The ululating cries of Solam's relatives – the women – could be heard outside the church. Glasses were raised, flashbulbs went off, children cried. The wedding party moved slowly from the church to the cars for the short drive to the hillside Westcliffe Hotel where the reception would be held. There were government vehicles, press cars, diplomatic licence plates, and a vast assortment of sleek, luxury cars. As they got into the waiting vehicles, a passage opened up between the cars that swiftly flowed closed again.

'Happy?' Solam asked her.

She nodded. 'Very,' she whispered. She looked out of the window at the crowds still pressing against the sides of the Mercedes. So many people. It was hard to imagine they'd all come just for her and Solam. Even now she found it hard to grasp how important he'd become. She caught sight of her father, his snowy white hair blown across his reddened forehead. He was talking to Oliver and Iketleng, both shadowed discreetly by bodyguards. She craned her neck to see if Kemi and Julian were following in the car behind, but there were too many people in the way.

'Are *you* happy?' she asked him, carefully watching his profile.

He turned his head and his face came round full upon her. A muscle trembled slightly in his jaw. It was a movement she knew well. It came upon him in moments of determined decision making. 'Yes. This is only the beginning, Jen. You wait and see.'

# 66

'It went very well, don't you think?' Julian said, tugging at his belt to remove his trousers. They were finally back in their plush hotel room. It was past midnight by the time the driver had dropped them at the front door.

Kemi paused in the middle of unzipping her dress. She'd kicked off her shoes in the car and walked through the hotel lobby in her bare feet, dangling them by her fingers. 'She looked absolutely amazing,' she said, struggling to release the zip all the way down.

'Here, let me.' Julian walked over to help.

'Thanks.' She wriggled out of the dress and hung it up.

'*He's* a funny chap,' Julian continued, peeling off his trousers. He sat down on the edge of the enormous bed.

'What d'you mean?' Kemi called, walking into the bathroom.

'He looked as though he was on a stage the whole time, almost as though he couldn't let his guard down. I've never seen anyone so aware of being watched.'

Kemi appeared in the doorway, toothbrush in hand. 'People *were* watching him. They couldn't take their eyes off either of them.'

'He's got real political ambitions. He's looking to be president one day.'

'Who told you that?' Kemi asked, frowning.

'Overhead a few people talking.' He picked up his own toothbrush. 'That's the advantage of being a middle-aged, white foreigner,' he smiled. 'No one takes you seriously. You hear all sorts of things.'

She got into bed beside him. His arms went around her, as usual. He found it impossible to sleep without touching or holding her in some way. They lay in peaceful silence for a few minutes. She smiled to herself. She could almost feel him judging whether to make the now-familiar move that would lead to lovemaking. But they were both tired and a contented lassitude crept over them both. She drifted off to sleep.

The following morning, she went to Hyde Park to have brunch with Ayanda. She left Julian to spend the morning reading by the pool, which he was only too happy to do. A holiday was a rare and precious thing for a leading cardiologist. There was always some conference to go to, colleagues to see, patients to check up on. Jen and Solam had gone to the Seychelles for their honeymoon immediately after the wedding.

'Sorry I'm late,' Kemi apologized, sliding into the seat opposite her. Ayanda was in a white trouser suit with a crimson silk scarf knotted elegantly at the neck. 'There was a lot of traffic.'

'Worry not,' Ayanda smiled, pointing to the bottle of champagne nestled in the silver bucket beside her. 'I've been keeping myself busy.'

'It's so good to see you.' Kemi touched her hand. 'And before you say it, I know, I know. I'm rubbish at keeping in touch.'

'So am I. So, we're even. You look well,' Ayanda said, looking her over with a careful eye. 'Marriage obviously suits you.

How's Julian?' She had been at their Marylebone wedding, one of the few South African guests. The three doctors had got along so well together; Julian hadn't stopped talking about Ayanda for weeks afterwards.

'He's fine. Asleep by the pool, I imagine. It was quite some wedding.'

'You OK with it?' Ayanda asked, looking directly at her.

'Yes, of course, I am. Absolutely,' she said firmly.

'Well, good luck to her is all I can say. Let's see how long he keeps it zipped up.'

Kemi looked at her. 'Is he really that bad?'

Ayanda shrugged. 'What you've done once, you'll do again,' she said dryly. 'Anyway, enough about Solam Rhoyi. Tell me all about *you*. How's work? How's married life?'

Kemi picked up her champagne flute. 'It's fine,' she said slowly. 'No, more than fine. Julian's wonderful. He's good to me and he's good *for* me. I sometimes wonder what *I* bring to the marriage, you know. He's so successful in his field, everyone respects him—'

'Everyone respects you too, Kemi,' Ayanda said quietly. 'Don't underestimate yourself.'

'I'm not, I don't. It's just . . . it's just that he's so much older and more experienced than I am. He's lived a whole life before me. He's fifty-five . . . I wonder sometimes if he doesn't want more. He's talked about doing something here, setting up a clinic or something, but I think he's reluctant to tread on my turf, or at least that's the way he sees it.'

'So why don't you?'

'What?'

'Set up something here?'

'Oh, Ayanda, I don't know. I don't think he's serious about it, to be honest. And I'm not sure I want to live here. At least not now.'

'If not now, then when? You said it yourself. He's nearly sixty. Maybe he's waiting for you to make the first real suggestion. If you take the idea seriously, he's free to act.'

Kemi smiled. 'I've missed you,' she said quietly. 'No one sees things as clearly as you.'

'That's why I'm twice divorced, my dear,' Ayanda said with a wry smile. 'Now, how about some lunch? I can't remember the last time I had champagne on an empty stomach. Student days – and believe me, those are long gone.'

Julian was nowhere to be found when she got back to their suite. He wasn't at the poolside or in the restaurant, either. She frowned. It wasn't like him to disappear without saying anything. She walked back up the thickly carpeted stairs, trailing a hand along the bannister, just as she'd done at the house in Morningside as a teenager, mooching around with little to do. She picked up a novel from the bedside table – one of his; she rarely found time to read – and slipped into a white cotton sundress. It wasn't yet warm enough to swim, but the sun was strong and the sky cloudless. She would spend a couple of hours by the pool. They were due to visit her parents in Pretoria the following day. An afternoon by the poolside was just what she needed.

She woke to feel a rather chilly breeze wafting over her. She put up a hand to shade her eyes from the sun. It was sinking rapidly behind the building opposite. She glanced at her wristwatch. It was nearly five thirty! She'd been asleep practically all afternoon. She got up hurriedly, picking her discarded paperback off the ground and thrusting her feet into her flipflops. Surely Julian was back by now? She wondered why he hadn't come to the pool to find her.

She was on her way back up to the room when she heard

a burst of men's laughter coming from the bar behind reception. She paused. Wasn't that Julian's laugh? She listened for a moment. It was him. She turned and walked into the bar. He was sitting with someone.

'Darling,' he said, sliding off the bar stool as soon as he caught sight of her. 'There you are! I stopped by the pool but you were fast asleep. There's someone I'd like you to meet.' He turned to the man sitting next to him. 'This is Mitch Levinson. Mitch, this is Kemi, my wife.'

The man slipped off the stool and held out a hand. 'Pleasure to meet you, Mrs Carrick. Although I understand from Julian that you go by your professional name. A good choice. Your father's an excellent man.'

'Mitch heads up the endocrinology department at Sunningdale,' Julian said quickly. 'We met in Sydney last year.'

'Oh.' Kemi was surprised. He hadn't said anything about meeting anyone whilst they were in Johannesburg. 'Nice to meet you,' she said, shaking his hand.

'We're meeting a couple of Mitch's colleagues for dinner,' Julian said, quickly looking at his watch. 'Will you join us, darling?'

Both men were looking expectantly at her. 'Um, yes, of course. I'll just freshen up,' she said, looking down at her sundress.

'Of course. We'll be in the bar. They should be here around seven.'

'I'll see you then.'

She took a shower, standing with relief under the powerful hot blast and washing her hair. She tied it up in a knot, finishing it off with a long black silk scarf. She took a black-and-white striped cashmere sweater off the hanger and selected a pair of black palazzo-style pants. She kept her make-up to a minimum and slipped her feet into a pair of flat black sandals. She took a quick look in the mirror – she looked chic and business-like – and made her way downstairs.

They were still in the bar, having been joined by three other men, all doctors, all around Julian's age. She was introduced, one by one. They made their way to the table in high spirits and took their seats. It was funny, she thought to herself as she watched them talking and eating, pausing only to polish off three bottles of excellent red wine, how it only required the company of one female in a gathering to bring out the show-off in most men. Julian was positively preening. She suddenly felt very young and rather out of her depth. This wasn't about medicine at all, but about business. Trusts, investors, management, sites, partnerships. She slowly drank her glass of wine, listening with half an ear and wishing she were curled up in bed in their room, watching a film.

She suddenly became aware of Julian looking at her expectantly. 'Sorry,' she said, bringing her attention back to the conversation.

'D'you think you could?'

'I missed the question,' she said, mortified. She saw two of them men exchange a quick glance. 'What did you say, darling?' she repeated.

'We need a favour,' one of the doctors butted in. 'Julian here thinks it's inappropriate to ask, of course, but look, I'm just a boy from Benoni—' He broke off to much laughter from the others. 'And I don't mind asking a favour from time to time.'

'What's the favour? What could I possibly do for you?' she asked, puzzled. She looked quickly at Julian. It was hard to read his expression.

'We'll need governmental go-ahead,' he said, lowering his voice. 'Setting up a private clinic's not a straightforward thing.'

'Yes, but—'

'Let me put it to you like this,' one of the other doctors said quickly, signalling for another bottle of wine. 'We're in a bind here. First World know-how, Third World delivery. A question of misplaced ideology, if you will. Since this lot took over, I don't mind telling you, it's got worse.' Wine had loosened his tongue. He warmed to his theme. 'We've put together the best package you'll see this side of the Mediterranean, but we can't give the go-ahead until we've got ministerial sign-off.'

Julian was watching her closely, she noticed. She could feel the heat rising in her cheeks. 'What Mike's saying,' he said hurriedly, 'is that we're going to need a little *help* in getting to the right ears, that's all.'

Kemi looked straight at him. Her heart had started to pound faster. 'I know what he's saying,' she said shortly. 'I'm not stupid, Julian.' She stood up. 'I'm afraid you're wasting your time. I don't know anyone in government, least of all someone who's looking to make a cut.'

'No, that's not what—' Julian started to say.

Kemi didn't wait to hear what he was going to say. She got up and walked out of the restaurant.

Julian held his hands up as he entered the room a few minutes after her. 'I know, I know. I should have talked to you about it beforehand. I'm sorry.'

Kemi stood by the window, her arms wrapped tightly around her waist. 'That was insulting,' she said tightly. 'I can't believe you asked me to do that in front of your friends. I didn't even know you had any here!'

'Kemi, what do you want me to do?' Julian's voice was quiet. He sounded suddenly angry. 'Has it ever occurred to you why I'm doing this?'

She stared at him. 'I . . . I don't understand what you mean,' she said uncertainly. Julian seldom got angry.

He took a step towards her. His face was tight with some emotion she couldn't identify. 'I'm a senior consultant surgeon. I've worked for the NHS all my goddamn life. Do you know how much I earn?'

Kemi shook her head. It was one of the agreements between them when they married. Separate accounts, separate finances. She'd readily agreed to it; he was the one with experience of marriage, after all. She hadn't questioned it. 'No,' she said. 'You insisted on that, not me.'

'And did it ever occur to you why? Rosemary got everything. I *gave* her everything I had. I couldn't give her children, a family or any of the things she really wanted. All I gave her was heartache. It seemed the decent thing to do, to give her the house and the savings and all the rest of it. But it meant I came into this marriage with next to nothing. Did you ever stop to think about that?'

'How was I supposed to know? You never told me any of this!'

'You never asked!' He turned away and walked to the window. 'Yes, I know it wasn't phrased well. Mike's an idiot. But I want to leave *you* with something. There's absolutely nothing illegal about it. We'd be doing *exactly* what I do in the UK. No difference. Saving lives. But I'd be able to give you something, instead of watching everything I've worked for disappear down the drain.'

Kemi was speechless. The anger she'd felt was replaced by something else: a childish fear that she'd somehow done the wrong thing. 'I'm sorry,' she said hesitantly. 'I didn't think . . . it just didn't—'

He turned back to face her. 'You don't *have* to, that's the whole point. You've got your inheritance and your rich uncle.

You're thirty-two years old, for Christ's sake! You've got your whole life in front of you. I'll be retiring soon. Did you ever think about that?'

'Stop.' Kemi moved towards him. 'Stop, please. I'm sorry . . . I didn't realize . . .' She put a hand on his arm. She'd never seen him like this. His eyes behind the convex glare of his glasses were wet with tears. It produced an alarm in her that was equal to, if not greater, than her earlier rage. 'Don't,' she said, unable to bring herself to say it: *don't cry*. She put her arms around him. 'I'll do it, of course I will. Just tell me what you want me to ask.' She hugged him, pressing him to her tightly. The sound of him choking back tears was the most terrible thing she had ever heard.

If her father was surprised to receive a phone call from her early the following morning, he chose not to show it. 'Yes, of course. I'll tell security to expect you.' His voice for her was still the disembodied voice of Prisoner 49865, heard over crackling airwaves. The enormous gulf that lay between them would not – *could* not – be crossed.

She slowed down, trying to remember the way. Eridanus Street, then left onto Regulus Street . . . there it was. Sharp turn onto Grus Street, third house on the right. She parked the rented car under a jacaranda, not yet in bloom, and opened the door. From the top of Waterkloof Ridge she looked down onto the city. It was just past eight in the morning and the sun was already high in the cerulean sky. The house, unlike many in the street, was fenced rather than walled, and set deep into the property. There was a discreet guardhouse just behind the gate pillars. A uniformed guard stood up as she approached. He wrote down her name laboriously, concentrating on forming the letters, she saw with a pang of sympathy. His bulletproof vest and gun couldn't conceal a lack of schooling. He spoke into the walkie-talkie – a burst of unintelligible static – then motioned for her to walk up the path, alone.

Her father was waiting in the doorway. He was nearly seventy but he still stood tall and strong. He was wearing a cream woollen cardigan and slippers. It was a far cry from the formal attire of suit and tie which was all she'd really ever known of him. He smiled as she approached. She was struck by the similarity to her own smile, the face she saw each morning in the mirror. It was there in the upward flick at the edges of her mouth – his mouth too, she saw now.

'What brings you here so early?' he asked, standing aside to let her pass. 'Come in, come in. We weren't expecting you until lunchtime. Is everything all right?' The hallway was dark and a little cool. 'Shall we sit outside?' he asked gravely. 'It's chilly but the sun's out. Your mother's still getting dressed.'

She followed him through the house to the *stoep* at the back overlooking the teal-green pool. How different it must have been to the twenty-odd years he spent in prison, she thought with a pang. She had never asked him about his years spent in jail, first on Robben Island with the others, then at the prison outside Cape Town from where he and Mandela had been released. There was a section of the wide patio that was in sunlight. He led the way to a grouping of white wicker chairs with brightly coloured red gingham cushions. A bowl of roses sat squarely in the middle of the low table. It was the sort of domestic, feminine touch her mother would never have thought of. The bowl had been carried out by a housekeeper, no doubt. As if on cue, a woman's tread could be heard approaching the patio, high heels on the wooden floor. A woman appeared. She was wearing a powder-blue woollen dress with a string of pearls. Middle-aged, with a low bosom, sturdy calves. Light-skinned, with honey-coloured straightened hair.

'Can I get you anything?' she asked politely.

'No, I'm fine. Thank you.'

'I'll have a rooibos tea, please, Victoria.'

Kemi sat down opposite her father. He busied himself bringing out his pipe and lighting it, giving her time to compose her thoughts. Perhaps there was more between them than she thought, she realized with another sharp pang.

She slid the brochure Julian had given her towards him, across the glass table, moving the heavily scented roses out of the way. She quickly explained why she'd come. 'They're hoping to start construction next year,' she said. 'Julian says most of the money's in place.'

'I see.' He took his time, not hurrying her, the finger of one hand pressed into the fleshy pad of his cheek.

'The thing is, they need governmental approval before they can go any further. The Department of Health needs to grant permission for a private healthcare provider in any case, but in this one particularly, since there are no South African investors.' She looked at him. 'Julian's asked me to see what I can do.'

Her father nodded. 'You say "we",' he said, picking up the brochure. He flicked through the pages. 'Are you financially involved?'

'No, of course not. This is Julian's project. He just asked ... *I'm* just asking you if there's any chance you could ... well, put in a good word for them. Get it through. I know it's a lot to ask,' she said carefully.

He shook his head. 'On the contrary. You've never asked me for anything. Not once, not ever. I failed you as a father. I know that.' He put up a hand to stop her protesting. 'You've never reproached me. How can I refuse *you*, my child? My only child.'

# PART NINE
# 2004

### Three years later

. . .

Politics: A strife of interests masquerading as a
contest of principles. The conduct of public
affairs for private advantage.

AMBROSE BIERCE

# 67

He ended the call and put down his phone. The caller's words still reverberated in his ears. *It's on.* He interlaced his fingers and brought his palms together, flexing them, then cracking his knuckles, one after the other.

'Darling,' a voice interrupted him. He looked up. It was Jen. Her enormous, distended belly almost blocked out the rest of her.

'You all right?'

'I'm fine. Just tired. I just wish it would *happen*.' She looked down at her stomach. 'I'm popping out to the super-market. D'you want anything?'

He shook his head. 'No. Let the driver take you. I don't want you driving in your condition.'

'I'll be fine.'

'No. Ring Gumede and ask him to take you. I'm heading out in a few minutes.'

'Oh.' She looked crestfallen

'What's the matter?'

'I thought we were going to have supper together tonight. I was just going to go out and get some fish. I was going to cook; I've given Dora the evening off.'

'I can't. I've got a dinner tonight in Rosebank.'

'We haven't had dinner together—'

'Jen, I can't.' He stood up, gathering his papers together. 'I've got a meeting with the mayor in half an hour and I won't be home tonight. You'll just have to eat without me.'

'That's all I ever do,' Jen said quietly. 'I eat alone, I sleep alone . . . I practically *live* alone.'

He shrugged. 'What do you want me to do? I have to be there.'

'Oh, fuck the World Cup,' Jen said angrily. 'That's all anyone talks about these days. I'm sick of it!'

'Yeah? Well, I hate to break the news to you, sweetheart, but that's all *I* care about at the moment. Have you any idea what this means? What this means to us as a nation?'

'I don't *care*! Forget South Africa . . . what about *us*, Solam?'

'Jesus, Jen . . . you pick your moments, don't you? I'm the Minister for Youth and Sport. It's my *job* to care about it. Now, I know you're overwrought and—'

'Oh, go to hell, Solam!' She turned on her heel and lumbered into the hallway.

He stood with his hands on his hips and blew out his cheeks in frustration. It was those two friends of hers – what were their names? Sasha, and the other one whose name he could never remember. That Sasha had a mouth on her like no one he'd ever met. A real ball-breaker. Jen had spent the first three years in Johannesburg complaining she had no friends and now, thanks to the two of them, she seemed to have more friends than sense. Thick as thieves, those three. Although you had to admit that Sasha looked good. Better than good, actually. She looked like one of those women who'd give as good as she got in bed. She was some combination. Honey-coloured skin, high cheekbones, black, black eyes and lips that looked stung all the time, thick and full. He stopped himself. He was smart enough not to let it show but

Jen repulsed him at the moment. She'd had three miscarriages in the past five years, leaving her thinner than she'd ever been. Now, with that huge bulge, she looked almost grotesque. Not what he *ought* to be thinking about the mother of his unborn child, he knew, but what was he supposed to do? He was scared to look at her stomach, never mind touch it.

His phone vibrated dully on the desk. He picked it up, relieved to have something other than his wife's body to think about. 'Hello?'

'Solam? It's me, Manny.'

He glanced at the doorway. Jen was nowhere to be seen. 'What's up?' he asked carefully.

'Ready when you give the word, boss. The driver will pick you and the guys up after dinner. They'll be in the basement parking lot. Silver Jaguars. Three of them. Cape Town plates.'

'Cool. Thanks.' He ended the call. He looked at the clock on his desk. It was 9.30 a.m. in Johannesburg. 10.30 a.m. in Zürich. They were expecting the announcement at noon. There was one more person he needed to see before he saw the mayor.

# 68

Jen lay on the pillows and put her hand over her mouth to stop herself from screaming out loud. She could hear the front door open and shut and seconds later, the throaty roar of Solam's car starting. Tears were leaking from her eyes. She slid her hand down to her stomach. She felt wretched. She shouldn't have sworn at Solam like that. It was pointless. All it did was get his back up. She could feel the baby kicking hard. He was probably feeling as miserable as she was. She levered herself upright. The sound of his engine died away as he sped down the road. She swung her legs out of bed with difficulty. There was a heavy, leaden feeling in her stomach that was new. She put a hand out to steady herself and stopped. She pulled her hand away. It was wet. She opened her mouth to shout for someone – anyone – but a wave of pain ripped through her, leaving her breathless. She gulped in a mouthful of air. The baby wasn't due for another two weeks! She tried to stand up but the pain hit her again like a jackhammer. She tried to remember everything she'd been told . . . *Breathe, breathe, breathe!* She staggered upright, trying to get to her phone. She'd left it downstairs on the kitchen table. She turned to look at the bed. It was soaked, but there was blood too. It was happening again. She'd managed to carry this one almost to full term but it was happening again.

'Dora!' she screamed, calling for the maid. She'd given her the day off but, please God, please let her be in. 'Dora!' she shouted again. '*Dora!*' There was no answer. She staggered to the doorway, holding on to it for dear life as the waves of pain began to intensify. Her abdomen felt as though it was caught in a vice, tightening to the point where she thought she would pass out, then stopping as abruptly as it started. She edged closer to the stairs. All she could think about was her phone. There was no landline in the house. 'What's the point?' Solam had said. 'Between us we've got about five mobile phones. Why bother? It'll only take Telkom a year to install it.' Christ, she wished she hadn't listened to him. She lurched forwards, grabbing the bannister. Another wave hit. She bellowed like an animal in pain, holding her breath until it passed. She put a foot out, trying to get up. Then she lost her footing and slipped.

# 69

He drove fast, aware of the hard knot of excitement in his belly. He reached Grayston Drive but instead of merging onto the freeway, he turned right, heading for Randburg. He looked at the clock. It was nine fifty. If he put his foot down, he'd be there in forty minutes. Just enough time to close the deal and get back to the mayor's office by noon. He touched the accelerator and the Mercedes C-class S63 responded immediately. He grinned. Nothing like a Mercedes to get you from A to B in a hurry.

Exactly forty minutes later, he pulled into the airport parking lot and looked around. At the end of the second row, a pair of hazard lights flashed once. He moved forward slowly. Row 3C of the Lanseria Airport parking lot was almost empty. He got out of his car and slipped into the back seat of the car next to his, breathing fast.

'Any news?' she asked, her distinctive profile showing as she looked straight ahead.

'It's ours,' he said. 'We won. Announcement's due at noon. I'm heading to the mayor's office now and from there it'll be press conferences all afternoon.'

She looked at him, nodding slowly. Her eyes were shining. 'So, here it is. *Finally.* I should have brought some champagne.'

'Later. Let's get the announcement out and take it from there.'

'And you're sure about this? No possibility of a mistake?'

'No, our man's solid.'

'And the other thing?' she asked, her eyes narrowing. 'You sure it's a good decision?'

He shrugged. 'What did Churchill say? "It's the worst possible option except for all the others." These sorts of things are never good or bad. It's never that simple. I'm thinking early next year. February, once everyone's back from summer recess.'

'So, we have a deal.' She held out her hand.

He took it. Her touch was firm. 'We do.'

'I'll see you in February,' she said briskly. 'I'd better go. My flight leaves any minute.'

'Yes, ma'am.' He gave her a mock salute. 'See you in February.'

'Solam?' She paused, her hand on the door. He looked up. 'Don't call me "ma'am". Makes me feel ancient.' She closed the door behind her with a snap. He smiled. Hélène van Roux was a class act. Ahead of him, the driver sat impassively. Solam got out of the car and headed back to his own. He flexed the fingers of both hands. The game was on. He fucking *loved* it.

By the time dinner ended, most of the men at the table were somewhat the worse for wear. Celebrations had begun the minute Sepp Blatter opened the sealed envelope at the FIFA HQ in Zürich and uttered the two words that changed everything: '*South Africa!*' The room erupted in deafening cheers. Six thousand miles away, President Mbeki held up the trophy, flanked by FIFA officials and senior statesmen. To describe the scene as euphoric would have been an understatement. The cameras rolled, soundbites were delivered, promises were made. It was an afternoon unlike any other.

Solam escorted the group of eleven men to dinner where the drinking continued, and from there to the parking lot where the cars were waiting, exactly as Manny had said that morning. It was a short ride to the club in Sandhurst.

'Where are you taking us, Solam?' one of the men slurred as they headed out.

'Somewhere fun. Don't worry, it'll go on all night.'

There were sniggers from the back seat. They were an assortment of prominent local and international businessmen, politicians and FIFA executives. Solam's instructions were clear: *take them out, show them the time of their lives and lay the groundwork*. He was good at all three. As the cars pulled out of the Hyatt parking lot, he felt his phone vibrate against his thigh for the umpteenth time that night. He pulled it out. There were eleven missed calls from Jen and three from an unknown caller. He glanced at the screen, then tucked the phone away. He didn't feel like dealing with a hysterically apologetic Jen right now. He'd deal with her in the morning. And he didn't take calls from unlisted numbers. Rule #1 of politics.

The girls were everything Manny had promised, and more. Solam led the way in. The tall blonde who held the door open was beyond perfection. She was wearing a white silk sheath slit all the way to her pelvis, and there wasn't a stitch of clothing underneath.

'Good evening, gentlemen. Welcome. May I take your jackets?' She had one of those theatrically Eastern European accents – Russian, Ukrainian, Czech, it was hard to tell, not that it mattered. They weren't there for the conversation. She handed their jackets one by one to a bevy of beauties who were standing by – brunettes, redheads, blondes; black, white, dark-skinned, light-skinned, milky white, Asian. Some of the girls were wearing next to nothing; others were masked, wearing leather. Solam felt his own pulse begin to race. He drew in a deep breath to steady himself. For once he wasn't here to enjoy himself. He looked around discreetly. 'She'll give you a sign,' Manny had said. 'She knows what you look like. Just wait for her.'

'Hi.' Someone spoke directly behind him. He whirled around. He was face to face with a girl with long, jet-black hair wearing nothing but a black thong and a lacy bra through which her nipples could clearly be seen. 'I'm Clara.'

He nodded cautiously. 'Hi.'

She brought up a cigarette to her face. 'Got a light?'

He reached in his pocket for a lighter. She cupped her hand around his. Her face was inches from his own. 'I'm the photographer,' she said quietly. 'Manny's told me what to do.' She stepped back. 'Thanks,' she said, twirling her fingers. 'See you around.' She walked off, her perfectly rounded buttocks shuddering lightly as she went. He was sweating, he realized. He walked over to the bar and ordered a soda water.

'Plenty of ice, plenty of lime. I'm driving,' he added, as the brunette behind the bar slid the drink in front of him.

'Pity,' was her only comment.

He turned around. His cock was throbbing. He looked at his watch. It was nine thirty. By midnight it would all be over. His phone vibrated again. He reached into his trouser pocket. Another unknown caller. He switched it off.


It was nearly two thirty in the morning by the time he was dropped back at the Hyatt where his car was parked. As he walked towards it, he kept fingering the memory card tucked safely in his left trouser pocket. Insurance. He opened the door and slid into the driver's seat. The familiar smell of leather and cigarette smoke washed over him. He started the engine and leaned his head against the headrest for a moment. Christ, he was tired. He pulled his mobile out of his pocket and switched it back on. His heart missed a beat. Six of the last calls had been from his mother's private mobile phone. He stared at the screen, then pressed call.

She answered on the second ring. 'Where the *hell* have you been?' she shouted.

'Ma? What's wrong? I've just got into my car. I was out with the mayor. What's the matter?'

'You'd better get here fast. I'm at the hospital in Sandton. You have a son.' She hung up the phone.

He tore out of the parking lot, tyres squealing. It couldn't be! Jen wasn't due for two weeks! A son! Those were her words. *You have a son!* He had a son!

# 70

Jen couldn't take her eyes off him. He was perfect. She had never in her life been so relieved when she heard his first cry. She'd thought she'd lost him. No, much worse than that, she feared she'd *killed* him. She still didn't know how it had happened. One minute she was standing on the landing looking down the stairs, next minute she'd started to fall. She'd had two stiches to the gash above her eyebrow and three to her lip where she'd hit the stairs going down. One side of face was swollen and already turning purple, and her wrist was badly sprained but she felt nothing. Her only thought as she was falling was, *Let the baby be all right!* Now, as she sat propped up in bed with pillows all around, her mother-in-law on one side and the baby on the other in one of those funny little cots, all she could see or think about was the tiny creature lying on his back, swaddled so tightly it was a miracle he could breathe. Her wrist hurt too much to hold him, so Iketeng had been the first to touch him. She'd arrived at the hospital in a blaze of sirens and bodyguards, running down the corridor to the suite where Jen lay recovering, an hour after surgery.

'Where is he?' She could hear Iketleng's urgent voice outside the room. The door opened and she stood in the doorway, bangles tinkling against one another, her brilliant headscarf blocking out the light. Jen tried to sit but the nurse laid a warning hand on her shoulder. Iketleng's attention slid from Jen to the cot. There was no sound other than her heels crossing the floor. 'Can I hold him?' she asked the nurse.

It was on the tip of Jen's tongue to protest, to say, 'I haven't held him yet,' but she stopped herself. Iketleng picked him up carefully, peering into his tiny, still-squashed face.

'He's perfect,' she whispered, and in that instant, Jen would have forgiven her anything. 'Absolutely perfect.' She turned to look at Jen. Her second question was not so gentle. 'Where the fuck is my son?'

# 71

Iketleng looked at him over the rim of the plastic coffee cup. Neither spoke for a few moments. Then she got up and walked to the sink. She poured the rest of the undrinkable liquid down the drain and turned to him.

'Your marriage is your business, Solam, not mine or your father's. Fine. We couldn't get hold of you. You tell her whatever you have to tell her, but let *me* tell you something.'

Solam lifted his head. 'It's not what you think,' he began slowly.

'How do you know what I think?' she snapped at him. 'Like I said, your marriage is not our business. But politics is. If you do *anything* to jeopardize either your father or me, *in any way*, I will personally destroy you. Do you understand me? I've been in politics since I was thirteen. I've been banned. I've been put under house arrest. My life has been threatened. I've been jailed. I am afraid of nothing. Do you understand me? *Nothing.*' She stopped and poured herself a cup of water. She took a few sips, then continued. 'But I have *never* been betrayed. *Never*,' she hissed. 'If I find out that you've done something I cannot condone, I *swear* I will destroy you.'

'That's not it, Ma.' Solam cut her short. He pushed back the chair and stood up. 'I told you. The announcement came out, I was with the mayor all afternoon, and then I had to take a visiting delegation to dinner. I left my phone in the car. She wasn't due for another couple of weeks . . . I thought it was fine. I'm sorry, Ma, honestly.'

Iketleng said nothing. She drained the cup and set it back on the rack. 'All right.' She looked at her watch, then at her son. He looked shattered. Her voice softened. 'Go in there. Look after your wife and *my* grandchild, you hear me? Nothing else matters for now. I'll get someone to come in and stay with her for the next couple of months . . . one of the aunties from home.'

'No need, Ma, we'll manage. Everything's going to be fine, I promise.'

Iketleng shook her head. 'Have you forgotten who I am? I'm your *mother*, Solam. I also gave birth. Do you know where your father was when you were born?' He shook his head. 'In jail. I was completely alone. The bastards wouldn't give my own mother permission to visit me. So, I know what she's going through. You've got enough on your plate at the ministry. I'll find someone in the morning. No argument.'

Solam nodded. They looked at each other. She looked as though she wanted to hug him but physical contact had never been their way – there was too much space, time and distance between them. She picked up her handbag instead.

'Thanks, Ma,' he said softly as she opened the door.


He let the driver take the wheel. He was so tired he could barely move. Jen and the baby were being kept in hospital for a few days. 'Routine,' the doctor said briskly. 'After a C-section we normally keep them in for a couple of days, but especially in her case with the fall and everything. She's doing fine. First one, is it?'

He glanced at the clock on the dashboard. It was nearly

8 a.m. He'd go home, grab a couple of hours' sleep and then go into the office. Everyone would understand. It was unlikely it would make the news, but with the announcement of South Africa's winning bid the day before, his ministry would come under more attention than usual; perhaps some keen journalist would pick it up. It would be better to hold off on a press statement until Jen was in better shape. It wouldn't look good. All those bruises and that ugly gash above her eye. Someone might misconstrue it. He suddenly remembered. The pictures. He slipped a hand into his pocket; the memory card was still there. He relaxed, settling himself more comfortably in the plush leather seat. He closed his eyes.

The house was silent apart from the occasional sound Dora made downstairs as she went about her daily cleaning routine. The chink of the dishwasher; the 'beep-beep' of the washing machine, the greedy suctioning gasp of the vacuum cleaner . . . the sounds drifted in and out of his consciousness as he studied the photographs on his laptop. They were all there. Mvusi. Mthembu. Lahoud. Petersen. Dlulane. He flicked through the images, one after the other. Then he closed the file, ensuring it hadn't been copied anywhere on his hard drive. He got up and walked to the closet. At the back was his safe. He put the envelope in and slid it to the back. He closed the door, changed the code, just to be sure, and shut the wardrobe door. He walked into the shower and quickly disrobed. Time to move on with his day.

# 72

*It'll get easier. I just have to wait. That's what the doctor said. It will get easier.* She repeated the words to herself every morning as she walked to the cot where Euan lay. He was sleeping now. She stared down at him, wondering where the euphoria that she'd felt only weeks before at the very sight of him had gone. In the first few days, she'd been unable to do anything other than stare at him. His perfect features; tiny flared nostrils, dark black eyes just like Solam's, tiny pursed lips already set in an obstinate line. He had her father's wide cheekbones and his slender, elegant fingers, even as a month-old baby. She couldn't see anything of herself in him but perhaps that was because he was male? No one said, 'Oh, he looks so much like you!' It was all 'Solam this' and 'Solam that'. Even naming him had been a battle. Iketleng seemed to think he'd be given a Xhosa name by automatic right.

'Lebohang,' she'd said firmly. 'It means "gift" in our language.' She'd looked to Solam for confirmation.

'I'm not naming him *that*,' Jen said, clutching him to her as though Iketleng might take him away from her by force.

She'd seen the look that passed between mother and son. 'We'll talk about it later,' Solam said, stepping in to stall an argument.

'No, we won't. I'm giving him a normal name.' It was the wrong thing to say, of course. She saw from the look Iketleng threw her that it had come out wrong. 'I mean, a Christian name.'

'And what makes you think Lebohang isn't a Christian name?' Iketleng could be terrifying when she went all quiet.

'I'm sure it is, but I'd rather have a Scottish name.'

'Scottish?' Iketleng pronounced the word as if it were blasphemous.

'Let's talk about this later,' Solam interjected again. 'We don't have to decide now.'

'Why do you never stand up for me?' Jen said to him later when Iketleng had finally gone home. 'You always do what *she* says; you go along with every goddam thing *she* suggests. He's *my* baby!'

'Jen, you're being irrational. It's only normal that she wants a say.'

'Normal? By whose standards? It's not normal at all! He's *our* child – we should be the ones to name him, not her!'

'And I want to name him Lebohang,' Solam said, his voice suddenly going cold.

'Well, you can't!' She stared at him. 'You can't!' She could feel herself getting hysterical. 'I won't let you!'

'Stop it, Jen.'

'No, I won't! I won't be told what to do like some naughty child! You're not naming him . . . wh-what are you doing? Get *off* me. You can't—'

'Give him to me.' Solam was standing over her. 'You need to take a nap. Give him to me. You'll make him cry.'

'I won't. Solam, no . . . please . . . no, *don't*.' She tried to stop him prising the baby out of her arms but she was afraid she'd hurt him so she handed him over. 'I'll stop . . . I promise, I'm—'

'Auntie Gladys?' Solam strode to the bedroom door with the baby in his arms, flinging it open. The baby started to cry.

'Yêbo.' Auntie Gladys must have been practically at the door. She took the child from him and disappeared. 'Hai, hai . . . wena, wena,' she cooed at him in Xhosa. 'Shhh. Stop crying.'

'Pull yourself together, Jen,' Solam said, his hand on the door. 'For God's sake.'

She sat down on the edge of the bed, too drained to speak. She had to speak to someone, anyone. As much as she hated to admit it, Kemi was the only person she could turn to. She picked up the phone.

# 73

'I . . . I don't feel *anything*,' Jen sniffed. 'That's the whole problem. I'm just numb. I look at him . . . there's nothing. I don't seem to have any feelings for him at all.'

Kemi nodded. Jen needed more than a shoulder to cry on. She needed medication. Citalopram or Prozac. And fast. 'How long have you been feeling like this?' she asked gently.

'I don't know,' she said, beginning to cry again. 'It feels as though it's always been this way.'

'Are you breastfeeding?' Kemi asked.

'I tried, but he wouldn't latch on properly. Auntie Gladys said I'd better stop.'

'Who's Auntie Gladys?'

'She's a relative of Solam's. His mother sent her to help with the baby as soon as he was born. She's with him now. She won't let him out of her sight.'

Which was surely part of the problem, Kemi thought to herself. 'Jen, I'm going to prescribe something for you. You won't have to take it for long . . . six months, probably not longer. But it's important you do, d'you understand?'

'Pills?' she said slowly, almost disbelievingly. 'You're going to make me take *pills*? I'm not taking them! I won't!' She sounded on the verge of hysteria.

Kemi gripped the phone. 'Jen . . . it's fine. It's going to be fine. You're not well. There's nothing to be afraid of. You are not your mother. The circumstances are just not the same, d'you hear me? You are *not* your mother. There's no danger of you becoming addicted or going mad, or whatever it is you're afraid of. You're in more danger if you *don't* get help.'

'Wh-what if I can't stop?' Jen asked, her teeth chattering. 'What if . . . what if I—'

'You *will* stop,' she said, cutting her off quickly. 'Just as soon as you start to get stronger. Trust me, Jen. You know I'd never do anything to hurt you. You know that, don't you?'

'I know,' she whispered. 'I'm the one who hurt *you*, Kemi. I'm so sorry. I think about it all the time. I think about what I did and I don't know what to say.'

Kemi was quiet for a moment. 'Where's Solam?' she asked carefully.

'I don't know,' Jen said weakly. 'I never know where he is.'

And that, too, was another part of the problem, Kemi thought. *Dear God, don't let Ayanda be right.*

She phoned the prescription through to the pharmacy and then quickly called Ayanda. 'I prescribed Citalopram. I don't think she's strong enough to get over this without it.'

'Yes, sounds right. What does the husband say? Or doesn't he notice?'

'We didn't really talk about it,' Kemi said, trying not to sound evasive. 'I know he's busy. There seems to be so much *noise* around the World Cup lately.' She trailed off. It was true. Every day seemed to bring forth new allegations of bribes and pay-offs, backroom deals and contracts that couldn't be explained.

'Well, you know what they say,' Ayanda commented dryly. 'Follow the money.'

'Oh, no, I don't think so,' Kemi said hurriedly. 'Solam's never been mentioned in that way. It's just his office. Besides, he doesn't need the money. They have plenty.'

'If you say so. Well, I think you've done the right thing. Where did you send the script?'

'Dis-Chem in Rosebank. I'll ask Julian to pick it up and I'll take it to her myself. Now, when are you coming over? We're only here for another week.'

'Friday? I'll leave work early.'

'Perfect. Julian wants to cook for you.'

Ayanda chuckled. 'A husband who *wants* to cook? Never heard of such a thing.'

Kemi hung up the phone just as Julian walked into the kitchen. They were staying in a guesthouse in Parkhurst for a month whilst they moved ahead with plans for the clinic. She pulled a quick, sympathetic face. 'That was Jen,' she said, turning up her cheek for a kiss. 'She's having such a rough time of it.'

'What's wrong? Baby blues or something more serious?' He opened the fridge door and pulled out a beer.

'I think it's serious. She seems done in. From the sound of it, Solam's too busy to pay much attention.'

Julian shrugged. 'He's certainly a busy man. Have you been following the news since we got here?'

'It'll die down. My mother said it's what always happens after that sort of announcement.'

'Meaning?'

'Oh, you know, the minute oil's discovered, or a new mineral's been found, everyone gets over-excited. People start seeing dollars where there aren't any. The World Cup's the same. Everyone thinks they're going to get rich all of a sudden.'

'From a *football* tournament?' Julian smiled faintly. 'They'd do well to look at history. I don't think there's a single city that made any money after one of those sporting events. Beats me why they even bother.'

Kemi pulled a face. 'Prestige. Glory. Tourism. It'll be the first time Africa's ever hosted one of those. *I* think it's good news.'

'Yeah, well, good job you're not looking to boost your pension. Speaking of which, we're close to finishing the first phase. And that, my dear,' he said, pointing at her with his half-empty bottle, 'means you and I have to go on a charm offensive.'

She rolled her eyes. '*More* money?'

'Clinics cost money,' he said. 'But don't worry. We'll get what we need.'

'How can you be so sure?'

'I'm yet to meet an investor who can resist you, my darling. Never mind your qualities as a surgeon, you're one hell of a fundraiser. And d'you know why that is?'

She shook her head. 'Go on, tell me,' she said dryly.

'Lust. Best fundraising tool there is. Trust me, they're all lusting after you.'

'You're full of shit,' she laughed, smacking away his hand. 'Seriously, though, she sounds almost hopeless.'

'Isn't that just Jen?' Julian asked carefully. 'You've said it yourself. She just seems to go from crisis to crisis.'

Kemi sighed. 'I know. But I suppose *I* feel responsible.'

'How?'

'Well, if it weren't for me, she wouldn't have met Solam.'

'That's the most absurd thing I've ever heard you say. She betrayed you, remember? *You're* not responsible for her choices. *She* is. She's an adult. She needs to behave like one.'

Kemi looked at him in surprise. 'I thought you liked Jen?'

'I do. But she's managed to get away with some pretty

Soul Sisters

questionable behaviour over the years. The whole "silly old me" routine, it was fine when you were in your twenties, but it just doesn't cut it now.'

'Julian,' Kemi said carefully, 'that's not fair. Jen's . . . she's different, that's all.'

'Sure. But I still don't see why you feel the need to take responsibility for her, that's all I'm saying.'

Kemi was quiet for a second. She bit her lip. 'It's complicated,' she said finally. 'She'll be all right. I'll get her started on Citalopram for now . . . when she's a bit more stable, we might recommend counselling. Sounds as though things are a bit rocky at home.'

Julian grunted. 'Can't say I'm surprised,' he said.

Kemi sighed. 'No one's pointing a finger at him, though. It's people around him.'

'That's how these things always start, Kem. Bit of smoke, a few sparks, and next thing you know there's a raging inferno and everyone goes down. Where there's money to be made, corruption follows. It's human nature.'

Kemi gave a short laugh. 'Funny, that's exactly what Ayanda said. "Follow the money."'

'Well, she's right. It's simple enough. If you follow drugs, you'll find a dealer. If you follow crime, you'll find a criminal. Trouble with money, though, is you've no idea *where* the fuck it'll lead.'

Kemi laughed. It was so unlike Julian to swear. She put her hand out to catch his. 'I love you the most when you swear,' she said, giggling.

He brought her hand up to his lips. 'And I love you the most when you're worried,' he replied. He brought his other hand to her face, smoothing the line that had appeared between her eyes. 'You get this little indentation, right here. I just want to keep on stroking it away.'

LESLEY LOKKO

She closed her eyes. His touch was light, almost feathery. He cupped her face in his hands and began to kiss her. It had been a while since they'd made love. His hands slid down her body, her own already busy unfastening the belt that held his trousers. It was quick and urgent and all the more pleasurable for it. He was uncharacteristically forceful, entering her roughly, and she could feel his excitement mounting with every stroke. He came with a short, strangled gasp, his whole body shuddering in delight. They lay in the tangled heap of clothing like two teenagers, panting for breath.

The faint buzzing of a phone dragged them both out of their late afternoon sleep. Kemi struggled to open her eyes and focus. The room was dark. She'd left the phone on the kitchen counter. She got up groggily and walked through to grab it before it woke Julian. It was the pharmacy. The prescription was ready.

'Who was that?' Julian mumbled, coming awake.

'It's Dis-Chem in Rosebank. I'll go over and pick it up.'

Julian shook his head. 'No, let me do it. You get ready for dinner. I'll book somewhere nice.'

'OK, I'll be ready when you get back.' She blew him a kiss and rolled off the bed. He stretched out a hand to grab her as she passed but she was already gone.

He pulled into the parking lot on Cradock Avenue, a block away from the mall. He fancied a short walk. His body felt supple and he was completely at ease in himself. He pulled out the note she'd scribbled. *Dis-Chem, 1st floor. Ask for Busewe.* He tucked it into his jacket pocket and reached for the door handle. It happened so fast he didn't even have time to react. A hand appeared in the window and grabbed his collar.

'Phone. Gimme the phone.'

'What the—?'

'Give it.' The hand holding him by the throat gave him a sharp shove.

'Phone? What phone?' He was genuinely confused. His phone was in his pocket.

'You was looking at it. Get out.'

There was another man standing behind him. Everything he'd ever read about how to behave in a mugging went out the window. His brain went into overdrive. Stay calm? Shout? Threaten? Obey? He simply couldn't remember.

'Get out!' The man holding him seemed as though he would drag him out through the window by force. He yanked the door open from the inside.

'I'm getting out, I'm getting out.' He put up his hands and did so. The night air was cool and sharp. His heart was thudding with fear. 'Just . . . just take it easy,' he said to the man still holding him. A sour smell came off him, sweat mixed with something else . . . weed. He swallowed. They were young. The man was jumpy, nervous. The street lights were off and the parking lot was shrouded in darkness. He should have noticed as he drove in. *Idiot, idiot!* He turned his head quickly to look at the booth where the attendant usually sat: it was empty.

'Don't look! Give the *fokken* phone!' The man spat the word forcefully, tightening his grip. His accomplice behind him said something in their language; his voice was panicked.

Julian put a hand in his trouser pocket to retrieve the phone and then he heard a shout behind him. He felt his knees go weak. A passer-by had noticed the tussle.

'Hey! Hey you!' Another man's voice. He shouted again, a

stream of unintelligible words in the same language as his attackers. There was a sudden flurry of movement. He felt his phone being snatched out of his hand and they bumped him, hard. He heard the scuffle of feet, footsteps running towards him as well as away. He turned in relief. His saviour ran towards him. It was a security guard from across the road. '*Ekskees mynheer*,' he began in Afrikaans. Julian recognized the words, if not their meaning.

He waved him away. 'No, I'm English. I don't . . .' He stopped. There was a dreadful shortness of breath in his chest, as though the air was slowly going out of him. He clutched a hand to his heart. He felt the stickiness and looked down in horror. Blood was seeping from his shirt.

'You hurt?' The security guard looked at him in alarm.

'I . . . I think . . . I've been stabbed,' Julian gasped. He felt his knees giving way, properly this time. He fell against the open car door, shutting it with his body, sliding down slowly towards the ground. 'Get me . . . help.' He forced the words out, even as he knew. The blade had penetrated his abdominal aorta. He knew what was happening to him. 'I need . . . help.'

# PART TEN
# 2004

## A month later

. . .

Do not fear death so much, but rather
the inadequate life.

BERTOLT BRECHT

# 74

The funeral service was held in England, at the local village church in Almondsbury, near Bristol, where Julian had grown up. Kemi stood at the graveside, too numb with shock and grief to speak. Both his parents were buried in the same parish; it was the only thing she could think of to do. *Get him home.* Rosemary came to the funeral, along with colleagues from all the hospitals where he'd worked, including the four clinic directors who'd flown from Johannesburg with her and Julian's body, stored at 2°C in the plane's hold, many feet below.

No one knew what to say. They stood huddled in small groups, breaking apart to admit a newcomer, closing ranks when they'd gone. Kemi moved among them like an automaton, unable to make eye contact or sustain a conversation beyond the usual mindless utterances. *I'm so sorry for your loss. I hope you're bearing up. What a shock.* It was Rosemary who said what should have been said.

'What a waste,' she murmured, coming to stand beside her as they made their way back to the church. 'What a fucking senseless waste.'

Kemi turned to look at her. She'd come with her new husband, a kindly, bespectacled man, a professor of history, something like that. The introductions had sailed over her head. Rosemary's hair was short now, and she'd gained weight since the divorce, which was when Kemi had last seen her. They'd never had much to do with one another, Kemi steering clear out of a sense of guilt. 'Th-thank you for coming,' she said, her voice still hoarse. She'd damaged her throat screaming when the news was brought to her, or so Ayanda told her.

'I shouldn't say this, not now,' Rosemary said suddenly, impulsively. She put a hand on Kemi's arm. 'He loved you. Properly, I mean. And he was happier with you than I ever knew him to be.'

Kemi swallowed painfully. She couldn't speak. They were almost at the parish door. The vicar's wife had organized lunch after the funeral.

'Here.' Rosemary had taken off her gloves. She tugged at something on her left hand. She put it in Kemi's palm. It was her wedding ring. 'It's my old one. The one he gave me when we were married, thirty years ago. I never changed it. Richard bought me one but . . . oh, I don't know. I'd always worn *this* one. I changed my engagement ring, of course, but I'd like you to have this.'

Kemi stared at it. It was similar to her own wedding ring, a plain gold band. She fingered it. 'I . . . I—'

'Please.' Rosemary squeezed her arm. 'Keep it. Or throw it away, if you can't bear it. Since neither of us will have his children and I'm no longer Mrs Carrick . . . you should have it. It just seems . . . fitting, somehow?'

Kemi bit her lip. She still couldn't speak. Rosemary squeezed her arm once more and slipped away to join her husband. Kemi was left alone. She saw a group of people coming towards her, including Harry, her old colleague and friend. She slipped the ring onto the third finger of her right hand. It was slightly loose. She fingered it lightly, twisting it round. It was the Egyptians who'd first started the tradition of wearing a wedding ring, she remembered. It was Julian who'd explained it to her. *They believed the vein in the ring finger ran directly to the heart. The Romans picked up on it, calling that vein the 'vena amoris', the vein of love. That's why you wear it on the left.* She could still hear his voice. Now she had his ring on both hands. It was exactly as Rosemary said. It was fitting. She would always belong to him and no other. She looked up. Harry was approaching. She looked at him through the blurry veil of her tears.

It took her a couple of months to settle things. She sold the house in Dulwich almost as soon as she returned from Johannesburg, and resigned from her job. It wasn't possible to live there without him. She had no clear idea what she meant to do. She listened to the will being read out at his solicitor's without really hearing the words. She hadn't even known he'd had a will. His shares in the clinic would have passed to her automatically, the solicitor told her, even if he hadn't specifically directed it. There was a modest life insurance policy payout and his share of the profits of their home. His car, clothing, files, a paper he'd been working on with colleagues.

She sat at his computer in the downstairs study, marvelling at the speed with which a person ceased to exist. His phone was gone, of course. Her mind was only able to recall fragmented details of that evening when she realized something was wrong.

*She came out of the shower, her hair washed and pulled back into a tight knot, ready to be blow-dried. She looked at the clock on the bedside table. It was nearly seven. She'd spent longer in the shower than she should have. He'd be back any second. She pulled a tan and dark blue jersey wrap dress out of the closet, and a pair of tan leather sandals with a small*

LESLEY LOKKO

*heel. She hurried back into the bathroom to dry her hair. At seven thirty, she was ready. She added a slick of red lipstick and a touch of mascara. She looked at her watch impatiently. Rosebank was less than twenty minutes away and he'd been gone nearly two hours. What was taking him so long? She grabbed her phone and dialled his mobile. It rang without answer. She picked up the novel she'd been half-heartedly reading on the plane and tried to concentrate. Ten minutes later, she flung the book aside and picked up her phone again. There was still no answer. She tried again five minutes later. This time it went straight to his answering service. 'This is Julian Carrick. I'm not able to take your call right now. Please leave a message at the beep.'*

*'Julian, it's me. Where are you? I'm beginning to get worried. Call me back, darling. Love you.' She tapped the phone against her teeth. Then she quickly dialled Ayanda's number.*

*'Hi, it's me. Listen . . . Julian went to pick up the prescription but he's not back yet. D'you think you could call your pharmacist friend and see if it's been collected?'*

*'Sure, I'll call you back.' After that, she couldn't remember much. She waited for what seemed like hours. The dread when she saw Ayanda's number, not his. Somehow, she already knew.*

*'Something's happened. I'm on my way to get you.'*

*She remembered screaming into the phone at Ayanda. 'What? What's happened?'*

This was what happened. *This.*


She flew back to Johannesburg a few weeks later. She was too drained to do anything. Her father had insisted she come and stay with them for a few weeks. She had no idea what her life was any more.

# PART ELEVEN
## 2005

### A year later

. . .

Corruption, embezzlement, fraud? These are
all characteristics which exist everywhere. It is
regrettably the way human nature functions,
whether we like it or not. What successful economies
do is keep it to a minimum. No one has ever
eliminated any of that stuff.

ALAN GREENSPAN

# 75

Solam studied his face in the bathroom mirror. It was his face, all right. Same as ever. There was a tightness around the jaw that hadn't been there a year ago. It was difficult to meet his own eyes. They were so dark that the pupil disappeared, darkness itself. He opened the cold tap and bent down, cupping his hands. He splashed water over his face, enjoying the coolness for a moment, then reached for a napkin. The phone in his trouser pocket vibrated soundlessly. He pulled it out. It was a message from Hélène. There was a date, *12 February*, followed by the words *bill immediately preceding SONA. Max. impact*. He slipped it back into his pocket and opened the door. It was less than a fortnight away.

# 76

Jen pulled her smart, dark grey Audi into the driveway and switched off the engine. She got out of the car with some difficulty. She was in her second trimester and her stomach had started getting in the way of the steering wheel. 'Twins,' her obstetrician had told her with a smile. 'Congratulations, Mrs Rhoyi. You're having twins.'

After the initial shock had worn off, she'd been pleased. Things were steadier now. Those first few months after Euan's birth and Julian's murder had been amongst the worst she'd ever known. She felt as though she'd been walking around in a dark fog, unable to see anything. It took a while for the medication to kick in and even now, she didn't know if her recovery had been down to the pills or to the fact that, for the first time ever, Kemi's loss seemed to be greater than anything she'd ever had to bear. To say Kemi was suffering seemed to make a mockery of the word. For weeks after she'd returned to Johannesburg, she'd sat in the upstairs sitting room with Jen and Euan whenever she came to visit, neither saying anything, just watching numbly as Jen bottle-fed him or put him to sleep.

After a couple of weeks, Jen had asked her to give it a go. She watched as Kemi gingerly picked him up or put him down, her heart in her mouth. It seemed to work. There was that first smile, perhaps a month after it happened. Then she'd come in the room one afternoon to hear Kemi singing softly to him. After that, and with surprisingly little objection, Jen persuaded Solam to add 'Julian' to Euan's name. Lebohang Euan Julian Rhoyi. There would always be a special bond between her first-born child and Kemi. After her own act of betrayal, it seemed only fitting that her son should be the one to bring Kemi slowly back to life.

Kemi came out to the patio to meet her. She'd bought a bungalow in Parktown North, one of Johannesburg's older, more graceful suburbs. She didn't want to live in the sterile, security-obsessed northern part of town, where Jen and Solam – and almost everyone else she knew – lived. It was a 1940s flat-roofed bungalow that she'd gutted and turned into a beautiful two-storey house, though it had one of those reed-filtering pools that Jen shuddered at whenever she saw it. It looked dark and creepy, not sparklingly turquoise and shiny, like their pool.

She kicked the door shut with her hip. It was February and unusually hot. She was almost tempted to slip into the pool. She walked carefully across the lawn. The two golden retrievers, Pablo and Lola, bounded happily towards Jen.

'Pablo!' Kemi shouted. 'Down!' He was the most affectionate animal Kemi had ever encountered. 'Down! Come here, boy. Come on, there's a good boy.' Pablo turned away reluctantly, obviously hoping for a reward. Lola, who was less energetic, trotted along beside Jen, happy to see a visitor.

'I'm all sweaty,' Jen said, hugging her. 'I feel as though I'm being boiled alive.'

'Well, there's always the pool. Come in, it's cooler inside.'

They went into the kitchen. There was a huge bowl of roses sitting on the counter. Jen buried her face in them. 'These are gorgeous,' she said, breathing in deeply. 'Where did you buy them?'

'I didn't. They're from the garden. Tea? Or water?'

'Can I have both?' Jen looked around. 'It's lovely in here,' she said, admiring the bright colours. 'Fresh. I love these colours.'

'Thanks. The decorators did a great job. How's your new place coming along?'

Jen pulled a face. 'It's a bit over-the-top for my tastes, to be honest. Solam loves it. He can't get enough of gold taps and built-in wardrobes.'

'Presidential tastes. That's where he'll wind up, wait and see.'

'God, I hope not. I can't think of anything worse.'

Kemi put a jug of water on the counter and fetched two glasses. 'Really?' she asked, sounding dubious. 'But isn't that what he wants?'

'It might be what he wants,' Jen said dourly. 'But I certainly don't want to be a president's wife.'

Kemi said nothing but turned back to the freezer. 'Ice?' She dropped a few cubes in Jen's glass. 'That's a long way off,' she said. 'It'll be years before he's ready for the top job. Anything can happen in that time.'

'How's the clinic coming on?' Jen asked. 'I'm bored of talking about Solam.'

'We're nearly there. The plan is to open on his birthday. What *would* have been his birthday. That's just over a month to go. Did I tell you Rosemary and her husband are coming out?'

'He'd smile at that,' Jen said. For a moment they both said nothing. Jen looked at her without the simulated horror that hides embarrassment in the face of terrible tragedy.

Kemi smiled. 'Yes, he would. His two wives.'

'Do you want Solam to be there? Or will that bring too much attention?'

Kemi pulled a face. 'Part of me would rather it was a quiet affair, you know? Just the directors, me, Rosemary. And you, of course. My father wants to come. But I also know the attention will be useful, especially with fundraising. That's what I spend most of my time doing these days. Julian said I was good at it.'

'Of course you are. You're good at everything,' Jen said. 'Well, if you do want him there, let me know. These days even *I* have to book in time with him through his secretary.'

'Isn't that just the life of a politician? I look at my parents . . . I don't know when they even saw each other last.'

Jen sighed. 'I suppose so. Goes with the territory.'

'A politician's wife,' Kemi said slowly. 'Funny, isn't it? Me a widow, and you a politician's wife. It's not quite what we planned, is it?'

Jen looked down at her stomach. 'I don't think I really had a plan, to be honest. But it sounds better than what some stranger called me the other day. I overheard her as I walked by.'

'What was that?'

'A trophy wife. That's the *last* thing I ever thought I'd be called.' She looked around the room. 'That's beautiful,' she said, pointing to a new painting. 'When did you buy that?'

'Last year, at the art fair. It's been sitting at the framer's for ages. Yes, it's rather lovely.'

'It's really *you*. This place is lovely. You've really turned it into a home.'

Kemi nodded. 'It gave me something to do at first. That and the clinic. But I enjoy it.'

Jen looked at her watch. 'I'd better run,' she said. 'Traffic back to Sandton will be hell.'

'I'll walk you to your car. Pablo'll be sad to see you go. He loves it when people come round. Doesn't happen often enough for his liking, I'm afraid.'

# 77

The vote on the amendments to the new economic policy bill was scheduled to take place at noon, with the President's State of the Nation address the following day. Hélène's timing was absolutely spot on. Solam sat in his usual place in the National Assembly, two rows behind the front bench, his eye on the monitor in front of him.

The gallery was more crowded than usual, due to the contentious nature of the bill being passed. It was ironic, he thought to himself, as they waited for the Speaker to call the house to order so that proceedings could begin. The Democratic Party was opposing the government's attempts to broaden the black economic empowerment policy that the ruling party had introduced a decade earlier. He and Hélène had decided to make it appear as though the bill was the proverbial straw that broke his back, yet privately, he was *entirely in favour*. She'd offered him the position of Shadow Home Affairs Minister in return for his defection, claiming his age would be a factor against him. He wanted more, much more. If there was ever a time to strike a hard bargain, it was now. He knew that the next few minutes were the most important of her political life.

'Order, order! Members, take your seats, please. We are due to begin.' The Speaker banged his gavel loudly. Groups broke up. People began to shuffle towards their seats. The bill was about to be debated. Solam felt the knot of anticipation tighten in his gut. He knew exactly the moment he would stand up and walk across the floor. First there was a message to send. He looked at his phone sitting on the ledge in front of him. He'd written it minutes before entering the chamber. It was short and to the point. *Deputy. Otherwise, it's off.* He looked across the Assembly to where she was seated in the front row. He pressed send. He saw her react. Her private mobile phone was never far from her person. She slipped a hand into her jacket pocket and, turning slightly away from the person next to her – the incumbent – she read the message. There was a moment's hesitation, then his phone vibrated. He looked at the screen.

*This wasn't the deal.*

*Deals change.*

*Need to consult with party members. Not my decision alone.*

*Yes or no. Your call.*

He could see her hesitating. He'd outplayed her. If she didn't respond and called his bluff, she would have to explain the text messages. His party would demand his resignation if their dealings were exposed. But he had insurance in the form of the photographs. He was no fool. He was in what the Americans liked to call a 'win-win' situation. His phone lit up.

*Fine. But I'll announce after the next party caucus.*

*Deal. And this time it'll hold.*

He looked across the room at her. She returned his gaze evenly. He liked that about her. Nerves of steel. She knew what would come next.

The press scrum was unlike any other. As soon as he stood up and heard the gasp from the benches, he knew with a certainty that was absolute, unmoveable, that things would never be the same. The sound went over his skin, like wind over water. 'Order! Order!' The Speaker bleated out his call, astonishment clear in his voice. Solam walked over calmly and took the empty seat on the opposition bench, three seats down from its leader. And then the pandemonium. All hell broke loose.


He heard Buthelezi's voice struggling to make itself heard against the din. 'Floor crossing,' he shouted into the microphone thrust in front of his face. 'It's like the H1 virus because it robs the political system of all honour . . .' He jogged lightly past. As soon as the reporters saw him, they abandoned their posts and ran after him, a pack chasing its prey. Hélène's official car was waiting at the foot of the steps, engine running, the back door open. He jumped inside and the car pulled away, leaving a trail of reporters hurrying after it until it powered through the gates and turned into the street.

Hélène's face was turned away from him. For a second, neither spoke. 'That was some move you made,' she said calmly, without rancour.

'You'd have done the same,' he said easily. 'Don't pretend otherwise.'

'True, but it was a risky move all the same.'

He shook his head. 'No, not really. You're unusual, Hélène.'

She turned towards him. He saw that her face was alive in a way he hadn't seen it before. 'How so?'

'You want to win. You've led this party for nearly twenty years. We both know you won't take the presidency, not in our lifetime. You're a middle-aged, middle-class white woman. You'll never get the majority vote. No offence.'

'None taken.' There was a smile playing around her lips. His respect for her doubled. Her clear blue eyes came to rest on his. 'But *you* will. So, here's what we're going to do. This is how we're going to play it and this time, there's no room for negotiation. As you say, this is *my* party. I've built it from the ground up, before you were even out of diapers. So, be quiet for once, and listen.'

# 78

Kemi's mouth dropped open, her fork halfway. She spilled her glass of wine. From her feet, Pablo growled in protest as the drops splattered over him. She stared at the television screen. Solam was walking down the steps of Parliament, two at a time, followed by a surprised pack of photographers and journalists. *Breaking news: Minister Rhoyi crosses floor to join Democratic Party.* The ticker tape surged across the screen. *Breaking news!* The newscaster broke off her story to make the announcement. 'In a move that shocked and stunned the nation, popular Minister for Youth and Sport, Solam Rhoyi, crossed the floor in Parliament this afternoon, joining the opposition party. DP spokesperson—'

Kemi muted the television and jumped up, scrabbling for her phone. Jen's line was busy. She pressed twice and on the third try, she got through. 'Jen? Tell me this isn't true! Did you know?'

Jen sounded dazed. 'I've no idea what's going on . . . his mother's been on the phone. They can't get through to him. I'm watching the television now but they're talking to the Democratic Party spokesperson. He's unavailable for comment.'

'Jesus Christ! His parents . . . his mother will kill him. What is he *thinking*?'

'I don't know, Kem. I'm scared ... what's going to happen?'

'I'll be right there.'

# 79

Jen put down the phone. She was shaking. She wasn't joking; she was terrified. She knew little about South African politics – or any politics, for that matter – save that it was brutal and short-lived. Solam was a government minister. They lived in a ministerial *house*. Their cars belonged to the government . . . or did they? She actually had no idea. Upstairs, she heard Euan begin to cry. The noise had woken him. Auntie Gladys was already on her way up. For once, she was grateful. She felt sick. Her phone rang again. It was Solam.

'Solam? What have you just done? What's going on? Where are you?' She was sounding hysterical but she was too frightened to care.

Solam's voice was oddly calm. 'Calm down. There's nothing to be afraid of, absolutely nothing. I'll be back tomorrow night.'

'Your mother's been trying to reach you,' Jen said, her voice shaky. 'You're all over the news!'

'I know, I know. The main thing is just to stay calm. I'm sending over two new bodyguards. They'll be there in the next ten minutes—'

'Bodyguards? What's wrong with the ones you have?' Jen broke in, even more alarmed. 'Where are they?'

'Jen, I've switched party. I haven't assassinated anyone. You change party, you change your job. They've arranged for two of their own to handle the transition, that's all.'

'Are we going to have to move again? I can't, Solam, I can't bear it! We've only just moved into this house!'

'Jen, just calm the fuck down! Go wash your face, call Kemi, do whatever you have to do. There'll be reporters all over the house tomorrow morning. I need you looking like a trophy wife, not some hysterical nutcase, do you understand?'

Jen was brought up short. A trophy wife. It was exactly what some journalist had called her. Did she know? Did she know what was about to happen? The small worm of fear that never really went away where Solam was concerned raised its head. She swallowed. 'OK,' she said, trying to steady her voice. 'Sorry.'

'It was a spur-of-the-moment decision. I just couldn't take it any longer. But let's talk tomorrow. And Jen?'

'Yes?'

'Don't talk to anyone about this, you understand? Not Kemi, not my mother, not anyone. Just tell them you've spoken to me, and everything's fine. You got that?'

'Yes, got it,' Jen whispered.

'OK. I'll see you tomorrow.' He hung up.

# 80

She and Jen were sitting in the living room talking softly when there was a tap at the sliding doors. Jen's head shot up. She clutched Kemi's hand in fright. 'There's someone at the door.' She was still jumpy.

'I'll go,' Kemi said, getting to her feet. There'd been three security guards on duty when she arrived half an hour earlier; it was unlikely an intruder had got through. She walked to the doors and looked out. There was a man standing outside with one of the guards. The guard gestured to her to open up; it was all right. She unlocked the door. 'Can I help you?' she asked, wondering who it was.

'Good evening, ma'am. I've been assigned to the Rhoyi family. Just wanted to let you know. Sbu and I will cover things for tonight with the rest of the team.' He indicated the guard next to him.

Kemi nodded, unsure of what to say. 'Sure,' she said. 'I'm just a friend. Mrs Rhoyi's inside, but I'll let her know.'

'Yes, I know. Thank you, ma'am. You have a good evening.' They turned and walked back to the gate.

'Who is it?' Jen called.

Kemi let the curtain drop. 'Looks like a new security guard. He said he'd be working with the rest of the team for tonight.'

'Oh, I forgot. Solam said he was sending someone new

over.' She stopped suddenly and put her hand over her mouth. 'I don't know if I'm supposed to tell you that,' she said, looking even more confused. 'He said I wasn't to say anything.'

'Then *don't* say anything,' Kemi said quickly. Some deeply buried memory of her own past surfaced. Silence had been one of the tactics of the Mashabane household for as long as she could remember. 'Give him a chance to talk first.'

Jen nodded doubtfully. 'What d'you think's going to happen?' she asked after a moment.

Kemi shook her head. 'No idea,' she said truthfully. 'I actually have *no* idea what he's up to.'

# 81

Iketleng was shown to a table tucked discreetly behind the column. The restaurant at the Mount Nelson Hotel in Cape Town was the perfect place to meet her son. She could be sure of at least half a dozen prying eyes and the odd roving photographer to capture the moment where she either slapped him, threw a glass of wine in his face or both, preferably. She was seething with rage and everyone, including the poor, innocent waiter who'd shown her to her seat, knew it. It emanated from her like a life force, sending waves of static running up through her body; her hair refused to cooperate, bursting out of the elaborate head-wrap she wore, shoved angrily to one side.

The waiter addressed her respectfully in what he guessed was their shared tongue: 'Something to drink, *Mamá*?'

'A white wine. No, make that a whisky. Double, no ice.'

'Yes, *Mamá*.' He withdrew as silently and unobtrusively as possible. She didn't even have the time to be angry at the word '*Mamá*'.

She saw him as soon as he entered the restaurant. There was a murmur of surprised recognition from the other guests when he appeared in the doorway, all 6'3 of him, dressed casually, as though it were an ordinary summer day. He wore a light blue shirt, no tie, black trousers. He cut such a fine, distinctive figure, she ought to have been proud. Heads turned as he walked past, and not just because of recent events. She was a woman. She saw the way other women looked at her son. But she was not proud. She was angry and ashamed. And by God, was she going to let him know it.

'Ma,' he said, bending to kiss her on the cheek. She offered it coldly.

'You're late.'

'Three minutes. I was stopped at the entrance by one of the doormen.'

'Wanting to know why you'd done it?' she hissed angrily.

'No, wanting my autograph,' he said mildly. 'What are you drinking? Whisky?'

'Your *autograph*?' She stared at him in disbelief. 'You're lying.'

'Ask him.' He raised his hand for the waiter. He hurried over. 'I'll have the same.'

'Yes, sir.' The waiter hastened to comply. Iketleng watched him, her eyes narrowing. There was something in addition to the man's professional demeanour, some other attitude she couldn't quite define. He hurried back with her son's drink. 'Anything else for you, sir? Not ready to order? No problem, sir. Just let me know when you're ready, sir.' As if she didn't exist.

'Cheers,' Solam said, raising his glass slightly.

'Don't you dare say "cheers" to me!' she snapped at him. 'This is not a cause for celebration.'

'Isn't it?' He leaned back in his chair and looked at her. As with the damned waiter, there was something in his manner she couldn't identify. He was relaxed, easy in himself . . . in complete command of his actions. He looked at her almost insolently. How *dare* he? The thought made her angrier still.

'What have you *done*?' It came out louder than it should. Through the damned potted palms and the gap between the columns, she could see people's heads turning.

He leaned forward, resting his elbows on the table, his hands clasped under his chin. He did not look like a man with regrets. 'Look, Ma,' he said calmly. 'I know you're upset, believe me.'

'Upset?' She couldn't help herself. 'I'm not *upset*! I'm *ashamed*, d'you hear me?' She took a gulp of whisky. 'How could you do this to us?'

He leaned back. 'I haven't done anything to you,' he said deliberately. 'Do you not realize what I just said? That man *wanted my autograph*.'

'Sycophantic creep!' Iketleng hissed angrily.

He shook his head. 'No, that's where you're wrong. "It's far easier to blame the past than to try and fix the future."' He leaned forward again. 'You said it to me once, remember?' He didn't wait for her to answer. 'You can't see it because you've done the one thing you always taught me *not* to do.'

'Which is *what*?' she spat suspiciously.

'*Not* to think short-term. *Not* to only think about the here and now. To think – and play – the long game.'

'What are you talking about? How does betraying your party manifest as long-term thinking? Have you lost your senses?'

'On the contrary. Look around you, Ma. You think the party's going to win the next election?' He shook his head, almost sadly, she thought. 'They've lost the plot. All they've managed to do in twenty years is line their own pockets, at the expense of everyone else, yourselves included. This bill was the last straw. I don't need to spell it out. You know exactly what I'm talking about. Don't kid yourself.' He stopped. He picked up his glass and held it to the light. 'The truth is simpler than we realize,' he said after a moment. 'This isn't the party you fought for. It's been disappearing ever since '94. Slowly at first, and now almost daily. Once the damned World Cup is over, the bubble will finally burst. The only question *you* need to ask yourself is this: are you going to take the fall along with the rest of them? You've kept your nose clean all these years, and well done to you for having the courage to do it. *I* know it, Dad knows it . . . *they* know it. But what's the point of having a clean nose when the music stops playing? That's what's happening, Ma, only you're too damn stubborn to see it.'

Iketleng's mouth dropped. The rage that had been building in her all day suddenly left her, replaced by an overwhelming sadness that brought tears to her eyes. It wasn't just the fact that it was longest speech she'd heard him make in more years than she could remember, it was that deep down, buried in her in a place that was accessible to few, she knew he was telling the truth. It wouldn't have been her way. He was right about one thing: she *was* stubborn. It was a trait that had seen her through things that would have broken anyone else. Her refusal to give in or to give up was the reason they were sitting here in the Mount Nelson Hotel today, drinking fine whisky and being waited on, hand and foot. Thirty years ago, they wouldn't have been allowed on the grounds of the hotel, let alone into the restaurant. So, stubbornness was useful. It made it possible to continue the struggle when all hope was lost. But now? Perhaps he was right. Her mind went back to the newspaper she'd bought at JFK, only weeks earlier. She couldn't remember the writer's exact words. 'There are only three necessary conditions for any society: a capable state, the rule of law and a culture of accountability, including account-able government.' Something like that. She'd read it on the long flight back home, her neck prickling uncomfortably.

*Accountable government.* She looked at her son, who was draining his whisky. Was it possible that he had seen what she couldn't?

He put down his glass and stood up. He walked round the table and leaned down. For a moment she thought she would clutch at him physically. He kissed her on the cheek, very softly, then straightened up. 'See you, Ma,' he said gently. Then he turned and walked out, heads turning, eyes following him hungrily in his wake.

# PART TWELVE
# 2008

### Three years later

. . .

An affair wants to spill, to share its
glory with the world. No act is so
private it does not seek applause.

JOHN UPDIKE

# 82

The new house was smaller than their previous home. As a
member of the opposition, Solam wasn't entitled to quite as
many perks, which was a relief to Jen. It was just off Oxford
Road, in a part of town that seemed to have no exact defin-
ition, situated halfway between Rosebank and Killarney but
belonging to neither. There was a small, nondescript gate off
the main road, a long narrow driveway and then the house
itself, hidden in the trees. There was a swimming pool, separate quarters big enough for one maid, and a sentry post
halfway down the driveway, which had obviously been
installed at a later date. It meant Auntie Gladys could no
longer live with them, another fact that pleased Jen. It also
meant the various security guards who'd been assigned to the
family no longer intruded on their presence every waking
moment, although the current lot were a vast improvement on
the old bunch, she had to admit. There were three new guards
assigned to the family. There was François van Niekerk, the
tall blond one with the quiet smile. There was Motsame
Dhlamini, cheerful, short and powerfully built. And then there
was Sbu Motsepe, tall and thin, respectful to a fault, who
hardly ever said a word. They kept their distance, unlike the
previous guards, and were always ready to lend a hand with
the shopping or the kids' prams. She could even call on

François or Motsame to keep an eye on four-year-old Euan in the pool or kick around a football with him in the garden.

Solam *seemed* happier. He spent more time in Cape Town with Hélène. Although there hadn't yet been an official announcement, the papers were full of speculation. Rhoyi was about to take over from Van Roux as the party leader. Solam said little to her, but Iketleng was uncharacteristically talkative. Jen had no idea what had passed between mother and son in those few days after he'd stunned the country by joining the opposition, but their meeting in Cape Town seemed to have initiated a thaw between Iketleng and her daughter-in-law. She'd always been pleasant, Jen said to Kemi over the phone one Sunday morning, but now she was positively kind. And it wasn't just towards her three grandchildren, either.

'In what way?'

'Well, don't laugh, but she rang up yesterday and said she wanted to take me to a hairdresser's.'

'Really? *Her* hairdresser?'

'No, don't be silly. What would her hairdresser do with *my* hair? No, some new place in Sandton. She says it's *the* place for white women.'

'She said that? She used those words?' Kemi started to laugh.

'Yes, I couldn't believe it. Anyhow, we've got an appointment on Saturday. She says it's about time she took me in hand.'

'What on earth does that mean?'

'I don't know. I guess I'll find out.'

Henning studied her with all the intensity of a surgeon about to make the first incision. He swivelled her round in the plush revolving chair, first this way then that, looking at her auburn tresses from every angle. Finally, when she thought she wouldn't be able to keep a guffaw of laughter in for one second longer, he turned to Iketleng.

'There's no way around it,' he said dramatically. 'It's got to come off.'

Jen put up a hand to lift her heavy mane instinctively. 'What d'you mean?'

'I mean, you've got to cut it. It's in terrible shape.'

'You're going to cut my hair off?'

'Every last scrap. You'll love it, darling. I promise. Oksana!' He turned around and bellowed to a woman who was busy drying another client's hair. She switched the hairdryer off.

'Yes, Henning?'

'When you're done with that, come over here. Wash, but don't bother conditioning. It's all going to come off.' He smiled at Jen in the mirror and puffed himself up. 'Trust me. You won't recognize yourself. You've been hiding under all this shit for years.' He lifted up her hair and let it fall. 'Time to let the *real* you out.' He strode off.

'You see?' Iketleng leaned forward proudly. 'I told you he was the best.'

Jen was too stunned – and scared – to reply.

*Snip, snip, snip. Head turned to the left. Snip, snip, snip. Then to the right. His fingers were gentle. She sat under his hands, a lamb to the slaughter, conscious only of the sound of his scissors slicing through her hair, through the air. Snip, snip, snip.*

She did not recognize the woman staring back at her. Her hair was feather-short at the back and sides with a long, dramatic sweep across one eye. Her jaw was square and well defined, her cheekbones high, her green-blue eyes staring back at her. Her right ear appeared as a delicate scroll pressed flat against her hair, the gold stud earring catching the light against her pale skin. There was a mole on her neck that she'd never noticed before, a dark beauty spot that caught and held the attention.

'You see?' Henning said, placing his hands on her shoulders as he willed her to look at herself. 'Where've you been hiding?'

Iketleng looked pleased. No, more than pleased, she looked *satisfied*, as though proven right.

She settled the bill, wouldn't hear of Jen paying. 'I can't recognize you!' She tucked her arm into Jen's as they left the salon, something she had never done before. Jen's head was reeling. Iketleng kept on talking, talking. 'Now we just have to do something about these clothes you like to wear. At least you've kept your figure.'

Jen was too stunned to reply. It dawned on her that she was being given what television programmes called a 'makeover'. She wasn't stupid. She was being groomed.


François looked up as she got out of Iketleng's Mercedes and approached the house. He said nothing, but from the look on his face she saw the new haircut had surprised him. He took the bags from her as the car rolled back down the driveway and disappeared.

'It suits you, ma'am,' he said suddenly, quietly.

Jen put up her hand to her newly bare neck in embarrassment. 'Oh, this? I . . . I just thought . . . why not?'

He smiled faintly and strode ahead with the bags. Jen stared after him. She was oddly touched. Although they were a constant but discreet presence in their lives, she knew very little about any of the men whose job it was, in Solam's own words, 'to take a bullet for me. They'll take one for you and the kids too, if the situation calls for it. So, treat them well.'

She walked behind him up to the front door, wondering what would prompt anyone to take a bullet for anyone else, or for *her*, for that matter? She hoped to God she'd never have to find out. She pushed open the door. Euan was standing in the doorway. His mouth dropped open in shock.

Well, there was one person who didn't like her new look, she reflected wryly when all the fuss had died down. Euan had taken one look at her and burst into loud, heart-wrenching sobs. He didn't recognize her.

Later that evening, when the children were asleep and the house was finally quiet, she took her plate through to the kitchen and put it in the sink. She'd made do with an apple and some cheese. No point in turning on the dishwasher for a single side plate and a wine glass. She rinsed both carefully and set them on the rack to dry. It was the second week in a row that she'd eaten supper alone every night. She'd almost forgotten what it was like to sit opposite someone and chat about their day, her day, the kids . . . her life, in other words. She glanced at the clock. It was only seven thirty. The empty evening stretched ahead. The bottle of wine she'd opened earlier was standing on the kitchen counter. She opened the fridge. There was still a large pot of curry left over from the evening before. She hesitated for a moment, then took it out.

She walked down the driveway, her heels crunching on the ground. Better to give it to François than throw it away. She half smiled. She could practically hear her grandmother's voice. *Waste not, want not.*

She heard the click of the gun before she realized what it

was. François was standing right in front of her, aiming straight at her head. She nearly dropped the tray in fright.

'Oh, Jesus! Sorry, ma'am, sorry.' He hastily put the gun away, tucking it behind him. 'I didn't see who it was, I just heard footsteps. You shouldn't come up on us like that,' he said, only half joking, as he took the tray from her. 'Are you OK?'

She nodded, still trembling with fright. She pulled herself together. 'No, please. *I'm* sorry. I just didn't think. It was stupid of me. You're bodyguards, after all.' She laughed jerkily. They stood looking at each other for a moment. 'I . . . I just thought . . . well, there was some leftover food. It was going to go to waste . . . would you like a bite?' It occurred to her that she'd never wondered how the men ate, or where they went after their shift, or what they actually *did* other than wait around for some idiot to strike . . . an idiot such as herself. 'And there's some wine, too.'

He smiled. 'Thanks, ma'am. I'll take the food, but not the wine, thanks. I'm on duty.'

'Oh, of course you are. Gosh, I *am* being a bit dense tonight. Sorry, I'll take it back.' Was that rude? she wondered. Offering someone half a bottle of wine? 'I hope you enjoy it. Mercy cooks rather well.'

'I'm sure I will. Thank you again, ma'am.'

'You're welcome. Have a good night.' She turned and walked quickly back to the house, feeling very foolish.

She poured herself a small glass of the wine and sat down at the kitchen table. She looked around. The kitchen was immaculate. There wasn't a surface that hadn't been wiped, polished, buffed; not a thing was ever out of place. She took a sip of wine. Was this all it came down to? A clean kitchen, someone else on hand to take care of her children, a husband who was never there? If he wasn't at dinner with colleagues, he was on a plane somewhere, giving a speech or preparing for a speech. Come to that, when was the last time they'd had sex? She actually couldn't remember. She put her head in her hands. A distant memory surfaced of her mother sitting alone in the kitchen in Morningside, in exactly the same position, right down to the glass of wine. She'd sometimes come upon her by accident, creeping down well after bedtime to fetch a glass of milk or an apple from the bowl that Mrs Logan always kept in the pantry. One night she saw her mother crying. Her shoulders were shaking. She cried in silence. Jen turned around soundlessly and crept back upstairs. She thought then it was the saddest thing she'd ever seen. Crying without making a sound.

Suddenly there was a tap at the kitchen window. She nearly jumped out of her skin. It was François. She hurried to the door. 'You didn't have to bring it back,' she said, taking it from him. The bowl had been neatly washed. 'I'd have sent the girl out to get it. Thanks.'

'It was very good.' They looked at each other again for a moment. There didn't seem to be anything more to say. 'Goodnight, ma'am.'

'Goodnight.' She watched him walk down the steps to the garden. 'Please call me Jen,' she called out suddenly. 'This "ma'am" business makes me feel so old.'

'Yes, ma'am,' he said, lifting his hand in a half-salute.

She smiled and closed the door. At least he had a sense of humour. She was glad someone did. She put her glass in the sink, turned off the lights and walked slowly upstairs.

# 83

There was a loud thud which went all the way through the house. It reached Alice on the second floor, whilst she was watching her favourite morning television programme. Her tea spilled over the lip of the porcelain cup, splashing into the saucer. Irritated, she pulled the cardigan around her shoulders and turned back to the screen. Suddenly a scream ripped through the house. The hairs on the back of her neck stood up. Then she heard someone running down the stairs. She turned the sound on the television up. She could hardly hear a thing! The thuds continued, doors banging and slamming and more screams, and then finally, footsteps pounding down the corridor and her door bursting open. It was the maid.

'It's Mr McFadden,' she all but shouted, her face wide-eyed with fright. 'He collapsed! Mrs Smith's called an ambulance! Oh, Mrs McFadden, he doesn't look well!'

Alice frowned at her, trying to work out what the silly girl was blethering on about. 'Who's that? Who're you talking about?'

'It's Mr McFadden. He was in his bathroom. Mrs Smith says she thinks he's had a stroke! Oh, Mrs McFadden, ye'd better come!'

'Me?' Alice frowned even harder. What was she supposed to do? 'Whatever for? Has she called the doctor?'

The maid's head went up and down vigorously. 'The ambu-ance is on its way,' she said breathlessly.

'Well, then. No need for me to interfere.' Alice turned back o the television, turning the volume up to maximum.

The maid stood at the door for a second, obviously unsure ₊f what to do, then she turned and ran down the corridor. ₊econds later, Alice heard the distinctive wail of an ambulance ₊oming up Jordan Lane. She stood up and peered out of the ₊vindow. Two burly men in green jackets were running across ₊he lawn carrying a stretcher. Yes, the ambulance had arrived. ₊Vhat more did they want from her?

₊t was a massive stroke, Mrs Smith informed her. 'Just like ₊hat!'

Alice rolled her eyes. 'Well, you'd hardly expect to be given ₊otice of your own stroke, would you?' she said tartly. 'Is ₊here any more tea in that pot?'

Mrs Smith got up without a word and poured her another ₊up. 'Will you no tell the bairns?' she asked after a moment.

'Catriona?' Alice considered the question for a moment. ₊Yes, I suppose she ought to be told.'

'And the other one?' Mrs Smith asked. 'Will you no phone ₊er?'

'Mrs Smith, I don't know *how* many times I've asked you ₊ot to mention her in this house,' Alice said crossly.

Mrs Smith wasn't to be put off so easily. 'I've nivver under-₊tood it,' she declared loudly, loud enough for the maid to ₊ear. 'Why ye've taken against her all o' a sudden. I dinnae ₊nderstand it. She's a lovely girl, she is.'

'Mrs Smith! I'll thank you not to poke your nose into our ₊ffairs. I've asked you not to mention her and that should be ₊he end of it.'

Mrs Smith walked through into the scullery, still muttering

Alice got up and walked into the hallway. She'd better phone Catriona. Now, how was she to know her number? She'd never phoned her before. Catriona was always the one to call, not that she called very often. She was forced to summon Mrs Smith for help. Together they went through Robert's phone, searching for Jen's number. Alice had never quite got used to those little handheld devices with names instead of numbers. They finally found it, a long number with lots of zeros and ones. She had Mrs Smith dial the number. She held it slightly away from her ear and shouted into it.

'Catriona? It's your mother. Your father has had a stroke. You'd best come home. What? I can't hear you. Is he alive? Yes, of course he's alive. It's a stroke, not a heart attack. I don't know. I haven't been to see him. All right, bye for now.' She put the phone down, ignoring Mrs Smith's questioning glance. Let Catriona tell the 'other' one.

# 84

Jen put her phone back into her handbag and stood still for a few moments. She was in the mall, shopping for the children. She had no idea how serious the stroke was, what hospital, whether he was likely to recover . . . nothing. She opened the flap of her handbag and pulled out her phone again. It took her two tries to get hold of him.

'Solam? It's me. Listen, my father's had a stroke. My mother just rang. I'm going to have to go home.' She heard him swear indistinctly. 'What's that?' she asked.

'Nothing,' he said quickly. Too quickly. 'Is he all right?'

'He's had a stroke,' Jen snapped. 'Of course he's not all right. Mother didn't say very much. He's in hospital. What'll I do with the children? I can't take them on my own.'

'Well, I can't come,' Solam said brusquely. 'Leave them with my mother. She'll be only too happy to take them. How long d'you think you'll be gone?'

'I don't know . . . a week? Ten days?'

'Have you told Kemi? Why don't the two of you go together?'

'I haven't told her yet. If it looks serious, of course I will, but it's better if I go alone for now.'

'Fine. Can *you* ring my mother? I'm in the middle of some-thing.'

'All right.' She hesitated. 'Well, I'll phone you later.' But he was already gone.

# 85

The plane circled lazily around the Firth of Forth before making its approach to Edinburgh Airport. Jen sat with her face pressed against the window, taking in the distant but still unbelievably familiar view of the city as they dropped below the cloud cover. Her heart lifted almost unbearably as they flew over the austere grey city centre, then across fields so green that it dazzled the eye just to look. There was a gentle bump as they hit the tarmac and then the screech of brakes as they skidded to a stop. 'Welcome to Edinburgh,' the flight attendant said disinterestedly into the microphone. 'The local time is just after twelve.' Jen peered out of the window. It was early autumn but the light was soft. After the fierce, blinding light of Johannesburg, it was a welcome relief.

She was one of the first passengers off the plane. She walked through the airport, which was still undergoing renovations, she noticed. It had been a few years since she'd been back but it seemed to be always in a state of repair or renewal. She walked downstairs to baggage claim, picked up her black case within minutes, and went out to hail a taxi. It was a typical Edinburgh day – windy, a little on the chilly side, but fresh. She inhaled deeply. She was home. Christ, she'd missed it. She clambered into the waiting cab and gave the driver directions to the house. She'd see her mother first, then

LESLEY LOKKO

brave the hospital. Kemi had wanted to come, of course, but she'd held firm. She would be absolutely fine on her own. Kemi had enough to do with the clinic only just opened. 'Let *me* handle it,' Jen said. 'For once. I promise I'll call if I need you.' The driver attempted to strike up a conversation – it was Edinburgh, after all, not London – but Jen was too tired to respond. He gave up after a mile or so and they continued to Morningside in silence.

She pushed open the gate to the house and stood in the driveway for a moment. The house looked exactly the same. Handsome in the way of all Edinburgh grey-stone homes, shuttered and austere. The Japanese maple in the centre of the lawn was in full, splendid bloom, its beautiful red leaves trembling lightly in the wind. She walked up to the front door, put her bag down and firmly pressed the brass bell.

The door opened almost immediately. The house smelled exactly the same; a mixture of beeswax polish, last night's supper, whatever it was, and cold, slightly stale air as though summer had never quite found its way inside. It was the smell of her childhood. 'What's your name?' she asked the slip of a girl who answered the door.

'Isla, miss,' she said shyly. 'I'm new here. I only started in January.'

'Is that her,' Mrs Smith shouted from the kitchen. 'She's a wee bit early, is she not?'

Jen walked down the two stone steps into the vast kitchen. Her feet had picked up the rhythm of the house without faltering. A step up into the hallway, a step down into the dining room, and then two steps down to the kitchen. The body remembers all. Mrs Smith was at the table, sleeves rolled up to her elbows, her thick, meaty arms covered in flour. 'Och,

384

there ye are! Oh, Jennifer . . . my, don't you look bonnie! What's happened to all yer lovely hair? Ye've cut it all off. I'd no hae recognized you!' She was genuinely pleased to see her. She held up her arms. 'I'd gie ye a wee hug but I'd get yer clothes all messed up. Oh, it's guid to see ye, so it is!'

Jen walked up to her and put her arms around her shoulders anyway. 'It's lovely to see you, Mrs Smith. You're looking well.'

Mrs Smith's face was pink with a mixture of embarrassment and delight. 'Get away wi' ye. Have ye seen yer mother?'

Jen shook her head. 'I came straight to see you. Where is she?'

Mrs Smith hesitated. 'Ye mustn't pay her too much attention,' she said quietly. 'She disnae know what she's sayin' half the time. She comes an' goes.'

Jen nodded. There was already a lump in her throat.

She left Mrs Smith giving instructions to Isla about where they ought to put her bag and what bed to make up and when to serve lunch and supper. She smiled faintly. Mrs Smith was still very much in charge.

She walked upstairs, passing the landing that led to her father's rooms. The door was closed. She paused for a moment. She knew the house so well, but not as a place of particular rooms or objects, rather as a *quality*, a feeling. There was something emanating from her father's closed door. She put out a hand as though to touch it . . . then let it fall. She gathered herself and turned to the next flight of stairs.

The door at the top had been painted since she'd last been home. It was now a creamy off-white gloss, where before it had always been varnished pine. There was a new brass plate and escutcheon, both diligently polished. She tapped gently on the door but there was no answer. She tapped again, louder.

'Who is it?' Her mother's voice came from behind the door, muffled and indistinct.

She turned the brass knob and the door swung open easily. There was a small entry hall, then another closed door. She pushed it open. Her mother was sitting with her back to her in an upright, upholstered chair placed by the window. When Jen was thirteen or fourteen, she'd come home one Christmas holiday to find the whole of the second floor converted into a small, self-contained flat for her mother. All her possessions – clothes, books, paintings, perfumes – had been moved out of the first-floor rooms and brought upstairs, along with the heavy, ugly mahogany furniture that her grandmother had so loved. Over the years pieces had been replaced . . . a more modern-looking chest of drawers, a side table, a new television and stand, and a new sofa. The paintings were the same though, a strange collection of pastel-toned watercolours of Scottish landscapes and a few abstract paintings, garishly colourful in the muted light. A shaft of sunlight briefly pierced the cloud and came to rest for a moment on Alice's face and hair. She turned her head and for a moment, the two women looked at each other. Alice clearly struggled to place her for a second, then the fog cleared.

'Oh, it's *you*,' she said, her face breaking into a smile. *She comes and goes.* Mrs Smith's warning rang in Jen's ears. 'Hello, Catriona. Where've you been?'

'Hello, Mother,' Jen said, advancing into the room. Alice was wearing a delicately patterned nightdress with a woollen cardigan draped across her thin shoulders. Her hands held it together at her neck. They were paper-thin, Jen noticed with a pang, and almost entirely covered in liver spots and large freckles. Her mother had aged suddenly, terribly. She bent down to kiss her on the cheek. She smelled none too clean, a faint trace of sweat and urine, as though she hadn't washed in a while. She drew back, afraid her wrinkled nose and expression of distaste might show. Next to her mother's feet was a large wicker basket, folded in two. She looked at it and her face broke into a smile. It was her mother's mending basket! She remembered it clearly. One half contained a bizarre assortment of needles, bobbins, scissors and cotton reels in a rainbow of colours, and the other contained old cigarette tins bursting with buttons and eyelets and cards filled with studs . . . As a child, it had been an Aladdin's cave of treasures. Every week, when Alice couldn't put it off any longer, the basket would come out and Jen would sit happily at her feet, watching her mother's hands dart about, her face a mask of concentration, as shirts were mended, lost buttons sewn back on, and skirt hems taken up or down.

'Are you mending, Mother?' she asked with a smile.

Alice looked at her feet. 'Oh, goodness no. I was just looking for something. I can't remember now.' She looked up at Jen and frowned. 'What have you done with your hair? You look like a boy.'

Jen put up a hand self-consciously. 'I . . . I had it cut.'

'I can see *that*,' Alice said tartly. 'Are you just up from London for a visit?'

Jen swallowed. 'You rang me, Mother, don't you remember? I live in South Africa now.'

Alice's eyes narrowed. 'South *Africa*? What on earth are you doing out there?' Then her voice hardened. 'Have you seen her?'

'Who?'

'Her.' Alice jabbed the air with her finger, pointing at something past Jen's shoulder. She turned around. There was an assortment of photographs on the mantelpiece. She walked over. Some of them she recognized. There was a school one of her, gap-toothed, her long red hair in pigtails. There was another of her parents' wedding day, both looking stiffly at the camera, neither smiling, she noticed. There was a picture of her maternal grandmother whom she'd never known, an even thinner, more washed-out version of Alice, and then the picture of Euan that she'd sent them soon after he was born.

'Oh, you got it,' she said delightedly, holding it up. 'He's completely different now. I've got some new pictures to show you of the twins. You remember I told you about the twins? Alicia and Bryony.'

Alice's voice was still hard. 'I've no need to see them,' she said clearly and distinctly. 'One's quite enough, thank you very much. I keep it to remind me.'

Jen looked at her in surprise. 'Of what?' she asked, puzzled.

But Alice's face had closed. Her gaze slipped away from Jen and she pointed to the remote control sitting on the coffee table. 'Will you hand me that?' she asked, her voice suddenly light, almost child-like. 'It's time for *Gardeners' World*. I do like that programme, I have to admit.'

Jen picked it up and handed it to her, still frowning. What on earth was Alice talking about? Her mother had already switched on the television. The volume was deafening.

She touched her mother lightly on the arm and left the room. She'd better go to the hospital. It wasn't a journey she was looking forward to, in more ways than one.

# 86

She looked down at the diminished figure in the hospital bed and her throat almost closed over. Her father was dying. Her first sight of him was a physical blow. He had always been tall and physically imposing, a giant to her as a child. The wizened old man lying propped up with pillows as white as his hair was shrunken, shrivelled, a presence that sucked at the air greedily though the plethora of tubes and pipes that were keeping him alive.

'He can't really talk,' the nurse said cheerfully, 'but he can hear you. Go on, don't be afraid. You can go closer.'

Jen's legs had turned to stone. She stared down at him. One hand was above the coverlet, the skin as wrinkled and papery as an insect's wing. The nails were yellowed and thick, and there was a dark orange nicotine stain on the third finger that almost glowed in contrast to the pale, ghostly figure he'd become. She swallowed. She moved closer, aware of the nurse's presence as she bustled around her, checking dials and screens. She put out a hand to touch his arm. It was like touching the bark of a tree, dry and leathery . . . the body returning to its elemental state. 'Father,' she whispered. 'It's me, Jen.' There was no sign from the inert figure that he'd heard her, let alone recognized her voice.

'Don't be scared,' the nurse said, more gently this time. 'It often helps them in these last few days. You know, to hear the voice of a loved one.'

Jen turned to look at her. 'Are we talking days, then?' she asked hesitantly.

The girl pulled a stoic face. 'Or hours. You can't really tell at this stage. It was a massive stroke. It's good you got here in time. The woman who came with him in the ambulance said you live abroad.'

Jen nodded. 'Yes, in South Africa.'

'Och, I've always wanted to go out there,' the nurse smiled. 'Could do with a bit more sun. Aye, he's only had the one visitor. Little old lady . . . Mrs Logan, if I remember. She used to be the cook, she said.'

'Yes, she was. A long time ago. It was good of her to come.'

'Aye. Well, I'll leave you for a wee bit. I'm only across the ward if you need me. Sit with him a while. Like I said, it helps them . . . and I dare say it'll help you too. Always better to have the chance to say goodbye, that's what I've noticed.'

Jen couldn't answer. She turned back to the bed and the rasping figure lying there, his whole wasted, beaten body engaged in the struggle to stay alive. She couldn't bring herself to stroke his hand, or whisper to him as she supposed others in her place might. She sat there in the deepening gloom as the sun dipped below the horizon, the sounds of the ward receding. It was so quiet. She was tired. She began to doze.

*She's not sure what it is that's woken her, but she lies in her narrow bed across the room from Kemi's, her heart thudding. She's always been afraid of the dark, but this time there's something else in the room that's more frightening, though she doesn't know what it is. She opens her eyes a tiny crack, and then a little bit more. It's her father, but from the way he's standing, she knows something's wrong. He's leaning over Kemi in a way that doesn't seem right to her. He's holding something in his hand. She opens her eyes a little more. He's stroking something but she can't see it properly. There's almost no sound in the room except his heavy breathing, then a little groan, a moan . . . a sigh of release. She's completely frozen. She doesn't know what she's looking at, but she knows it's wrong. Kemi is still fast asleep. She watches her father reach out and touch Kemi's forehead, so gently, so lightly . . . he's never touched her like that, she thinks to herself enviously. He barely looks at her. And then he straightens up and walks away, light as a feather. He's in his pyjamas. She closes her eyes.*

Her eyes flew open. Her heart was thudding. She surfaced from a nightmare and focused her eyes blearily on the figure in the bed; he had slipped sideways. She knew immediately then that he was gone. His face carried an expression that was beyond sleep. His mouth was open and the fingers of the hand that still lay on the coverlet were relaxed, although the sheet was bunched up as though in the last moments before death, he'd tried to grasp hold of life, to hold on. It was unnaturally quiet in the room. The desperate see-sawing sound of the respirator had suddenly fallen silent. She got up as quietly as possible, tiptoeing out of the room without understanding why she felt the need to be silent. She tapped on the glass window separating the nurses' station from the ward. The girl looked up from her computer. Suddenly tears leaped out of Jen's eyes. They didn't well up and trickle down her face in the usual way; they seemed to spring straight out. The nurse got up immediately and came to her, leading her to a chair. All around her, the routine hospital procedures for dealing with a person's passing kicked into place. Someone brought her a cup of sweet, weak tea. *Was there anyone she'd like to call?* She shook her head. The chances of getting Solam on the phone were slim to none. It was pointless telling Alice over the phone and she wanted to tell Kemi in her own way, privately, not in the hospital corridor or nurses' station with people traipsing past.

'When's the funeral?' Kemi asked softly.

'In about a week. It's strange. It still doesn't feel quite real. Mother switches from tears to laughter in the space of five minutes. She doesn't quite get it.'

'She doesn't, at least not in the way we think. That's what dementia does to the brain. I suppose it's probably better that way. It spares them at least some of the pain.'

Jen nodded doubtfully. From her perspective, what was happening to Alice was far worse than her father's passing. 'I suppose so. Anyway, I'll let you know the exact date. I'll get someone to meet you at the airport if I can't get away.'

'Is Solam coming?'

Jen shook her head. 'Not a chance. Anyway, I'd better go. You can't imagine how much work planning a funeral is.' She clapped a hand to her mouth. 'Jesus, I'm sorry, Kem . . . that was thoughtless of me. I'm sorry.'

'It's OK. I'll see you soon. Hang in there.'

Jen put down the phone. She could have kicked herself. Downstairs the big clock in the hallway chimed the hour. It had never sounded so solemn and final. She picked at a loose thread in the bedspread. It was five o'clock. There were still papers to be sorted out in her father's study before the solicitors arrived the following morning, and she'd been putting it off for nearly a week. There was nothing for it – it had to be done.

\*

She pushed open the door to the study cautiously, as if she expected him still to be sitting at the vast mahogany desk by the window. She stood for a moment in the doorway, her heart thumping. Here on the first floor of the house, the ceilings were highest. The walls were pale blue, as they'd always been, with elaborate white cornicing and a picture rail in the style of the period. The furniture was all dark polished wood, and one wall contained only his books, rising all the way to the top. There was a bureau in one corner, and a row of silver-framed pictures hanging on the wall just above it. She looked nervously at the desk. Something hovered at the edge of her mind but she wouldn't allow herself to dwell on it. She walked over to the bureau. All his legal papers were kept in it, Mrs Smith had told her, including the will. She was the only person allowed into the room to clean it, she whispered, not wanting Alice to hear. She knew where everything was kept. It was a good job she did, Jen thought, otherwise she'd have been completely in the dark. Her father had not been one to divulge anything, least of all his business affairs. She knew where he banked – a private bank in St Andrew Square where her dividends and trust monies were paid every quarter – but beyond that, nothing. She had no idea how much money there was. Like everything else, it wasn't a subject every broached in that house.

She put out a hand to open the drawer, but her eye was caught by the photographs. She peered at them. She picked one carefully off the wall and looked at it curiously. It was her grandfather, George McFadden. She had no memory of him but the resemblance to her father was striking. The same high, sloped forehead, upright bearing. There were two children in the photograph; a young, light-skinned girl and a darker girl who stood shyly in front of a thickset, very dark-skinned woman in a chair. She looked at the photograph more closely.

It was uncanny. The light-skinned girl looked strangely familiar. She put it back and then saw another one of the same girl, this time older, as a teenager. She was dressed formally, in a high-necked white blouse with a fussy brooch. The photograph looked as though it had been taken somewhere in Scotland, perhaps even in Edinburgh. Her face was carefully composed for the photographer, the light-coloured, crinkly hair pulled back and held in place with a flowered comb; lips made into a lovely shape with lipstick and dark eyes with long, thick lashes. The girl's image ended in the photograph at her shoulders. She wondered who they all were.

The clock downstairs chimed again, making her jump. It had been a long time since she'd heard the measured division of quarters and halves of time in its companionable way, soothing her fear of the dark when she was little. It was 5.30 p.m. She pulled open the drawers and carefully lifted out the files. It would take her days, not hours, she realized, as soon as she opened the first one. There were records going back almost a century. She sighed deeply. Silence in their family was so deeply entrenched that it had become its own tradition, part of the culture of the McFaddens. Silence was who they were. Her mind kept returning to the picture of the girl on the wall. Who was she, and why was she hanging in her father's study in what seemed like pride of place?

# 87

Whenever she heard an explanation she didn't like, Hélène had a way of tucking her forefinger into the soft pad of her cheek, saying nothing, but following the speaker with an expression on her face that transmitted her message clearer than any word could. *You're trying to fool me?* Solam had seen it many times. Now he felt that gaze upon himself. His voice petered out.

Hélène leaned forward. 'He's your father-in-law. The father of your wife. Your children's *oupa*.' She used the Afrikaans word, uncharacteristically sentimental. Grandpa. 'Of course, you must be there.'

Solam swore silently. He didn't *want* to be there. He wanted to be here. The closed tenders for a host of World-Cup-related contracts were due to be opened that week. He had to be here. Hélène didn't know that, and neither should he. He swore again. 'Jen's got her hands full,' he began, then stopped. He knew when he was beaten.

'All the more reason for you to be there,' Hélène said crisply. 'Didn't you say there was some connection with Tole Mashabane?' she asked, getting up from her desk.

'Yes. I think her grandfather was the one who sent Tole to medical school in Edinburgh.'

She walked to the window. Her offices looked directly onto

Table Mountain. She turned back to him. She was smiling. 'It's a perfect opportunity,' she said firmly. 'Perfect.'

'Perfect for what?' he asked, confused by the sudden switch in tone.

'Public reconciliation, three families bound by history as well as love. You couldn't script it any better. I'll arrange for coverage. There are a few journalists who owe us one. Wear your best suit and play the part of the supportive husband. This could turn out to be political gold.'

You had to hand it to her, Solam thought, as he walked back down the corridor to the lift. The woman didn't miss a damn thing. All that *oupa* business? She was thinking two steps ahead, as she always did. She was right. Properly handled with a few key images . . . his popularity would soar. He punched the button, a smile beginning to form. He wouldn't tell Jen, either. He'd let it be a surprise. He'd take along one of the bodyguards, probably François. He liked the way the man handled himself. He was very quiet, very discreet, didn't say much but nothing got past him. He stepped into the lift and pulled out his phone.

'Get me two tickets on tomorrow night's flight to London with a connecting flight to Edinburgh. Myself and François. We don't need to sit together but keep him close. Oh, and find me a black suit, will you? Something formal, classy. I'll be attending a funeral.' He hung up and walked out into the dazzling sunshine.

## 88

The silence was so loud you could hear a pin drop. Mrs Logan stared at the photograph, but not in the way of someone looking at something for the first time; rather in the way of someone who'd been waiting decades for a moment like this to take place. Her throat pulsed softly, almost like a frog's.

'Who is she?' Jen asked.

Mrs Logan sighed, one of those sighs that seem to come from so far away as to have nothing to do with the lungs that produced it. 'She's the bairn. The African bairn. Auld McFadden's bairn.'

Jen looked at her, puzzled. 'You mean my grandfather? How is she his child?' She stared at it. She looked up at Mrs Logan. Suddenly, the significance of her words began to take shape. 'Are you telling me,' she began haltingly, the words coming out with difficulty, 'that she's my grandfather's *daughter*?'

'Aye. Yer father's sister. His half-sister. That's her mither in the picture, the wan sittin' doon. She passed away no long after that picture was taken. She was aboot eighteen, I think. She had an illness . . . I dinnae ken the name o' it.' She put her hands around her mug. 'I said to yer ma . . . I think that's the reason, ye ken?'

'For what?' Jen was struggling to make sense of everything

Mrs Logan had said. Her father had a half-sister? Her mind was reeling.

Mrs Logan looked up. 'I reckon that's why he done it. He couldnae help hisself.' Mrs Logan fell silent.

'Mrs Logan, what are you talking about?'

Mrs Logan gripped her mug with both hands. She was trembling. 'Do ye no remember?' she began, her lip quivering. 'Those nights when he used to visit the both of ye in yer room? I tried to stop him. Told him he'd go to hell if he ivver touched her, but it was nae use. He couldnae help himself. She reminded him of her, ye see . . . his sister.' She stopped suddenly. She pointed at Jen's face. 'Yer face, Jen. Ye're bleedin' again. Just like ye used to.'

Jen put up a hand. Her lips were sticky with blood from her nose. It all came flooding back. Those nights when she'd seen her father at the end of Kemi's bed, staring at her. He'd never touched her. She knew that, but she knew too that there was something wrong with the way he looked at her. Now for the first time, it began to make sense. In some strange, deeply buried way that she had never properly understood, he confused the two girls, and his desire to be closer to Kemi was part of a long-buried desire to be closer to her . . . to the girl everyone thought of as a servant . . . but who, in reality, was his blood. Her head started to spin. The whole room began to crowd in on her. Mrs Logan's voice seemed to come from a very great distance. She felt her legs give way and she pitched forwards, striking her head on the side of the table as she fell.

# 89

The house was quiet. The funeral had taken place two days earlier. Solam left the following morning. Kemi and her father were leaving early the next morning. They were staying at the Waldorf Caledonian in the centre of town. Jen needed a day or two on her own. She had two stitches above her left eyebrow, and a dull pain in her temples that the doctors said would disappear in a few days. Solam had arrived with François, to her surprise. He'd insisted on leaving François with her and travelling back alone. 'It'll only be for a couple of days,' he said, seemingly in a hurry to get away. It crossed Jen's mind to wonder why he'd rather be without his bodyguard but she was too drained to enquire or wonder further. She was numb.

It was nearly nine o'clock. Alice was fast asleep, knocked out by her cocktail of sleeping pills, antidepressants and whatever else she took. Jen walked downstairs in her nightgown and bare feet, forgetting for a moment that François was in the house. He was so quiet and unobtrusive at the funeral that she'd barely registered his presence.

She went into the kitchen and then into the pantry. Mrs Smith usually kept a few bottles of wine in there. She pulled out a rather dusty bottle and went back in search of a glass and an opener. She poured herself a glass and lit the single cigarette she'd been saving all day. A sudden noise came from outside. She cocked her head. It was the sound of a chair scraping against the stone-flagged floor. She got up and pushed open the kitchen door. A cigarette glowed in the dark. 'Is anyone there?'

The chair landed back on the ground with a thud. It was François. 'Sorry, ma'am,' he apologized immediately, quickly stubbing out the cigarette. 'I saw the light come on but thought you'd go back upstairs. Sorry to disturb.'

'But it's cold outside. Why don't you come in?'

He looked down at the still-smouldering cigarette. 'A rare luxury,' he said sheepishly.

'No, it's fine. Mrs Smith smokes up a storm in here. I was just having one myself. You're off duty.'

He hesitated. 'Well, thank you, ma'am, but please don't let me keep you up.'

'You're not keeping me up,' she said, standing back to let him pass. She was suddenly aware of her attire. 'Just wait here a second,' she said, locking the door behind her. 'I won't be a moment.'

She left him standing there and ran upstairs to get a dressing gown and a pair of slippers. She caught sight of herself in the mirror in the hallway. She looked like a waif.

When she came back down, he was sitting at the kitchen table with his back to her, sleeves rolled up to the elbows, finishing his cigarette. She stood in the doorway for a moment, watching him. There was a stillness about him that had nothing to do with the professional wariness that all the bodyguards displayed. She walked over to join him and pulled out a chair.

For a few moments, neither spoke. There was a packet of cigarettes beside him. He tapped it open and drew one out. He handed it over without a word. 'Here,' he said, offering a light. She reached behind her for a second wine glass and pushed the bottle over.

'Just one. To keep me company.'

He smiled faintly. 'Sláinte,' he said, lifting the glass.

She blinked. 'How d'you know about "sláinte"?' she asked.

He took a small sip. 'Just one of those things you pick up,' he said with a shrug.

'Really?'

'Really.' He gave another faint smile. 'My CO was Irish.'

'Your CO?'

'Commanding Officer. In the army.'

'You were in the army?'

He nodded. 'I was called up in '87. I was eighteen. We had three months of basic training, then we were shipped out to Angola.'

Jen didn't know what to say. 'So, what made you get into this line of work?' she asked finally.

He took a moment to reply. 'Put it this way. There aren't too many jobs out there for someone with my specific skill set,' he said delicately.

'What's your specific skill set?'

He shrugged. 'Shoot to kill. Sounds dramatic, but it's true. By the time the war ended, there just didn't seem much point in doing what everyone else was doing. South Africa back then was a very different place. It was chaos. It's hard to remember it now,' he added, almost as an after-thought.

'I suppose it could all have turned out so differently,' she said quietly. 'Everyone was predicting civil war.'

He nodded. 'It was hard to know what to believe. That's why this job is so simple.'

'What do you mean?'

'It's pretty straightforward. Whoever hires me pays for pro-tection. That's it. I don't ask questions; I don't pass judgement You pay me to be your eyes and ears, not your conscience.'

There was a sudden shift in the conversation, as palpable as a drop in temperature. 'Are you married?' she asked, her eyes going surreptitiously to his left hand. There was no ring.

He shook his head and took another sip of wine. 'Nope Never.'

'There must have been *someone* once?' She was prying, but a sudden and unexpected intimacy had surfaced between them that made it suddenly possible for her to ask.

He shrugged and raised his glass again, subconsciously shielding his face, perhaps. His eyes were an unusual colour she noticed. Greyish green, with flecks of brown, like splin-ters. They were very still, she'd noticed, lids closing slowly when he blinked, but still somehow giving the impression of intense concentration. His hair was dark blond, greying at the temples, cut very short. At this late hour, the beard growing impatiently beneath the sun-grained surface of his cheeks and neck was visible only as a shadow. But it was his mouth that held her attention. It was full, the lower lip covering the slight misalignment of his lower teeth, and yet tight at the same time, as though he were perpetually holding himself in check. It hinted at a sensuality that his grave, quiet manner forbade. It was strange, she thought, frowning. Despite his formidable physical presence, he was someone you might miss in a crowd . . . as though he'd trained himself to be so still as to dis-appear. And yet once you were aware of him, as she was now, he was impossible to ignore. She supposed it was a particular feature of his job, but it wasn't present in the other body-guards, except perhaps for Sbu. Perhaps that was why Solam consistently chose him over the others.

'Funeral must have been hard for you,' he said suddenly, breaking the silence. 'I'm sorry for your loss.'

She blinked slowly, as if coming out of darkness. 'It was.' She fingered the stem of her glass.

'And your mother? How's she taking it?'

The tenderness in his voice hit her like a blow. It was his job, she tried to remind herself. Nothing got past him. 'You've probably noticed,' she said slowly, 'that we're hardly your typical family.'

'Few families are.'

'I suppose so. But these days I find myself wondering if *all* families treat the past this way.' She lifted her gaze.

'What way is that?'

'With silence. Nothing ever gets said. No one says *anything.*'

He was quiet for a moment. 'It's also a form of self-protection,' he said slowly. 'In some cases, silence is the last form of protection, the only form there is.'

'What d'you mean?' she said, struggling to keep her tears in check. It wasn't just his words. There was an aching sadness in his voice that cut straight through her. He knew exactly how she felt.

'Well, take the situation back home. Those of us who fought apartheid's dirty war in Angola, after it was over, we said nothing. Partly to protect those who *didn't* see it – women and children and so on – but also to protect ourselves. If you didn't *talk* about it, *write* about it, *speak* about it . . . well, it didn't happen.' He gave a slow, ironic chuckle. 'Of course, it doesn't quite work like that. But it's useful.'

She stared at him. *No ordinary bodyguard.* 'So how do you break the circle?' she asked. 'When does it ever end?'

He pulled a face. 'You're asking the wrong person,' he said. 'I don't go in for all that unburdening. Oh, we had the whole truth-and-reconciliation thing.' He shook his head wearily. 'The state turned confessional. Ironic, if you think about it. Anglicans and Lutherans turning to a Catholic ritual for absolution. What did it actually resolve?'

She took hold of the bottle and poured herself another glass. She thought back to the commission that had been set up in South Africa after the end of apartheid. She remembered watching some of the harrowing testimony on television with Kemi, victims and perpetrators coming face to face in front of a barrage of reporters. Kemi thought it was a necessary process but for Jen, it was hard to hear the stories of state-sanctioned killings and torture. Scotland, with its buttoned-up respectability and centuries-old tradition of civility and good neighbourliness, might as well have been another planet. *Nothing like that could ever happen here.* That was what she'd felt, viewing the scenes from the comfort of her couch, munching her way distractedly through a packet of biscuits as though methodical chewing might keep the revulsion at bay.

Now she was not so sure. Revulsion, it seemed, could happen anywhere. She only had to think of the past week to understand that. Suddenly, she began to talk.

She had no idea how long she spoke for. She talked quietly, letting it all tumble out. The nosebleeds, the fear outside her father's study, the strange dream she'd had just before he died. It all came out.

When she stopped, so drained she couldn't even think straight, she got up and walked to the window. She lit a third cigarette, blowing the smoke carefully to one side. She wrapped her arms around her waist, hugging herself tightly. It was still dark outside, but it was the porous, tinged-with-light darkness of late summer. It could have been any time, any hour between sunset and sunrise, not registered on any watch or clock.

'What would you do if something like that had happened to someone you love?' she asked, not turning round and not really expecting an answer, either. Perhaps there *were* no answers. Perhaps that was the point? She heard his chair scrape against the floor as he got up. He said nothing but walked over to stand beside her. She was still holding her cigarette in one hand. Very, very gently, he turned her around to face him. He took the cigarette away from her and stubbed it out on the windowpane behind her. He said nothing. His arms went around her shoulders, pulling her towards him. She gave herself up almost luxuriously to it, laying her cheek against the starched blue shirt, feeling the terrible tension in her slip away, bit by bit. He was warm; she could feel his strong, steady heartbeat through the padded muscle against her cheek. They stood there for a minute . . . two? Three? Time seemed to slow to a halt. Then her own hands went round him, slowly sliding up his back. He bent his head at the same time she raised hers. They looked at each other. Then he dipped his head and kissed her, solemnly, but with great passion. There was absolutely no sound in the room except their own breathing. He turned her round very carefully so that the kitchen table was behind her. She was moved by him in a way she'd all but forgotten, her own exquisite pleasure mounting until she clawed at him, drawing him inside her with an urgency that took her breath away. He yielded entirely, collapsing at the end with an inarticulate, strangled cry, as if he'd allowed her into that part of himself that he kept hidden, locked away.

They lay in each other's arms, clothing half shed, half unbuttoned, the space behind them cleared suddenly, violently, so that the half-empty bottle of wine had spilled onto the surface and now pooled, like blood. His heart was thudding in his chest. Jen closed her eyes against his probing grey-green gaze. She wanted nothing more than the feel of his arms around hers. Nothing else mattered. For now.

# PART THIRTEEN
# 2010

Two years later

. . .

This is the strange thing about
South Africa – for all its corruption and
crime, it seems to offer a stimulating
sense that anything is possible.

JUSTIN CARTWRIGHT

# 90

The stylist ran a brush through her hair for the final time. 'Ready, ma'am?' Jen nodded. 'I'll just fix this,' the girl murmured, spraying the sweep of hair that fell over her right eye. After the accident, she'd had to change the direction of the cut. You could barely see it. A small, thin red line that disappeared into her fringe. 'There. All done.' She stepped back, allowing Jen to get up from her seat.

'Thank you,' Jen murmured, making a mental note to send the stylists – hair and make-up – a bouquet and an envelope of cash as soon as the swearing-in ceremony was over. She walked across the bedroom a little unsteadily in her exceedingly high heels and opened the door. They were all waiting downstairs for her. Solam, Hélène, their advisors and press officers, the whole damn shebang. They would drive to Pretoria in convoy. The swearing-in of the new President was expected to take an hour, but the after-party and the festivities would probably go on all night. Both Solam's parents and Kemi's were already in Pretoria with the children. She would meet Kemi after the last official reception and together they would pick them up. She took one last look at herself in the mirror, reached for her clutch bag and made her way slowly down the circular staircase.

Solam looked up briefly as she reached the bottom, but it was Hélène who came over and complimented her.

'You look beautiful,' she said warmly. 'I must say, you're one of the few white women who can pull it off.' Hélène was openly admiring. It was one of the things Jen had come to like about her. For all her political manoeuvring, she was that rare person who spoke her mind.

Jen looked down at her elaborate dress a little self-consciously. It had been made for her by one of Iketleng's Congolese dressmakers. It was modelled on a Fendi cocktail dress pattern, with a wide neckline and tight sleeves to the elbow, opening out into an elaborate flounce. The skirt was tight-fitting, skimming over her waist and hips, then opening into a dramatic fishtail. It was made of brightly patterned West African cloth, a riotous swirl of deep aubergine, dark green and black, with highlights of coppery gold. When she'd seen the fabric, she'd nearly baulked. But with her alabaster skin, short red hair and crimson nails, it worked. She wore very little jewellery – her wedding ring, a thin gold bracelet and a pair of discreet gold-and-diamond stud earrings were all that was needed. 'Thank you, Hélène,' she said, meaning it. 'I guess we're ready to go.'

Solam overheard her and nodded. 'Yep, let's hit the road.' He had never looked better, Jen thought as she followed the group out of the house. He was wearing a suit by one of his favourite designers, Ermenegildo Zegna: a charcoal-grey jacket and trousers of pure jacquard silk, so dark it appeared black until the light caught it, giving it a discreet sparkle that drew the eye. It fitted him to perfection. He looked the epitome of a suave, urbane leader, a man at the height of his power, both physical and intellectual. He was forty-five years old, the youngest President in the country's history, but in the run-up to the World Cup, everyone agreed there was no better image to project. His wife and children were equally photogenic. She, a cool, slender redhead with impeccable family connections and an heiress in her own right; the children were carbon copies of their parents, perfectly well behaved and pleasingly cherubic. *A rainbow family for a rainbow nation.* The press was having a field day.

They walked out into a barrage of cameras, shutters going off like gunshots. The bodyguards kept a tight cordon around them as they made their way to the waiting cars. 'Jen, you go with François and the press officer!' Solam shouted over his shoulder. She nodded and turned around. François was standing behind her, already in position. Their eyes met and she followed him to the car. She got into the back, carefully lifting the train of her dress and making sure it didn't get caught in the door. He shut it behind her and got into the front. The press officer sat up front, next to him. François expertly manoeuvred the Mercedes out of the tight forecourt and turned into the street. Her heart was beating fast. There were six official cars, all carrying one high-ranking official or another. Ten security vehicles, a dozen outriders, sirens blaring. The noise, as they progressed onto the highway, was deafening. Every so often, his eyes met hers in the rear-view mirror. Grey green, the irises flecked with brown, long lashes. She knew what he was thinking.

The stately Union Buildings slowly loomed into view, the sounds of the motorcade filtering through the windows. The gardens below were packed to capacity, a crowd of twenty, thirty, forty thousand; the figures were mere guesses. In place of the gold, green and black bunting and flags that the ruling party had trotted out on every state occasion since '94, the bright blue and white colours of the Democratic Party held sway. As the cars glided onto the forecourt high above the capital, the taut flags of almost every nation blew stiffly in the wind. There were television crews from all over the world camped out; everyone wanted a glimpse of this special first family unlike any other. François brought the car to a gentle stop behind the car carrying the President and his deputy. He waited until the guards in front were in position, and then he opened the door. Jen got out of the car and straightened up. She stood for a moment next to him, conscious that all the cameras were pointing at Solam, and drew a deep breath to steady herself. It was noon and the overhead sun was already fierce. As she prepared to step forward, she felt a light pressure at her elbow. To anyone looking on, the gesture was simple professional protection, appropriate for the wife of the President-elect. But there was a message in its grip that was for her alone. She was too experienced to return it, but her eyes met his for a brief second. *No ordinary bodyguard.* And she was no trophy wife.

# EPILOGUE

*Cape Town, South Africa, 2010*

The two women stood at the edge of the rented property, looking out to sea. In front of them, the Atlantic Ocean heaved in slow-moving, sinuous swells. A few gulls flew overhead, their shrieks uncannily child-like, screaming into the wind. There was a glass balcony protecting them from the vertical drop of the cliff edge, which plunged at least ten metres down to the patio of the property below. They were in Clifton, a decidedly upmarket suburb of Cape Town, just days before the opening ceremony of the World Cup. The pressure – and the expectations – were at fever pitch. The major stadia were still not quite ready; there'd been the threat of a strike by the unions, affecting everyone from construction workers to the hastily assembled security force who'd been hired to protect the hundreds of thousands of expected tourists arriving any day now. Solam was in a fury, swearing at anyone who'd listen, threatening ministers with sacking if they didn't bring the union leaders to heel. It was all on his head, he'd screamed at her that morning.

She turned to Kemi who was leaning on the glass edge, mesmerized by the view. 'So, what are you asking me?'

Kemi tilted her head sideways to look at her. There was a small line between her eyes that Jen hadn't noticed before. It came from all the reports she had to read in her new role as director of the foundation that had been set up after the

413

LESLEY LOKKO

success of the first township clinic. There were now eleven such clinics dotted around the country. The Julian Carrick Foundation was becoming a force to be reckoned with in terms of healthcare provision. The past wasn't forgotten. On the contrary, it had forged Kemi, just as it had forged her. All the sorrows and secrets Kemi had endured had shaped her into the person she'd become. Jen could not have been more proud. 'I'm asking you to join me,' Kemi said patiently.

Jen felt the blush spread across her face. 'Me? But what use would I be to you? What would I do?'

'Whatever you like. It's ours to do with as we please.' She turned back to look at the ocean again. 'This won't last forever, you know. You do know that, don't you?'

'Of course I do. He'll want one more term. He'll get it, too, but he'll only be in his mid-fifties when it's all over. I don't know what he'll do next. Something else, I suppose.'

'Why d'you stay?' Kemi asked carefully, still looking out to sea. 'It's your life, Jen. You can do whatever you want. There's the money your father left us. You'll never have to earn a living if you don't want to. The kids will be fine. Hell, they barely see him as it is.'

Jen looked down at her hands. She twisted her wedding ring. 'Think of the scandal,' she murmured.

Kemi gave a soft laugh. 'D'you think yours would be the only one?' she said quietly. 'If you love each other . . . what's stopping you?'

Jen swallowed. 'How did you know?' she asked in a low voice.

Kemi turned round. 'Jen, I've known you almost all my life. I can tell by the way your eyes light up whenever he's around. I'm not blind.'

Jen's face was on fire. 'I didn't think it was so obvious,' she muttered.

414

'Don't worry, *I* see it because I know you so well. I doubt Solam's noticed. In fact, I'd swear he hasn't. What are you going to do?'

Jen's shoulders went up and down. 'I've no idea. I just can't seem to think straight.'

Kemi was quiet for a moment. Then she levered herself away from the balustrade and began to walk back into the house. At the sliding doors, she stopped and turned. 'Whatever you do, do it for *you*, Jen. Don't do it for anyone else.' And then she opened the doors and walked into the gloom.

Jen stood looking after her a little uncertainly. It was a typical Kemi comment, profound but cryptic, as though there was another message lying dormant within. She wanted to go after her, as she'd always done, asking for an explanation or at least the chance to thrash it out. But something stopped her, kept her back. She laughed a little embarrassedly, both at the sound of her voice out loud in the darkness and at her train of thought. *Do it for me. Don't do it for anyone else.* Kemi had always been so decisive, so knowing, so self-possessed. She'd used Kemi as a barometer for her own indecisions, as if by measuring herself against her quieter, steadier nature she might see in Kemi some future, better version of herself. Her certainty had been a powerful warning to her, all the years of their shared life together when she thought that being passionate and full of longing was a sign of weakness, no doubt passed down to her from Alice. But she was beginning to understand that nothing was quite as clear or fixed as she thought, or, perhaps more accurately, as she *liked* to think. She'd used Kemi as a crutch. What had happened in the twenty-odd years since her first impression of her was that Kemi had simply outgrown Jen's idea of her, and Jen had been too blind, or afraid, to see it.

The breeze picked up, whipping a few loose strands of hair

across her face. She put up a hand to touch her scar, the tiny ridge that her fingertips now understood as belonging to her, a real part of her now and for the rest of her life. *Her* scars were visible but Kemi's were not. She felt her skin prickling. Silence, truth and lies. Maybe, she thought to herself, turning back towards the sea, even the lies we tell ourselves are a form of truth. Perhaps the *only* form of truth, better and truer than our desperate attempts to evade it.

A light went on suddenly in the living room. She could see Kemi's silhouette moving around, plumping the cushions on the couch, opening a bottle of wine. They were alone for the weekend. Iketleng had insisted on taking the children for a few days, revelling in her unexpected role of favourite grandmother. Somewhere in the city below, François was waiting. When the time was right . . . Jen's heart had started to lift. She began to walk determinedly towards the light.